OUT OF THE DEN AND INTO THE FIRE

Printed in the United States of America
Cover design by: MiblArt

First Printing, 2025

ISBN-13: 978-1-966238-06-5

OUT OF THE DEN AND INTO THE FIRE

ARIANA TOSADO

CONTENTS

CHAPTER

ONE

"**I**'m Tristan Atera's daughter."

The words resounded off the walls of my mind with cruel regret. Two Secret Service men had me gripped by my arms while the President of the United States stood tall and proud in the middle of the heavily guarded Oval Office, his thin lips lifting into a knowing smile. Before he could reply, the room flashed.

"—long before you knew I knew something," I was saying.

President Caldwell leaned against the front of his grand desk, crossing his arms. "Yes, because Americans trust me to keep them safe from threats like her—"

Flash.

My palms slammed against the royal-blue rug under me as I

fell. Glass shards speckled the floor. Secret Service agents shouted into their earpieces, swarming the president lying still in front of me. A gunshot rang out.

Flash.

Someone was dragging me out of the Office, through a glass-paned door and to the gray-skied outside. My eyes desperately searched for a target as another gunshot boomed. Just as I looked right, through the shrubbery and across the street, a pang burst in the side of my stomach.

Flash.

Wet. My clothes were wet on my side—warm. Frigid, jagged stone supported my body as I lay there, a gaunt man with a light beard firmly pressing against my wound.

"Keep talking to me!" he commanded. "Don't go to sleep, don't close—!"

Flash.

Another familiar male voice quieted into the distance. Three people were calling my name. A cacophony of other shouts ensued. My head fell limp in someone's hold as the world around me shut to black.

My eyes shot open, a sharp gasp cutting through the disorienting silence. Instinctively, I made my breaths shallow, staring up at the dark ceiling above me. My fingers curled around the coarse comforter on top of me until my vision adjusted to the darkness.

This isn't my ceiling. These weren't my blankets.

The motel.

I swallowed the rest of my adrenaline and carefully sat up with a soft creak from the bed I shared with Aunt Becca. I glanced at her, unsurprised that I hadn't woken her up. When I looked over at the bed next to ours, Mom and Dad lay soundly asleep, their snores practically whispers. Driving for a total of thirteen hours across Saskatchewan and then Alberta must have taken more out of Momma than I'd thought, despite the brief breaks from Alejandro teleporting us whenever he was ready to. Considering nobody had murmured my name in the dark yet, I was pretty sure that Jak and Alejandro were still asleep in their sleeping bags at the foot of the beds, too.

I closed my eyes. My hands subconsciously reached for the locket around my neck. I was in no condition to fall back asleep, not after that vision. Not after my confession to the President of the United States himself, after the gunshot that had rung out and torn a hole in my side.

What was going on? What happened at the end, when—?

I cringed at the memory. The burn still lingered. My hand gripped the silver heart tight.

Shot.

Like she *was.*

An image of those emerald-green eyes freezing on me for the last time flashed in my mind. I swallowed. I definitely wasn't falling back asleep.

Today was officially the worst Christmas ever.

I slid out of bed, tiptoed past Jak and Alejandro, and grabbed one of the keycards off the TV stand. With that, I slipped out of the motel room.

Momma hadn't purposely chosen a motel with a 24/7 pool, but I was grateful that my druid vision had happened on the night we were staying at one; one of the perks of being in *rural* Canada was having an entire area to yourself in the middle of the night without the threat of local or federal authority stopping by. With a soft clack, I closed the black metal gate behind me and firmly crossed my arms over my chest. The pool was closed for the winter, but the hot tub in front of me was steaming with a welcome. I walked over, took my sneakers and socks off, and set them down by the edge of the tub. Pungent chlorine tickled my nose as I sat down and rolled up my pajama pants to stick my feet into the hot water—*piping* hot compared to how it was more than cold enough to snow. A shiver racked my body. I hugged myself tighter. The water reached halfway up my calves, illuminated by a light installed at the bottom of the tub.

I was tempted to throw myself all the way in, pajamas or not. Alberta was brutal. Canada was brutal, especially since magic was outlawed here, too, and we were only getting by because we were practiced undercover wielders and Canada didn't know we were fugitives yet (as far as we knew). That, and the appearance spells we put ourselves under helped a lot.

The black gate softly clanged on my left. My head snapped up. Alejandro strolled toward me with his hands in his sweatpants pockets.

"*Hola*," he said once he was close enough to not have to shout it. He ran a warm-brown hand through his messy black hair. "What is going on?"

Since we'd met in October, his verbal English had noticeably improved. He already understood it well, and being in a group chat with me, Annisa, and Kamose had helped. The group chat was one of the things I missed most now that we'd transferred our photos, videos, and contacts to a hard drive and destroyed our phones. Alejandro was exempt from that because the government didn't know anything about him, let alone to track his phone.

Still, it was easier to talk to him in Spanish for smooth conversation. Momma learned it when she was a Hunter-in-training, and she taught it to me while I was growing up. Thankfully, my year and a half at the Callistro Academy had kept it intact.

"I'm surprised that you're the one here and not Jak," I said.

"He would be here if he were awake." Alejandro sat down next to me on the hot tub edge, his legs crossed. Even sitting, he came up two inches shorter than me. "The jet lag is still affecting me. I saw you walk out."

I nodded, swaying my feet back and forth in the water.

"*Amiga*," he crooned, nudging my arm. "What's wrong?"

I kind of wanted to snap at him for the ridiculous question, but stopped myself. "Well, we're spending Christmas undercover at a motel. What do *you* think is wrong?"

We needed to get as close to British Columbia—the western edge of the continent—as fast as possible. His teleportation demanded a lot of energy, and his required energy multiplied for every person and object he took with him. We were six people total with an SUV that had all of our stuff, everything we hadn't burned or destroyed back home in our house, Dad and Becca's apartment, and Jak's house in Topa. The drives were long while we waited for Alejandro to recuperate—but we *needed* to find out more about the base under Mount Steele, if Dad's magic had made it there safely, and more about everything Alexa had told me before she died. And I needed the full story of what had happened that morning the US Government captured Mr. Dawson.

He wasn't dead: a locator spell only works on someone who's alive, and every time I used it on his tie we'd taken with us, he was somewhere in DC—no longer in the containment facility I'd seen him in the night we left home. The spell only showed me blackness instead of his perspective, which meant he was knocked out, and I didn't know why it wasn't giving me his exact location—but he was alive in DC, and we still weren't being pursued. With more time than I deserved, I needed to be a Hunter to survive for him.

"Save them." Alexa had used her last words on that plea. But *how*, how was I supposed to save anyone right now? Things had fallen apart to the extent that the girls back home knew why we were gone—mostly. They knew Momma and I were "friends with Tristan Atera's daughter" and needed to protect her, and that was all they needed to. At least they knew something.

Sarah knows.

I hadn't been able to stop repeating that to myself since the night we'd left Capperson. She'd cried. But it wasn't her glistening eyes amidst the dark or the silent sobs that I remembered the most harshly. It was when Sarah Duncan told me in response to my confession, "I should've known." Not like she was disgusted, like she felt stupid for never realizing it sooner—but like she'd missed out on carrying the burden with me. Every hour, I prayed that I had that right, because now she was covering for me to Breanne and Opal in case they became too curious. Without Sarah's protection, all of our secrets would be breached... if Caldwell hadn't exposed us to the American public yet.

I hope the girls did take my stuff from our dorm and told Adrien and Wyatt to do the same for Jak. That request had been short but necessary in the letter I'd given them.

"Are you comfortable talking to me?" Alejandro asked.

I shrugged. "There's not really anything to say."

He let the quiet, freezing night surround us for only a couple of moments. "I can wake up Jak if you want."

"No. He needs to sleep."

"So do you."

I'm not telling him why that's basically torture at this point. Nightmares about that morning at the hideout—watching Alexa die in front of me, sometimes watching Mr. Dawson or my parents be killed instead—I hadn't managed to avoid any of it.

"You don't understand." I cast my eyes down to the glowing water. "Jak's been through more than you can imagine."

For my sake, I didn't add.

The water softly rippled. In my peripheral vision, Alejandro stared at me with sharp brown eyes. I could practically hear his thoughts simmering, but I wasn't ready to entertain any of them.

"He means a lot to you, doesn't he?"

Ha. Those words didn't even begin to cover it; I felt something for Jak far beyond friendship, beyond care. I just didn't have a word for it.

"Yeah," I said simply. "He's protected me since he was seven years old, nine years before we even met. A Grand Hunter raised him to kill people like us, but he's fought like he's one of us. I don't wanna say he's 'valuable' like he's an object, but... he's invaluable to me."

Alejandro vaguely nodded. For some reason, he scooted an inch away, like the words had zapped him. The gap left behind a cold draft, and I shivered.

"Let's go back inside," he said.

I shook my head. "I can't. Believe me, freezing is much better than lying awake and worrying."

"I'll be ready to teleport us in the morning," he assured me. "But if you freeze first, it defeats the purpose of the mission."

The hot tub seemed to cool the longer my legs stayed in the water. I took a second to look at Alejandro, to study his eyes and concave jaw and shaggy black hair. It all contrasted with his otherwise gentle, rounded features that belonged on a sixteen-year-old boy who just wanted to have fun. He was trying to grow up for us, forced to because of us. He shouldn't have been dragged into this life yet. Then I remembered that I'd been just barely younger than him when it began for me.

"Thanks for doing this," I muttered, shivering again. He closed the gap between us and wrapped one arm around me, his hands rubbing my arms. "We literally wouldn't have been able to escape, let alone get into Canada, without you."

"Thank my parents for letting me come," he teased. "We just won't tell them that we're fugitives... I'm thankful that I met you and the others. Someone else like me."

The others. Annisa, Kamose, and now Alejandro. I often caught myself wondering if there were more people like us—someone else who could potentially help us. We weren't going to take down Caldwell, let alone save Mr. Dawson, on our own. I couldn't help but wonder if, *hope* that, I wasn't done finding allies for whatever plan magic had for our alter identities.

Adara. The day Mr. Dawson told me about her felt ancient now.

He's not here.

I closed my eyes to alleviate the stinging pressure behind them. He was a wielder and a lead to the Ateras, and the man *would* lay down his life if it meant protecting us. The government would do everything in their power to get information out of him.

"*Amiga...*" Alejandro whispered, gently shaking me. "Are you okay?"

I nodded, flaring my nostrils so I could breathe without sniffing.

"I know you're worried," he told me, "about getting there safely and saving—"

"I'm okay," I said, needing to cut him off before I did snap. "I can't wallow in it. We have no hope of saving him if I can't be who he needs me to be."

Alejandro simply nodded and stopped rubbing my arms. I took that as my cue to take my feet out of the water (something I regretted instantly when the air swallowed my legs whole with ice) and slip my socks and shoes back on.

Alejandro stood, offering me his hand. I took it. He squeezed mine for a second.

"We can do this," he assured me. "No matter what."

No matter what. Mr. Dawson had said that about making it out before we had split up in the hideout. Well, I was still fighting under that rule. What Alejandro didn't know was that I'd added Caldwell's downfall to the list.

Two

"Just the essentials," Momma told me and Jak from the front seat, turning her head to look at us. Her refined features seemed to sharpen with her amber eyes. "We have one short trip after this and it's broad daylight, so be quick."

Brookmere, British Columbia was basically in the middle of nowhere, but I was still on edge: this last gas station was one of the bigger ones we'd been to, which meant more open space to be spotted. We were too close to Mount Steele for everything to fall apart now.

"I want a coffee, then," an invisible Aunt Becca said behind me, "to calm me down."

"Caffeine's gonna make it worse," Dad grumbled from the passenger seat, also under an invisibility cloak—we weren't taking any chances, especially now.

"Coffee makes me happy, so it'll *calm me down*," Auntie shot back. "If you want a donut, Tristan, just say so."

"Okay," Momma said, mediating again. "Emma, Jak, the essentials, quick."

I turned to Alejandro on my left. He shook his head, denying my silent offer. Jak opened his door and climbed out with me behind him.

Tensions were high every time we stopped; we didn't know exactly how much the US knew, let alone what Canada knew, let alone what any individual we came across—any of which could've been undercover—knew. But at least this was our final stop. Next we'd drive down to Deroche two hours away to give Alejandro the rest he needed, and then teleport straight to our coordinates near Mount Steele. The mountain was also a public hiking peak (which raised a lot of suspicion in me regarding the safety of a magician *safe haven*), which meant we risked someone watching us teleport in. There was a cabin for hikers at the base of the mountain, and that was our biggest lead. As soon as we found someone who worked at the haven, we'd finally be home free.

As long as Alexa wasn't lying and it really is a safe haven.

The overcast sky threatened a different kind of shiver down my spine as Jak and I approached the store. He pulled open the glass door, letting me walk in first. With a welcome ding, a puff of heat pushed my hair back. I dreaded our first stop as we approached the refrigerated beverages in the back.

Jak opened the door and grabbed four large cans of espresso drinks. I couldn't help but notice how he came a head shorter than the height of the door. Even though he was nearly eighteen, he'd grown an inch or so in the almost year and a half we'd known each other. His jaw had become more prominent, now a defined oval-square shape, highlighting the intense warmth of his russet eyes that complemented his light-brown skin—still noticeably marked by the long scar on his left cheek. His dark hair stopped at the bottom of his ears, the tips curling a little upward, something I always really liked about him. It was nice to have something familiar when everything else was changing.

"I hope this actually is our last trip," he muttered, letting the refrigerator door fall shut. "Remind me again how Alejandro is able to... do what he can? I thought that was impossible."

"It is," I replied. The plastic aroma of packaged pastries teased my stomach. "But he's—different."

"Like, a different class?"

I glimpsed the man browsing the instant ramen choices down the short aisle next to me. "I don't think this is where we should be having this conversation."

Jak strolled by me and went toward the aisle over. I stood in the quiet buzzing of the fluorescent lights overhead, my eyes traveling down the scar on his cheek. That was the only *glaring* evidence left of his torture in November, but it still glared at me. The small one under his right eye was fading, but that long, taut scar on his cheek glared.

I followed him into the aisle, the answer to his question about Alejandro weighing on my mind. He knew I was a wielder, but he hardly knew anything about magic. Let alone about the four wielders with powers that were supposed to be impossible, or why Alejandro, a complete stranger to him, was helping us.

"How did you meet him?" Jak asked me in a flat tone that

was strictly surveillance, gathering information. He scanned our food options. "He's all the way in Spain, he has this impossible thing—how did you guys run into each other?"

"On the cruise," I answered, taking a loaf of bread off the shelf. "We stopped in Barcelona."

Even though Alejandro met me in Paris.

"So, you two just knew the other was trustworthy and he happened to have a—special talent?"

"It's a bit of a story, I can't tell you right now."

His voice dropped lower, his eye meeting me in the corner. "Does it have anything to do with what you told me about Caralyn Callistro and her being an ally?"

I'd almost forgotten that we'd told him about that; he needed the full context of the situation if he was going to come with us on our Steele mission. A sliver of me felt relieved about it, but the other part didn't know how to shut down his fatal curiosity in public.

"I just need to know why we can trust him," he said, reading my silence. He grabbed an overpriced jar of combined peanut butter and strawberry jelly. "It looked like your parents had never even met him before, and Becca was super hesitant about him."

Becca's super hesitant about everyone, I kept to myself.

"Look, I'll tell you." I followed Jak farther down the aisle. Maybe it was the defensive adrenaline starting to build from this conversation mixed with the blazing heater, but my body was starting to warm up like a radiator. "When we're not in *public.* But you can trust him."

"We're not in a position to take risks." He faced me in full in the middle of the aisle. "Do you *know* for sure?"

"Jak, I said I'll tell you," I hissed. "What's going on? We're literally one trip away from Steele and *now* you're cautious?"

He straightened, jaw firming like he was holding something back. "I kind of have the least to go off of out of everyone," he said flatly. "You know why I'm here to begin with, what my main goal's always been, and I barely have any power to make it happen. All I can do is watch and help"—he nodded to the groceries in his arms—"where I can. If there's a chance that someone could demolish everything I've spent my life protecting, then..."

I stepped up to him with the bread in my arms and took the jar of peanut butter and jelly from him. "You don't know why you can trust him yet, but you can trust me. And I can trust him because... magic said I could."

"Magic?"

I opened my mouth with the words, but they froze in there. Now wasn't the time to tell Jak what I was—and I wasn't sure if I'd ever find that time. Sure, he felt okay about magicians in general, but a hybrid? Someone who wielded all seven classes of magic in her veins? What if *that* was what would make him look at me differently?

—Emma!—

I paused, glancing out the floor-to-ceiling window at the front of the store. Momma was supposed to be pumping gas with Alejandro on lookout. Instead, she was throwing herself back into the SUV with him.

Oh no.

—¡Vuelve al coche, ya!—

Get back to the car. Get back to the car!

Black vehicles barreled down the highway on both sides. No

emblem or seal.

"Go!" I urged, pushing past Jak. Without question, he dropped the groceries in his arms. The cashier behind the front counter shouted after us as we dashed across the store and barreled through the front door.

—*Alejandro, destroy the tires on the left side!*— I told him in Spanish.

Jak and I ran off the sidewalk and onto the hard asphalt lot. My gaze locked on the three SUVs zooming down the right side.

Anullo!

Twelve tires burst into scraps of rubber, sending the cars winding into each other. On the left side of the road, four vehicles scraped against the pavement, rear-ending each other. My feet pounded harder on the asphalt, Jak right behind me. He flung open the back door, and I threw myself inside. Before he could shut the door, Momma slammed her foot onto the accelerator, throwing us against our seats. The car swerved around the gas pumps and the edge of the station, bullets booming from outside.

Is this the Canadian Government? US?

Both?

"Alejandro!" Momma exclaimed.

He put one hand on her shoulder and his other on mine. The rest of us locked hands as his eyes squeezed shut. Amber waves of bright magic enveloped the car, making me shut my eyes with fear that I cursed.

The gunshots went silent. I opened my eyes. The trees and mountains of the highway whizzed by on both sides. Our car hummed steadily under us.

Alejandro curtly exhaled next to me, releasing me and

Momma. "I couldn't go far," he said in Spanish. His usually sharp eyes sagged with tiredness. "I'm sorry, it—it was rushed, I didn't have time to think or recover from the last time."

Now he has to regain more energy before getting us to Steele. And it mattered this time: the government was *officially* after us, and we didn't know which one. Based on how nobody in public had recognized us yet, our pictures still hadn't been broadcasted across the United States or Canada. Nobody in public had received a National Alert, either. What was going on? We had the last two generations of Ateras in this car, and Caldwell wasn't sending every force he had, including the ones that came with the US's alliance with Canada?

"Someone needs to destroy *their* tires, too!" a still invisible Aunt Becca snapped from the seat behind me.

I turned around, looking through the back windshield. Four black SUVs were hot on our tail.

Alejandro could only take us farther down the road.

One bullet went off. My instincts jolted awake.

I threw my hands out to the side. *Agger vis!*

With resounding clinks, bullets flew off the air surrounding the car. Each one awoke a flash of amber upon impact. The force field would only hold up for so long if these agents kept shooting.

I need more.

"Keep driving," I told Momma, looking ahead—and noting the curve we were flying toward.

"Emma, their tires!" she commanded, Jak joining her.

"No," I barked at Alejandro when he looked behind him. I didn't have the heart or the bravery to remind anyone that destroying the tires up here would make those government vehicles veer off the road and tumble down the mountainside, killing those agents. And I couldn't bring myself to be responsible for that.

"Emma," an invisible Dad snapped from the front seat, "they're trying to kill us, you can't hesitate—!"

"Hold on," Momma called as we approached the curve.

Bullets barraged my force field. The trees on both sides of the highway loomed tall over us, almost threatening to crash down.

Crash down...

"We need to get out of here before they block the road up ahead or kill our tires!" Dad exclaimed.

My mind decided. *I have to.*

Our car swerved, throwing me into Alejandro and Jak into me. When we straightened, I locked my eyes on the hood of our car, holding out my hand to help me visualize the spell.

Accelera.

"What's going on?" Momma cried as the car sped up. She pumped the brakes, but my magic worked against her. Dad asked me the same thing as I looked behind me, still holding out my hand. My gaze focused on the trees on either side of the highway as the government vehicles drew farther away.

An entire tree would take too long to fall, but...

I called upon the warlock in me as we passed a dense grove. Forming a claw with my other hand to visualize my move, I thrust it up. Just behind us, enormous, thick roots slithered from over the edges of the road, intertwining with each other in the middle. I released our car from the acceleration spell and then locked my eyes on the SUVs in the distance.

Tarde.

Their tires screeched against the asphalt, echoing across the mountains—but I never heard a crash as the government came to a halt in front of the tree roots.

Jak's stunned gaze stopped me as I started turning back around. I quickly remembered: I'd enacted the hybrid part of me.

Warlock. Green eyes.

"What—" he asked tightly, "what was that?"

I opened my mouth but then froze. Whirring purred in the distance above us.

Helicopter.

"Emma," Mom and Dad exclaimed, my attention snapping to the front. Three more black vehicles were zooming down the oncoming side of the highway. Suited arms stuck out the back windows and threw something metal onto the road: tire spikes.

Protect the force field for as long as you can.

I threw my hand out and to the side, swiping the spikes off the road. *Tarde-uro!*

Steam billowed out from the hoods of the slowing SUVs on the other side of the road. The cars swerved before quickly regaining control. Bullets clattered against our car again as Momma zoomed down the highway, approaching another curve.

We're going too fast, I realized, *we can't slow down in time!*

A clang struck the side of the car. They'd broken past part of the force field.

The helicopter whirred louder above us, lowering. Four SUVs charged forward behind us. They'd breached the tree roots.

We were surrounded. We had no other choice.

"Alejandro," I said, grabbing his and Jak's hands, "do you know the coordinates near the cabin?"

"Yes—"

"Get us as close as you can, *anywhere* near it!"

His lips parted for only a second before he looked at Momma. "*Pare el coche.*"

"Are you crazy?" Jak exclaimed in Spanish, his eyes aflame with terror. "If we stop the car, we're dead!"

"Trust me, do it now!" Alejandro turned to me. "Emma, help me."

"What?" I said. "I can't—!"

"You are a mage!" he cried. "I need your will!"

I didn't have time to argue. Momma slammed on the brakes. The cars behind us hurtled forward. The helicopter's whir stirred the trees towering over us. Gunshots from the other side of the highway barraged the force field. I looked over at Alejandro, forcing my will through my veins as I squeezed his hand and we shut our eyes. Our car screeched before jolting to a forceful stop, throwing me forward. In a blink, a bright amber light illuminated the darkness behind my eyes.

A couple of seconds later, it faded to black.

Silence. Stillness.

I pried open my eyes. To my surprise, I slouched back in my seat with it, my body as heavy as lead and chest heaving with breaths too big for me. I'd never been so drained in my life. It felt like Alejandro had zapped my very magic from me and taken some of my life source with it.

The entire car exhaled with relief. Even the sun managed to poke through the overcast gray of the sky, brightening it as if to congratulate us. Dad and Aunt Becca threw off their hoods upon realizing that we sat alone in a snowy field lined with trees—

No, I realized, barely managing the energy to look out Jak's window. The upward, snow-blanketed terrain of a mountain loomed over us. Looking ahead, through the clustered branches of the evergreens our car sat hidden behind, was a wooden cabin.

No way.

My heart thundered in my head. The heat in my body was already combatting the winter air that had dropped at least twenty degrees. "Mom?"

Dad took her hand, panting deeply with her like we'd just run the whole way here. My heavy breaths ravaged my throat, which was starting to burn with adrenaline-infused fire.

Momma took the GPS off the dashboard. "He did it," she whispered. "Our coordinates are right. We're at the cabin."

Mount Steele. We'd made it.

Another point for Hunter training, I thought, closing my eyes. Even if Momma hadn't taught it to me while growing up, Spanish was one of the first languages Hunter schools taught. That included Redway, Dad and Jak's school, which meant they were included in our conversations with Alejandro. I almost felt guilty that Becca—who was slouched against the back window of the car, trying to catch her breath—had been the only one who couldn't understand anything we'd said, but at least she was safe.

I turned to the mage on my left, ready to thank him. "Alejandro—"

Alejandro was out cold.

THREE

"Alejandro," I said, shaking his shoulder with what little strength I had in my lead-heavy arms. "Alejandro! Can you hear me?"

"What's wrong?" Momma stated, turning her head with Dad.

"He's unconscious," I said, patting his cheek, an exhausted ache pulling back my arm. "I think he pushed himself too far, Alejandro, can you hear me—?"

"Amy!"

I jumped at Dad's warning, following his finger that pointed through the windshield: three people in white winter gear, black fabric covering half of their faces, were marching out from around the edge of the tree line hiding us. The two on the side—a burly light-skinned man and a short brown woman—aimed their rifles at us. The skinny man in the middle kept his hand outstretched.

We'd either made it to a wielder's safe haven, or death's door.

"*Ou!*" one of the men called, his voice muted outside and behind his fabric mask. "*Noh!*"

"What?" Becca asked anxiously behind me.

"*Ou!*" the voice shouted again. I realized it belonged to the man in the middle when he rapidly waved his outstretched hand with the command. The three of them continued toward us, the details of their two rifles coming into view. "*Righ noh!*"

"Get out of the car," Momma muttered quickly, undoing her seatbelt with a click. "Hands up. Becca, Emma, you know what to do if these aren't people we can trust."

"But Alejandro—" I began.

"Now," she stated, opening her car door with reservation.

I looked back out the left window, at the three strangers and their aimed weapons. They'd stopped yards away.

"Out of the car, now!" the man in the middle commanded, his voice clearer. An Indian accent—Punjabi, I was pretty sure.

Jak slowly opened his door, holding his hands up in surrender according to Momma's instructions. With severe exhaustion still pulling down my limbs, I shakily followed his lead. We came to stand with Momma and Dad in front of the car's left side. Aunt Becca came out and around the back, arriving on Jak's right. The cold was twice as merciless as last night in the settlement of Mount Currie, all the more so with our lives in these people's hands.

Mount Steele stood tall, grand, and white behind us, the highway running behind the strangers. An avalanche almost felt like our biggest concern when the short brown woman on the right slightly lowered her rifle, muttering something behind her mask in what must have been Punjabi to the man in the middle. He replied in the same language.

"Three of you have magic," the middle man said, his voice as strong as his nose that stuck out. Amber flashed in his umber irises before he asked, "Can we trust you all?"

I suppressed my sheer confusion as I swallowed. *How do they know that three of us specifically have magic? And how did they know to come out here fully armed and aimed when we're at a* public *peak?*

The weight of a truth spell seized my words when I opened my mouth. Truth spell. That was why he'd blatantly asked that question.

"Yes, you can trust all of us—" I began.

"Are you here to hurt anyone?"

"No," Dad immediately said, his breath clouding in front of him. "Not at all. We were looking for the cabin."

"Are you here because you need refuge?" the middle man said. I envied him for the fabric covering half of his face, pushing his warm breath against him.

"Wait," Mom said, keeping her hands up. "We need to know we can trust you, too."

The Punjabi man stayed rigid, neither of his companions letting their eyes leave us for a glance. "Okay. Do your spell."

Momma looked at me—or at Aunt Becca—and Becca cast the truth spell. "Can we trust you, too?" she asked.

"If you are refugees, yes," the man answered. "We protect refugees. What brought you here?"

This was it—*This is it.* We'd made it to the base.

Alexa wasn't lying. The woman might've been under a truth spell when she'd told me about this place, but the verification was nonetheless relieving—bittersweet.

"Refuge," Momma answered, like the man should have known the answer. "We just traveled across the continent to find a magician base of some kind that's supposed to be here. Our friend is unconscious and needs medical attention."

"Alexa Delphine said you could help," Jak added, much to my surprise. When I glimpsed upward at him, his lip was pale and shivering, telling me that the cold was the only reason he *had* spoken up. "Do you know her, did you ever work with her?"

Only at her name did the group lower their weapons. Now the two on the side looked to the man in the middle as if for instructions.

"Your names?" he said, his hand staying tense beside him.

None of them recognize Dad or Aunt Becca. How sheltered are they out here?

For what I was pretty sure was the sake of our body temperatures, considering my very bones were now shivering, Momma was quick to reply: "I'm Amy Atera. This is my husband, Tristan; our daughter, Emmalynn; my sister-in-law, Rebecca; and our friend Jak. Our friend Alejandro is the one unconscious in the car."

"You're the Ateras?" The burly man on the left narrowed his icy deep-set eyes, his gruff voice no less subdued by his mask. "We thought Tristan and Rebecca Atera were dead."

"Well, I can't lie right now," Momma argued, the cloud in front of her mouth thickening with every word. "When was the last time you received an update on us?"

"Two weeks ago, when Rebecca Atera was found dead."

If they're part of the security here, they'd keep up on news like that to stay updated for safety reasons. If not, they're going out way too much.

Did that mean that that was their last update they'd gotten on *us*, or their last update period?

"Well, here I am," Aunt Becca remarked, her pale hands now shaking above her. "Look, we can tell you how we did it, but not if we freeze to death."

With my nose numb from the cold, my arms were begging me to drop them, still drenched with fatigue. I watched the Punjabi man in the middle press a button on his watch, silently begging him to take us inside already.

"It's the Ateras," he muttered. "Alexa Delphine sent them. They need medical attention."

Several seconds of bone-shivering cold passed, the snow ready to melt into my boots and give my toes frostbite.

"Okay," he eventually said, lowering his watch from his mouth. His eyes flashed amber again, and the truth spell released me. He nodded behind him. "I'm Karan, this is Pranjeeta. Luke will get your friend in the car. Follow us inside."

"Wait, what about the car itself?" Momma asked as my arms dropped to my sides, on fire. I caught a flash of amber from Auntie's eyes as she released our rescuers from her truth spell. "Everything we have is in there."

"We'll drive it to the base," Karan replied as Luke heavily walked past Aunt Becca. "We won't touch your things."

Wait, what?

"Hang—hang on," Dad said tiredly but warily, stopping in his tracks. "This isn't the base?"

The car door shut behind me, turning me around. Luke carried an unconscious Alejandro in his arms.

"We'll explain, but we need to get inside," Karan answered,

his accent thickening when he emphasized the words. "Please."

Needless to say, we understood the urgency. With Luke behind us, the five of us followed Karan and Pranjeeta around the tree line and toward the wooden cabin a little farther down along the highway.

Karan opened the front door with a creak, and we filed inside. It was barely ten degrees warmer but still, well, warmer, and had a saturated air of wood shavings and old rubber. Pulling down their face masks, Karan and Pranjeeta led us across the creaking floor and through an open lounge area with rustic furniture. A small office sat in the back, "STAFF ONLY" printed in white on the plaque nailed to the door. With Luke carrying Alejandro, Pranjeeta took his rifle from his back and mounted it with hers on the left wall.

"We have sensors here that detect activated magic so we know when to come out and greet refugees," she began, her accented voice sweet and rich. "We also keep a sensor on us so we can detect real magicians and mortals, just in case. You gave off a large wave, that's why we had to be extra cautious in case you were harmful magicians."

With the guns. And that's how they knew three of us have magic. They have government-level technology... For now, I had to pray that that was the blessing it seemed to be.

We arrived at a collapsible elevator door in the back of the office. Karan took off his thick winter glove and provided his handprint on the scanner on the wall. After a confirmative beep, he pressed the button underneath the scanner. The elevator door folded in on itself as it slid to the side.

"The base built this cabin," he said, "as a cover to the hikers that visit, but primarily so we could build an infirmary under-ground in case refugees need medical attention. They often do."

"So," Aunt Becca asked slowly next to me, "is it *just* the infir-mary down here?"

"Yes," Karan said, stepping aside to allow us into the elevator car. "The head nurse is calling in the chief and will address your friend. She'll explain everything else while we take your things up to the base."

"Wait." Momma stopped us all before we could enter. "Where exactly is that? We told you, that car has everything we own."

"Please, Mrs. Atera, you know you can trust us," Karan urged. "I promise, you'll have your things again after you receive treat-ment and are escorted to the base. Our settlement situation is not simple."

I knew my mother: because she had no other choice (and be-cause once she had a target, they never escaped her hunt), she stayed quiet and stepped into the elevator car. The rest of us fol-lowed, Luke with Alejandro at the front, before Pranjeeta pressed the down button.

The awkward silence only lasted for a second before I closed my eyes, fighting to keep my thoughts from taking the frontlines. The last five minutes started replaying before trickling down a dozen trails into other memories, so distant and yet vivid like they couldn't let me forget that a different part of my life still existed. Someone softly nudged my arm. I looked up next to me. Jak couldn't offer me his signature warm smile—like the scar under his eye and the one down his cheek would've made it easier to believe, anyway—but with those brown eyes alone, he was trying to reassure me. He was letting me see that right now. I didn't have a response, though; my adrenaline was still fading yet somehow heightened by the chill sending my body into survival mode so it could warm itself up somehow.

The elevator dinged before the collapsible door slid aside. Our three guards stepped out first, and the temperature plummeted again, the air damp but clean. With gray-speckled white tile below us, rectangular fluorescent lights hung all the way down the ceiling, the room big enough to comfortably store a dozen SUVs. Medical cots lined both walls sandwiching us, only a handful accompanied by an IV stand.

"This is the head nurse—" Karan began.

"Eun-Ji's been notified and wants to meet our new guests as soon as possible," a woman announced from the back, a chair squeaking as she stood. Her sweet yet deep voice tugged on my memory. "So I hope you're okay with staying behind for a bit to drive them up, Karan."

Aunt Becca was last in. The collapsible door slid closed behind us. But when I stepped up to my frozen mother's side, I didn't see anyone else in the excruciatingly bright room except the fair-skinned, auburn-haired, green-eyed woman strolling toward us from her desk.

The name fell from my lips, like saying it was the only way my mind would believe it: "Julia."

FOUR

Auburn ponytail dangling behind her, Julia moseyed down the white infirmary and to us in her teal scrubs—the inelastic fabric of which highlighted the small distension of her belly.

Is she...?

My stun stole the rest of that thought. The sterile smell of medical equipment almost burned my nose as she finished her way to us. Memories flashed in my mind of every conversation I'd had with "her" from October to March of my sophomore year. None of them real, none of them actually her—all of them her sister posing as her as the Callistro Academy school nurse.

Did she know yet that her sister—her entire family—was dead?

Her gaze instantly landed on me like she knew me. An image

of those emerald-green eyes losing their light in front of me pierced my memory. I stumbled into Aunt Becca behind me, Jak grabbing my arm to help keep me upright.

"Whoa," Becca whispered, straightening me. "You okay?"

"Julia," Momma said numbly. She knew, she'd been there. She'd seen her already like I had.

Yet Julia snapped into action once she saw the Spanish boy in Luke's arms, and she guided Luke to a cot on the right side of the infirmary. Upon her turning, there was no mistaking the humble bump in her belly.

"Do you already know each other?" Pranjeeta asked next to Karan, whose furrowed brow exposed that he had the same question.

"Not... directly," Momma replied, sticking close to Dad as we followed Luke. "We, um..."

"What?" Dad mumbled to her.

—*She's*— I began before remembering that he didn't have his magic and, therefore, couldn't hear telepathy. "Julia... the Callistro school nurse."

That was all I needed to say—and my dad and aunt had never looked more like siblings than when both of their mouths fell slightly agape and they stared back at each other with the same bright-blue eyes.

All those memories from sophomore year continued blaring in my head, conflicting with everything I saw right now.

"We're familiar with each other," Momma told Pranjeeta and Karan.

Julia remained unfazed as we all gathered around Alejandro's cot, her small hands feeling his pale-brown forehead and cheeks.

She slid out a narrow flashlight from her shirt pocket and opened one of his eyes at a time, moving the light back and forth over his irises before clicking it off. Then she grabbed the stethoscope around her neck. Her concentrated and firm yet gentle features reminded me so much of Alexa. Too much. I remembered everything about Julia, and yet I didn't know a single thing.

"Pale, low blood flow, dilated pupils," she noted. That sweet, kind voice. I hadn't heard it in almost a year. "What happened before he passed out?"

"He cast—a spell," Momma replied, apparently not yet wanting to get into the conversation that his teleportation would prompt. "He had to cast it to get us here."

"Exhaustion," Julia answered without missing a beat. "I'm gonna get an IV in him and elevate his feet, we need to get his blood flow circulating again."

The room stayed silent as she turned around and wheeled over an IV stand, then pulled down a lift strap from above the foot of the cot. She put both of Alejandro's legs into the lifts and then slid her sterilization tools over on a small metal tray. So practiced, like she was doing what she was meant to do, and it somehow wasn't hunting. Luke helped her remove Alejandro's coat and roll up his sleeve for the IV. As she slid on a pair of blue nitrile gloves, he faced the rest of us.

"Hey, I understand you folks wanna stick close to your belongings," he began in his gruff voice that made me doubt his sincerity—that and his dull-blue eyes that sat deep in his head, like he was always daring the earth to stop spinning. "But for safety's sake, considering your car's full to the brim, Pranjeeta and I gotta get it to the base as soon as possible."

"The license plate," Dad began, almost slurring his words like his tiredness was finally catching up to him. "That's—we switched plates back in the States, but it's been compromised. I don't think you wanna drive that thing for long."

"We have a discreet road we take," Pranjeeta said. "Much of it isn't a real road. We could probably take off the license plate completely. Either way, it'll be safe."

Dad took his gaze to Momma as if to verify she was okay with it. She nodded lightly, hugging his arm. "Okay," she said. "Thank you. Just please be careful."

"Yes, ma'am. Karan will drive you up when you're ready."

I tried to hide my swallow as Luke and Pranjeeta left the cot and walked back to the elevator. Part of me couldn't help but worry about our things, but the other part had to trust the truth spell we'd put them under outside.

"I'll keep lookout in the cabin as usual," Karan announced. "Please come up once you're ready."

Julia thanked him, and he walked away, joining Luke and Pranjeeta in the elevator car. When it went up, Julia returned her attention to the six of us, matching her eyes again with mine. My heart skipped a beat.

"Well, hello, Emmalynn. It's nice to formally meet you." Her gaze shifted to the tall boy next to me. "I'm surprised to see you here with them."

Jak didn't reply, casting his stare to the floor. I was right there with him; my lips had been stapled shut.

She tricked me echoed louder and louder in my head. *She cared about me* fought for its place. *She was never real* whispered back. I couldn't shove down the panic upon seeing her again, seeing her but never meeting *her*. But when Dad looked at me from the other side of the cot, his rugged eyes struck a deep chord in me. A reminder somehow.

I swallowed, sending everything into the pit of my stomach. We were here to get an explanation, to find out where Dad's magic was (and now the entire facility we'd come here for). The sooner I buried emotion to make room for rationality, the better.

"Your friend's vitals are otherwise normal and his breathing is regular," Julia told us. "He's just sleeping. Whatever spell he did zapped all his energy from him."

Like what I feel, I thought. Teleporting us here, even with my alleged "help", *had* pushed him too far.

I didn't understand, though: wielders can cast the same spell on something to give it extra power, but I couldn't cast whatever Alejandro did to teleport. Was it really my will that he had drawn from? Since when could magicians lend their energy to someone else for a spell?

"Now," Julia added, "if I knew what spell it was, I might be able to give you a more accurate prognosis."

"That's..." Momma murmured at the foot of the cot. Dad wrapped his arm around her waist. "Look, we're all exhausted, wildly disoriented, and still trying to convince ourselves that we can trust you or any of the people that just left. Alexa told us to come to the base under Mount Steele in British Columbia, and now you're all telling us that we're not there."

"Your friend Karan said you'd explain everything," Auntie remarked next to me.

"Okay, sure." Julia smiled, softly clapping her gloved hands together and looking between Aunt Becca and Dad. "First of all, it's good to see you guys aren't dead."

Alexa nailed *her personality.*

"Second of all, this *is* a base of some sorts, just not our main one. The main one's under Mount Steele in the Yukon."

"There are two?" Dad asked, arching a brow.

"Yeah, which serves us well. The Yukon is almost completely remote, and the Saint Elias Mountains are a great hiding place for a magician facility. We have a lot of security measures in place that the chief can tell you about when you meet her. This one serves more as a cover and immediate treatment center than anything else. It's infinitely more accessible to refugees because it's right off the highway, and then we're able to drive them up to the Yukon once we get them treated. If any hikers come around, we advise and equip them for the hike up the peak. Perfect cover story."

How long has this place been around? Someone clearly did their research before establishing it.

"So that's how Alexa kept it a secret after marrying William?" Jak muttered. I was kind of surprised that he'd spoken up, but he had business with the Delphines, too, in a way.

"One of the handful of ways," Julia said, resting her hand on the thin metal railing of Alejandro's cot. "Honestly, if you had magic, we might've been able to include you in the mission."

Dad sighed, rubbing Momma's side. "Well, if you haven't been caught by now, I guess it works."

"Our double agents do a pretty good job at keeping us hidden, too," Julia said. I mentally held on to my questions as they gathered. "Again, Eun-Ji can explain our logistics later. May I know what your friend tried before he passed out now?"

Momma pressed her lips together. "Alejandro's... unique. He

can teleport, which is the only reason we were able to escape the government to get here without being followed."

I guess she's ready for that conversation, after all.

Julia narrowed her eyes, tilting her head down. "*Teleport?*"

"I promise," Momma said tensely, "this is the last thing I have to lie about right now. None of us can tell you how, just that that's the case."

Julia must have been ready to ask how anyway, but then she caught my gaze, and her mouth closed. I realized then that Alexa had probably shared my blood test results exposing that I was a hybrid with her family. If I could be a hybrid, Alejandro could probably teleport.

With Jak in my peripheral vision, I straightened and widened my eyes slightly, praying that Julia would get the message. Thankfully, she left Momma with a simple hum of confusion.

But Jak's stare fell onto me like he was asking me the same question, and I reset. I glimpsed him solely for the sake of acknowledgement, letting him know that I wouldn't ignore the question forever—especially because he'd already seen me activate the warlock in me. It was only a matter of time until he knew.

"So if this isn't the main base," Dad said, readjusting his hold around Momma, "you don't store anyone's magic here, do you?"

"Exactly," Julia replied. "But Alexa did warn me before Christmas that we'd be getting your magic. Our retrievers on the East Coast usually take about two weeks to get back."

The tension in my chest flared. Dad's magic was supposed to be on its way to the base because the Delphines had taken it from him, but after what had happened that morning...

Did its deliverer even survive the raid? Or the trip here? If not, that left too big a chance that Caldwell had it. We only had four days until we'd know for sure. Somehow, paying the nore's price to find out exactly where it was right now felt steep.

"Now it makes sense that you're here days before they'd arrive," Julia added, looking down at Alejandro and snapping me out of my head, "since you had him. It doesn't sound like the trip went smoothly, though. And if Alexa sent you here directly... things must be bad down there."

I met Momma's eyes with the thought: *She doesn't know. We can't tell her that her entire family is dead, not right now, at least.* Especially when she was carrying the very last generation of Delphines.

"They are," I began, surprising myself. When my stare dragged itself to hers, the courage found me. "You have no idea what we've been through since they took my dad's magic, but Alexa said we'd get answers here that we can't get anywhere else. I've had questions about you guys since I found out you were magicians, so I need to know the truth about you and how you ended up here before I can trust you and the base in charge of our lives."

She pressed her thin lips together, nodding at me. "Fair enough. Okay. I'm not a Hunter, never have been. My parents just shoved that onto me and my siblings, but I never joined an agency after graduating."

Like what Alexa told me.

"So not only am I not recorded in any agency's files, but I'm also under an alias. Yeah, the world knows the Delphines as mortals, but that's never a guarantee that you won't have enemies. Let alone enemies who want to kill you if you or someone you know hits the right nerve. Hatred's always hungry for an opponent. So as far as the Hunter world is concerned, Julia Delphine doesn't exist."

"But to the federal government, you do," Momma argued.

"Yes, but I'm also a registered resident in Rome, where magic is legal. Even if they suspected me under my alias, the US can't touch me."

"How did you manage that?" Dad asked, the furrow in his brow deepening. "Moving internationally is a suicide mission for magicians."

"That's why it matters that I wasn't the only one in America whose last name was 'Delphine'. I came here so I could forget the mess America was tangling itself up in. Long story short, I stored my magic at the base while I got residency in Rome. That process alone took almost a decade. But then I came back here—I just knew this was where I had to be. Met a lot of good people, a great man, got married last year..." She placed a loving hand over her small bump. "Now I go back to Rome every once in a while to maintain my residency, but yeah—the US Government doesn't bat an eye at me because I don't have magic."

There were probably a million different roadblocks included in that story that she was sparing us from, but I almost wanted to hear them. After all, I didn't know if we'd ever see her again after getting to the Yukon.

"When did all that start?" I asked. "Your family being *protectors* of magic when Alexa always pretended to be the bad guy?"

"Well..."—she exhaled and rested her hauntingly green eyes on Alejandro's sleeping face—"after a few generations, someone realized that people don't attack someone they fear first. So to flip the tables and convince the world we hated what they did, we said we were hunters of magic—protectors of mortals. Half the world

respected us and the other half feared us, and anyone who chal-
lenged us paid a steep price for it. Obviously we stayed that way
for a long time until the kids in my generation started promoting
the idea of individuality and breaking free from our parents' mold
more and more. That was when my siblings and I started getting
iffy about the whole career, mostly because we wanted to be something that was... for us, I guess you could say, not for someone
else's legacy. We wanted our own independent lives."

I didn't expect the solemnity that fell over her face as she
crossed her arms. "Around then was when Alexa told us she was
pregnant, how it happened, and then about the magician facility.
She's the one who helped us realize we could fulfill our legacy with
a different purpose—*really* kick the mold. I immediately signed up
while my siblings continued their work in the States. We keep tabs
on each other all the while."

Kept. They died for all this. I trapped the words in my head.

"So Alexa was the one who found the facility?" Momma
asked. "When she was seventeen?"

"One of our instructors at the Callistro Academy was an
ally," Julia answered with a humble smile. "And someone she
trusted. So when she told them about her pregnancy, they referred
her to there. That's actually where Anthony was born."

Too many memories. Too many memories were stacking up
against me like a wobbling tower.

Jak placed his hand on my back, like he sensed every thought
going on in my head. He did have a terrifying ability to read me.

"I have to ask, though," Julia began, caution encroaching on
her tone as she looked at Jak across the cot. "You didn't leave an
accidental trail for William to follow, did you?"

He merely shook his head and muttered, "No."

She nodded. "Okay. Then I think we should focus on getting Alejandro awake and getting you up to the Yukon. The drive is *long*, but it's safe. And if Alejandro can make a full recovery, he can shorten the drive by... teleporting, evidently."

I looked down at his pale-brown face and wondered how long we had until then. After pushing himself to the extent of passing out, I wasn't sure if he'd have the energy to teleport for the rest of the day. But that was for him to decide, and I knew he was just as anxious to get us to safety as I was—that way, none of the last week and a half would have been for nothing.

C H A P T E R

FIVE

Karan didn't want to "spoil" anything for us about the facility until we could meet the chief, Eun-Ji Park. He did, however, warn us about the twenty-hour drive we had ahead of us to the Yukon, but that made Alejandro waking up a couple of hours later all the more exciting: after recovering more, he'd probably be able to shorten our trip by one or two hours.

"We can't ask you to do that, honey," Momma said, rubbing his shoulder as he sat on the side of his cot. Dad stood next to her with his arm around her waist. Aunt Becca, beside me, nodded along like she understood what we were saying. "You hurt yourself by taking us *here*. We'll be okay."

Jak glanced down at me on my other side, subtly cocking his

brows with no doubt the same thought I had: *Maybe you're okay with a drive that long, but some of us would love the shaved-off time.*

Alejandro took another swig of orange juice before shaking his head. "Taking you to the *base* is the job I came to do. I respect you, Mrs. Atera. But please respect my mission. You won't be safe until I take you there."

She looked between me, Dad, Aunt Becca, and even Jak before Dad took over for her.

"I can honor that," he said, his Spanish a little rusty and slow. "You're the only reason any of us are alive right now."

My stomach fluttered with unease. Both Alejandro and my parents were right: we weren't home free until we were at the main facility, and we wouldn't know exactly how protected it was until we saw it for ourselves.

"Be gentle with him," Julia remarked in Spanish, one of the three foreign languages she remembered from training. She wheeled Alejandro's IV stand to the cot over. "Do not let him push himself too far again."

Karan stepped away from the elevator door. "Will he be ready for the trip soon?" he asked.

Alejandro looked at me for the translation; Karan's accent made it difficult for him to understand English as well as he usually did. When I translated for him, he nodded. "I can—rest," he said slowly, awkwardly, to Karan in English, "in the car for... one hour or two hours? Yes?"

Karan nodded. "We should leave, then."

My parents helped Alejandro up from the cot, for some reason sending my heart thumping. As if he sensed it, Jak placed a light hand on my upper back, reassuring me again. I gave him a brief smile of acknowledgement.

"So we're ready?" Aunt Becca asked, stepping backwards and toward the elevator.

Momma confirmed, steadying Alejandro. Dad offered him his arm, which he politely declined but thanked him for.

Unexpectedly, Momma turned her head, meeting her gaze with Julia's. "Thank you," she said earnestly. "I wish I had more to say right now."

"You don't even have to say that."

I followed Momma's eyes, finding the soft smile that pulled up Julia's pink lips. Her role was down here under the cabin, and I highly doubted we'd need to come back here, so this very well could be the last time we'd see her. Part of me couldn't help my gratitude that we wouldn't be the ones to tell her about her family, but the other part announced my guilt for it; in a way, shouldn't we have *been* the ones to tell her?

I'm sorry, I almost said. Instead, I followed suit with Momma: "Thank you."

"You're welcome," she said. Just like all those times I'd left the nurse's office after "she" had treated me at Callistro. "It was nice to finally meet you."

I turned away and stepped in line with Jak and Aunt Becca toward the elevator, cutting off my thoughts at the stem. Roughly twenty hours lay between us and what was supposed to be our final destination for answers, refuge, and somewhere safe to start planning Mr. Dawson's rescue. I loved my family too much to let my guard down for one second.

🔥

At the end of what ended up being seventeen hours thanks to Alejandro, we found ourselves in the rocky, snowy wilderness of the Saint Elias Mountains, face to face with a mountain three times the height of Mount Steele in British Columbia. Amidst the barren territory and jagged peaks that surrounded us on all fronts, we got out of the crossover and met with two agents that had been sent up to restock our six empty jerrycans and drive back to the cabin. Karan then escorted us to a particular "incline of snow" that, surprise, was a metal door.

"Yes," he muttered into his watch. "I'm here with the Ateras and two friends."

Seconds later, the incline split apart, chunks of snow crumbling off it. The seven of us walked inside and into a dim, cramped elevator lobby. Two elevators sat a few feet apart from each other. Karan opened the left one, and we gathered inside before the doors slid shut and the car jerked down.

Nobody had anything to say, and I only realized why when I thought it myself: *This is it. This is really, finally it.* And saying it out loud kind of felt like it would make it all disappear.

Was the last week and a half, even the last twenty-four hours, about to be worth it?

The stainless-steel doors slid open with a quiet grinding sound. Karan led the way out, stepping onto a concrete floor, and I cautiously followed with my family.

My eyes didn't know where to land: a cavernous lobby of gray walls and steel support beams stretched out in front of us, entryways branching off on either side. Long industrial fluorescent lights overhead almost gave the same brightness as morning outside. A concourse continued straight down in the back of the lobby, accommodating the entrances of more hallways on both sides. Concrete echoed our steps before we wandered onto a dark-yellow rug that muted them. A grand oak coffee table sat in the middle of it, vinyl armchairs set up in pairs and sets of four across it. At the other end lay a large secretary desk.

Where is everyone? I thought, right when Karan turned around to face us.

"It's still early," he said. "A lot of residents are asleep. Eun-Ji should be here soon to address—"

"Karan?"

A melodic voice floated down from the concourse ahead, turning his back to us. With raven-black hair locked up in a simple bun, a short Korean woman sauntered past the secretary desk in a yellow blouse and gray pencil skirt. Her heels were stifled on the rug as she approached, her petite hands folded in front of her. Despite her soft features, her every step seemed to command respect, deep smile lines kind but authoritative on her round face.

Her dark-eyed gaze fell onto Dad and Aunt Becca, her hands mindlessly unfolding. "Mr. and Ms. Atera," she said, her melodic voice hollowing. "I'm... I'm sorry, it's just surprising to see that it really is you."

Huh, I thought. *I wonder how* she *recognizes them.*

"Right, um,"—she quickly shook her head, readjusting—"let's see if I have this right from what Julia told me." She looked upward at Momma standing beside me and offered her hand. "Of course, there's Mr. Atera, and I'm assuming you're Amy, his wife."

"Ms. Park?" Momma asked, accepting her hand after Dad.

"'Eun-Ji' is fine," she replied reassuringly. Her eyes moved over to me. "You must be the beautiful Emmalynn Atera, their daughter."

I was too exhausted to be shy, so I mustered a polite smile and a thank-you.

She looked up at the tall boy on my other side. "From Julia's description, you're... Jak. Jakson Bleu, her nephew-in-law."

The words were bitter to hear, but we all knew better than to correct her on that.

"And then..."

I perked up when Eun-Ji's gaze landed on Alejandro, when the air shifted into unchartered territory.

"Alejandro," she mused. "The boy who teleported his friends to safety, do I have that right?"

After the curious way she'd said it, I kind of wished that she *didn't* have it right.

But to my blatant surprise, when Alejandro looked down the line of us, Momma nodded with encouragement at him.

"Yes," he answered warily, "*pero*—I mean, but I can't speak English well."

"You understand it, though?"

"Yes, ma'am."

"Then don't worry." She turned to Karan behind her. "Thank you for bringing them here, I'm glad you're all safe. Get some much-deserved rest before going back to the security ward."

"Yes, ma'am," Karan replied, facing us with the friendliest smile he'd mustered since we met. "Welcome to Bouchard, Ateras and friends."

It wasn't until he walked off the rug and toward one of the hallway entrances on the upper-right side of the lobby did Eun-Ji speak again. "He's actually going in the direction I wanted to take you all to—if you'd like to speak privately in your room. But we can also talk out here if you're more comfortable with it."

"Would anyone here recognize us?" Aunt Becca asked.

"A select few," Eun-Ji said, doubt narrowing her eyes. "But new refugees are few and far between—you'd have some unwanted attention either way once more people start waking up."

"And you already have a room for us?" Dad asked.

"Of course." Eun-Ji nodded once slowly, like we needed time to process her every move. "We set it up as soon as Julia called in with the news that you'd arrived at the cabin. Speaking of,"—her kind yet now urgent eyes looked over us again—"you said Alexa Delphine sent you?"

The name still wrenched my gut every time I heard it, especially because we were the only ones who knew she was dead.

"Yes," Momma replied stolidly, refusing to expose too much emotion. Part of me envied her for being able to do that so well.

"Good. Please follow me."

Eun-Ji turned in her heels toward the upper-right corner of the lobby. Only when my parents started following her did I feel safe to do so, and apparently the same went for Auntie, Jak, and Alejandro. My parents stayed ahead of us, their hands intertwined with each other. Despite that, I'd never seen their backs, their postures, so rigid before. Almost like they had to hold on to each other to stop the other from physically falling apart right now after the last twenty-four hours.

A full breath swirled in my lungs before I quietly released it. But the boy next to me always heard those kinds of things, especially when I didn't want him to.

When I caught his eye, Jak gave me a tight and all-too-subtle smile. It wasn't even enough to dent the scar down his cheek. I reminded myself that just over a month had passed since his torture. That wasn't enough time; of course he still wasn't himself. Half of me was scared that he'd never be himself again.

None of us are ourselves right now.

Aunt Becca and Alejandro walked on my other side. I'd never seen Auntie's soft, heart-shaped face so stone-like, so... masked. Like a Hunter's. Even the icy blue of her gentle eyes seemed harsher, all the more so with the platinum blond she'd dyed her shoulder-length hair last year. The bright lights overhead further defined the profile of her straight nose and small lips. Despite her usual hesitant-yet-ready-for-sarcasm-to-save-the-day demeanor, something felt amiss.

"Hey," I whispered, letting my steps fall a little behind. She, Jak, and Alejandro matched me. "Are you okay?"

"Why're you asking *me* that?" she asked incredulously.

"You're so serious."

She nudged my arm in her half-teasing, half-assurance way. "If I'm not running, I'm fine, Em."

I wish I didn't feel that so heavily right now.

I tried to let the weight of that fall off as Eun-Ji led us down a narrow white hallway illuminated with circular lights installed above. Dark, tight-woven carpet covered the floor of this section instead of echoey concrete, absorbing our footsteps. Despite that, some of me remained uneasy, and I was pretty sure I wasn't the only one. I tried reminding myself that this place was safe, we were supposed to be here, but instinct is next to impossible to override, even when your rationality has all the evidence it needs.

Midnight-blue doors sandwiched us on both sides as we

walked. The hallway pattern of dark carpet and bright circle lights repeated as we turned right and then left. For a second, I almost felt like we were walking through a hotel.

"Your rooms are close to the end of this sector," Eun-Ji murmured, telling me that too many people were asleep behind these doors to use our regular voices. "We expand as needed to accommodate new residents, always a few steps ahead of the population. Your sleeping arrangements are up to you, of course, but I put Jak and Alejandro in one room and the Ateras next door for now."

In the corner of my eye, I sensed Alejandro's stare. I didn't have time to meet it before I heard in Spanish, —*I don't think Jak will like that.*—

—*It's fine,*— I assured him as we slowed toward the end of the last hall and faced the left side. The boy was convinced that Jak wasn't his biggest fan. —*You won't be roommates for long, you're leaving soon.*—

Eun-Ji slid out a key from her gray pencil skirt pocket and unlocked the door. It opened with a soft click and a squeak on its hinges, and we filed inside after her.

She flicked on a light switch when, last inside, Alejandro closed the door. We ambled out of the short entry hallway, passing on the left what I assumed was a bathroom door, and stepped into a quaint, minimalistic bedroom. Against the right wall stood a hickory-colored credenza, a simple lamp situated on the corner and alit. That contributed to the soft-yellow bulbs in the ceiling illuminating the entire room. In the corner beside me sat a reading chair, a lamp standing tall next to it. Two full-sized beds lay in the middle with our suitcases sitting on top of them.

"Glad our things made the trip," Dad said, rubbing his chin.

"If I'm being honest, I'm amazed that any of this is real."

"Of course, please, take a seat anywhere," Eun-Ji said, gesturing across the room. "I want to explain as much as I can. The pressing matters for now, at least."

"Security is our number one priority," Momma began, going with Dad to the second bed and taking a seat on the edge of it. Aunt Becca and I did the same with the first bed, and Alejandro took the reading chair. Jak leaned against the wall the bathroom shared, keeping his arms firmly crossed over his chest. "Julia was saying that the base—Bouchard—has a lot of security measures in place. What do those include?"

"A number of things," Eun-Ji replied, standing tall and prim in front of the credenza. "But broadly speaking, if I may, our two immediate measures include our sensors that detect magic on the surface in case there's something, or someone, supernatural we need to investigate. The other is a bit tricky."

Momma tiredly chuckled. "Try me."

"Bouchard is guarded by a spell that prevents external magic from acting upon it, say, if someone were to try to use a locator spell on any one of you while you're here. Magicians can still cast inside, but magic can't penetrate us from the outside."

The whole room seemed to wake up at that news. "That's possible?" I asked.

"Well, considering its difficulty and complexity, as you can imagine, it's a *rare* spell few are aware of—a select few governments are. Our founder, though, always thought two steps ahead."

I can tell by them picking "Mount Steele" to set up camp at.

"Okay, the spell makes sense," Momma began, "but I'm pleasantly surprised about the sensors. Usually only Hunters have access to devices like that in the US."

"We do have a team of Hunters who serve as undercover agents," Eun-Ji told her. "Otherwise, for everyone's safety, tech advancement is an absolute priority here."

Her nearly black eyes landed on Dad, causing the air to shift again. It was astounding how a woman so petite had such authoritative power. "All of which reminds me, Mr. Atera, we should be receiving your magic within the next couple of days."

We can only pray, I thought, and I can guarantee that I wasn't the only one in the room who did. It was a good thing that Eun-Ji kept talking before any of us could react.

"That said, I'm glad you all made it here safely after what I know was a *long* journey, with or without teleporting. Please, just do your best to breathe and settle in right now. The last thing I want any of you to do is relive what brought you here."

It was a *great* thing that Eun-Ji had kept talking.

"I like you, we're on the same page," Aunt Becca remarked next to me. "Because I'd kinda like to know more about this place, how all this happened, especially after hearing how Julia ended up here. I mean, how did *you* end up here? And as chief?"

"Bouchard has been here a long time," Eun-Ji said, lifting her chin with pride. "1827."

Wait, what? Canada hadn't been formally founded yet, let alone had its mountains named. Had the Mount Steele coincidence been intentional?

"My parents immigrated here from South Korea just before Canada completely outlawed magic. After that happened, it was a miracle of mercy that the Hunter who caught my parents was an ally and sent them over here. I was born a few years later."

"And you've stayed here your *whole* life?" Momma asked.

"Fifty-two short years, yes."

Even as I write this now, I still have the same reaction to that: *Whoa.* With smooth skin marked by no more than five wrinkles, Eun-Ji didn't look a day over thirty-five.

"My life is founded on our mission: to protect and preserve the wielders of magic. For any refugee who's actively being hunted by the local, state, or federal government, they're able to lead a safe life here until they're forgotten about. From there, they can decide if they want to reenter society as a mortal, or continue their life here. We store everyone's magic in a high-security vault farther underground. Seeing as how you're all here, the Delphines joining us was nothing short of destiny—especially if you're running from whom I think you are."

"Caldwell," Dad mumbled, his eyes falling to the floor. "Never announced that he *was* after us, just... came."

Eun-Ji simply nodded. "I sincerely wish I could say that doesn't make sense."

"What do you mean?" Momma asked warily, a divot forming between her brows.

Eun-Ji shifted her weight, squaring her shoulders. Her smile had dissipated, replaced by the professionalism of a facility chief. "We've been gathering intel on him since he first assumed the presidency. Something's never been right about him. That's why the Delphines have been so critical to our operations: they work directly under him, they have the best leads. Alexa's even spoken to him at some points. We have a couple of theories about his intentions, but they're far-fetched. We can't say for sure that any of them are true, but he has something underway. I wouldn't be surprised if the Ateras had something to do with it."

I leaned back on the bed with a small huff, supporting myself with one hand and lifting my other to the locket around my neck. I caught Jak's eye and could practically hear the same thought in his head: great—*more* theorizing about an enemy we knew too little about and had no access to without plunging into certain death.

"Actually, if I may be so bold," Eun-Ji began, her scrutinizing gaze moving to Jak, "how did William Bleu's son wind up with the Ateras? Considering your father's history—no offense."

"I was..."—Jak cast his eyes down, shrugging—"like the Delphines. I wanted to protect, not kill, I didn't want to be my dad. My mom taught me better."

"Your mother was mortal but an ally of magic?"

"She was the one who told me about the Ateras," he said, his body going rigid as if to protect itself. "She was killed during a hunt when I was seven and told me to protect them before she died. Her mission became my mission."

"I'm sorry." Eun-Ji's features somehow softened beyond their natural state, her tone following suit. "You're right, she taught you much better. What was her name?"

"Um..." Jak swallowed, like he couldn't let the memory of his mom fall into the wrong hands. "'Aastha'."

Eun-Ji's shoulders fell slack. I almost thought she'd taken offense somehow to his answer until she asked, "Aastha Virani?"

The entire room, even Alejandro, dared to look at Jak again. His eyes seemed to empty. "Yeah..."

I glanced at my parents sitting on the other bed like they'd somehow know what was going on, but their expressions were just as blank with confusion. I returned to Eun-Ji when she stepped away from the credenza and to Jak. Raising her small hands and looking up at him, she whispered a simple "May I?" that he hesitantly gave his permission to.

—*What's going on?*— Alejandro asked.

—*I don't know.*—

Her left hand hovered above his scarred cheek, her other pushing a few strands of his dark hair away from his eyes. She ran her index finger down the narrow bridge of his nose. Ultimately, she came to cup his face.

"It makes sense now," she murmured, her hands falling to her sides. "Of course, I remember. Your mother was the most kindhearted Hunter I knew."

C H A P T E R

Six

The words seemed to slam into Jak with almost enough force to knock him into the wall behind him. Aastha, a natural-born Hunter, had been involved with and contributed to a safe haven for wielders? At what point with her magic-despising husband?

"You knew my mom?" Jak murmured to Eun-Ji, his stun suppressing his voice. "How? When—when was she—did she ever come here?"

"As often as she could," Eun-Ji said. "It's funny how someone so kind and compassionate to the world around her was so naturally deft at a Hunter career. She was one of our best and a favorite around here with the residents. One of the last times I saw her, she came to tell me that she'd found the man she wanted to marry.

I never knew her William was William *Bleu.*"

Jak glanced at the rest of us in the bedroom like we had the right response for him. If his mother had found some roots here, it was no wonder she'd kept the outlook on wielders that she had. It was no wonder that Jak had ended up the way he had, either, for the sake of keeping her legacy intact.

"She kept..." he eventually managed, "she kept this place a secret from us for their whole marriage."

"She told me she'd try to persuade him to join. But that was the last conversation we ever had. I had no idea that she'd passed..."

I blinked, swallowing. Had Alexa not told *anyone* she'd accidentally killed her, not even Eun-Ji?

A moment of silence settled over the room. I wondered how long it'd been since Aastha had last had one.

I looked up at Jak standing in front of the wall, wondering if he was still with us right now. Something was hiding behind that blank stare, and I'd seen those eyes on him before: wild and sporadic on the inside, trapped on whatever was in front of him like a caged animal waiting to be released. I'd seen them the day my family and I had sat him down and told him that the Delphines were actually magicians, and it'd hit him like it had changed his whole identity. What thoughts were going on behind those eyes right now?

"I'm..." he began, stepping sideways and toward the short entry hallway, "I'm gonna be out in the hall for a minute."

He turned away before any of us could fit in a word and strode off.

The door shut gently behind him, and I looked at my parents

sitting on the foot of their bed. Momma's lips parted before she swallowed. She didn't know what to say, what to make of it, and Dad's stare on the floor told me the same thing about him. They were still reeling from everything.

So is Jak.

Unlike last time, I had no hesitation going after him.

I took comfort in my muted steps as I darted into the hallway and to the door. I swung it open with ease and made sure to close it carefully behind me, mindful of the sleeping residents. Jak was pacing down the white hall back the way we'd come, and I hurried toward him.

"Hey," I murmured, turning him around. I almost ran into him when he stopped dead in his tracks. "Everything okay?"

"Yeah," he said with a strangely tight voice. "I just... I need to think, that's all."

"Are you sure? Because—you can talk to me. If you need to."

"I know." He nodded. "I just... I need—I don't know."

I didn't, either. But that was mostly because I had no idea what was going on in his head right now.

"I can go back in the room," I said softly, pointing loosely behind me. "Unless you—do you... need me right now?"

He pressed his lips together, sticking his hands into his jean pockets. "I feel like I do, but..."

I waited.

He shrugged lightly, helplessly. "I always feel like I do."

I didn't know what to think of that—not when something was clearly wrong and I was 90 percent sure he was suppressing it for everyone else's sake.

He never acts for his own sake.

But someone needed to. So I nodded at him with encouragement. "Tell me."

"I just..." He closed his eyes like he was already too tired to have this conversation. "My mom died when I was seven. I suppressed a ton of stuff from back then, so now I know even less than I did when I was a kid. But now I'm finding out that she was part of *this*, all this,"—he gestured to the empty hall around us—"she practically led a double life here and was, apparently, supposed to take my dad with her. But then, like I said, she always kept this place a secret, she never told him about it, and I bet you I know why. He showed her again why she couldn't trust him with this before she had the chance to. He gave her the same reasons she only ever trusted *me* with your name and not him, he was the same ignorant, *hateful* piece of—!"

Jak snapped his mouth shut, firmly rubbing it as if to hold it closed. His voice climbed in volume with every sentence, each one dribbling out faster than the last; it was like even he didn't know what struck him so wrong about Aastha's involvement with Bouchard, but he was slowly uncovering it.

Or this was the thread making him unravel.

The circular lights overhead betrayed the glisten appearing in his eyes. He closed them, pressing the heels of his palms against them. Resetting.

I took a step toward him. "It's okay."

A lump passed in his throat. He kept a hand over his eyes, shielding them from me. "He could've been part of this," he muttered. "He could've done something good if he'd just listened to my mom. All he had to do was *listen*, even Alexa was better than that when she had the same cover as him." He dropped his hand, exposing the red flooding into his nose and cheeks. For the second time since we'd known each other, Jak let me see his bottom lip quiver with his caged tears. "He always wanted to avenge my mom when people like him were the ones who killed her. The man he chose to be spat on her memory, abandoned me, put me on a federal list I'm never gonna escape! He physically tortured me, *his son!*"

The truth that Alexa was Aastha's killer had never rested so bitterly on my tongue, but for Jak's own good, I swallowed it back down; Momma once told me on the cruise last year that not even the best Hunter in the world is strong all the time because they know it's a death sentence. Right now, Jak was crumbling and avoiding that sentence, and I needed to let him.

"It was all for nothing..." he whispered, his broken words for him only. He leaned his back against the wall of the next-door room, his room. My gaze stayed loyal to him—to the tear that broke free and trickled down along the taut scar he'd earned on his cheek for my sake. "His own plan was what killed him in the end. Everything he did to our family was for nothing. My mom died for nothing, he hurt me for nothing, I was orphaned..."—Jak's tears finally won out, sliding down his face without mercy as his voice gave out—"for nothing."

I stepped in front of him, reached for his shoulders, and pulled him into me. His forehead fell onto my shoulder as he inhaled, his arms locking around my torso like I was the only thing to hold on to in a raging flood. He let out a ragged exhale and jerked with every stifled sob into my coat, chipping away at my heart with each one. Jakson Bleu doesn't cry, not unless you've broken him. And my heart couldn't let him break alone when he was an integral part of it.

"It's okay," I whispered again, trying to keep myself afloat with him. Tears pressed against my eyes, and my hands tightened on his back. I understood now: if William had been willing to serve this place like his wife had been, he wouldn't have set his son on the path he'd spiraled down—been tortured on. Jak still blamed his father for everything that had happened to him and his family, and he couldn't even lash out at him for it.

"All he had to do was listen," he whispered hollowly.

"I know."

His head rose and he stepped back, pressing his back against the wall again. He dragged the heel of his palm across his eyes to dry them. "I'm so sick of—"

He locked his jaw so tightly that I was scared his teeth would shatter. Then, he shook his head.

"What?" I asked.

Another hard lump passed in his throat. Nothing.

"Hey." I leaned my shoulder against the wall, trying to put myself on his level, let him know that I was willing to go down there with him. "You're hurting. You were set on a path you didn't deserve, you've lost a lot, too. Don't care about being right or polite right now. Just give me what hurts."

He still refused to look at me as he said, "I'm... sick of this."

I fought tooth and nail not to regret my decision, to remember that he *was* hurting. "'This'?"

"Magic," he stated. "Running, hunting, being part of it, losing everything because of it. Losing everything I've ever had because of it."

With that, I let him talk—because a fraction of me shared that exact sentiment.

"All because of people like *him*. And my mom had the mortal capability of *fighting* for something like this despite not being inherently part of it. But my dad—"

He rubbed his mouth again, then wiped his watering eyes. I was surprised at how long it took him to find his steadiness to speak again. "I guess I just realized that I lost him the moment she died... I lost them both on the same night."

He leaned his head against the wall. The fluorescent lights illuminated the red in his face as he looked up at them. "My parents are dead, Emma."

My hand rested on his arm. He still wouldn't look at me, and I couldn't tell if that was a curse or a blessing; the heartbreak screaming in his eyes right now would rip me apart. It would threaten my own resolve, and I now needed to shield him under it, too.

I kept my gaze on him. Just watched him. I didn't know what else to do. My heart twinged at the fact that I didn't have anything for him right now.

"I want to help," I whispered. "I don't want you to hurt alone."

He nodded, closing his eyes. "I know."

I swallowed. *Don't hurt,* I begged in my head. *Please don't hurt. It hurts me.* My care for him bound me to his pain as if it were my own. I knew nothing else except that it hurt.

The last time we were both like this... both hurting together—it was the night he'd cried with me on my living room carpet before we left town. Despite how he'd been falling apart in my arms, he'd still managed the only piece of comfort my grieving heart could accept at the time.

"Remember what you told me at my house the night we left Capperson? How the last thing I'll ever be from here on out is alone?"

"Yeah."

"That goes for you, too. And if you ever let yourself be alone when you need someone..."

My mind trailed off to the last conversation I'd had with Sarah right before we left that night. *"Don't do this alone."*

"Don't do that to yourself," I told Jak. "Or me. Please?"

I couldn't make the grand speeches he could, but I could try. I think my effort was what he saw in that moment, because after standing there for a bit, he huffed, rubbing his face with a tired hand. "I'm—I'm sorry," he whispered. "I'm trying to deal with it, I am. We're supposed to be on a rescue mission and I'm supposed to be—literally anything but this."

Mr. Dawson. I couldn't believe I'd managed to forget about him for even a second.

He's right. We had to keep going. Getting here had always been the goal: we could only save Dawson once we were safe, and now we were safe to plan.

"Don't apologize." I stood up straight. "We're finally allowed to rest, so we should while we can. Let's get settled in."

Jak stayed against the wall. I almost contemplated leaving him to gather his thoughts more until I took his hand. Cold and a little rough. Finally, he looked up at me with those russet eyes that were enough to warm me up even in the heart of the Saint Elias Mountains.

"Then we'll never have to leave each other again," I told him.

A wave of relief swelled in my chest when his frown softened and he pushed himself off the wall. His hand stayed cold in mine as we walked back to my family's room.

C H A P T E R

SEVEN

Bouchard was, of course, always prepared for worst-case scenario, which Security and Defense had calculated as unlikely at any given moment. Still, the alarms were always ready to sound, and all eight hundred residents knew to flood into the panic room under the eating hall if that day ever came. All that was why we started feeling *actually* safe as we went with Eun-Ji for our formal debriefings and interviews (protocol). Then we were officially welcomed to Bouchard Base and wished a happy New Year's Day.

Needless to say, the new year had snuck up on us. But that gave me all the more motivation to start it right:

"I need Mr. Dawson's tie," I told Dad, flipping open the lid of my suitcase on my and Auntie's bed. Thankfully, Karan had been telling the truth when he'd said our things would be taken care of. In the corner of my suitcase, my gaze caught on the small black box with the three Atera family rings Jak had gotten me for my birthday last year. I wondered if we'd finally get to regularly wear them now that we were here.

"Hope Thomas is actually awake," Dad mumbled from his and Momma's bed next to ours, making me look up. "And that magic will give you an actual place this time."

Auntie unpacked her suitcase at the foot of our bed, and Momma mimicked her, taking her clothes out and putting them in the dresser next to the credenza. Dad drew Mr. Dawson's navy-blue plaid tie out of his coat pocket and tossed it to me.

I rubbed the stiff fabric with my thumb, closing my eyes. *Invenio.*

Sheer amber waves of light burst in my vision. Just when I had hope for a real answer this time, the light ultimately faded into the same black nothingness we'd gotten every time Auntie and I had cast the locator spell.

That same whisper of magic resonated in my chest, too: *Washington, DC.*

I huffed, opening my eyes and tossing the tie next to my suitcase. "It's still black and I'm just getting 'Washington, DC'. For all we know he's in a coma in the White House."

Dad took a deep breath before tightly pursing his lips, shaking his head. "You know what—all we can ask for right now is the fact he's still alive."

"Exactly," I said, refusing to unpack a single piece of clothing. "He wouldn't still be in the city unless he was still in custody, and the only place I can think of for that is the White House. It's been a week and a half, we can't stay here when we have a lead and his life depends on it. Alejandro and I can—"

"Okay, stop," Momma said, turning around from the dresser. Flyaways stuck out all over her chestnut hair, a sight I'd only ever seen in the middle of the night and after she sparred with me. "You're right, we're not staying here any longer than we have to. But we need a plan before we jump in. If he *is* at the White House, he's in a top-secret, heavily guarded, *well-hidden* facility. Alejandro can't teleport with just an idea of where he wants to go, and if you teleport to anywhere in the White House, you'll be caught with the first step you take."

I was almost tempted to take that route and use an invisibility cloak to sneak around—but with the agents, technology, and security measures in that place, someone was bound to sense the active magic and find me almost as fast. The same thing went for using an appearance spell.

"Then I can figure out where he is with the nore part of me," I argued instead. "One of you can pay the price, just one question."

Aunt Becca tightened her small lips, Dad shaking his head again. My least-favorite reaction, though, was Momma lowering the pair of pajamas in her hands, her refined features on her narrow face dropping in disbelief.

"'Just one question'?" She stuffed her pajamas into the open drawer behind her before turning back to me. "No, not anymore. You are the government's *most* wanted target right now because of your magic alone. Your bloodline makes you all the more so, and what happens when they debrief you about your family and you have our answer sitting in your head? Becca already had to use the nore part of you to find out that Thomas was even alive before we left Capperson. Don't let them use you against us, no."

The words buzzed with conviction in my chest, especially because of what I'd seen when Aunt Becca asked me her question: her grabbing an invisibility cloak the night Dad was kidnapped and leaving the apartment to walk around the neighborhood. It turned out, she'd started doing that almost a year ago. I'd asked her why, and she'd admitted that it was a coping mechanism to feel a little normal after getting so down and restless about staying in one place for so long. It might've been small, but it was still a weakness of hers I now had stored in my mind that anyone could exploit if they wanted to use it against her.

I almost let Mom have this one before remembering that I wasn't just a nore. That I had knowledge about every one of my class identities except the one I was by lineage: a sorceress. And my parents had promised to tell me about it by New Year's.

"Then what about my identity as a sorceress?" I said. "Would that help?"

I carefully watched as Momma pressed her lips together and, surprisingly, looked over at Dad as if to ask for help. But to my disappointment, he gave another tired sigh in response.

"Emma," he began, "that's a long conversation that none of us have the capacity to have right now, please don't do that to us."

I bristled. *Do that* to them? "So it would help?"

"No, it wouldn't." He looked up at me with drooping yet rugged eyes. "And again, we're not ready to have this conversation."

"It really wouldn't help," Aunt Becca assured me from the foot of the bed. She pushed her white-blond hair behind her ear. "Trust me, you don't have to worry about that. One thing at a time—right now, it's concerning enough that the spell isn't giving you the actual place he's at like it should."

My very jawbone was tense with my thinning patience. Unfortunately, I already knew where this conversation was heading toward, and it wasn't going to help us or get us back on track to Dawson. Which only made me angrier that I had to let it go.

I took a few seconds to rein in that anger until I could forget the issue for now. That left me with the one thought that none of us had been brave enough to address yet: "He shouldn't still be alive."

"Why would you say that?" Becca asked, leaning down for a shirt from her suitcase.

"Because he shouldn't be, it's Caldwell." I plopped down in the reading chair in the corner behind me. "They'd only keep him alive for this long in custody because he's a lead to us, but he'd never give that information up. They probably know that, too, they're probably doing everything they can to make him give it up like Jak's kidnappers did to him—"

"Emma," Momma stated. Her long fingers tightly gripped the jeans in her hands. "Trust me. The last thing we want to do is leave him in Caldwell's custody. The only reason your dad and I aren't grabbing the car and driving across the continent is because we'd lose exponentially more if we tried to get him right now. We don't even know which government located us in Brookmere or how they did it when we've been in rural Canada this long with a false license plate, and we don't know why they didn't come after us again the entire time we were at the cabin. Our faces weren't officially wanted yet because, for whatever reason, Caldwell hasn't publicized us. And when we escaped, we gave away that someone in our group has the impossible ability to teleport, making us *infinitely* more valuable than we already are! We can't find out where Thomas is without sacrificing something we can't afford, and none of us are in the mindset to plan something that has a greater-than-5-percent chance of saving him. Drop it."

"He knows how to survive," Dad added from his spot against the wall—too calmly for someone talking about his best friend the US Government was likely torturing as we spoke. "He helped fake my and Becca's deaths, and he was one of Redway's top students. As long as he's alive, we have to be smart about our every step forward. We only get one chance, and we need to heal before we take it."

"*Save them.*"

Alexa hadn't been talking about Dawson when she'd said that to me—so why did I feel that pressure so intensely right now? Why did I feel like I needed to fulfill those words however I could before I failed them?

"Have any of you ever had someone be physically tortured for you?"

That was why. *Because I've failed them before.* I barely got there in time to save Jak, and if I couldn't succeed now with my own godfather, not even Adara could help her people.

"And then been forced to see what it did to them, how it left them, and still see it every day on their face?"

"Em, that's not fair—" Becca began, prompting me to stand.

"We didn't need to wait this long when it happened to Jak, we went after him almost immediately!"

"Emmalynn," Momma spat, her back to me.

"Why are we putting off at least *trying* to fix things?"

"You think we haven't been trying?" she exclaimed, whirling on me. "You think *this* is our first choice of action? That man has been part of this family since he was fourteen, he helped me raise you, he sacrificed everything he ever wanted for us! Everything in me *screams* to go after him, that there's something we can do right now to fix putting him in this position in the first place!"

"Listen to me, Emma."

Dad's unfamiliarly low voice froze me in my spot. I forced myself to look at him.

"None of us would be here without him," he stated. "His visions were the only hope I had half the days I was in captivity. Now he's going through the same thing for my family, MY family, how dare you think I'm prolonging his suffering on purpose?"

Anger bubbled in my chest. "I never said—"

"Since we escaped that morning, I've been trying to think of something that'll get him out." He stood from the wall. His voice rose unsteadily, like his last strings of self-control were starting to snap the tighter he pulled on them. "And it kills me that I still have enough rationality to stop me from doing any of it, because it'll all get my family killed. His sacrifice is for nothing if we throw our lives away trying to save him when we're not ready."

"So drop it," Mom said again, throwing her clothes into the dresser—hiding the red in her nose and the glisten in her usually strong eyes. And with the tremble that not even she could conceal in her voice, it hit me: now that we finally had a real moment to sit down and process, we were a lot closer to the verge of breaking than I'd thought. If Aunt Becca was in the same boat, she'd somehow gotten better at hiding it than any of us.

In full honesty, it was knowing I wouldn't win this argument that made me give up. I knew how this would end: I'd blow up, Mom and I would fight, and I'd commit an impulsive and fatal mistake that my family would have to clean up.

"Fine," I spat. Not this time.

I strode into the short entry hallway and to our door, swinging it open. Sure enough, Momma's ragged, tear-filled breath in caught my ears just before the door shut behind me.

"The walls must be pretty soundproof," Jak noted when he opened his door to me. Leaving it open, he stepped aside to allow me in and followed me down the short hallway into his room, a mirror image of mine. "What happened?"

Thankfully, Alejandro had gone to the eating hall to start fueling up for his trip back to Spain, so it was just me and Jak in a free space my anger could flow in. "They won't go after Dawson," I told him, plopping down onto the foot of the closest bed. "We're safe, so why aren't we figuring out a plan?"

Jak took a respectful spot next to me. "If I were as mad, exhausted, and still recovering from adrenaline like you are... would you want me forming an elaborate, absolutely can't-fail-under-any-circumstances plan right now?"

A rock of frustration hardened in my chest; I wouldn't. Mostly because any suffering I could endure would fade in comparison to watching my loved ones die from a poorly conjured and executed plan.

"I didn't hesitate with you," I argued, staring at the tips of my boots that scraped the dark carpet of the floor. Jak's lay flat. "We came up with a plan the second I found out where you were."

"So what's the case with him?"

"We only know he's somewhere in DC, we don't have his exact location. The locator spell isn't giving it to us for some reason. But we can easily find out if I—"

I cut myself off before the hybrid truth could fly out. One problem at a time.

"You what?" Jak asked.

I slouched, the mattress pushing back against me with a slight bounce. "If I asked a nore. They can answer any question about external present circumstances if you give them an answer they want. But when you ask them something, they get access to every event of your life—that's how they know what they want to ask you for their price. My parents don't want a nore getting insider information on us in case Caldwell could use it against us somehow."

I almost wanted to involve Kamose, considering he was safe on the opposite side of the world—except Alejandro was also from the other side of the world, and now the government knew that teleportation was a thing.

Jak slowly nodded. "Okay..."

I tilted my head, searching his eyes. "That's it?"

He shrugged at me like he didn't know what else to say. "I

told you, I know the least out of everyone here. I'm not in a position to make plans or suggest them. My mission's the same as it's always been, and I just do what it takes to get there. Which now usually means following your mom's lead."

I wondered what his opinion would be if he knew that I was a hybrid. As much as I hated to admit it, when Becca told me that my identity as a sorceress wouldn't help us here, I knew it was true—but if he knew what I was, would he be just as adamant about testing my ability with every class so we could get Dawson back sooner?

"Hey," he said softly. "You okay?"

Jakson Bleu's signature care. It was the first glimpse of the old him that I'd gotten in weeks.

I realized I'd started fiddling with the locket around my neck—that was probably why he'd asked. I dropped it and told him, "Yeah."

"I'm glad. Because can I ask you something?"

I paused. "I don't like that question anymore."

I wanted him to chuckle, to lighten the mood, but he licked his lips—and I braced myself. "You can be honest with me about everything now, right?"

It felt like a trick question. The only two things I hadn't told him yet were—

"What happened while we were driving down the highway? The tree roots came up and—your eyes went *green*. Then Alejandro said you were a mage. I thought the Ateras were sorcerers, what was any of that about?"

The second my mouth opened, the conversation I'd just had with my family shushed me: we'd alerted the government about the existence of someone who could teleport. Telling Jak that I was a hybrid now could be fatal. Being a lead to the Ateras was one thing, but if they ever tortured him for information again, or if Caldwell ever found out that more people like Alejandro existed... I couldn't put Jak through that ever again.

"For your sake," I answered slowly, "I can't tell you that. Trust me, please."

His brows pinched together as he turned to face me better on the bed. "What do you mean?"

"For the same reason I couldn't tell my best friends who I was, I can't tell you that."

"Em, I think we're way past the point of you endangering me by making me a lead."

I opened my mouth to argue until something bigger than the truth closed it: reality. In fact, there wasn't just that, but also the fact that I'd been in this exact situation before—*with* my best friends. I'd wanted to protect them from becoming even bigger targets by knowing I was Tristan Atera's daughter, and that had blown up in my face. They hadn't *needed* to know that for my worst fears to be realized.

Jak was the same: the government was already after him because of me.

If we're gonna form a plan to save Dawson, let alone take down Caldwell, excluding Jak from this isn't an option anymore...

"Okay." I brought my leg up onto the bed to face him in full. My heart thumped like I *was* telling him I was Tristan's daughter. "Look. There are a lot of things about magic you don't know yet, so this is gonna sound really confusing. You're right, Alejandro's teleportation is supposed to be impossible, and I only know him because I have—I'm... we're both wielders with impossible abilities."

"What do you mean?"

"We don't know exactly what's going on yet or how, but Alejandro can teleport, we know someone who can transmogrify present circumstances, we know someone else who can time travel, and... I'm a hybrid. I have all seven classes of magic."

I expected the blank stare stamped on his face, but I didn't hate the silence after any less. Before I could say anything else, I needed something indicating how he felt, to know the direction I had to take the conversation in.

"What?" he asked.

I mentally facepalmed. "You're gonna have to give me more than that."

"Okay," he said skeptically, blinking as if into focus. "Um... The guy who can change present circumstances—if that's true, why hasn't he just changed Dawson's location? Or—ha, make it to where magic's not illegal anywhere, we're not being hunted down?"

I recalled the first conversation with Kamose I'd ever had, on the phone and in my bedroom last summer. "We all have limitations. Kamose can't 'teleport' anyone or make dimension-altering changes. It's more like... changing your clothes or the food on your plate, or even what gate your boarding pass says. Basically anything you can cut out the middleman for."

"And he can't tell us where Dawson is?"

"Not unless we answer a question from him—he's a nore. But then we run into the same 'issue' of someone potentially using him against us."

"Why?" Jak's eyes narrowed in confusion. "Why you guys, what's the pattern, how is this happening?"

This is it. I had to connect the two dots for him.

"Do you remember when Alexa…" I began, trying to digest the name, "called me 'Adara' in her body cam footage? Right before she was shot?"

Jak tilted his head slowly. "No. The footage was all muted."

Wait. What? "It was?"

"I thought it was weird, but yeah, someone had turned off the mics in the body cams before the pack went on the mission that morning."

Like someone had known that the footage would be a liability. We now knew that Alexa had been on our side (in a twisted way) since the beginning; was it possible that she'd somehow predicted that things would go wrong and sabotaged the audio? Why just the audio and not the footage altogether?

So Jak would know what happened in worst-case scenario and come find us. Had she really thought of him that far in advance?

My heart skipped a beat. *He didn't hear her confess to killing his mom, either.*

I shook my questions out of my head; I didn't need to know the answers right now, and I definitely didn't need to deal with that second topic yet. "I'm gonna backtrack a bit: the patterns with the four of us, we all have an impossible power and we're each a 'one hundredth' generation of our families. And we all have a name we're known by in the magic world to protect our identities."

"Wait, hang on," Jak said. "Protect you from what?"

"We're all, apparently, meant to play a role in uniting the

mortal and magic worlds for good, and there are a lot of people who'd love to make sure that doesn't happen. Enter Nicholas Caldwell."

Again, I'd expected the blank stare; after all, the only thing I'd been able to accept since meeting Annisa was that I wouldn't figure any of this out soon. So I'd anticipated Jak's bewilderment, but not the accusatory "Are you messing with me?"

I narrowed my eyes at him. "You saw the proof in the car, and you're asking me that?"

"No, okay, that's not what I meant," he said quickly. "Like you said, there's a million things I don't know yet. But right now you're telling me you're supposed to... *save the world* one day, is that it?"

"I thought it was ridiculous when Mr. Dawson first told me. *Believe* me, I get it—I'm just being honest with you."

He took in a breath to speak, but something closed his mouth. To my relief, his shoulders deflated.

"Telling you this is hard for a lot more reasons than the obvious," I said. "Yesterday was never supposed to happen. We have *no* idea how the government found us when we covered all of our tracks. If that can happen in rural Canada when the US isn't even supposed to know we're here, it can happen anywhere. I'm secretly terrified that that includes here, even with the shield against external magic."

Jak took a few moments for himself, gathering his thoughts. I couldn't make heads or tails of if they were in my favor.

Then, his hand hesitantly rested on my knee.

"Thanks," he said. His tender touch was the only thing that told me he meant it.

"Are you... okay?" I asked.

"Honestly, I can't believe it right now. But that's probably because I'm still coming to terms with a million other things about our situation." His soft irises met mine, switching back and forth like he didn't know which one he liked more. "I've spent the last few months choking on secrets nobody wanted to tell me for the sake of protecting me. But I still wound up here, I'm still running, that was always the problem with that."

His hand tightened around my knee, that skeptical divot in his brow finally melting with the rest of his features—back into my Jak. "Thanks for not doing that to me this time. That's what matters to me, that I can go through this *with* you instead of uselessly watching."

I barely stopped a scoff in time. "Stop. You've never *once* been useless—"

A knock pattered on the open door down the hallway. "Jak? Emma?" a shy yet crisp voice called—Aunt Becca.

He and I shared a glance before standing from the bed. I followed him to the door, where Auntie waited outside in the hall.

"Alejandro's ready to leave," she told us. "Let's go say bye."

"Oh," I said, "um..."

Wow. I can't believe this is it.

I faced Jak, warily tilting my head. "Are we good? Am I still relatively normal to you?"

He nodded, a familiar stiffness in his smile—his professional smile, nothing more. "We're good. Don't worry. But, um—you go ahead, I need a bit of time."

I stepped out into the hall with Aunt Becca. "I'll tell him you weren't feeling well."

He leaned against his door, his smile growing a tad. "Tell him
I said thanks."

NINE

"Are you sure that you'll be okay getting back on your own?" Dad asked Alejandro in Spanish, standing with us in the dim, cramped elevator lobby we'd gone into when we first arrived this morning. The elevators sat behind us, ready to take us back down. I didn't know if I was jealous of Alejandro going back out into the open world, or worried for him.

"Yes, I'll be fine," he told Dad, smiling with reassurance and tossing the orange in his hand back and forth. "It'll take a lot less energy. I can stop when I need to."

I quietly took a deep breath in, ruminating on that. He'd demanded so much of himself to get us here despite how the two of us had only known each other for two and a half months. Our alliance in magic must've meant enough to him for some reason.

"Jak says thanks by the way," I said, offering a smile.

"Really?" he asked. "I thought he didn't like me."

"It's more like he doesn't completely trust you. The teleporting thing was—suspicious to him."

"*Teleportación*, teleportation, I got that one," Aunt Becca remarked in English, perking up from the seat she'd taken in a stray chair in the corner.

Alejandro beamed at her effort (and probably at her harsh American accent on the word). "*La tele*transportación," he said, correcting her.

"Right." She nodded once. "I said that. Right?"

It was some relief that his smile deepened before he looked back down at his orange, his thoughts seeming to grab him. I think he switched to English then for Auntie's sake. "We should—tell to Jak about... *nuestro equipo, ¿cómo se dice en inglés?* Our group of special magic?"

I looked up at Momma to verify. With her nod, I could take comfort in the fact that she knew something like that was inevitable—so hopefully she wouldn't be upset at how I'd already taken initiative on that.

"We'll tell him after you leave," she told Alejandro.

"Are you completely sure you'll be safe here once I do?" he asked in Spanish, apparently giving up on including Becca in the conversation. "We won't be able to contact each other. I thought about that a lot on our way here. I... I could ask my parents and stay here with you in case you need me."

Hang on—that didn't sound like a bad idea. If anything, once we did start planning to save Mr. Dawson, we'd need Alejandro more than ever.

"Bouchard already has a room for you," Dad noted. "But that's a big request for your parents. This is a *Hunter's* mission."

"Something you don't have any training for," Momma added.

"Um..." Alejandro licked his lips, running a warm-brown hand through his shaggy black hair. "I'll talk to my parents. I can leave here easily, and you can't. But if you need me, it will be for an important reason."

"I like the idea," Momma said, "but again, it would be dangerous. Talk to your parents and see what they say."

I translated for Aunt Becca, who immediately nodded with approval. "This kid is smart, I like him."

Alejandro offered a timid thank-you before exchanging his eyes with each person in the tiny lobby. Without warning, they landed on me. "Are you okay, *amiga?*"

"Yeah," I told him on instinct. "Now I am."

"I'm glad," he said, nodding. "I'm sorry if I hurt you when we teleported here. But thank you for helping me."

I hadn't known that he was asking about my *physical* state, but that was just as well; apparently I'd lied so well that he couldn't tell the difference.

After bringing us lunch, Eun-Ji wanted us to stay in our rooms until dinner to avoid unnecessary attention so we could focus on resting instead of introducing ourselves to everyone. Twenty minutes before dinner, she escorted us to the eating hall and started familiarizing us with Bouchard's rituals. We were slowly getting our appetites back after all the adrenaline, so when we got back to the hall our room was in, our plates were full of pork chops, mashed potatoes, and green beans.

"Remember, you're free to eat wherever you want during meals," Eun-Ji said again, ever the leader as she strolled in front of us. "Just don't forget to put your plates in the dish pile in the eating hall once you're done. For tonight, I'll send someone to pick them up for you."

A door behind us opened, and padded footsteps went down the opposite direction of us. A scratchy yet eager voice chirped, "Smells like they've got pork chops tonight!" I wondered if I'd get to know the owner of that voice any time soon.

"How do you make sure you have enough food for everyone?" Aunt Becca asked next to me, already shoveling a bite of mashed potatoes into her mouth. "When you're all stuck down here?"

"Most of us aren't being hunted," Eun-Ji replied, slightly looking over her shoulder at Auntie. "We have a team of those people that we send up to grab supplies every month, anything we can't grow or produce here. Those potatoes, for example, were grown down here in our community garden. Our warlocks are a huge help with that."

"With what funds do you buy the other supplies?" Momma asked curiously ahead of me.

"The short answer involves the wealth of our founder, Joseph Bouchard, and the collected salaries of our double agents out in the field."

"Who're all magicians," Dad said next to Momma, "but they can work for the government under a generous salary because they store their magic here."

"On the nose, Mr. Atera," Eun-Ji remarked, throwing him a proud smirk.

Up ahead, a lean brunet walked into the hall from his room, holding his little girl's hand. Eun-Ji greeted them before they squeezed by us on the left. The father kept his eyes down after a quick nod of acknowledgement. The blond little girl's round brown eyes looked up at us as she passed, snagging on me. I instinctively slowed as our stares followed each other, even as she and her father passed and continued down the hall. Something stirred in my gut, whirling... What was this? Who was she?

I caught Jak's gaze as I came back. He tilted his head with a question, but I shrugged in response.

"Tomorrow I'll be more than happy to give you an orientation tour," Eun-Ji said, arriving at our doors and facing us. "Meet me in the lobby at 10 and I'll show you more about how things work around here."

"Thank you, Eun-Ji," Dad said with a respectful nod. "Needless to say, we're beyond grateful for everything you've done for us today."

"It's what we're here for," she replied as Momma unlocked our door with the key we'd been given. Eun-Ji's short, petite stature moved past us, and she started back down the hall. "Rest well tonight, and I'll see you tomorrow morning."

Aunt Becca ambled by me and Jak, sticking a green bean into her mouth. A third of her plate was already gone. I was about to follow her until Jak took a step back, toward his door.

"Hey," I said before thinking, "you wanna eat with us?"

He opened his mouth as if to speak, glancing down at his

plate. I was surprised by his hesitance, all the more so when Dad stepped up to my side.

"Jak, how about we eat together, you and me? No girls allowed."

Momma scoffed beside me, and I forced a half smile. Jak simply nodded before unlocking his door with his key.

I wished that Dad had his magic so I could telepathically ask him what he was doing—and why he was leaving me, the closest one to Jak out of all of us, out of it. But I silently watched the two of them walk into Jak's room, where Dad shut the door with nothing more than a see-you-later wave.

"What is he doing?" I asked Momma.

"Your dad's good for him right now," she told me. "He doesn't just need another guy, he needs a father figure, considering he barely had one even when his dad was alive."

With that, I realized that Jak not denying Dad's offer—whether out of politeness or secret relief—said enough.

We still have a lot of settling in to do.

I turned toward our room next door, but Momma blocked my path. "Hey," she crooned, "you okay?"

I rolled my eyes, shifting my weight. I'd grown up hearing that question with that tone from my mother, so I immediately knew what it meant. "Mom."

"Em."

"Yes," I said, like it was as simple as that. I raised my plate. "I just wanna eat."

"Don't insult me," she deadpanned. "Master training *and* you're my daughter. Alejandro asked you how you were doing physically and I could *still* read right through your answer."

I scolded myself for forgetting to perform in front of *everyone* in the elevator lobby, not just him. But it didn't matter if I was okay or not—I wasn't dying, and that was all everyone needed from me right now.

"I'm tired," I told Mom. "I helped him teleport us all the way from Brookmere to Steele, we had a seventeen-hour drive over here almost immediately after, then we had that argument about Mr. Dawson and the sorceress thing—Dad said it earlier, we're settling in. We finally don't have to run, ration our food, or take shifts sleeping. I'm *crashing.*"

Momma's honey-like eyes were all the warmer against her beige skin as they softened on me. "Sometimes settling in also means letting go. I told you, you don't have to be strong all the time."

I wanted to tell her that, in this case, she was wrong. Saving Mr. Dawson needed every ounce of strength I had. I couldn't give any of it up for a second.

"I'm not being strong all the time," I assured her. I took a brief look around the bright hall, then down at my plate of food. "I'm... grateful."

That became completely true when Momma didn't respond. Instead, we walked into our room together and shut the door.

C H A P T E R

Ten

Breakfast the next morning went well until we had to leave our rooms to put our dishes in the eating hall and meet Eun-Ji in the lobby for our orientation tour. The stares and whispers we got were, apparently, normal for new refugees, but no less intimidating—so when my family, Jak, and I were set free to get more comfortable on our own, I headed for the library for some enforced quiet.

In a room as cavernous as the main lobby, rows of tables spread across the center with a cluster of round tables in the back. Grades three through five were taught there, I remembered Eun-Ji saying. Thankfully, people were too absorbed in their books to notice me as I passed by and drew closer to the back. Class was going on, the kids maintaining strict focus on either a worksheet or a book.

Bouchard's kids made up a fifth of the base's population, 163 of them, and that was just ages four through thirteen. Over half of them only had one parent. A handful had none.

Walking along the right edge of the room, I stopped just before my foot could cross the threshold from carpet to the wood of the educational section. The blond girl from last night in the hall sat at the table ahead of me, reading with her classmates. Her crimson sweater sleeves were too long for her arms.

I bit the inside of my cheek. A year and a half ago, in August, Breanne needed to get her Callistro blazer a size down after the medium's sleeves were way too long. Why did I miss that uniform so much?

I realized too late that I was staring; the girl's big brown eyes jumped up from her book and locked on me.

I turned to the towering bookcase beside me and started "browsing for a book". My thoughts ran as I mindlessly scanned the titles and spines. What was it about that girl that I couldn't shake away? She seemed just as curious about me.

I might see her at lunch. My family and I had agreed this morning that lunch would be our first *social* meal, and the only reason I wasn't dreading it was that I'd have Jak to fill in the potential awkwardness we were already betting on. Momma and Dad knew how to push through their baggage and put up a front, and I flat out didn't have to worry about Aunt Becca, but Jak and I were still untangling more than we'd thought we even had. Socializing was kind of the last thing we wanted to work through next when we probably wouldn't be here for that much longer, anyway.

"Hey."

I blinked myself out of my head and turned at the whisper. Jak was walking toward me with his hands stuck in his jean pockets, thumbs sticking out.

"Hey," I whispered back.

"Wanna take a walk?"

I tilted my head. "What?"

He nodded to the open doors of the library on the other side of the room. "Walk around and talk."

The words settled—the idea settled. *Like how we used to. I guess he needs this right now.*

"Yeah," I whispered, "sure."

He let me take the lead, and I crossed the room. Despite the heater running across the entire base, it could only do so much for a place so large (and under an entire mountain range); the temperature lowered as I walked into the hall and pulled my coat tighter around me. I wondered how Jak was managing with only a gradient hoodie to keep him warm.

"I saw your parents wearing the rings I got you last year," he began, crossing the threshold. "It's really nice to see them wearing them."

I looked down at my own comfortably hugging my right ring finger: a thin silver band with "A" engraved on the top, my name engraved inside it. "Well, it's nice having something that identifies us as a family," I said, sticking my hands into my coat pockets, "and that we can finally wear 'publicly', so we're gonna. Um..."—I hesitantly looked up at him—"how're you feeling today?"

For the first time in I didn't know how long, Jak chuckled. And for a brief half second, his smile lingered. "Well... last night I was finally able to think about everything without any—pressure.

No threats, no time limit, nobody else around. I thought about old things and the... new things. So that was a first."

I couldn't help but wonder what "things" meant—how he felt about them, maybe even the decisions he'd made about them.

"It just... hurts," he admitted, a crack entering his voice. We approached the end of the library hall. "Somehow, the situation hurts. I don't know why, it's not like the Delphines were my family—but I still hate that I'm so conflicted about my dad. It feels like there's this underlying kind of... ache, I don't know. I can't get rid of it and I don't even know what it is or why I feel it."

"These things take time," I said gently as we turned the corner. "You've barely had two weeks, and you lost your entire household of the past, what, six, seven years?"

"And the only blood family I have left is either in Pennsylvania or India. Not like it matters, I'm not close with any of them. I only really have..."

Us. I wanted him to say it, but not for my sake. For his, for him to know that he did have someone.

"Actually, can..." he asked in a voice too small to be Jakson Bleu's, "can we not talk about it?"

With that question, I knew everything I needed to about how he was doing.

"Of course."

He took a deep breath as we passed through the entryway of the educational sector, as if erasing the last minute. "Whenever we do leave, I kind of wanna go to the art room first and take advantage. Seeing it motivated me to start sketching again."

I stopped in the threshold between the entryway and the main lobby. "You sketch?"

"I've never told you that?"

I gestured to the surprise on my face. "Obviously you have."

Another crack of a smile nudged the corners of his lips, and I started thinking of any and everything that could keep it there. At least we were making progress.

"I like observing," he said.

"That part was obvious."

He shrugged. "That was how I got so good at it. Sketching taught me how to study details. There's something in it that Hunter classes can't teach."

So that's how he's so good at reading me.

"How come you've never shown me anything you've done before?" I asked, stepping into the main lobby with him. The temperature rose a smidge. "Or even brought it up?"

"We were always dealing with something more important than what I like to do for fun."

"Not on our dates," I argued without thinking. My stomach fluttered, and I scolded myself for it. "I'm pretty sure that's partly what they're for, half of it was *about* you then."

Jak pressed his lips together, locking his jaw.

"What?" I asked, stopping behind one of the vinyl armchairs toward the edge of the lobby's dark-yellow rug. I was only brave enough to ask because of how, whatever he was keeping inside, he was caging a smile with it.

"It's cute to hear you call them 'dates'," he admitted, leaning against the back of the armchair and looking down at me.

"I kind of have to when you flat out asked me out for two of them."

The old Jakson Bleu would've bitten his lip and grinned,

would've looked away and chuckled under his breath. I didn't have the old Jak anymore, but the new one was starting to heal: his reserved smile was finally big enough to poke a dimple in his left cheek again, right next to the clean scar.

"Still," he said. For the first time in weeks, he gazed at me—he didn't just look at me, his eyes weren't lost. He gazed at me with vibrant-brown irises that truly believed I was the only thing they *could* see. "I like that you count them."

I let a soft smile trace my lips. A kind of peace settled into my chest. This type of conversation hadn't happened between us in way too long. I'd been subconsciously counting the weeks this whole time, and now they had finally capped. I could stare at Jak again and remind myself of some of the things I had to be grateful for rather than remind myself of every reason magic was a burden I'd been forced to carry.

In the corner of my eye, I caught sight of a few people traveling across the lobby into the other hallways that branched out on the sides. Some walked down the concourse in the back, toward the eating hall. I wondered where Jak and I would head to next.

"I'm sorry."

I blinked, questioning if I'd actually heard that come out of his mouth. "What're you talking about?"

He shifted his weight against the back of the armchair, his gaze stuck on his sneakers. "I haven't... I wanted to deal with all this a lot better. I didn't want to take anything out on you—"

"No, stop. We've never had to deal with *anything* like the last couple of months since we met, we're gonna hit some learning curves—"

"Em," he murmured, eyes leaping up to mine. I shut my

mouth. "I didn't want to be so hard—closed off from you and your family after everything you've done. The last thing I wanted was to push you away but that's all I know how to do because—"

He cut himself off, but I was able to finish that sentence: *Because he was forced to after his mom died.* He hadn't had a father who understood or would even try to.

"I feel like I've just been a—rock. I'm... I'm sorry if I ever hurt you the last couple of weeks. Because you're right, I don't wanna do this alone, but I don't know how to do it with someone else..."

I took in a deep breath, digging my fists deeper into my coat pockets. "I know firsthand that admitting that is the first step. The whole time, though, I was just worried about you."

To my sheer relief, he drew his hands out of his jean pockets and reached out his arms. I walked into them, letting him rest his cheek on the side of my head. He straightened so our weight wouldn't push the armchair back. His warmth took a few seconds to seep through his hoodie and then through my shirt where my coat was unzipped, but we eventually reached each other. And when Jak sighed and sank into me, we connected. I closed my eyes, letting myself float in a respite I hadn't gotten since... I wish I could flip through my old journals to find out.

"Thanks," I said. "Because I'm here for you like you've always been for me. Since the beginning."

For a second, I felt his head lift and then lean in close. But hesitation broke his flow, and he rested his cheek against me again instead.

Was he about to kiss my head?

For obvious reasons, the subject of romance hadn't popped up since our kiss at my house after Thanksgiving. Before that, Jak had confessed that he loved me. The fact that he was hesitating now meant that he either was finally learning how to read a room, didn't want to assume I felt the same way, or both...

Why doesn't he feel safe assuming it? I kissed him back, I said yes when he asked me out, I visibly had butterflies whenever he did anything remotely romantic or suave... but I guess all those things could be attributed to the fact that, as he knew, I'd never experienced any of those things before him. I'd never outright told him that it was *him*, I didn't have feelings for the things that sent my heart racing. I had feelings for him.

I froze in his hold. I'd never confessed those words to *myself* until now.

Jak pulled away somewhat, looking down at me. "You okay?"

"Yeah," I said before he could question it. Because those eyes looked different now somehow. Something I didn't want to pull away from, I *really* didn't want to pull away from. They weren't the pretty eyes of the cute boy I had a crush on anymore; they were the rich, beautiful eyes of the boy I had feelings for, and they had been for some time.

But when I remembered all the times I'd caught myself falling into them before, I remembered why I'd held my feelings back since day one: it was always too dangerous. It would have always put us at a risk that wasn't worth it. Now that we weren't running, though, we were in the middle of recovering from being fugitives and emotions were at an all-time high.

We don't know what tomorrow or even this evening is gonna look like. Does that mean I have to keep holding back? Is it still the wrong time to pursue something with him?

More importantly... *did* Jak still feel the same way?

As if realizing that we weren't, in fact, a couple, his hands fell to my waist, telling me to pull away. When I did, his arms dropped to his sides. A signal for me to break away, nothing else.

Can we talk about this now that we're finally not being chased? Wasn't bringing up this topic after what he'd just told me completely insensitive, or was it exactly what he wanted to hear?

"I was thinking about..." he said as he stuck his hands into his hoodie pockets, "asking Eun-Ji about my mom. Since she knew her."

My head caught back with surprise. Well, that answered my second question...

"That's—" I began, forcing all thoughts of feelings aside, "that's big. Why don't you?"

"I think part of me is still hesitant to learn about her. After she kept her whole alliance with Bouchard a secret, I'm..."—he scoffed—"I'm actually kinda scared. To *know* things about her instead of just the vague memories I have."

"Your mom kept this place a secret for good reason," I told him. "William probably did give her multiple reasons to hide it from him. But she protected hundreds of people in the process."

"Yeah..."

Fragile silence sat between us, augmenting the volume of the passing normal talk around us—and my guilt. I was part of the reason Jak *should* be afraid of what he could learn about Aastha, because only I had the answer to one of his questions about her. But after he'd finally begun a path of healing, not just moving forward, news of Alexa being his mother's killer would shove him straight off. Didn't I risk putting him in a darker place with the full truth because there was nothing he could do about it? He needed to heal more before he could know.

Another topic there's never a right time to bring up.

"Do you trust me?" I asked.

"You've never given me a reason not to," he replied. "Everything you do, you're a protector of your people, too."

I am. That includes you. He'd just have to trust me when I believed that keeping the truth about Aastha from him, for now, was best. He'd have to trust that I wasn't hiding it out of malice, but for the sake of his emotional protection right now.

I guess that answers my first question, too: completely insensitive timing to bring up feelings right now. I don't know if I'm even allowed to bring it up unless I can give him some kind of direction or straight-up answer about—

I glanced over his shoulder. A man in a worn T-shirt was stepping onto the rug. His name jolted through my head like an electric shock. I stumbled backwards before Jak caught my wrist.

"Emma—?"

But my gaze was glued to the young man continuing toward us, passing the coffee table in the center of the rug. Forest-green eyes, oval-shaped face, dark-auburn hair. I could never forget any of that. I could never forget a Delphine.

Jak looked over his shoulder. His grip on me loosened.

"I know," Anthony said, holding up his pale hands. "But I need to talk to you. Please."

CHAPTER

ELEVEN

"I hope for your sake you can fit all this in before lunch," Jak said gruffly under the ceiling light of Anthony's hallway, refusing to take another step into his room. "Because that's how long you have to explain."

I turned to him. "Jak—"

"He has a *lot* to give us and I don't even think he realizes it!"

Anthony stood at the end of his bed. "About what happened a couple weeks ago?"

"A lot more than that, buddy," Jak growled, his hands clenching into fists. "But that's a great start, the fact you let that happen at all. *Your* mom gave Emma a code there's no way you didn't know about and you never translated for us, so you let that morning happen, you let *this*"—he traced the scar on his left cheek—

"happen, are we gonna forget how you also sat back and watched your mom beat Emma half to death—?"

"Okay, first of all," Anthony stated, holding up his hand, "none of us knew you'd be tortured. That's why those agents were transferred to a different pack. Alexa and William were furious."

They were both *furious—?*

No—wait. Anthony's words sounded familiar. At the hideout, after William captured me...

"He was never *supposed to suffer! They were never supposed to hurt him! That's why they were transferred!"* William told me that when I'd accused him of willingly sending his son to be tortured. *This was what he'd meant?*

Jak scoffed like he wanted to spit on Anthony. "Right, that makes sense. They couldn't just interrogate me themselves so they sent two agents who had no attachment to me. They sent the only two agents capable of doing that to me, and it wasn't like any of you came running to save me when I was gone for too long. Not even the one member of the pack who wouldn't even *be* a member if not for his mom."

"My mom, the same woman who saved you from getting arrested the night you were debriefed after the carnival," Anthony argued. "Why do you think the polygraph didn't catch anything you probably lied about? She rigged it before hooking you up to protect *her*." He nodded at me, making me internally shrink. "She's the sole reason neither of you were ever arrested."

My jaw fell slack. *The day we met. That's why she let me go, then why she let me go when she first kidnapped me. She was buying time until she could safely get my magic here without sabotaging her family and Bouchard. Playing her role in front of William and Caldwell...*

"No, wait," I said, my memory going back further. "It's not just what happened last year with Jak and me and Opal—she *stabbed* a man named 'Steven' when she told me I was a hybrid. He almost bled out in the forest! Was that part of 'protecting' us?"

"Alexa Delphine was one of the best Grand Hunters in the *country*," Anthony shot back. "Do you really think she couldn't've killed him with one stab, that him surviving was a miracle?"

I bit my tongue—because I'd even noted that fact in my journal: Steven's wound, much to my and Cara's surprise, hadn't been as deep as we'd thought. It'd almost been fatal, but also like Alexa had stabbed him with... calculated precision.

"She needed to incapacitate one of you and hold you for 'ransom'," Anthony said. "None of you would've listened to her otherwise, you were ready to capture her and turn her in."

"She needed a *knife* to do that?" I deadpanned.

"She didn't care what method she used. As long as you believed what she needed you to. She kept you afraid and on your guard, that's what saved you and us from Caldwell. Ever since she got the Atera descendant case, ever since she found out how powerful you are, everything she ever did since you met was to protect your family's magic from Caldwell—including involving Jak when he refused to stay out of things so Caldwell and his dad wouldn't get suspicious. Alexa covered both of you for over a year."

Jak bristled. "'Covered' as in tortured?"

"You wanna know how that was actually supposed to go?" Anthony snapped, daring a couple of steps toward us. "Because you're not gonna like it. Alexa and William sent those agents to interrogate you to 'find out what you were telling the enemy', but it was to get them—two *mortal* Grand Hunters—away long enough to plan our trip to South Mountains State Park. William hated magic, but he had no problem working with us if it meant catching his biggest target of the year. He couldn't do that with those two Hunters in our pack."

We were nowhere close, I thought, recalling that afternoon at Waverly's that Jak, my friends, and I had attempted theorizing the story behind Jak's kidnapping in the first place. *Not even Breanne would've figured out the truth.*

Jak's chest rose with a huff, but Anthony didn't let him speak. "Your kidnapping was supposed to be a distraction for them, that's it. Alexa approved it because she knew you wouldn't break and it was supposed to *end* at interrogation. They crossed the line because they suspected you really were hiding something, and then they were immediately transferred for violation of protocol and assault on the leaders' son."

We had so much of it wrong—

"And William was so angry that his son was tortured that he ignored me when I finally came back?" Jak exclaimed, startling me.

"He was ashamed." Anthony matched his volume, like he couldn't lose any part of this argument. I was thankful that Jak had closed the door. "He couldn't stand the fact of what *his* choice led to but he was too much of a coward to tell you that."

"Well, I'm glad you disapproved of him so much that you're defending him now."

"You know what?" Anthony held up his hands like he was warning us to stay back. "Fine. Blame me because I'm the only one you can, blame me when you know well and *good* I wasn't responsible for anything the pack did. No, you have nobody but your own father to thank for that."

Jak charged forward, but I grabbed his arm and pulled him back. "Stop it!" I snapped at them, directing my glare to Anthony. "You have ten seconds to tell us why we should stay, did you just need someone to blame for what happened?"

"No." His oval jaw clenched before he huffed, his body loosening. "I needed... I needed to talk to someone else who went through it. Julia knew what it meant when I was the only one who showed up at the cabin yesterday... That's when I found out that I was the only one who'd made it at all."

Those words breathed a chill down my back. Now that I was really looking at him, his nose and cheeks did have a subtle swell and faded red to them—like he'd spent the entire drive up here crying.

I crossed my arms over my chest; it didn't feel "safe" to reach for my locket in front of him.

"I needed to talk to someone," he said again, looking at Jak, "who lost something that morning, too."

Jak scoffed under his breath. "All I lost was a dad and a stepmom."

"Exactly." Anthony's eyes stayed narrowed on him. "I lost family."

I closed my eyes. I knew those words. I'd experienced them that morning, too, when Mr. Dawson was taken.

Except Anthony had lost his entire family. And even beyond that, Jak might have lost his dad, but Anthony had lost his mother. It wasn't like Anthony's dad would win a medal, either, and considering his dad was the whole reason Alexa had started her new legacy, he was probably dead, too.

These two had more in common than they'd ever admit.

"I want to know what happened to my mom," Anthony said, tired, forest-green eyes settling onto me. "I'm owed that much."

Jak had nothing left to say, and I didn't have anything I felt *safe* to say; how was I supposed to tell this man that his mother had died protecting me?

"Please, Emmalynn," he murmured.

How was I supposed to not tell him?

"She told me some of what you guys were doing with the innocent magicians," I began. "Then Caldwell's Hunters broke in. They shot her before she could tell me everything, but—she made sure I'd make it out."

All he did was nod. Forced understanding probably. After all, if he'd been on board with the Delphines' plans, all Alexa had done that morning by protecting me was make sure that none of it had been in vain. I just wished the price hadn't been so high.

"So Eun-Ji knows?" I asked quietly.

He nodded, sniffing and then scratching his nose. I guess her reaction had been just as devastating.

"Is Julia okay?" I found myself asking.

"Yeah," he said. "Physically, yeah. I stayed with her until she sent me up. I just sent Maverick—her husband, sorry—down there to be with her for a bit... She said you're here with your family."

"Yeah."

"So you got Tristan?"

"Yeah."

"Good." He stuck his hands into his wrinkled jean pockets, turning to face the rest of his room. I wondered if he'd shared it with his mother whenever they'd stayed here. "I just risked my life bringing his magic here."

I paused. "You're the one they sent for that?"

"Before William betrayed us." He lightly shook his head. "That's probably the only reason I survived, I left right before hell broke loose."

Jak leaned against the wall of the hallway, crossing his arms; he didn't feel threatened anymore, but he still didn't want to be here any longer than we needed to be.

I looked back at Anthony, his back still to us. As much as I hated to admit it, there *was* something different about him right now. Some kind of new presence, one that I was tempted to say I'd felt before. Connection...? The reassurance that he was finally okay to be around?

It's definitely not trust. It can't *be connection.* What was it about him that was different, besides the fact that he'd brought Dad's magic here safely?

"Wait," I said, the question dawning on me. "How did you get my dad's magic that fast? Taking someone's magic is a dangerous process, and it's definitely not *quick*. Even that bracelet Alexa got took days."

"Why do you think our plan took four months?" Anthony replied, facing me. "We were in contact with Bouchard the whole time trying to figure out something that could extract someone's magic fast and safely. We needed our best mages to do it, and to get our only two high priests in on it."

"Why did you grab him and not Becca?"

He exhaled, lazily shrugging. "She wasn't there when we came."

Because she'd gone on her walk, I remembered. *At just the right time. And she didn't notice Dad was gone when she got back because it was the middle of the night.*

"So," I said, "you grabbed my dad's magic but not Alexa's from Breanne? Or Opal's?"

"William sent them back before we could." Anthony spoke about the man like every word pricked his mouth. "We needed four hours, we only had them for two. Magic's like a string: unless you use the right method, you can't transfer only some of it. It'll fall back to the source that weighs more—our hearts."

I glimpsed Jak in the corner of my eye. He was merely listening, watching the hard carpet under our feet. In full honesty, part of me was angry *for* him; every time he managed to grab a curveball, another flew at him just as he went to throw back the last one.

It wasn't that I was upset that Anthony was alive. But him being here did threaten to complicate a lot of things, like...

"If you're here now," I began slowly, tightening my arms around myself, "what do you want? I mean, what's your main goal now? With us—?"

He shook his head, cutting me off. "Everything I ever did was for my mom. I was twelve when she told me who my dad was. We were already close, but that put us in the same pack. Same mission. I *hate* that I'm anything part of my dad, so I did everything I could to be more of my mom. People like him, I wanted to bury. Accomplishing that is all I have now. All I have left of my family. My mom. Everything I do now... everything I do is for her. I'm the only one who can keep her memory alive the right way."

Jak knew those words all too well, too. Maybe he wasn't ready to accept the fact that he and Anthony weren't complete opposites, because he uncrossed his arms and said tightly, "Let me get this straight: you wanna claim you're the good guy after doing all that stuff to Emma? You choked her after luring her into the forest, never helped solve Alexa's riddle, and—again—watched her get beaten black and blue no problem, but that was all for our benefit, is that right?"

"Don't act like you don't know how important a cover is," Anthony replied with strain. "If both of you believed the Delphines were ruthless Grand Hunters, so would the members who weren't Delphines, so would Caldwell. He was *always* watching."

That's what Alexa told me.

"Were we supposed to let you in on one of the biggest double agent cases of the millennium and hope you acted well enough so the US Government wouldn't find out everything faster?"

Those words rang a bell, and it only took me a second to place them: Jak's reasoning for having never told me that he'd always known my identity as Tristan's daughter. He knew that the best way to keep his cover was to make sure that he was the only one who knew he had one.

I dared to look over at him: Anthony's argument was definitely resonating. Jak understood it firsthand, and he stayed silent because of it.

When I returned to Anthony, his eyes were already on me. "And you guys were never completely innocent. That night in the forest with you and Opal helped us keep our cover, but it didn't happen because of it. Take one second to remember every reason Alexa had to be angry after the month you'd put her through."

I scoffed. "That doesn't justify—"

"I'm not saying it does," he stated. "I'm saying she was still human. She did what she thought was right when she could, but she was just as capable of being hurt."

Even now, I didn't want to think about last summer; I still had some remaining guilt about it, especially since the woman had died to protect me despite what my family and I *had* done.

"Okay. Fine." I took a deep breath to reset. "None of the last year matters anymore. We're fighting a common enemy now in a world that's against us." My gaze landed on Jak. "*All* of us."

He pressed his lips together before standing from the wall. "Okay," he said just as calmly. "If that's it, we're gonna go."

"Wait," Anthony called before we could turn around. "Eun-Ji wants all of us to meet in her office in half an hour. She wants the full story of what happened last month, and to talk about Caldwell."

"Caldwell?" Jak asked.

"Yeah. We did a lot more undercover work than you think."

Those words were familiar: Alexa's final warning to me. "*It's Caldwell, it's all Caldwell.*" He was the one she'd been protecting magicians from, and now it was my responsibility.

"Lead the way," I told Anthony.

C H A P T E R

Twelve

Evidently Eun-Ji liked to keep things minimal, shown by her gray office that solely consisted of metal filing cabinet walls; one desk in the middle with two chairs in front of it; a credenza behind it; and a yellow rug to, I guess, brighten things up. She likely spent most of her time walking around the base, because I couldn't imagine anyone spending most of their working hours in an office so depressing.

"I'm so glad you're okay, Anthony," she said upon the six of us walking in. Black hair pinned up in a neat bun, her ivory skin betrayed the remaining flush in her cheeks—especially her low nose. Sorrow pulled down her kind features as she looked across us. "All of you."

Congestion faintly subdued her words. I remembered Julia

telling us that Alexa and her siblings had been with the base since Alexa was seventeen—Anthony had been *born* here. Eun-Ji hadn't just lost a few agents; she'd lost residents, allies, probably even friends.

When I looked down at the concrete floor, my peripheral vision caught everyone else doing the same. And for the first time since December, my family and I had a moment of silence for the Delphines.

After a minute, Eun-Ji gestured for the six of us to approach her desk. "Mr. Atera, I wanted to let you know that Anthony brought your magic to our keepers down below. Let me know if you'd ever like it back."

"That's allowed?" Dad asked, arms loosely crossed over his chest.

"We store the magic of those who can't reclaim it or who don't want to risk keeping it," she replied, "but you're welcome to keep it as long as you're staying here. It's just wisest to store it in the event of worst-case scenario, especially for a sorcerer as powerful as you."

A sorcerer who's barely ever gotten to use that power, I thought bitterly.

Momma matched her eyes with Dad's as if to ask about his decision. He opened his mouth but then quickly closed it. "Well, first of all,"—he leaned forward, nodding at Anthony on the other end of the lineup—"thank you, Anthony, for keeping it safe." He returned his attention to Eun-Ji up front. Tiredness still drenched his voice like it had when we'd first arrived here, the dark circles under his dull eyes exposing his lack of sleep. "We can talk about it later, I don't think that's why we're here."

"No, you're right." Eun-Ji stood and walked to the side of her desk. "If you're all willing, I'd like the story of what happened a couple of weeks ago."

The room came to a halt. *Nobody* wanted to start that story. Unfortunately for me and my parents, though, we were the only ones who could give it; Jak had only gotten a limited perspective on the body cam footage he'd watched before coming to our house, and Aunt Becca hadn't been taken with Dad. To get those reasons, we had to start talking—so Momma did.

I still remembered everything too vividly: after kidnapping Dad and they couldn't find Aunt Becca, the pack took Breanne and Opal from our dorm in the middle of the night to the Hunter hideout in South Mountains State Park, hoping to lure me and Sarah there. Mom, Mr. Dawson, and I left Sarah at Callistro to keep her safe, but when we got to the hideout, Breanne and Opal had been sent home and William had betrayed the pack. Caldwell's Hunters swarmed the hideout in pursuit of the Ateras and the Delphines, but after we escaped, they took Mr. Dawson into custody, thinking he was Dad because the two of them were under an appearance switch spell.

Then Anthony gave his side of the story: like he'd said, he'd been sent to Bouchard before Momma, Mr. Dawson, and I got to the hideout. That journey involved an invisibility cloak, the Russo Diversion I'd learned in class last year, an essay-long list of spells, and two underground travel systems.

"I see."

Eun-Ji had sat back down at her desk halfway through the whole story. By the end of it, her hand was stuck on her chest like she was looking for her heartbeat. I sneaked a glance at Jak, whose downcast frown stayed quiet. He was blocking off his thoughts from the world again.

I wish I knew what he was thinking right now.

"You've all experienced more in the last two weeks than I could've anticipated," Eun-Ji muttered. "I'm... I don't know what to say."

"We didn't mean to keep what happened to the Delphines from you when we first got here," Dad said. "It was just—"

"Too much for one day." Eun-Ji nodded. A subtle glisten had formed in her dark eyes. "I understand."

"It'd be great to hear that it wasn't all for nothing," Momma said, then gesturing to me. "Alexa told Emma that morning that Caldwell is behind everything the Delphines were working against. You mentioned when we first got here that Bouchard's gathered incriminating intel about him. Are those two connected?"

As if that were his cue, Anthony approached the desk. Eun-Ji quietly patted the side edge of the surface, allowing him to fully come up.

"They're the same thing," he answered, facing us. "We think Caldwell is forming a plan against magicians on a scale the country's never seen before: potentially wipe us out on a national scale all at *once*."

"What makes you say that?" Momma asked, twisting her Atera family ring on her right ring finger.

"The Hunter world's been changing. For one, in the last year, Caldwell's lowered the federal standard for a Hunter to become a Master and a Master to become a Grand. The number of Grand Hunter packs is about to approach the Master Hunter population, which has never been seen since the industry started—in any part of the world."

And he would know, considering his family started the industry.

"As of August," he added, "the United States has the biggest Grand Hunter population in the world, rivaling Canada, Indonesia, and Argentina. On top of that, some Grand Hunter missions have the orders *not* to kill their targets on sight. Only pack leaders know where they're ending up after that."

"And both of our leads to whatever Caldwell's up to are dead," Momma said, sighing.

"*Save them.*" Alexa's last words had never echoed so loudly in my head before. What if *this* was what she'd been urging me to save my people from...?

"Didn't Alexa give you any insight on this?" Jak asked Anthony.

"If she did, I'd be telling you right now, believe me," he replied bitterly. "I'd love to watch our Hunters storm the Oval Office and shoot down the guy who ordered my mom's death just because of what she was."

"Couldn't this just mean he's buckling down on getting rid of wielders before he's out of office?" Aunt Becca asked next to me. "That's been his goal for the last fourteen years, it makes sense if he's growing desperate in his last two. There's no way they'd give him a *fifth* term."

"We'd almost like to think that," Eun-Ji said, resting her folded hands on her desk, "but if he was able to weasel his way into doubling his maximum term limit, something the United States never saw before FDR in 1944, he may just be capable of being the first US president to ever snag a fifth term. Time is most likely not his motive here.

"In August, Zachary Delphine was entrusted with a file transfer and uncovered a budget report showing an abnormally large sum allocated to 'targeted medical research' under a *discreet* branch of the United States Department of Defense—something that doesn't show up under the publicized budget reports. Caldwell wrote a note under his signature that said 'Ensure compatibility.'"

"Another reason we took four months to enact our plan," Anthony said. "We had to tailor everything around what he was doing. He worked fast."

"Do you have a copy of that report?" Momma asked.

"Right here." Eun-Ji slid one of the papers off her desk and handed it to Momma.

Her sharp eyes narrowed as they ran across the photocopy. I counted the seconds until she said, "I'd need a budget report from the year before. The numbers for Public Health and Safety Programs seem lower than standard, but I can't say for sure without reference. The technologies for National Defense shouldn't be one and a half times bigger, though. Caldwell's putting the country's resources toward eradicating magicians with a full-on purge instead of weeding them out like he's been doing."

"This is why I never paid taxes," Aunt Becca muttered.

"We can't say anything for absolute certain about what the president is doing," Eun-Ji said, "but we're worried about the safety of American magicians more than ever. Caldwell is looming over the country like a stationed missile. We've started sending our agents across the border under the cover of federal aid and reinforcements, but whatever he has planned, he's keeping it locked up tight. We're likely going to see a noticeable increase in refugees this year once it begins unless we can figure it out and prevent it somehow."

"It's a miracle Thomas has survived for this long..." Dad mumbled, eyes downcast. He rubbed his stubbled square chin. "It's not a possibility they're involving him in this, is it?"

I wondered what Anthony knew or even remembered about Mr. Dawson as he huffed and replied, "I have no idea what they'd do with him. Caldwell's already keeping select magicians alive when they're first captured for whatever reason, but if Thomas Dawson is still alive and in custody, he's a direct lead to his most wanted target. If Caldwell is desperate enough for you, he'll keep him alive for as long as it takes to get information."

"Do you have any idea where he could be?" I blurted, instinctively taking a step. "Since you were part of the pack. We've been using a locator spell on him ever since he was captured, and all we get is a black void and the fact he's in Washington, DC. The spell doesn't tell us the specific place he's in."

I braced myself as Eun-Ji and Anthony both straightened, sparing each other a glance. "He *has* to be at the White House," Eun-Ji said with finality. "Those are the results of a locator spell when the target is in a facility protected by the magic shield Bouchard has over it."

I bit the inside of my cheek. That made sense, and I regretted not connecting the two dots when she'd first told us about that protection spell.

"The US is one of the few governments aware of it," Anthony said. "For obvious reasons."

"What do people see when they use the spell on one of us?"

Jak asked, analytical again.

"Same black void," Anthony answered. "For any location that's protected, the spell moves to the next established place. We protected the mountains around us for that reason so the spell passes over the Saint Elias Mountains and lands on the Yukon as a whole instead."

Ha, I thought, beaming inwardly, *that narrows it down.*

"Someone's definitely thought the spell was malfunctioning on them when they tried to find someone here," Becca commented, biting her lip with amusement.

That knowledge made me feel safer about our situation, but a couple of weeks had already passed with Mr. Dawson in custody. How long would the government keep him locked up for before they wrote him off as a useless source?

"So Dawson's at the White House," Dad mumbled, nodding to himself. "Makes sense..."

Momma's glance at his dejected face snapped her back into action. "Okay," she began, setting the budget report down onto Eun-Ji's desk, "if you can get a copy of the budget report from the year before, we can start investigating, especially that 'Ensure compatibility' note. I wish I had more to go off of—and that my face wasn't officially a target for the US Government."

"We're happy to have you, Amy," Becca remarked.

I elbowed her. She rolled her eyes.

"Well, I'm glad we were able to trade answers of sorts," Eun-Ji said, laying her hands flat on her desk. "This conversation contributed a lot to our current investigations. I really appreciate you all being willing to share—"

The door behind us banged open, spinning us around. A boy

in a black jacket and ripped jeans panted furiously in the doorway, bent over and leaning on the knob for support.

Alejandro. *Alejandro?* He was back? Why was he so out of—?

"Em—Emma," he breathed. "Kamose—*¡un mensaje por Kamose!*"

What? A message from *Kamose?*

I crossed the office, helping Alejandro stand. "What's wrong?" I said in Spanish. "Are you okay? What did Kamose say?"

"It's about… Dawson," he whispered, my blood running cold. Kamose, a nore who knew all present circumstances without needing an enquirer, had news about Mr. Dawson. If Alejandro had come bursting in here with *urgent* news…

No, no, no, no, no.

"Alejandro, please!" I exclaimed.

"Don't—don't go after him." His hand fell onto my shoulder as his chest heaved. "If you want him—and your family to live—you can't save him."

THIRTEEN

hat? For Mr. Dawson to survive—for *all* of us to survive—we couldn't save him? How? What had Kamose seen, how had Alejandro ended up here with that?

"What do you mean?" I whispered.

"What's going on?" Aunt Becca said behind me. I remembered that she was the only one in the room who didn't understand Spanish.

—*I need to talk to you,*— Alejandro told me, still depending on the knob of Eun-Ji's office door to hold him up.

My brow furrowed. Why was he using telepathy? If this news was about Dawson, we all needed to know it...

He has something for my ears only.

—Okay. Into the hall.—

"Give us a second," I announced, guiding him out the door.

"What's wrong?" Momma said, stepping forward.

"He needs to talk to me." I kept an arm around Alejandro's waist to hold him up. "We'll be right back."

Momma's glower told me she *really* didn't like that, but the only reason Alejandro would keep something from my family right now would be Anthony and Eun-Ji being around. If Kamose was involved, we'd be talking about the *other* impossible wielders that existed, and now definitely wasn't the time to dive into that with everyone.

I shut the door behind me and then leaned Alejandro against the opposite side of the concrete hall. "Kamose said," I whispered, "we'll only live if we *don't* go after Dawson?"

He tried to straighten but staggered against the wall. "I'm sorry," he breathed. "I teleported—here. As fast as I could. They said you—were—in here, I still—can't breathe."

"Okay," I said against my mounting fear. Cringing at the soft echo of my voice in the cold, humid hall, I closed the gap between us to keep our conversation quiet. "Catch your breath and then tell me."

He swallowed a couple of times, his breathing eventually slowing. The bright round lights in the ceiling exposed a concerning paleness in his warm-brown face. I wouldn't be surprised if everyone on the other side of the door was trying to listen in, and I bet Alejandro felt every ounce of that weight.

"Kamose said..." he whispered after a few moments, "Annisa texted him. She had... a vision. It involved us and started—with you, you were saving Dawson. So Kamose—looked for him."

"Did he see him at the White House?" I asked anxiously.

Alejandro shook his head, swallowing again. "He can't see him. But his magic—can still speak to him. He knows what Caldwell is doing—with Dawson. You can't go. Caldwell's plan—depends on you rescuing him."

"If we know that, we can outsmart him! We don't have to fall into his trap—"

"Emma," Alejandro said, still on the verge of panting. "Kamose begged me. He is begging you. Don't leave. It has—*deadly* consequences."

"What was Annisa's vision?" I demanded, leaning in. "Was he dead at any point?"

Alejandro's throat bobbed, sharp eyes piercing me with conviction. Instinct warned me that I wasn't ready for that answer.

"Him and your dad—and Rebecca. You were fatally injured. Because you tried to save him."

My body went rigid. That sounded familiar. That sounded horribly familiar to...

The morning I went to save Breanne and Opal after Mom told me not to. The Delphines were shot down. One of us was captured.

And that had happened with a plan—with an enemy we were familiar with. I didn't need to try to connect the pieces of how a rescue mission could end up fatal. I'd already lived it.

My parents were right.

"But..." I finally managed, crossing my arms against the cold, "we can't do nothing—"

"I don't know where we were—in the vision. But Annisa told Kamose that people died. Because you went after Dawson. We all witnessed it somehow."

"Maybe we can talk to her." Pressure built behind my eyes with anxious desperation. "She's in Ontario, I need to know what she saw—"

"Emma, I say this for you and only you." He exhaled, running his hand through his hair and bringing my attention to the sweat glistening on his forehead. "If you involve yourself—you will kill your family, maybe even yourself. Kamose said he will inform you as the situation changes. He will message me whenever I go back to Valencia. But don't do anything—"

"Does he know what Caldwell's doing to him?" I snapped, more out of helpless frustration than anything else. "Anything about how he's probably being tortured? How he might not even get to confess something before he drops dead?"

"He didn't tell me—"

"Can we find out?"

Alejandro shook his head. "You can't ask him. He could only tell me what he did because I didn't ask him for those answers. He can't tell you what you want to know unless you ask him and pay the nore's price."

"Then I'm paying it," I stated. "If I'm forced to stay here while my godfather is in custody because *I* was dumb enough to follow him on a mission, then I'm going to know why!"

"You *can't!*" Alejandro hissed, startling me. "None of us can! He suffers without you right now, but he dies with you if you change that."

I blankly stared at the boy in front of me. Part of me cursed his boldness; if Alejandro, of all people, had gathered enough courage to snap at me, the situation was dire. But were we really supposed to stay here and wait for Kamose's green light? Were we not allowed to do anything other than *wait?*

No, no, no, no, no, I snapped in my head. *It wasn't supposed to go like this, we aren't supposed to stay here.*

Mr. Dawson was the government's biggest lead to us—but they didn't have infinite patience. If his stubbornness persisted for too long, eventually, they'd write him off as a dead end.

I fought an uphill battle against the burn in my eyes, the stinging in my nose, the furious quiver in my jaw amidst the stifling underground atmosphere. The man had given up everything for us, and now he was willing to give up his life.

"*Amiga...*" Alejandro stood from the wall with effort, reaching out a shaky arm. "I'm sorry. I didn't mean to speak harshly to you. I know you're afraid—"

I shook my head, stepping back from his touch. Breaking down wasn't an option; now more than ever, I needed to hold myself up to keep my head on straight. I couldn't do anything, least of all let this sweep me away.

"I'm fine," I told him, glancing behind me at Eun-Ji's door. "I just don't know how I'm going to tell all of them."

Alejandro took a deep breath. "Wait. There's something else that I need to tell you: Annisa saw five of us in her vision."

I paused. Five?

"She couldn't clearly... remember their face," he added, leaning against the wall again for support, "but they were there with the four of us."

There *was* a fifth one of us. And they'd somehow been involved with Dawson's rescue? Had they helped us with it?

Why would magic give just Annisa that vision and not me when we were both directly involved in it?

"So we're going to meet this person soon," I mused.

"I don't know," Alejandro said. "Annisa and Kamose are hesitant about that part. But with or without them, we can't go after Mr. Dawson, Emma. I wish Kamose could tell you why, I wish *I* could tell you why. He knew that the more you knew, the more likely you would be to go."

My teeth were almost chattering, but with angry regret. *I nearly forced Alejandro to take me to Annisa just now because of impulse.* I needed to hold on to the Hunter in me for dear life, especially if Kamose could predict from the other side of the world my biggest weakness.

I started pacing the width of the hall, finally feeling the last threat of tears drop back down into their well. "Someone will have to hold me down for the first few weeks."

Alejandro lightly shrugged. "I can help with that—I'm also here to tell you that my parents said I can stay here for a while."

My head caught back with surprise. "How did you get them to agree to that?"

"The conversation lasted for the whole night. As long as I visit them every week and update them, it's okay."

"That's a relief..." I didn't realize how much so until my body relaxed. "You're our only connection to the outside world."

"I'm here to help. And about that—does Eun-Ji know about you—about *us* yet?"

"No, but Jak does. We're probably going to tell Eun-Ji soon." I looked behind me again at her door across the hall. "The base has a theory about what Caldwell is planning, and it's big. Who knows, our abilities might be meant to stop him—since he's our main target."

He nodded thoughtfully. "Let's tell your family about Daw-son together."

I exhaled in defeat. Hearing those words made the situation no easier to accept. "Thanks."

Unfortunately, Kamose was dead right about how the more I knew, the more I'd want to go after Mr. Dawson. I hated, cursed myself for the fact, that I was that readable to someone who'd never even met me before.

FOURTEEN

As (easily) predicted, waiting until Eun-Ji excused us for lunch and then telling my family Kamose's message about Mr. Dawson didn't go all that smoothly, or without argument. But Momma and Dad couldn't be upset for long before we got to the eating hall.

In a concrete room without windows and with round tables all across (instead of a long rectangle for each class), I didn't have to worry about mealtimes at Bouchard feeling too much like eating at the Callistro Academy. People were also a lot nicer than their curious whispers and stares now that they were starting to get to know us. So in a small way... lunch did kind of feel like my first-ever meal at Callistro.

I had to quickly shove that thought away as I ate. I didn't

want to continue my high school education here, let alone "graduate" here, but with how we were now housebound because of Mr. Dawson's situation, I didn't have the luxury of choice. I hadn't gotten to mourn the fact once since we'd left Capperson, but I didn't want to let myself, either.

After dinner that night, we told Eun-Ji about our "group of impossible wielders". To my surprise, she hadn't been, well, *surprised* at how Alejandro wasn't the only one of his kind. I guess even she needed time to process it like Jak had, because she ended up giving us all a week off to "cope" afterward, like we hadn't said anything. Evidently, though, my parents wanted a distraction. Or teaching *was* how they coped, because three days later they were Bouchard's newest self-defense instructor duo. Aunt Becca was already in contact with the bakers about opening a café, but I stuck to whatever wouldn't remind me of present circumstances, which often meant the library. The forced quiet was therapeutic when I had no control over the chaos in every other part of life.

My eyes ran along the spines of the books on the shelves as I strolled along the right wall. The dusty smell of old pages and leather covers hovered in the cold air like incense. The silence was (literally) unheard of. The third through fifth graders were having class in the back, but the teachers were nearly as quiet as the rest of us. I was halfway down the library when the kids stood up and pushed their chairs in, the sliding wood muted by the educational section's carpet. The kids strolled down and between the long tables in the middle of the cavernous room, never sparing me more than a glance.

I looked back at the now almost empty tables. In the corner, the blond girl from a few nights ago returned my stare, whispering to a girl with straight black hair and bangs.

Instinct turned me toward the wall of books beside me. Those girls were definitely talking about me, but I didn't want to scare them by either approaching or running away. I'd just raise my hand and pretend that I was contemplating pulling out *A Separate Peace* until—

"Excuse me," a young voice whispered, in sync with the blonde sauntering up to me in my peripheral vision. I looked down. Round and grand chocolate-brown eyes looked up at me with an excitement I hadn't expected from the shy girl I'd been trading glances with over the last few days.

"Hi," I whispered back, offering a light smile.

"My friend and I have some questions for you." She pointed at the other little girl straight down and at the table in the back. "We'd like you to answer them please."

I suppressed a chuckle at her boldness, at the nearly adult-like quality of her speaking manner. She *was* as curious about me as I was about her. I guess I was about to find out why.

"I'm new here," I replied, "so I'll try to answer, but I can't make any promises."

"That's okay," she whispered. She stuck out her small hand. "I'm Michaela, the long way to spell it."

My smile poked through wider. I took her hand with gentleness that she returned with thrice as much strength, shaking our hands three times. Wow. She'd definitely rehearsed her handshake and wasn't afraid to show it.

"I'm Emma."

Michaela let go of my hand and waved for me to follow her. We went down the other half of the library until she tugged me to her previous spot at the round table, next to her friend, and then pulled out her chair for me.

As I sat down and she came to sit on my other side, there was still something about her that I couldn't place... No, wait. *Both* of them. Something I couldn't explain, just feel. I wasn't hesitant around these two girls like I was around most people. Then again, who ever is around little kids?

Michaela's friend leaned forward on her folded arms, grinning at me with joy sparkling in her dark-mahogany eyes. "Hi," she whispered, easily the loudest in the room, "I'm Li! I like your necklace."

I looked down at the silver heart around my neck that boasted my name with a small sapphire at the top. Another smile formed on my lips. "Thank you, Li."

"Do you wanna try a dumpling my *waipo* made? Oh, sorry, that's my grandma. '*Waipo*' is how you say 'grandma' in Chinese when it's on your mom's side."

"Huh, good to know," I whispered sincerely, tilting my head. "We're allowed to eat in the library?"

"No, but I got good at sneaking." Li reached down for her pastel-blue backpack next to her chair.

"Don't, we'll get in trouble," Michaela whispered, leaning forward on the table. "Ms. Hannigan said we have to give her our food if she catches us again—"—she looked up at me—"that's the librarian, do you know her?"

"I've met her, yeah," I replied, starting to wonder what kind of secret meeting I'd just been inducted into.

"Okay, cool." She shifted in her seat, firmly folding her hands on the table like she was formally beginning our conversation.

"You're an Ateria, aren't you?"

I barely suppressed my chuckle in time. "An *Atera?*"

"Yeah." She swept her straight hair out of her face and leaned in to lower her voice more. "My dad thought you guys were dead."

"You can't say that!" Li hissed quietly. "That's rude!"

"No, it's not," Michaela argued. "It's true." Her eyes rose back up to me. "He was really surprised when he saw Tristan Ateria with you guys a few days ago, but then I saw you and thought you were cool. And then I saw you some more and thought you were cool, and I wanted to talk to you because—okay, wait, so my dad thought you were dead but then Auntie Jennifer told us that the students at her school were talking about Tristan Ateria's kid. She works at the Callistro Academy in North Carolina—"

My brain stopped for a second, and I had to shake my head back into focus. I hadn't thought anything of it when Michaela had said "Jennifer", but a teacher with that name at the Callistro Academy?

"Wait," I whispered. "Jennifer *Durrett?*"

"Yeah." Michaela nodded. "My dad's sister, she's an English teacher at the Callistro Academy, did you have her?"

My sophomore year. She'd taken Sarah's phone from her after catching her studying for Ms. Perketti's physics final.

"Durrett is a magician...?" I whispered, stunned. Was this how Breanne had felt when she found out that Mr. Dawson was a druid?

"*Yes,*" Michaela said, like she was over this part of the conversation. "But that's what we wanted to ask you about. Auntie always tells me about Callistro when she sends letters to us, but she's a teacher, what's it like to be a *student* there?"

"Wait," I mumbled, fighting to keep my volume low enough, "how did you know I went to Callistro?"

"Eun-Ji told me. And she said your mom taught there."

I wouldn't be surprised if this girl had walked up to Eun-Ji within the last few days and blatantly asked for the details about the newcomers.

"I always wanted to go there," Li whispered, resting her chin on her small fist. "When Michaela and I met, she told me about Callistro. But my *waipo* says it's dangerous."

The irony in how many wielders had wound up at Callistro was still spinning in my head: me, Alexa, Mr. Dawson, Mrs. Durrett, Opal, even Breanne (albeit only technically). At this point, I couldn't be sure that anyone at that school was who they said they were.

No wonder Caldwell's growing desperate in his attempts to eradicate us, I thought. *There are a lot more imposters in the Hunter world than even I would've thought.* And Bouchard was a large contributor to that, considering their double agents. If there were this many of us hijacking the mortal world, what if Bouchard's purge theory was closer to the truth than they were assuming?

"It's super dangerous, right?" Michaela asked, but in a manner like she was investigating—not like she was excited to talk about big-kid stuff. "Because it's a Hunter school?"

I took a breath in, but truth and experience shushed me. Callistro was *supposed* to be dangerous for any wielder who dared a step into its halls, but its founder hadn't necessarily intended for that; Caralyn Callistro had been an ally of magic. But that didn't mean the staff today felt the same way.

Mrs. Durrett is probably the only reason these girls know that it is a Hunter's school, considering it's just an advanced self-defense boarding school to the rest of the world.

"Well," I began, "it depends on who you ask. Caralyn Callistro, the founder, has a much more interesting story than what the world knows."

"What's the story?" the girls whispered in sync.

"Both versions," Li added.

A library was no better place for story time: I told them all about how a young woman teamed up with a mage who was after her father, Henry, to stop him from stealing his victims' magic. That young woman wanted to build a Hunter school to help a magician's descendant centuries later because she knew that descendant would be the one to help make the world a better place.

"How did she know who the descendant was?" Michaela whispered in her detective fashion. "*Did* she know?"

I thought back to the night I'd found Caralyn's second document exposing the truth about her intentions. She'd written that the "ultimate connection" to the world's hope lay in the Atera family, but she'd addressed the "Soul of Unity" directly. And she'd marked the Delphines as not only our enemies, but Adara's, too...

I paused before I could answer. Caralyn had written Adara's fate on that paper and *associated* it with the Ateras—but had she known that Adara would be an Atera herself?

"I don't know," I told Michaela. "But she wrote in these secret documents I found that she wanted to help magic. She used Callistro as a cover for her alliance."

Li bounced in her wooden chair, fighting to keep her voice

in a whisper. "So I can tell Waipo it's not dangerous! Because Caralyn didn't wanna hurt us."

"No, she didn't," I said, "but Caralyn's gone now. And the people there today do want to hurt us, so your grandma has a point."

"Those *documents* are dangerous." Michaela leaned in right beside me as if one of our enemies were listening in. "Because can't you be killed for not hating magic?"

"Yep," I replied. "What Caralyn said about her dad is arguably just as dangerous."

"And if somebody found them and there are other magicians there like Auntie, they could be caught because it's suspicious," she whispered. Wow. Bright kid. "So the documents are safe, right?"

That was the one question I'd forgotten to ask Anthony amidst everything else going on. I knew that Alexa's pack had been the last ones to have them, and Alexa herself had said, way before she'd exposed who she really was to me, that that information was flammable. The pack had supposedly been keeping the documents hidden away for safekeeping, but now that the pack was dead... now that Caldwell's Hunters had most likely ransacked their lairs...

Where were Caralyn's documents now?

"Emma," Li sang quietly, waving a small hand in front of my face.

I blinked, suddenly aware again. "Sorry. They're safe, they've always been really well-hidden."

I had to believe that—if Caldwell *did* have them and Caralyn's story still hadn't gotten out. Not that I had any way of knowing while stuck down here. And call me pessimistic, but I doubted that Caldwell would keep that information confidential, especially if he found a way to harness it for his own benefit.

"How did you find them?" Michaela asked me.

I smiled. "I was exploring Callistro's secret passageways."

Li traced circles on the wooden table. "Bouchard doesn't have things like that. But I'd be too scared to go in them."

"It's not scary when you have friends. My friends and I used to explore them a lot together, we even did our homework in the secret rooms sometimes."

"Were they magicians?" Michaela asked.

"Two of them were."

"Are they here?"

I shook my head and forced myself to keep my smile before my mind could twist the situation into something worse. My best friends weren't here, my godfather wasn't here, and I wasn't going to subject these girls to why that was the case. They were too young for that.

Michaela took over before I could respond. "You probably miss them, sorry. I wish I could go to Callistro when I'm old enough. It sounds so pretty, Auntie Jennifer says nobody gets to teach in a mansion. And she said I would've made a great Callistro Girl."

"I wanna be a Callistro Girl, too." Li pushed her black bangs out of her eyes before resting her chin on her fist again. "I'd be so excited."

"I'd feel special," Michaela said, mimicking her position.

I remembered the day Momma first told me that I'd be attending the Callistro Academy; I'd thought she was insane, or that she wanted a cruel laugh. But after orientation, after seeing the gray plaid skirt and crimson blazer with the sword-through-a-rose crest, after seeing why Momma thought I'd be a good fit there... I'd been excited, too. I'd felt special, too. And after finding out why Caralyn Callistro had founded her school in the first place, I'd felt like I belonged there—because I think that was when I'd discovered what a real Callistro Girl was, what she was always meant to be.

"I think that's how anyone should feel about being a Callistro Girl," I whispered to the girls on either side of me. I could say that with confidence because no matter our differing beliefs about what the world should look like, even in Alexa's case, one thing was universally true: "Callistro Girls always want to change the world for the better."

"Even though they're Hunters," Michaela added.

I wasn't sure how to reply to that, which made me all the more grateful when a short woman approached our table.

I looked up. With her raven-black hair pinned up in a simple bun, Eun-Ji wore her professional smile on her small lips. Her hands were locked behind her back instead of folded in front of her like usual.

"How are we doing back here?" she whispered.

"Good!" Li answered, struggling to match Eun-Ji's volume. "Emma is telling us about the Callistro Academy."

Eun-Ji's thin brows rose with intrigue, dark eyes landing on me. "What a coincidence, I wanted to talk to her about the same thing. May I?"

Wait, what?

"Take her," Michaela whispered, sliding out of her chair. Li followed suit, both grabbing their backpacks on the floor. "We're done with school now. Bye, Emma."

"Bye, Emma," Li sang softly, moseying past Eun-Ji as she swung her backpack onto her shoulders.

To my relief, Eun-Ji's smile didn't leave when the girls were out of earshot. Neither did her kind eyes fade as she walked around the table to take Michaela's old seat. She moved whatever was behind her back into her lap, the table covering most of it. A book.

"I knew Michaela wouldn't leave you alone for long," she began quietly, back perfectly straight as she placed her elbows onto the table and folded her hands together. "She's remarkably intuitive for her age."

No kidding.

"Am I in trouble?" I whispered with a light tease.

"No, no." She rested one hand in front of me, her other bringing the book out from her lap and onto the table. "I just felt that it was a good time to give you this."

My eyes had already snagged on the title by the time she slid the worn crimson cover to me: *White Lies for Sacred Ties.*

I froze in my chair. Caralyn Callistro's autobiography.

FIFTEEN

I mindlessly pointed at the book in front of me, daring to look up at Eun-Ji. It wasn't even the fact that we were in the library, but my shock that trapped my voice in a whisper: "Where did you get this?"

"This was our founder's, Joseph Bouchard's. It's the first-ever copy of Caralyn Callistro's autobiography, and it's been protected by every Bouchard chief until one of us could give it to the person Joseph saved it for: Adara."

I knew her reaction to the truth about us was off! Apparently when we told her, she hadn't needed time to process it, after all; she'd been thinking about when to give me this book.

Every piece felt like it was part of a different puzzle: yes, you can find a Hunter's autobiography in almost any facility with a bookshelf, but Bouchard was the furthest thing from a Hunter's archive, and its founder had somehow snagged the first-ever copy of the one belonging to the woman who had built the first Hunter school. And he'd saved it for *Adara*!

"I should be honest about the evening you told me that you were Adara," Eun-Ji whispered. Maybe it was the fact that we were sitting at one of the kids' tables in the educational section, but I felt like a child shrinking into the chair. "I had a vision about you a *long* time ago: the day you and your family would arrive here."

That was why she was so surprised to see Dad and Aunt Becca that day. Confirmation, something she had already seen but maybe forgotten about somehow, or hadn't expected to actually happen.

"As I'm sure you know," she told me, "druid visions can be triggered by specific events tied to the future. I first had that vision after meeting Aastha for the first time—so I knew better than to doubt the timing."

"Did you tell her about it?"

"I did. And I had that vision again after I assumed my role here as chief. Then I saw a slightly different version where Jak was with you. That was the one I got your name in."

I straightened, pausing. "Did *you* tell Aastha my name?"

"Yes. Once I realized exactly who you were and that you were meant for something that had to be protected."

It was Eun-Ji. Aastha found out my name from Eun-Ji and told it to Jak before she died. My path had been intertwined with Bouchard since I was a little girl, if not before that.

"You have to understand, though,"—Eun-Ji laid her hand down next to Caralyn's book—"contact with her was *extremely* limited at that point. Like I told you the day you got here, the last time I'd spoken with her face to face was before she got engaged to William. I'm guessing she married him at around the same time she suddenly pulled back from us. She wasn't able to help us in Canada anymore, but she was still eager to do her part in the US. So I made you her priority. Her top mission was to find you and protect you however possible."

I wondered exactly when she'd given Aastha that assignment. And I wondered exactly what she'd told her to communicate the significance of it for Aastha to have entrusted her seven-year-old son with it when she knew she was going to die.

"So," I whispered hesitantly, "did you recognize me and Jak when you first saw us?"

"It all began coming back to me once you arrived. Slowly, but especially when I realized that Jak was Aastha's son. When I knew for a fact that you were Emmalynn Atera, I decided to let you tell me the significance of that."

"Does Jak know about this...?" I asked, leaning in like someone was eavesdropping. "How his mom knew my name?"

"I have a feeling that he wants to know more about his mother now that he can. But if he were ready to know, he would've asked me by now. I'll tell him once he is."

My eyes fell onto the worn book in front of me. "And all of that has to do with this?"

"In a way, yes." Eun-Ji straightened in her chair, changing gears. "I doubt any chief knew why Joseph grabbed this for Adara, let alone how we were supposed to know her identity so we could give it to *you* if any of us met you—we just all believed in the same cause he did, and we knew to take him at his word when he wrote that this was for you."

I shifted in my seat to face her better. "I'm confused, *how* did he get this? Did he know Caralyn, how would they've ever crossed paths—?"

She placed a calming hand on my back, quieting me. "I'll tell you what I was told when I took over as chief: 'Guard this like you would the magic downstairs. If you meet Adara and there's no mistaking that it's her, give it to her. She should know what to do with it.'"

Who said that *lie?!*

I reached for the book, Caralyn's secrets whispering in my memory. My hand froze halfway, and I looked back at Eun-Ji. "Do you know the truth about how Caralyn really felt about magic?"

She took in a breath to speak like she needed to prepare the words first. "I guess it shouldn't be a surprise that you do, too."

"How did you find out?"

"I can tell you that story anytime," she whispered, subtly waving the matter away. "I didn't want to overwhelm you with all this, but I think I missed the mark. The point is, considering this book is supposedly as valuable as the magic we're keeping in the vaults down below,"—she slid it closer to me, toward the edge of the table—"I'd put it somewhere safe in your room."

My head was still swimming with frustrating questions I knew I wouldn't get the answers to any time soon. How had Joseph Bouchard ended up with the first-ever copy of *Caralyn Callistro's* autobiography? Had she exposed her darkest secret to him? How had he known to trust her? How would they have ever met? Had she been partially responsible for Bouchard being built, too? How had she known that I'd end up here two centuries later?

"The Callistro Academy has a copy of this, obviously," I finally managed, "but the only thing special in it are the riddles that tell you where the school's secret passageways are, that's it... Nobody knows how Joseph got this? Or even if he knew Caralyn personally?"

Eun-Ji shrugged. "From what we know about him today, she's never come up. He never told his successor how he got this, either. All I know is that it's yours, and you should guard it like you do your own magic."

When I dared to open the book and flip to the table of contents, it was identical from what I remembered about the copy in Callistro's library. Nothing stuck out. What was so special about this copy other than it being the very first?

Caralyn Callistro and Bouchard's founding. How can there be a connection there? None of this makes any sense at first glance.

At first glance. Yet another riddle Caralyn had left behind for me to solve.

How?

"Um... thank you." I mustered every ounce of sincerity I could into my whisper; I did mean it amidst the dense fog of confusion. "I appreciate you waiting. I'm honestly super confused by this."

Eun-Ji lightly rubbed my back before standing. "Don't worry," she murmured, pushing her chair in, "your identity as Adara is safe with me. Whatever Joseph Bouchard and Caralyn Callistro wanted you to find in that book, you'll find it. If it could wait two hundred years, it can probably wait however long you need."

As she strolled past the table and toward the library entrance on the other side of the room, I clung to those words. I didn't know how long I'd need to solve a conspiracy theory that blew all

the others out of the water, and I definitely wasn't ready to start
right now.

◊

The frigid atmosphere of the dim, gray room dampened my skin
yet barely mattered on my hot cheeks. Cuffed to a chair at a long
silver table, I looked a suited rectangular man in the eye. "People
have known about Adara for centuries," I was saying stiffly. "But
they—"

Flash.

"Okay, Emmalynn."

The agent, three more behind him, opened the lapel of his
suit jacket. Three flashes cut up the scene as a zipped-up plastic
bag landed in front of me and was pushed over to me. Before I
could catch what was inside, a flash interrupted.

"What did you threaten them with?" I demanded. "Their
lives in exchange for help in finding us?"

The rectangular man blinked, tilting his head. "'Them'?"

"My other—"

Flash.

Watrous, Saskatchewan. Those words were echoing with a resounding realizing chill across my mind.

"Seems like we're getting somewhere," the agent said, satis-
fied. "So let's skip the back-and-forth—"

Flash.

Startlingly bright daylight contrasted against the Secret Service agents guarding the curve of the beige room, two holding me
captive by my arms. That light clashed even more so with the navy-

blue suit the tall man in front of me wore as he told me, "I want her ability and then yours."

"Emma, stop—!" a familiar voice beside me cried. Mr. Dawson.

I kept my eyes locked on President Caldwell. "I'm a hybrid wielder—"

Flash.

"Americans trust me to keep them safe from threats like her," Caldwell said firmly, standing rigidly.

The details, I thought rapidly, *remember the details! "Threats like her". He's spent millions—*

My mind snagged on a realization, one my magic refused to give me, before everything flashed again.

"You didn't just have the Delphines killed because they were magicians!" I cried, writhing in the loosening hold the two men had on me. "You had them killed because they had—!"

"I said SHOOT HIM!"

A gunshot rang out. The window behind Caldwell shattered. I dropped to the floor. Friction caught my palms on the blue carpet. When I glanced up, a gaunt Mr. Dawson had dropped with me. Another shot boomed.

Black swallowed my vision as my eyes snapped open and I gasped.

The firm mattress under me bounced with a slight creak as I propped myself up on my elbows. I tried quieting my breaths as quickly as I could, but the vision I'd had at the motel in Alberta had darted to the surface with that gunshot. I slowly laid myself back down onto the bed, trying to no avail to suppress it. Those images throbbed in my head like a heartbeat.

Mr. Dawson... I fought to calm the pressure building behind my eyes. *He is at the White House. And Caldwell said to—*

I pursed my lips and shut my eyes despite how nobody would know if I broke down right now. That was my first time having that vision since that night at the motel. Almost three weeks apart. I cursed that fact with every fiber in my being. They weren't supposed to be that close together unless that event, if it would actually happen, was imminent. I wanted to excuse it with whatever I could: a couple of *weeks* had passed since Eun-Ji gave me Caralyn's autobiography in the library, my family had been just as lost about Joseph Bouchard having it, and we were already over halfway through January. No wonder I was so on edge about Mr. Dawson. I had to wonder how long it would be until I could emotionally accept the facts of the situation—or if I'd never truly rest again until I could save him.

If I'd ever be able to save him. Now I knew there was a reality where Caldwell ordered his death right in front of me.

What if I lose him first?

What if he wasn't the only one I would lose?

Breaths threatening to speed up at the thought, I was surprised that I hadn't woken up Momma and Dad by now—but the sincerely *deafening* quiet down here probably helped them feel safe and get a good night's rest better than anything they'd ever had in their lives.

That was why Aunt Becca stirring next to me startled me. My mouth clamped itself shut.

"Em...?" she murmured with the rasp of sleep, turning over onto her back. The night-light plugged into the wall next to the credenza in front of us illuminated her rubbing her eye. "You okay?"

I swallowed, wiping my damp eyelashes dry. "Yeah, um..." I whispered, thankful that my voice couldn't betray me. "Just..."

No. No, it's not okay.

For some reason, it was always easier to let Auntie know when something wasn't right with me, even when nobody else was allowed to. There were some parts of me that were only safe with her.

"I had a vision," I admitted, staring up at the concrete ceiling. My fingers numbly rested on the white cotton sheets on top of me. "Caldwell was there. Mr. Dawson—was there, he's at the White House..."

The potential aftermath of that vision was wrapping around my mind like a python, squeezing it. What that gunshot meant. What it could have meant. What it *would* mean if we didn't figure out a plan to save him.

My jaw quivered, but in the dim light of that yellow nightlight, I locked it. Aunt Becca turned onto her left side to face me, propping herself up with her elbow. I closed my eyes to hide the glisten I felt forming in them.

"Caldwell ordered someone to shoot him," I croaked. "And then a gunshot went off and everyone was dropping to the floor, and I don't know if he was on the floor to protect himself or because he was—shot—"

An arm wrapped around my waist, holding me against my aunt. Her other arm slid under my neck so she could pull my head under her chin. I held my breath to avoid exhaling a hot cloud and further suffocating myself.

"Vision or nightmare?" she whispered.

"It felt like a vision," I replied, sniffing back tears. Auntie was allowed to know that I was missing a few pieces, but because of that, I didn't want her to see me fall apart. "It was just like the other ones I've had."

Including the one where Alexa was shot in front of me.

"Okay," Aunt Becca said, "but you know that going after Dawson is what'll kill him—especially if you know now that he's at the White House. Right?"

"*Yes—*" I quietly groaned.

"Then how do you know that vision isn't what happens if you try to save him anyway?"

Finally, my breaths stopped long enough for silence. I didn't. That was a blessing and a curse, because what if that vision was what would happen if I waited?

"I don't know," I whispered.

Becca knew that I wasn't talking about her question—she knew me like that. That was a big part of the reason I could let a few chips fall in front of her. Before Dad came into my life, before I knew that Mr. Dawson was a druid, Auntie used to be not just the only one who knew *every* part of me—magic and all—but shared it. She could see me a little broken because she knew the pieces and where to put them back.

She squeezed me. "That's okay. You don't have to know right now. Enjoy that while you can. I'll take you to the café tomorrow, we'll grab some coffee together."

I liked the sentiment, but half of me was left uneasy; I still had the magic of a druid in me ready to ruin another night's sleep (and my days with anxiety), and I couldn't escape it no matter how much I wanted to.

"Okay," I told her anyway. Partly because I wanted this conversation to end, partly because I was getting hot and wanted her to release me, and partly because I didn't have another choice. I couldn't escape *anything* right now no matter how much I wanted to, but I could feel the anxiety in my brain slowly starting to drain into the rest of me, threatening to set everything on fire and take control. Sooner or later, something was going to have to give.

C H A P T E R

Sixteen

"Y ou here to finally take me up on sketching lessons?" Jak teased as we both approached the doorway to the main art room. I'd finished assisting Ms. Hannigan in the library, and I guess he'd finished with cleaning duty in the kitchen at the same time. And with that smirk, his pleasant surprise about it beamed on his face.

"I'm *never* giving you that ammo," I said, strolling inside with my journal tucked against my chest. The half-full room was so large that it was more like an art *hall*. "You'd never let me live anything I draw down."

"Yeah, hence the lessons," Jak said, coming up to my side. "I'll let you roast my teaching skills if I can roast your drawings."

"You're a bad person."

"You're mad I make you laugh."

I playfully shoved him, and he nudged me back. I *was* mad, but only because, well, I still felt like I couldn't tell him how I felt about him. Every time I'd thought about bringing it up, I realized that I could only give him a confession, no direction after that—because pursuing something with him still didn't feel... *safe.* We'd all spent the past three weeks settling into an industrial bunker, and I was still wrapping my head around the fact that *someone* in the nineteenth century had known that I'd end up here one day and made sure Joseph Bouchard had Caralyn Callistro's first-ever autobiography to give to me; it still felt like we had eyes on us everywhere, watching. I wasn't used to a life without forbidding eyes, and I wasn't even convinced yet that I was living one. On that front, I was the one who needed more time. For now, I just had to keep looking away every time Jak smiled at me like that and, I guess, stay mad about it.

The art room did its best to make you forget the outside world: one half was dedicated to the art folk, and the opposite wall was lined with a few writing desks and three bookcases of writing materials. We could even store our projects in the lockers against the wall behind me and Jak.

They try so hard to make being stuck enjoyable.

I noticed Dakota, a brunette my age whom I'd met last week, peacefully crocheting in one of the rocking chairs in the back of the room. On my left, a boy sitting in a beanbag chair in front of the art easels waved up at Jak, and he waved back.

"That's Joshua," Jak told me. "The one who managed to bring his drawing tablet when he got here with his uncle."

Oh, that's Joshua. Jak had talked a bit about the friends he'd met so far, but I hadn't gotten the chance to meet any of them yet. Joshua was born deaf and preferred digital art. Save for his round, short features, his forest-green eyes and spruce-brown hair reminded me of Anthony. I wasn't sure how to feel about that.

Jak gestured to the dark-blue journal I held. "Gonna write again?"

I took the book into both of my hands, my thumbs rubbing the smooth cover. "I think so—I'm almost done with this one, but I don't... want to be. It's the last thing I have from Mr. Dawson. And it talks about my friends and going to Callistro—"

Jak's hand landed on my upper back when I cut myself off and didn't continue. "I get it," he murmured.

"I had to stop at when Alexa died. So next is everything we did before we left, when you got to our house..." I swallowed, forcing a chuckle. "I don't know why I write it all down when it makes me feel like this."

Jak rubbed my back. "If getting it down helps, it helps."

It'd always helped before, and maybe it still did just a bit, but how was I supposed to write about something I didn't want to remember? Something that would only reignite my fury about a situation I couldn't do a single thing about right now?

Especially with Caldwell's all-out purge he's almost definitely planning.

"Hey!" a rich, smooth voice chimed behind us, turning me and Jak around to face the entrance. A boy taller than Jak, with black skin and tight curls, strolled into the room with his hands in his jean pockets. "Jak, what's up? This your girl?"

Right as I opened my mouth, Jak was already saying, "No, no, no, this is Emma, we're friends."

I'm not allowed to be upset. I'm not allowed to be upset.

"Right on, right on," the boy replied, nodding with a kind grin and bright teeth. He offered his left hand to me. "Hey, Emma, I'm Omari. Heard a lot about you."

I recognized that name, too, and the second Omari's other large hand clasped over mine, my impression was made: I liked him.

Huh, I quickly realized, slowing. *There's... something about him.* Something warm and familiar, but in a way that I could physically feel. And not just familiar in the sense of comfort, but also like...

Like Michaela and Li. Maybe even Anthony. What was going on with my senses when it came to meeting new (or renewed) people? Were my nerves that shot after everything?

"I've heard about you, too," I told Omari, noting the way his dark eyes protruded slightly. "All good things."

"Right on," he said again. He faced and gestured at Jak. "You got something I can paint today?"

"Not yet, but I can," Jak replied. "What were you thinking?"

"I'm gonna ask Joshua." Omari looked down at the teenage boy sitting in the beanbag chair behind me and Jak, peacefully drawing away on his tablet. "Usually has something in the bank when I'm dry."

As if feeling our stares, Joshua looked up at us and leapt from his seat. Smiling, he placed the side of his hand on his forehead near his ear and moved it outward, mouthing with a grin, "Hello."

My knowledge of American Sign Language didn't really extend beyond that—if Joshua even used ASL specifically. But I could read the excitement in his hands as they wildly flew with gestures I couldn't translate.

"All right," Omari chimed, nodding enthusiastically and then looking at Jak, "he's been wanting to know if you could do a sketch of his aunt for his uncle. He wants to give him something to remember her by."

I furrowed my brow while Jak blinked. He held up his index finger and bent it a few times, the rest of his gestures slow as he articulately asked Joshua, "Are you sure? Why me?"

Joshua signed, and Omari kept his eyes on him as he said, "He says, 'Why not you? My aunt was really special to us, and my uncle appreciates traditional art more. I trust you to do it right.'"

Jak thought about it before politely pointing at Joshua. "For you, I'll do it."

Omari translated, and Joshua beamed as he signed and mouthed, "Thank you."

Jak faced me as the two of them took their seats in the bean-bags in front of the art easels. "His aunt was killed when they were all on their way to Bouchard. She protected Joshua while they were being shot at because he couldn't hear where the bullets were coming from."

My jaw fell slack. I wanted to think it was because of shock, but I knew better: it was because I knew that pain, how it felt to be more important to someone than their own life—even though it was my magic that Alexa had been protecting. I didn't know how Joshua felt about it, but I knew the guilt that came with it.

"Oh" was all I could think to say.

"Joshua and his uncle ended up giving the base their magic. They'd gotten into a lot of trouble because of it, so giving it up was a coping mechanism of sorts."

I was surprised at how much I related to that.

When I said nothing, Jak touched my arm. "I'm gonna warm up with them."

"Okay," I said, letting him turn to an easel.

Our third week had been easier than the first for obvious reasons. I wanted to keep that momentum going as I looked over at the line of writing desks against the opposite wall, over half of which were occupied. A couple of days ago, I'd met a woman who wanted to publish a novel if she ever came out of hiding. She was pushing thirty, but she would be happy if she could get it out by forty, she'd told me. I hadn't caught her name and she wasn't here today, but she was all alone here. No family. Apparently her roommate had become like a sister to her in the last fifteen years she'd been here, but I could more than sense her longing for someone she could call her own.

I looked down at Joshua in his beanbag chair, thinking about how he'd ended up here. I didn't know about Omari, but obviously something had brought him here, too, if he hadn't been born here like a portion of other residents.

I couldn't believe how different yet identical everyone's stories were. And they all had one.

Amidst the chatter floating around, laughter erupted from the back of the room: Dakota, in a pastel-purple hoodie, with one of her friends. She and her parents were among the residents who saw no purpose in keeping their magic while down here, so they'd stored it down in Bouchard's vault below. Out of those who weren't federally wanted, a lot fewer than I would've thought wanted to try starting a normal life in the outside world. Then again, without a watertight backstory (and legal evidence to back it up), that was drastically easier said than done.

Dakota's bright-blue eyes landed on me and widened. "Emma!" she chirped, setting aside her crocheting on the wooden table between the two rocking chairs. She jumped up from her seat, sending the chair into oscillation, and practically skipped across the room and over to me. "I'm so glad you're here, I made you something!"

What? This was the second time I was seeing her, and she'd already made me a present?

She reached into her hoodie's pocket and pulled something out that was the size of her hand. "Here!"

Oh, wow...

I carefully took the crocheted yellow-and-orange flame like it'd unravel at any second. A moment later, I saw what had been crocheted all around the circumference.

"You fit my whole first name?" I said, rubbing my thumb over the dark-blue yarn spelling it out. "This is beautiful, thank you, I don't know what to say."

"Of course!" She pushed a long brown bang behind her ear. "My pieces have *really* brightened my room, I consider that an accomplishment for a place with no windows."

I didn't know if I was laughing at the joke or in disbelief.

"Don't make fun of me, but I picked a flame because it seemed fitting," she said, sticking her hands into her hoodie pocket. "When we first met, I *instantly* got the vibe that you have—a kind of fire in you. I know I've only known you for, like, a week, but I also know you've been through a lot to get here. It was just a vibe, I don't know, it felt right."

I reached my arm around her shoulders and pulled her into a hug, getting a waft of her sweet perfume. "Thank you. I really wish I knew what to say."

"You already said it, lovely." Pulling away, she nodded at the two boys sitting in the beanbags beside us, sticking her hands back into her hoodie. "What're we doing?"

"Trying to find some inspiration for my next piece," Omari answered, looking up at her. "Joshua's just practicing."

Jak turned from his easel, setting down a graphite pencil and revealing a few lines and elementary shapes on the large sketchpad in front of him. "Warming up," he said, glimpsing me. "I got a new idea for a portrait sketch."

"I wanna watch!"

He stepped to the left side of the easel, letting Dakota take a spot next to him.

"Hey, you have to let the artist breathe," Omari remarked, signing the words for Joshua to understand. "Otherwise he'll draw you and it won't be pretty."

Dakota stuck out her tongue at him just as Joshua back-handed Omari's shoulder. He firmly signed his reply.

"What did he say?" Dakota asked.

Omari looked up at her with a grin. "He said no drawing of you could be ugly."

If only I could verify that. ASL hadn't originally been on my list of to-learn languages, but if Jak was learning it for Joshua, I should, too.

A red tint bloomed on Dakota's light cheeks. She covered half of her face with her hoodie sleeve. "*Joshua*, stop, I'll cry."

Omari made a few more gestures, mouthing his words that I could almost fluently read: *She's—pri—ee yute—you think?*

Dakota kneeled down and quickly patted his shoulder.

"Stop, what're you saying?" she asked.

"Nothing, nothing." Omari held up his hands. Joshua elbowed him and replied again with narrowed eyes. I understood that every word was in good fun by how Omari signed as he added, "But he wants me to tell you that he likes your hair."

Joshua shoved him, earning a laugh out of Dakota and even a smile from Jak.

"I wanna learn sign language!" she chirped, leaning on the bulging side of Omari's beanbag. "How do I say 'hello'? Oh, how do you say my name?"

Definitely *learning ASL soon.*

Jak and I met each other's gaze as the three of them talked. I quietly exhaled with relief from how his smile wasn't just there—it was warm. It was reaching out to me again; it had enough to share again. He and I had a lot more between us now, but we were finally surfacing from it all together.

His eyes fell back down to our friends. Dakota laughed again, tossing her long, wavy hair over her shoulder in a way that reminded me of Sarah. Joshua patiently taught her the first three letters of her name in ASL, his eyes lighting up in a way that reminded me of Breanne. Omari teased and laughed with them about silly mistakes in a way that reminded me of Opal. And for Jak, Omari had the calm humor and two inches over him like Adrien did. Joshua had the quiet intelligence that Wyatt did.

Friends.

As wonderful as the people in front of us were, they weren't *them.* We'd been forced to leave them behind. Made them start the new semester without us. Left them to depend on each other because they couldn't count on us anymore.

A hole burned a deep cavity in the center of my chest, but not in the way it did for Mr. Dawson. This was duller, a heavier ache, pressing down on me instead of pushing me to my feet with a readiness to act.

I could easily visit any of them with Alejandro right now. Even just get close enough for telepathy. I could walk into Callistro before the day is over...

Except I couldn't. I couldn't and I wouldn't because how could I? What was I supposed to do once I got there?

Dakota shoved Omari off his beanbag when he tricked her into saying "You're pretty" in ASL to Joshua. I remembered when that used to be me and my best friends. This felt... wrong somehow without them here. Yet the longer I studied the joy brightening the faces in front of me, I couldn't help but feel like this was exactly what the three of them needed: a kind of drink in the middle of a desert. At least, if they were as thirsty for relief as I was.

C H A P T E R

SEVENTEEN

Thanks to the decorations going up around the base when February hit, I remembered to wake up early on Valentine's Day to meet with Charlotte, one of the breakfast cooks, to make something special for the birthday boy. I just had to pray that my idea of a heart-shaped chocolate chip pancake wasn't as stupid as I was tempted to think it was.

I'd asked Charlotte to do that for three reasons: one, in parody of Valentine's Day; two, to spite Jak; and three... if the topic happened to come up, I wanted to take it as a sign to confess how I felt. Nothing had outright threatened us for a month and a half now, and I was finally starting to shed the paranoia of watching eyes. Plus, his birthday felt like cute timing—

Wait, I thought, walking into the lobby with Jak's breakfast tray in hand. *Is it cute or tacky?*

No, no. If it came up, I'd ride the wave. I only had to know *if* the time came.

—Alejandro,— I began in Spanish as I strolled across the lobby and toward the second residential sector's hallway, —*are you guys awake?*—

Instinct told me to pause once I stepped inside the entryway. —*Alejandro?*—

—*Yes, sorry,*— he replied sleepily. —*It's only me in here. Jak went to the gym. I'm still waking up.*—

I turned around and headed back into the lobby. —*Okay, thanks. I'm sorry for waking you.*—

Traveling down a couple of hallways, I entered the first half of the recreational sector with Jak's steaming tray and iced vanilla latte. Despite how it was only 7 in the morning, I ended up passing a few people and greeting a couple of acquaintances already on their way to work. I almost worried about how many people would be at the gym getting in an early workout, but I kept my thoughts focused on Jak. We'd be the last thing on their minds.

The rubbery aroma of the gym was so potent as I stepped inside that I was almost scared it'd seep into the pancake somehow. After a quick glance around, a small handful of the equipment occupied, I looked down my right and found a signature head of dark-mahogany hair. Jak was doing pull-ups at the bar in the corner, in front of the mirror wall.

I'm surprised he didn't see me come in.

The acoustics echoed the metal equipment use across the gym hall as I strolled down the glazed wooden floor. Jak still didn't notice me when I got close enough to hear the small grunt in his breath as he peaked above the bar again. I set down the tray onto the low plinth sticking out of the wall. When Jak lowered himself again, I tapped his shoulder.

He spun around, wide eyes landing on me. "Oh, hey," he said, relaxing. "What're you—?"

His gaze fell onto the breakfast tray on the black plinth. It only took him a second to make the connection.

He deadpanned at me. "You didn't."

"I did."

"I told you, you know I don't—"

"I didn't listen," I said simply, picking up the ceramic plate with his heart-shaped pancake and dollops of whipped cream around the edges. A strawberry slice sat perched in each one. "Happy *Valentine's Day*."

A smile played on his lips as he shook his head. Thankfully, he took the plate. "You're a bad person."

"You can't say that, I brought you coffee, too. Sit."

He obeyed, carefully sliding the tray over to make room for himself. "I'm literally at the gym and you bring me carbs with chocolate."

"And strawberries." I took a close spot next to him. "I care about your health."

He picked up the plate and showed me the full face of his breakfast. "A heart," he noted, narrowing his eyes. "Cute."

"There's a reason for that," I argued, causing my own heart to skip a beat and a wave of nerves to crash into my stomach.

No, no, I can't bring it up. He has to. Then I'll know if I should tell him.

"Valentine's Day, for one," I said. "And because I had to spite you."

He picked up the silver fork from the tray. "You're right, I totally deserve this."

He cut a bite, and I couldn't help but notice the tone of his smooth light-brown arms, left exposed by his gray tank top. He looked really good in a tank top. Somehow, despite the exercise, he'd managed to keep a trace of whatever cologne he'd put on this morning, too. Or that was just my memory acting up.

My hands grew clammier by the second as they gripped the edge of the plinth we sat on. Part of me hoped that he *wouldn't* bring up the topic of feelings. Actually, maybe I should just let him enjoy his breakfast since this was the only celebration I'd planned because he didn't like people celebrating his birthday. Should I leave now so he could eat in peace, let him forget that he was officially eighteen—?

No way. *I can't believe I forgot.*

"It's a big day," I told him, eyeing the bite stuck on his fork. For some reason, he wasn't taking it. "Like, a really big day."

He nodded lightly, jaw tight. It almost felt like he was forcing himself to agree with me, or at least pretending to.

"Congratulations." I offered the word as lightheartedly as I could.

"Thanks," he said, matching my tone. He gave me his eyes, a gentle smile in them. "Thanks for this, I appreciate it."

"I know you don't like people feeling obligated to do things for you today, but... it's not an obligation to me. This was me wanting you to know that today is special to *me*, and I wanna celebrate you."

Now his lips matched mine with a smile. That was a relief. "I can't tell you not to, I guess."

"We both deserve a little celebration right now."

I wondered if I'd somehow said the wrong thing with that: Jak simply stared at me in response, irises switching back and forth between mine like I was keeping something from him and the answer was in my eyes.

"How're you holding up?" he asked, so softly that I almost didn't hear him.

I processed the words and then blinked. "What?"

"I never got to make sure you were doing okay," he admitted, gazing back down at his plate like he was too ashamed to look at me. "But I've wanted to. I know it's been hard for me—I can't imagine what it's been like for you."

I fought to stop an eye roll. Sure, he hadn't blatantly asked me how I was doing, but it felt like everyone else had. Even Eun-Ji at two points, a week after we'd arrived at Bouchard and a few days ago. Half the time it happened, Jak had been around, and he had heard the same answer every time:

"*Yes,* I'm fine." I nudged him again with my shoulder. "Eat your pancake."

"Are you sure?" he asked. "Not to dig around or pry, I promise, I just—obviously this is the last place we thought we'd be this month—"

"I've had a great support team," I said, easing my tone, "including you. I'm just as okay as you are, but thanks."

He let me have another small smile before finally taking the bite on his fork.

"Don't worry," I told him, "this is the only thing I planned, and my family knows how you feel about today. You can have a normal day after this."

As he chewed and then swallowed, his fork held his attention as he subtly twisted it. Okay—I'd definitely somehow said the wrong thing.

"I asked Eun-Ji about my mom yesterday."

My eyes widened. "*What?* That's... that's great, isn't it? What made you choose yesterday to finally ask?"

"You're gonna think I'm weird."

I scoffed. "Please."

He rolled his eyes halfway. "I didn't wanna make a big deal out of today, but I still wanted to do something. I figured getting her story would... I guess... make me feel like she's celebrating today with me."

"That's not weird. That's totally normal, sorry to tell you."

He cut another bite and quickly took it. "Mmm. Great work by the way."

"Mostly Charlotte," I said. "So...? Can I know what Eun-Ji said?"

He set his plate down onto the tray beside him and then grabbed his iced latte. I started regretting (and disbelieving) that I hadn't gotten myself one, too.

"It's pretty crazy," Jak said, stirring the drink with his straw. "And a bit of a story."

"I don't have to be at the library for another hour."

After a gulp of his coffee, he took in a deep breath. "Like I told you a long time ago, my mom was basically born to be a Hunter. Her parents immigrated from Gujarat to Boston to send her to a nearby Hunter school so she could earn a 'secure' living. Eun-Ji was a guest speaker at her school one day because she was doing undercover work for Bouchard and trying to find more people to recruit. Guess why my mom went up to talk to her after."

"Why?"

"She wanted to know how Eun-Ji committed her 'first kill'."

My head caught back with surprise. "What?"

"Yeah... because my mom saw something messed up a few years back." Jak lowered his voice to a murmur. "While her family was still settling into Boston, she witnessed a group attack on a couple of magicians. Obviously they tried to defend themselves, but one of them was..."—he didn't dare meet my eyes now, letting his fall to the space between us—"you know."

Murdered. I bit the inside of my cheek. *In cold blood.*

"Your mom saw that," I whispered, "as a *kid?*"

"Yeah. Then a Hunter showed up and—took care of the other one. And then he *thanked* the group for 'helping him out' with his mission."

My breathing went hollow, like I couldn't let Jak hear how deeply those words cut.

"My mom never wanted to be part of what she saw that day. So when she talked to Eun-Ji, she told her the story and asked how Eun-Ji got over the guilt, supposedly as a means to help her overcome it. But Eun-Ji ended up asking her how she felt about magicians as a whole. Long story short, Eun-Ji told her the truth about herself and Bouchard. Gave her a number and address if she ever decided to go down a different route." Jak shrugged. "So my mom joined the cause."

Wow, do I wish I'd been there for that conversation. Aastha had definitely said the right thing, or Eun-Ji had already seen something that had exposed her in a druid vision, for Eun-Ji to just give up the truth like that.

"And then your mom became a Hunter?" I asked.

"She had to finish school if she wanted to become a useful agent for Bouchard." Jak took another gulp of his iced latte. "Then graduation happened, and guess who she met at the airport when she was on her way to an agency in North Carolina."

I didn't need to. Now I wasn't sure how to feel.

Jak slouched against the wall, resting his drink on his thigh. "My parents had their love story, my mom decided she wanted to spend the rest of her life with him, and then she made one last trip to Bouchard to update them. She also promised to still do her part however she could. Which apparently meant marrying my dad anyway."

"Wow," I breathed. "It really is no wonder you turned out so great. She planted a better seed."

He sighed, a small lump passing in his throat. The air shifted, a barrier hardening around us that the clanging exercise machines couldn't breach.

"I miss her," he finally said. "I wish she could've seen today."

I placed my hand on his warm shoulder. His muscles tensed under my touch but then relaxed, and I rubbed his damp skin with my thumb.

"I wish she could've, too." It was the only thing I knew to say. "I would've never stopped bragging about you."

"She would've beaten you to it," he teased. "Except she would've had every right to."

"So do I," I said without a single thought.

He peered at me in the corner of his eye, then brought his straw up to his lips. "You must really like talking about me."

I shoved him, almost spilling his latte, which he promptly covered with his hand. "Shut up."

"Now you're contradicting yourself."

I rolled my eyes, a familiar laugh teetering on my lips. I'd missed this. I'd missed our normal conversations, letting him out-wit me for the sake of a skipped heartbeat. I wanted more of it, I wanted it to be our normal again. I wanted to let him know that it was okay to have more of these moments... to let the conversation veer into how we felt like it used to.

Wait. Did he just bring it up? Was that flirting?

I licked my lips, but no words were ready. I wasn't sure I'd been the best at detecting his flirting before, but knowing *how* deeply I felt about him only further sabotaged my logic. Did this count? Should I wait longer? Considering everything we just talked about, *would* he even bring this topic up?

Is it bad timing again?

He chuckled. "You okay?"

"*Yes. Okay, no. Because I have feelings for you and really wanna say that, but I can't bring it up because I'm scared that I'll be sentencing us somehow, but you won't bring it up and tell me it's okay now.*"

I can't even say that... Can I? What if his birthday is bad timing because it pressures him? What am I supposed to say right now?

"Your food's getting cold."

Never in my life have I mentally facepalmed so hard that my head started throbbing.

"Oh, right," Jak said, merely turning to set down his drink and then grab his plate. The whipped cream had started melting off the edge of the pancake. He cut his next bite with his fork and eagerly took it, chewing until a bright smile shone on his face.

"Okay, the chocolate was a great touch."

I wanted to say it. I did. But every time I put the words into my mouth, it replaced a brick that had fallen from my wall of paranoia, rebuilding it. Every time I went to open my mouth, I started feeling those prying eyes too heavily somewhere—like my rationality and my emotions were playing tug-of-war with my brain every waking moment. And he wouldn't say anything about it, which was honestly starting to make me think that he didn't feel as strongly as he used to...

"I have feelings for you, but I'm still too scared for us to do anything about it."

No. Saying that wouldn't be fair to him.

"Please don't tell the guys I ate a heart for breakfast on Valentine's Day," he said after swallowing. "They'd harass me about it for the rest of the month."

"You can blame it on me," I joked back, straightening and looking out at the gym in front of us. Like I'd predicted, the few other people here barely knew that Jak and I were talking in the corner, too busy with their workouts.

I hate that I need more time. Why does it always feel like I can't afford to let out a single secret without catastrophic consequences? I could explode government tires and escape from a federal pursuit *despite* the repercussions, but not tell a boy I liked him *because* of the potential repercussions?

Yeah—because that's the key difference. One risked my own skin, but the other risked his. We were in the middle of an all-out cold war with the American and possibly Canadian Governments—both of which could use Jak against me like his two kidnappers had last year. Taking a chance on my fears only being paranoia took the smallest chance on his safety, and that was a risk I'd *never* take again. I couldn't, I couldn't do it, I couldn't do it again.

I guess until I could tell Jak the full scope of how I felt, I'd just have to continue showing him how much I cared.

"Thanks for keeping that on no matter what."

I blinked out of my head, refocusing on him. Before I could ask, I looked down at my fingers that had taken my locket again.

"It's my stress ball at this point," I told him. "It's actually the sole reason I *am* allowed to do this for you today, because you started it on *my* birthday."

He rolled his lips together, smiling through them. "Fine, you win. Say it."

My heart dipped a little lower as I stood—because that was my cue. "Happy birthday."

"Thanks."

I regretted staring at his smile when I felt my lips reflect it, when Jak was so fluent at reading me. I ambled backwards, waving at him.

Thankfully, the wall next to me wasn't a mirror; when I turned around, he couldn't see me cursing myself under my breath as I walked back to the gym's entrance.

EIGHTEEN

"Can we eat with you?" Michaela asked just before I reached our table in the eating hall. Li stood next to her, both of them carrying a plate of lasagna and broccoli. "Dad's working in surveillance tonight and Li's grandparents said she could eat with me."

I glanced at Jak on my other side, who simply nodded and sat down at the circular wooden table. "Sure," I told the girls. "If you don't mind grown-up talk."

"I'm gonna grow up sometime," Michaela said, setting her plate down two seats away from Alejandro sitting on the left side. Li took the spot next to him, and he shyly waved.

I sat next to Michaela, looking up in time to catch Momma's smile on the other side of the table. "Hello, Michaela, hello, Li," she said. "Nice to see you again."

"I had so much fun in your class today, Mrs. Atera!" Li chirped, pushing her black bangs out of her eyes. "I can do a perfect jab now."

"Good!" Momma set a napkin into her lap. "What about a straight?"

"Michaela's helping me, I help her with jabs."

"I'm proud of you both. You did great today in—"

"Mr. and Mrs. Atera?"

A stout girl had come up behind my parents with a boy who matched her height. Thin-rimmed glasses sat at the top of the girl's bridge, but they couldn't hide how identical her hazel eyes were to the boy's. Their noses and fawn hair mimicked each other's without discrepancy, too.

"Bram and I were wondering if we could sit with you," the girl said.

"Hey, Sofia!" Dad gestured to the two seats next to Momma, his Atera family ring boasting itself proudly on his right ring finger. "Sit, we'd love to have you."

I recognized them as two of Mom and Dad's students from their self-defense class—they would've been freshmen if they were enrolled in high school. After a few weeks, Momma was still trying to upgrade to the beginner Hunter courses, but evidently, teaching with Dad made her lessons more effective and vice versa; Eun-Ji didn't want to lose that when the students were doing so well.

"Thanks." Sofia set down her plate and slid into the seat next to Dad. Bram took the spot on her other side. "Our parents have the swing shift in the security ward tonight, and our friends' table is full."

"Funny Becca's not here yet..." Momma noted, glancing around the gray eating hall.

I followed suit, scanning the dozens of round tables scattered across the spacious room. Eventually Auntie's dark roots and platinum-blond hair caught my eye at a table a few down behind Dad: she'd just sat next to a man with commanding features, silver streaking his gelled-back auburn hair. Despite the harsh point of his nose, his chin, and the corners of his eyes, he'd whispered something to Auntie that made her backhand his arm and burst out laughing.

"*That's* new," Momma remarked with her head turned to them. Dad followed her stare.

"Well, if he doesn't pass my interview, it probably won't last," he said, cocking his brows.

"That man is probably ten years older than you," Momma deadpanned.

"Doesn't matter." Dad stabbed his lasagna with his fork. "If Dad's not here to approve, Little Brother's next up."

"She's a forty-four-year-old woman—"

"She's my sister."

I looked up at Jak, who was already smiling at me. Relief like this still felt tentative, like we had to value every second of it—especially Auntie. She'd waited over twenty years for excitement that didn't involve a board game or a screen. Out of all of us, she probably needed this the most.

I wonder how Grandpa is doing back in the States after everything... The last time Momma and I had been able to visit him, I was thirteen. He was fairly off the grid with no technology and no trail leading to him, and he moved every other year just in case. He was also the one who'd taught Dad and Aunt Becca everything they knew about powerful magic. It was always easier to assume—hope, more like—that he was safe. But after the last few months...

I didn't allow myself the thought for long; the last thing I needed was another situation I had no control over.

January had been hard, and February hadn't helped too much, either. I'd spent every morning waking up and wondering if today would be the day I'd somehow hear from Kamose saying that Caldwell had executed Mr. Dawson because he hadn't cooperated. That never came, but no matter how many times Kamose sent Alejandro back with reassurance, I couldn't stop thinking that it would because it *could*.

I glanced around our table: Jak, my parents, Sofia and Bram, Alejandro, Li, Michaela—and those were just the people sitting with us. I thought about Dakota and Omari and Joshua, about the regulars that came into the library while I was working, about the friends I'd made in the art room. Admittedly, the more I missed home, the more I had to be grateful for Bouchard. I just hoped that my best friends were coping well—if they didn't completely despise me for leaving despite mostly knowing why I had to. I hoped that they were safe.

"My dad has to work tonight, too," Michaela told the twins when my parents stopped bickering, denying silence a single moment as always. She rested her round cheeks in her hands, ignoring the warm plate of food under her. "In surveillance. What's your parents' names?"

"Aini and Luuk," Sofia replied next to Dad. "Interesting that they're both working security tonight."

"*Loooke?*" Michaela asked.

Bram smiled. "No, 'Luuk'. It's like 'Luke' but with two u's and no e. Our mom's parents came here from the Netherlands, but she and our dad were born here."

"Were your mom's parents forced to come here?" Li asked.

"Yeah. Magic started tearing the country apart." Bram scraped the baked cheese on top of his lasagna. "Opa—our grandpa—got caught as part of a resistance group. He and Oma were helping a friend find their 'missing family' they'd supposedly lost during a riot. But that 'friend' had been bribed by the government to corner them."

"That's mean," Michaela said, scrunching her face.

"No joke," Bram said. "Oma and Opa got out because of magic but became fugitives. So they tried to go back home to pack, but... They lived above the bakery that was in our family for three generations. When they got there, everything was ash."

My mouth fell open as Momma asked the twins with disgust, "The government *burned down* their home?"

"Everything they had," Sofia answered. "It took them two years to make it over here. But it turned out that the Canadian Government coming after them was the best thing to happen to them because the Hunter worked for Bouchard."

The base's relief efforts really do come through.

"I wonder what happened to their friend," Li mused softly.

Sofia shrugged. "Oma and Opa don't know. But a lot of the time, when Oma thinks she's alone, I hear her praying for them. In case they're still out there."

"Why?" Michaela asked, her face still scrunched.

"I actually don't know." Sofia pushed up her sagging glasses on her slender nose. "I've never understood it but I'm not gonna question it."

"I'd never be nice to the people who tried to kill me and my dad."

"What?" I said, my head spinning to Michaela.

"Yeah, some people broke into our house and tried to kill us," she replied, still resting her cheeks in her hands like she was telling us about her favorite color. "Dad's girlfriend got jealous one night because she was a psycho, went through his stuff, and found out he was a magician. So she called the cops on us and these big vans and trucks came but Dad hid us with invisibility cloaks and made them go away. But then I smelled smoke. They set the house on fire."

The whole table froze, all but Li, the rest of our attentions gripped by the nine-year-old girl sitting next to me. How could she say all this so casually, like she was talking about her day?

"Fun fact, that's how I got this burn scar." She rolled up her sweater sleeve. A half-foot-long patch of taut, pale-pink skin marred her forearm, illuminated by the bright lights far overhead. "I was reaching for... something in my room. But Dad had to pull me out when I got this."

I didn't know what to say. I kind of hated that I didn't know what to say. I was worried that Michaela was only able to tell her story like this for the same reason Jak had been able to tell me about his mom a year and a half ago without crying. Why was she so strong at just nine years old?

"It's fine, we're okay now," she added, slouching in her seat like she was sincerely confused about the long faces around the table. "Dad likes working here and I got to meet Li."

—*Understanding English has its blessings and curses,—* Alejandro told me in Spanish.

All I could do was look at him three seats down in response.

"That was my favorite day at school when you came," Li said, her smile matching her soft tone as she held her fork. "I *finally* had something exciting here."

"'Finally'?" Jak asked curiously next to me, leaning forward to see her better.

"Yeah," Li answered. "I was born here, but it wasn't fun until Michaela came. She made me feel better about a lot of things—we both don't have a mom, and she said we could share her dad."

"I'm glad you have your grandparents," I said, reaching behind Michaela to rub Li's small shoulder.

"Me, too. They actually saved me," she told us, perking up. "My parents took me to the surface after I was born because they didn't want to live here anymore for some reason. My *waipo* said she and Waigong realized I was gone and then found me in my parents' arms after they died from the cold. Waipo says their warmth kept me alive for long enough to be saved."

"Your parents went up to the surface with no plan to stay warm?" Dad asked across the table, his brows furrowing.

"No, they *wanted* to freeze," Li replied matter-of-factly. "I don't know why, I heard it's *painful*. But I was only a week old, I think, so I don't remember how it felt. I know my parents wanted us to be together, though."

My blood ran cold. Cabin fever. Li's parents had *intentionally* died on the surface and wanted to take her with them.

How many times has that happened here? The thought echoed across a canyon in my head, reverberating deep down. As large as Bouchard was, staying in one place for so long had to have some kind of toll eventually. Even Aunt Becca had grown restless when she was living at our house and then her apartment with Dad. How did people stop that here?

I think that thought plagued everyone's mind after Li finished, because nobody dared a word after that. I noticed Momma across the table twisting her Atera ring, like she was holding on to her family with that. Li and Michaela looked at each other in sheer confusion.

"For anyone wondering," Michaela began casually, "we're fine. Like, things are okay now."

Was she okay because she really believed it?

"It's just..." Dad said, taking Momma's hand on the table. He rubbed his square chin in thought. "You've all been through more than I would've imagined."

"I don't remember it," Li said again, finally taking a bite of her lasagna. "I didn't know my parents and I love Waipo and Waigong, so I'm fine."

"We're just sad for Oma and Opa, is all," Sofia assured us, pushing up her glasses again. "*They* went through a lot, not us."

"And plus, we got the better end of the bargain." Michaela scooped a big bite into her mouth. "Dad could *never* make this at home."

"*Home*". She still considered that burned-down house her home, not Bouchard.

Yet she'd sent everyone around the table chuckling with that, seeming to remind us that we all had food in front of us. As the rest of my family and friends picked up their forks to eat, something unsettled bubbled in my stomach. I looked around the eating hall, at the sea of people surrounding me and eating while happily conversing and joking with each other. Everyone here had a story like the three I'd just heard. Some of them had been forced to come here like my family and I had been; meanwhile, the rest had been born here because of the sufferings of their family before them. And they'd probably spend the rest of their lives here. If they wanted to survive, live well into old age, they had to be okay with that. They had no other choice. They were *trapped* here like we were.

I thought back to Caralyn Callistro's autobiography that Joseph Bouchard had reserved for me. Even though he didn't seem to have known what Caralyn had hidden in it for me, he'd been dead set on making sure that I'd get it one day. I still hadn't brought myself to read it or research Bouchard's founding to see if I could find a trace of Caralyn in it—but they'd obviously *both* seen something in my future. What I could do for the people of today, starting with the people right in front of me.

"Adara. Save them."

This was what Alexa had meant: Bouchard needed something powerful to save its people from living like this. Even great Master Hunters like Mr. Dawson needed a savior right now. Our people needed someone with power, something impossible, something like what Annisa, Kamose, Alejandro, and I had...

I'm sick of waiting for permission to move in Caldwell's war. I'm gonna move where I can.

I could still be productive and form a plan to rescue others in need—even those I was meant to help in the future. But my group of "impossible wielders" couldn't do it alone, and we weren't meant to.

I looked up from my plate and at Alejandro, telepathically

sending him the message: if we were powerless everywhere else, we were going to track down our fifth ally and prepare for war.

NINETEEN

That night, I laid out my plan to my family. It took a lot of convincing that finding the fifth person in our group was our wisest course of action right now, but it was *because* we had time for once that my parents wouldn't let us go unless we had every individual step mapped out. That meant, Momma quickly told me, if we planned everything over the course of two days, we'd need another two to make sure we hadn't forgotten anything.

I was more than on board with that; as much as I wanted to find this person, I wanted to find them without getting caught even more.

"You're *sure* you've thought this completely through?" Momma asked me and Alejandro again as the six of us walked down the concourse and into the main lobby. Next to me, Alejandro popped the rest of a blueberry muffin into his mouth.

"You made us spend a *week* planning this," I told her, sliding on my second backpack strap. "Get across Canada, make our way to Egypt, get information about our next ally from Kamose, and then track them down. We have a backup plan for everything that could go wrong."

"You just made your first mistake," Dad said on Momma's other side as we stepped onto the dark-yellow rug. "You can *never* have a plan for everything that could go wrong. All you can do is be prepared."

"That's why Alejandro is taking baby steps," I said, "so he has enough energy to teleport us away in case we get into trouble."

"Sleeping and memory spells first, remember?" Momma said, pointing at me. "We don't need anyone else knowing he can defy the laws of magic."

"I still don't like that Em's face has definitely made international broadcasts by now and she's going out," Aunt Becca remarked next to Jak, arms crossed as we came to a stop at the edge of the rug. "Appearance spells can only take you so far."

"Nobody's gonna recognize us as long as we switch fast enough," I assured her.

I looked behind me at the elevator doors. Ever since he discovered his teleportation at fourteen, Alejandro had spent the last two years traveling across Europe whenever he wanted, sometimes with his best friend back in Spain, which had helped him strengthen his power fast. Now he could comfortably teleport almost six hundred miles with one other person. (He'd really pushed himself when he'd teleported us from Paris to Valencia last year; he'd just kept that from me until now.) That made New Hazelton in British Colombia our first stop. I felt safer knowing we could leave anywhere at a moment's notice if we had to.

"You have your phone, right, Alejandro?" Momma asked, worry slightly widening her eyes. "And everything else in your backpack?"

"Yes, ma'am, I do," he replied, giving himself time to find the proper English. He'd improved a noticeable amount over the past few weeks after getting a tutor and constantly having to speak it with the other residents. "Don't worry."

I exhaled, preparing myself. "If we're still not back after two weeks—March 16, 11:59 P.M. is our deadline—*then* you should worry. But no sooner than that."

"It's not that easy, Em," Momma said softly. I was surprised to see her eyes droop; the last time I'd seen those eyes was that morning in the hideout in December. "I'm trying to remember that you've done worse with less. But I'm still worried."

Dad wrapped his arm around her waist, looking at me the same way.

"It's okay," I told her. "We need to do this sooner or later, and we're gonna do it sooner when there's nothing else *to* do. If anything, trust in the job you've done training me."

"Oh, then she should feel especially good," Aunt Becca remarked. She ran a hand through her hair finally growing past her shoulders. "Please try not to die, kid."

"Sure thing."

The air was suspiciously quiet after that. I dared a glimpse at Jak standing next to Auntie. His silence was loud with his thoughts as he looked between me and Alejandro, his thumbs snagging on his jean pockets.

I wish you could come with us.

The small scar under his right eye had finally faded, the one down the left side of his face softer but somehow just as loud as before. Looking at that scar now reminded me that the next time I'd see him—any of my family—wasn't guaranteed. I guess because, if I didn't come back, I'd be leaving a lot of things never said, things none of them would have any other way of finding out. If there was anything last year had taught me, it was that plans were entitled to fail. As much as my mind wanted to deny it, bad things could happen to the good guys. And I had no idea what would happen here while Alejandro and I were gone.

Come back to them. No matter what.

The air in my lungs tensed as my family's attention fell onto me, putting me in command of our next move. This was it.

I made myself turn to Alejandro and ask, "Ready?"

"*Sí.*"

"Be careful," Momma said for the millionth time, opening her arms to me.

"We will." I walked into her embrace, squeezing her. Right before I could let go, I felt Dad latch onto us. Momma slipped away, letting us have our own hug.

He leaned his cheek against my head before kissing the top of it. "I love you."

"I love you, too."

Aunt Becca was next. Then Jak. He wrapped his arms around my torso and firmly held me like his embrace alone had the power to protect me.

"Come back," he whispered into my ear.

Earlier this morning, I'd taken off my Atera family ring so that I wouldn't risk losing it—so the only thing I'd have to remind myself of Jak on the journey was my promise to him: "I will."

He pulled away just enough to kiss the side of my head. I told myself that there wasn't a wave of butterflies in my stomach, that it was all just nerves set aflame by fear—which Jak's gaze alone quickly quenched.

I stepped back and toward the elevators as I heard Alejandro press the button. Facing the four people in front of me, I took a final mental picture. "We'll be okay," I assured them.

The doors dinged and slid open behind me.

"Take care of each other," Momma called.

Alejandro and I entered the car, waving at them until the doors closed.

"Okay," he began in Spanish, pulling out his phone from his backpack's side pocket, "I have a picture and the address of where we will go. It's likely that nobody will be there, but keep your cloak's hood on until I tell you that it's safe."

"Got it," I said. "Are you ready?"

He reached for the gray velvet hood under his jacket, prompting me to follow. I took his hand. We flipped our hoods over our heads, and my eyes squeezed shut as the world around me surged in a powerful swirl.

C H A P T E R

Twenty

Valleyview, Alberta was just as quaint and discreet as New Hazelton, and that was all Alejandro and I could ask for. Still (after he let me overcome the shock and sheer gratitude of being outside again), we limited our time in both towns to a twenty-minute rest.

I'd teleported with him on foot, not in a car, once—when he'd first shown me his ability in Paris last October. It turned out, teleporting on foot was a means of transportation that needed a lot more than one time to get used to.

With my eyes closed for our third jump, only my stomach could detect the wave of magic that suddenly coursed around us, right through my being like a torpedo. My body hung in free fall before, in an instant, the ground solidified beneath me again.

I opened my eyes, my backpack weighing heavier on me for a second and causing me to stumble. An invisible Alejandro tightened his grip on my hand to keep me upright.

"*¿Estás bien, amiga?*" he asked.

"Yeah," I said, gaining a bit of stability after my eyes focused on the cracked cement under us.

I inhaled a deep breath of fresh oxygen, just as quickly scrunching my face in disgust. Sulfur?

I looked up: a green dumpster sat against the exterior wall in front of me. That made sense. Still, after two full months underground, I wasn't used to being outside again after less than an hour, and I'd take any part of it that I could.

A crème metal door stood next to the dumpster, matching the rest of the single-story building. Besides the sulfuric odor... were those fries and charbroiled meat I smelled?

I should not be hungry already. I ate before we left.

All was quiet except for the low late-winter wind, and the occasional car whooshing by on the street in front of the building. Another mostly empty street lay on my right, intersecting with the one upfront.

"Alejandro—?"

I just as quickly took a step back. Whoa. There it was again—I'd felt this every time we landed so far. I didn't know what it was, just that Alejandro's presence... felt different whenever my stomach tried to settle. I'd been this exhausted upon landing, too. We weren't moving too fast, were we? We could only afford *to* move this fast.

"I'm—I'm here," he replied in Spanish with slightly shallow breath, his voice traveling from somewhere in front of me. "Do you need us to wait—?"

"No," I said, attributing the discomfort in my stomach to the teleportation lag, "I'm fine, just settling. Are *you* okay? Why does your breath sound like that?"

"I... I pushed it a little," he admitted. "We're in a town called 'Watrous', not Battleford. I'm sorry."

"Watrous". That sounds familiar. Why do I feel like I've heard of that before?

My stomach clenched at the brain activity, and I immediately dropped the question. What mattered was how much farther out Watrous was than Battleford, and it sounded like just enough to push Alejandro more than I was comfortable with.

"Trust me," I said, "I want to get there as fast as possible. But we need to take small steps in case we get into trouble. Even though we're being careful, it still worries me that we've gone through two towns without any problems."

Silence. At least I didn't have to add "I'm so used to everything going wrong"; he knew better than to argue right now.

"What is this place?" I asked, stepping backwards on the gravel for a better view of the building.

His voice stayed close by as he answered, "It's a burger restaurant. I thought it would be a good place to recharge."

He must need it if he wants to dig into the allowance Momma gave us instead of the snacks we brought.

"Okay. We need to find someone's appearance to take on before we take off our hoods." I started my way down the left side of the restaurant slowly to give him time to hear my steps and match me.

"Let's pick anyone who stops at the intersection," he said.

"There's a stop sign there."

I went down the length of the building, bumping into Alejandro a couple of times as we tried to gather a sense of each other's presence. We passed a black-and-silver neon sign on the wall that read "Burger Bishop", a bishop chess piece alit next to it and stuck into the top of a cheeseburger.

I should try to eat if my stomach isn't feeling well, considering we have a lot more jumps to go. Hopefully these burgers would be hearty enough to rejuvenate Alejandro, because the last thing I wanted—and that we could afford—was staying in one place for too long, disguised or not.

"I can't believe you're gonna eat a second one," I told a disguised Alejandro in an elderly voice I wasn't used to. It sounded even stranger in Spanish. With my new "grandmother hands", I polished off the last bite of my own burger, which had almost been too big for me to squish together to bite into it. How would Alejandro be able to down a second one?

"My stomach works fast," he replied. The appearance spell had traded his brown eyes for a pair of sky blue, his warm-brown skin two shades lighter and lined with a few wrinkles. Dark facial hair carpeted the lower half of his short face. I, on the other hand, looked old enough to be his grandmother with my new saggy face, bony hands, and knee-length flower-print dress. It was just the two of us and another couple, sitting on the other side of the small restaurant, eating inside, so we were relatively cozy.

"After this,"—I swallowed the last of my bite—"we're going to

Winnipeg in Manitoba, right?"

"Yes," Alejandro said. "I think we should stay here for a little longer, though. If I start to digest my food, I'll have more energy. After Manitoba, we have to go to Ontario, then Quebec, and then Newfoundland and Labrador. I'll need as much energy as possible then—from Newfoundland, we have to go across the Atlantic and to Spain. I may need your help with that because I'm taking both of us across the ocean this time."

As long as we're responsible about when we buy food and where, our allowance should get us through the trip.

I leaned back in my metal chair, stretching and recalling the day we'd first teleported to Mount Steele in British Columbia. Even though I seriously doubted that anyone in the restaurant spoke Spanish, I switched to telepathy just in case: *—I've never been able to make sense of that. Do you know what you did that day that I "helped" you? Because I didn't know it was possible to share energy between wielders. How did you know that that would work?—*

He shrugged, taking another bite. For a smaller boy, even though he had the appearance of a middle-aged man right now, I was still impressed with his appetite. *—I had a feeling,—* he replied. *—Since you're a mage and you can cast with your will, I decided that if you knew what we were trying to do, you could somehow help me cast it. It was like you were "creating a teleportation spell" as a mage, or like I was borrowing your will.—*

I still wasn't sure if it made sense to me. When Dad and Aunt Becca destroyed Alexa's bracelet last summer, they hadn't borrowed each other's strength to do it; they'd *combined* it on the same object. Unless I could teleport now, this wasn't the same thing.

—Do you know all the rules for how far you can teleport?— I asked.

—Any limitations besides needing to know exactly where you'll end up?—

He shook his head, wiping his bearded mouth with a napkin. —It's a matter of energy, what I take with me, and knowing where I want to go. So if I were to strengthen my energy and my ability enough, in theory, I could teleport however far I would like. And you know already that I can't teleport to an idea or desire, only to a place whose physical location I have. I haven't found other limitations.—

—So you feel for when you're ready to go?—

—More or less. I can feel it when I prepare my next location in my head. It tells me how much energy it will take from me if I teleport there... if that makes sense.—

I furrowed my brows as he took another bite. —You can feel what teleporting somewhere will do to you?—

—I have a sense of it, yes. I know how much it will cost.—

I sank in the chair, my vision gone with my thoughts. It hadn't been intuition alone telling him to ask for my help to teleport us to Steele; he'd known how much it was going to take out of him. He'd known that it would be too much.

But he did it for us anyway—for a family and a guy he barely knew. And now he was potentially risking his life again going on this trip to Aswan, Egypt with me to get intel about the fifth "impossible wielder" who was just like us. That part made more sense to me, though; Alejandro seemed interested in what his destiny as Azariah entailed, but not so much like he was attached to it. He was a curious boy in general... Was all this just a curiosity chase for him? Or was he sincerely helping me like how Annisa and Kamose did?

"It's Kamose," Alejandro announced, regaining my attention. He was looking down at his phone screen. He switched to

English to read out, "'Give me time to clean the place up.'"

Despite having never met the guy before, I smiled to myself and thought, *That sounds like Kamose.*

My stare froze on the table with realization. Wow. I was on my way to Aswan to meet Kamose for the first time. I wondered if his real-life persona at all differed from his charming digital one.

"Tell him that he'll have plenty of time to clean," I teased as a red sedan drove into the parking lot, visible through the floor-to-ceiling windows at the front of the restaurant.

Instinct flared in my chest as the sedan turned off. Whether it was the Hunter's or the magician's in me, I couldn't pin down. Maybe both. Why did the bald, stalky man climbing out of the car wave a red flag in me? It was only me and Alejandro and the other couple in the restaurant, and I'd been fine until now...

The stalky man took off his sunglasses and pulled open the front door, a black heavy-duty vest protecting his torso. I took in as much comfort from the appearance spell as I could, hunching forward in my seat as if I really were nothing more than an old woman who couldn't digest her food well.

"What's wrong?" Alejandro whispered.

—*Him.*— I never dared a glimpse, especially as the man called to the cashier at the front counter. —*I think we should leave.*—

"I'm looking for two kids," the man said behind me. My body went rigid, trapping my breath in my lungs. I heard leather flip open. "Agent DuPont with the CSIS, sent in after a report saying that two teenage American fugitives, both magicians, were located here."

The Canadian Security Intelligence Service. Canada's CIA.

—*We need to leave,*— I stated. —*Go, not too fast.*—

"No minors have come in this morning, sir," the young woman at the register said.

"They could be using an article of clothing known as an invisibility cloak to stay hidden, have you seen any sort of suspicious activity around the area?"

With his second burger more than halfway gone, Alejandro took my hand. I forced a tremble into my legs as I stood. "Thank you, hon," I murmured. The small details mattered the most—which made me start to question how we were going to reach for our backpacks in a non-suspicious manner.

"My manager could check the security cameras in the back to see if they've been around the building."

"Do those cameras have infrared lenses?"

"Yes, sir."

I locked eyes with Alejandro. Cameras in the back. We weren't visible to the naked lens, but not even magic could conceal our body heat. We were on those infrared tapes.

I never checked for cameras, I thought with bitter resentment. I hadn't felt physically well enough to remember.

—Go,— I urged to Alejandro. —*Calmly take our things, put up your hood when we get outside, and then teleport us in the back after I erase the footage.*—

He supported me by my arm as we turned to face the front door. A tall, stiff man in a white shirt and the same protection vest swung it open, a square black gadget in his hand. It was beeping, fast.

"Thaumometer's picking up a signal," he announced to his partner, "magic is in the area."

In the split second I needed to telepathically tell Alejandro to run, the tall man's narrowed blue eyes squared onto me.

—*Run!*— I shouted anyway just as he pointed the thaumometer at us, the beeping quickening.

"Targets confirmed and located!" the stalky man behind us called. I whirled around right when he lunged toward me.

Dormio! I said, his beefy hand clamping around my wrist.

My eyes widened when he stayed upright and awake, trying to grab my other wrist against my twisting. He wasn't asleep. The sleeping spell wasn't working!

"*Dormio!*" I called again, thrashing as he gripped my other wrist.

"Emma, it's not working!" Alejandro exclaimed in Spanish. So he was trying his magic, too. Why weren't these men dropping, why couldn't our magic touch them?

"It's not gonna work, kids," the tall agent behind Alejandro said, cuffing one of his wrists. Alejandro's middle-aged man appearance evaporated, exposing his young, warm skin and black hair. "These vests are enchanted, they absorb whatever magic you cast on us."

And they have neutralizing handcuffs. Our magic was suspended with those things on. I needed to escape before the man behind me locked those cuffs around my wrists.

I bucked my head back and square into his chin. Metal clanged against the tile floor. I shut my eyes and called upon the warlock in me, letting a surge of my will dominate in my veins. These agents were immune to my magic, but the world wasn't: the ground quaked beneath us, distracting the stalky man long enough for me to swing my leg under him. He crashed backwards into the table Alejandro and I had sat at, sending the rest of

Alejandro's food splattering onto the floor beside him. I spun around. The tall agent had released Alejandro to grab the table next to him for stability.

I locked my eyes on Alejandro's cuffs. *Exsolvo!*

They snapped open and fell from his wrists. The ground slowed to a stop.

Our backpacks sandwiched my stumbling agent on the floor. I commanded my telekinesis, and they flew into my grip.

"Put this on, hood up!" I exclaimed, shoving Alejandro's bag into his hand and then grabbing his arm.

We sprinted out the door, pulling both of our cloaks' hoods over our heads. Keeping my hold on him, I turned around, setting my gaze on the five stunned people in the restaurant. Two security cameras in the corners caught my eye.

I can't rip off the agents' vests or make them forget. Something physical has to stun them.

I squeezed Alejandro's wrist, urging another earthquake forward. The entire block trembled, threatening to knock us off our feet. When I saw the agents stumble, I locked my eyes on the cash register sitting on the front counter. I grimaced inside, my throat tightening, until I forced the Hunter in me to override it: my telekinesis flung the cash register at the stalky agent, then at his partner with full force. Both fell unconscious to the floor—and hopefully with traumatic amnesia, something magic couldn't reverse.

—*Make that couple and the cashier forget the last half hour,*— I told Alejandro. I whispered the same memory-wiping spell over the cameras at the front of the building before shattering them.

—*Okay, let's go to the back,*— he urged.

He yanked me down the side of the restaurant and around

the corner. Two more cameras sat mounted above.

Obliviscor-anullo.

The cameras burst into a hundred pieces, scattering across the cement. Alejandro tugged on me just as I cried, "Go!"

Bright waves of amber magic swelled around us, the ground beneath me falling out.

Twenty-One

I crumpled to my knees, opening my eyes. Dewy grass cushioned my palms, winter's cold whooshing by me. I swallowed a painful bit of my adrenaline, urging my mind to grip the new reality in front of me.

Where were we?

I didn't realize I was trying to catch my breath until Alejandro's winded voice sounded closely next to me. "Amiga, ¿estás bien? ¡Necesitas que decirme!"

I couldn't translate the words for a second. They needed to repeat in my head before a familiar, small force pushed me backwards and onto my feet, my hands falling into my lap. "Yeah..." I breathed, needing to use English. "I'm fine. I'm okay, are you?"

I still have the old woman's voice. I need to get a new appearance as soon as possible.

"Yes," he told me in Spanish, his invisible hand finding my shoulder after a few moments, "but that was still sudden for you. I'm sorry—"

"Don't be." A fragile tremble shook my arms even when they were still. I looked up at the grassy field in front of me, cement paths winding through it with benches and outdoor lamps standing along them. Nobody was around, which meant nobody to take an uncompromised appearance from yet. "You had to do that. That wasn't supposed to happen, I... I don't know how they..."

The facts weren't lining up. We'd been in Watrous for half an hour. No government on the planet could've tracked us that easily, not even with a locator spell because they didn't have anything that belonged to either of us to track us with. My family and I had destroyed or gotten rid of everything at the apartment and our house. What could we have missed, and even then, how could someone have known to look for us *now*? The chances that the government had used a nore to find us ran into the same issue: just happening to ask where we were at the same time we were out? Those chances were too low for even magic to make probable.

On top of all that, using a thaumometer to detect magic, in this case, was only useful if its user knew not only where to look, but whom to look for. CSIS had somehow known where *Alejandro and I* were, and I had no idea how.

"Come on," Alejandro said, finding my arm and helping me stand on the grass. "We need—to find new appearances."

"Where—?" I tried to force my head past the nauseating dizziness whirling around. "Where are we?"

"A park in Winnipeg," he answered. Both of us still invisible, he guided me to the concrete path next to us with a bench. "Manitoba. I studied maps of all the cities I would take us to. I needed to know the places we could teleport to in case... *that* happened."

We didn't rest long enough. Alejandro had needed more time, and I was feeling an exhaustion suspiciously similar to what I'd felt when I'd helped him teleport us to Mount Steele in British Columbia. If I'd accidentally helped him get us here, too, we were both at a physical disadvantage.

The bench thumped with his weight as he plopped down beside me. I heard him huff. At least he'd managed to put down almost two burgers, but he deserved more time to rest and digest. That was what bothered me the most: he *should* have had more time. Those agents had been with the CSIS, not a Hunter agency—which told me that they'd been called in on emergency because they were the closest federal agents nearby. The higher-ups knew where we were. How? *Who* knew?

"*Amiga,*" Alejandro said, his voice traveling toward my left side. I looked over, finding a group of kids with backpacks on across the street. A woman was leading them down the sidewalk.

"I'll use the woman," I said, switching to Spanish and trying to let the rest of my shaky adrenaline fade.

Conveni speciem.

When a lookout spell verified that nobody else was in the park, I took off my cloak's hood. The skin on my arms had lightened a shade, blanketed with blond hairs. My jacket had transfigured into the beige winter coat the woman had on. I still had dark-denim jeans, but my boots had given way to gray sneakers.

I exhaled, slouching against my backpack.

"You're more tired than I am," a young voice noted. I opened my eyes to a little boy sitting on my right side: large hazel irises, a button nose, and full cheeks with freckles dotting his pale skin. "To be honest, I'm surprised that I'm doing better than I thought I would. Are you sure that you're okay?"

"No. I don't think so," I muttered with a surprisingly silvery voice. "Unless I'm crazy, I think I'm having the worst case of déjà vu ever."

"What do you mean?"

A breeze fluttered through the branches overhead. I shuddered, pulling my coat tighter around myself. *—How the government found us too fast and suddenly, and forced us to teleport to safety.—*

The boy next to me said nothing, contemplating.

—I don't think we'll be okay here, either,— I added, distrusting of our empty environment. *—You need to rest and then get us to Ontario as soon as possible.—*

—That device the agents had,— he said, facing me better on the bench, *—what was it? Do you know?—*

—A thaumometer. It's a magic detector.—

—So any time we use magic while we're close to it...—

—Yep. They can't detect telepathy, unless that's changed in the last year, but everything else is a death sentence. We should move.—

"Do you feel well enough to keep going?" he asked.

I stood from the bench to prove it. "We have to."

Now more than ever, my instincts were on the prowl. A lifetime of being in hiding, a year and a half at the Callistro Academy, and a few near-death experiences were more than enough for me to trust them by now.

Nobody came after us after Watrous. A few hours later, we got to Spain and then Sousse, Tunisia in North Africa (where magic was legal) without issue, save for my nausea and lightheadedness worsening with every trip. I didn't know why I was getting increasingly sensitive to teleportation travel, but I had to hide it long enough to convince Alejandro that I was okay to keep going. We didn't have time to waste.

"I think we should rest here longer," he said anyway with his new deep voice, setting down his coffee mug on the table outside of the café we'd stopped at. This time, we'd taken on the appearances of a young tourist couple. Alejandro had kept his brown eyes but inherited a bulbous nose and small lips with it. We sat in front of the café window, the yellow fairy lights bordering it seeping into the night. "You look pale. I don't think traveling this way is good for you."

"Remember what happened the last time you said we should stay somewhere longer?" I argued with a voice higher pitched than my real one. "I'm tired, that's it. That's why I'm drinking coffee."

The street next to us bustling with tourists, cars, and the locals of Sousse—all of which apparently preferred the lively night life—wasn't helping. Even the aromas of fresh coffee and spiced Arabian pastries were starting to nauseate me instead of soothe my shot nerves, for which not even the cool, humid wind was doing any favors.

"You didn't eat in Newfoundland or Spain because you were too sick. Coffee alone isn't good, you need food."

"We have *one* more jump," I said. I took another sip of my latte that my stomach dared me to swallow. "I'll sleep for as long as you want once we're safe at Kamose's house."

"We can find somewhere to rest—"

"No. We're almost there."

"Emma, *I'm* doing something bad to you," Alejandro stated, leaning forward on the black table between us. Even though his new brown eyes weren't his, I could still see him in them. "My magic is making you sick. What if I make this last jump when you're not ready and there are serious consequences?"

"Don't think that way," I said—mostly because I didn't want to hear that. "Once we get there, it'll be time for bed anyway, and this will have all been worth it!"

"Do you think we'll be safe to *stay* there after what happened this morning?"

I chewed on my cheek, almost reaching for my locket—technically I still had it on, but while it wasn't visible under the appearance spell, I couldn't grab it. Right now, I wasn't sure if I *could* answer Alejandro or if I didn't want to.

"The Nasirs are a powerful family," I said. "They're a big reason that magic is legal in Egypt, and they have a lot of influence and protection. If anything goes wrong, not only will we be able to defend ourselves, but so will they. And Kamose can change the circumstances if he needs to."

Alejandro leaned back in his chair, giving me a small nod that I barely caught in the soft light of the fairy lights. "Okay. Then let's go."

Leaving our mugs on the table, we grabbed our backpacks, stood, and then weaseled down the street. Lamps lit up the whole way, drinks and appetizers mixing together in the air and floating down the road. We passed multiple stores, businesses, and alleyways until the cars in the street and crowd on the sidewalk thinned. An alley lay on the other side of the street. Alejandro kept a firm grip on my hand while we crossed and entered. Only a few tourists were strolling along on the stone, and their backs were to us.

"Behind there," Alejandro whispered, pointing at a tall potted bush standing beside a lamp-lit door.

We positioned ourselves next to the bush, which was just tall enough to block the blinding light of the mounted lamp. Safe in the shadows, one last time, Alejandro and I threw our hoods over our heads. My hand squeezed his as the waves of his teleportation magic billowed around us. I tightly shut my eyes. The swirl surged in my head, ready to knock me clean off my feet. The ground felt as gelatinous as my legs, even when the bright waves faded and the world solidified again.

This time, Alejandro was the only thing keeping me upright when I slouched against him.

"Emma," he called, pushing me up.

A white brilliance shone harshly in the slit in my vision. I forced my eyes open a little more: two outdoor lights mounted proudly on the thick stone pillars of a front gate, glaring against the void-like night sky above us. A giant, regal house lay beyond the gate, boasting geometric Egyptian architecture and lit by multiple small lamps clinging to its walls.

"Emma, what's wrong? Talk to me!"

I couldn't tell where night ended and my blackening vision began. I couldn't feel my own body trying to support itself without Alejandro's help. My words sat heavily on my tongue, trapped.

Two hands squeezed my arms as the large metal gate in front of us screeched open. The blood in my head drained to my feet in a cold rush. My body fell limp against Alejandro, his voice fading as the world shut to black.

CHAPTER

Twenty-Two

For once, the darkness was still.

No nightmare. No vision. No *tears*. Only the dark that soon glowed with orange.

I pried my eyes open. A yellow room blurred around me, and I had to blink a few times before it came into clear focus. Long black desk straight ahead. Sleek matching dresser next to the left window. Flatscreen TV mounted in the corner. Door in the other corner with the closet in the wall. Woman sitting in a cushioned chair on my right side—

Wait, what?

I jolted to the side, entangling myself in the midnight-blue covers on top of me. I didn't know this woman, I didn't know this bed, and I didn't know this room.

"Shh, it's okay," the woman crooned with a heavy Egyptian accent, picking up a glass of water from the nightstand. She held it out to me. "You worried us, my dear, I'm glad you're awake."

"Us"? Who's "us"?

"My name is 'Najwa'," she said, pressing a slender brown hand to her chest. Coffee-brown eyeshadow and eyeliner drew out the kindness in her deep-set hazel-green eyes. She was almost a combination of Momma and Sarah. "Kamose is my son."

Kamose's mother. We'd made it—we were inside the Nasir home.

"Do you remember what happened?"

I took a sip of the water, mindlessly eyeing the covers on top of me. The memory hit me like a truck, the moments before it dragging regret behind them.

I didn't want to admit my stupidity out loud, so I nodded.

"Okay. Alejandro informed me," Najwa replied, continuing with the same patient speed and considerate tone. "The boys are waiting in the family room. I know you're here for an important meeting with Kamose."

That was one way to put it. But for someone who knew why Alejandro and I were here (and who definitely knew what Kamose was, possibly the rest of us, too), Najwa was considerably calm about it.

"Thank you," I said, remembering my manners. I reached to put the glass back down onto the nightstand, but she took it with a surprising gentleness and set it down for me.

"Do you feel well?" she asked.

"Yeah. I think I can—" I tried sitting up against the headboard until the water dropped into my stomach, sloshing around.

"Um... I'm still a bit nauseous."

"Take it slowly, my dear. I can wait until I bring in the boys."

I swallowed, letting the water settle. "No, that's okay... I can still rest while we talk."

"Then I will get them." With a smile that somehow reassured me a tad, Najwa rose from the chair with a slight creak.

Watching her walk across Kamose's bedroom, I saw just how big it was: the size of my living room, dining room, and kitchen combined (which were all small, but still). I recalled the glimpse of the house I'd gotten before I passed out. This wasn't a "house", we were inside a small mansion. *And* magic was legal in Egypt? The Nasirs were living their best possible lives here.

I brought my fingers to the locket around my neck, consequently realizing that my appearance spell had disappeared. Thinking about the industrial facility that Alejandro and I had come from... well, I couldn't help my jealousy. Sure, he and I were welcome here as visitors, but the government wouldn't accept us as citizens without proper documentation. And unless our fifth ally had the impossible ability of conjuring things out of midair, we were stuck here as visitors and nothing more.

The door in the right corner of the room opened. Alejandro was first inside. Behind him strolled in a tall, lanky boy with fluffy black hair and the darkest beads for eyes I'd ever seen.

With flat, full lips, a grin brightened his brown face, displaying the world's straightest teeth. "Hello, commander."

Kamose.

Whoa. He had a presence, too. Upon looking at him, something slightly pushed me back against the pillows, something strong and familiar...

Like with Alejandro whenever we teleported.

No, maybe this was different. From the moment Kamose first called me last summer and I sat down on my bed to talk to him, I'd felt something about him. I'd never been able to pin it down, but seeing him in person now, I could pick out part of it: respect. Despite his "commander" nickname for everyone, with a round yet defined jaw and intense eyes, he naturally commanded a room, like he knew he could take over whenever he wanted but chose the backseat.

"Hey..." I breathed, mindlessly moving the covers off me. I slid my legs off the bed, slowly planting my feet onto the hardwood floor. "I can't believe this is how we're meeting."

"I usually ask for dinner first before we have a sleepover," he said with an accent only a little less prominent than Najwa's, ambling to the corner of his bed. It was almost like he was afraid to catch something from me if he got too close. "But magic has determined that you're an exception."

I stood, stabilizing with relieving speed. "You're tall."

"You're short."

He held out his arms and I walked into them, embracing him half as tightly as he held me—a hugger for sure. I'd only known him for half a year, but hugging him felt like meeting up with a lifelong friend I hadn't seen in just as long. Then I remembered why: I hadn't been able to even *text* him or Annisa since we'd destroyed our phones and left Capperson.

He was taller than Jak, able to rest his whole cheek on the top of my head. His hugs were just as warm and yet... less heavy, I noticed. They felt as light as when Sarah, Breanne, or Opal hugged me: no strings attached, only friendship despite proximity.

"You've been through a lot," he murmured, rubbing my back. His cologne was spicier than Jak's, less musky. "I'm surprised you're trying to add 'saving the world' to that list."

"Well, we kind of have to," I said, breaking away.

"Right. You're only here for a *spell* so you can find our next friend, yes?"

Standing in front of the desk chair, Alejandro furrowed his brows. "We are here for a spell?" he asked slowly in English. "I thought that... we are here for the information."

"'Spell' is another way we say 'period of time'," I told him. "It was a pun."

"Ah, *¡el juego de palabras!*"

"Play on words, yeah," I said, sharing his excited smile.

"*Yo comprendo*," Kamose added with his Egyptian accent, saluting with two fingers. "I'm learning."

"*Muy bien*," Alejandro said, gratitude lifting his lips.

Kamose faced me, taking out his phone from the back pocket of his sweatpants. "Okay, firstly—Alejandro told me that you were almost caught in Canada." He scrolled twice on a text conversation. "Watrous, Sas—*katch*—e—wan. What happened there?"

"We don't know," I said, plopping down onto the foot of his bed. "We were there for half an hour when two CSIS agents came in looking for us. They had a thaumometer to detect magic and caught us almost immediately. After that, we rushed through the rest of the journey here because we didn't know if the same thing would happen again."

"Emma remembered," Alejandro began awkwardly, lowering himself into the padded desk chair, "that this happened—when we teleported to *la*—I mean, the mountain. The government found us, and it... made me teleport to there before I felt good. We don't know anything."

"A locator spell is unlikely because we destroyed everything we didn't take with us," I said, twisting the silver heart around my neck. "And I told my friends to take care of my stuff from my dorm. But beyond all that, how would anyone have known to locate us at *just* the right moment, and with time to track us down? We were good everywhere else we went. I don't even wanna stay *here* for long because if a locator spell is involved, your government will swarm your house for international fugitives."

Kamose shook his head, hands deep in his sweatpants pockets. "Our house is protected. No magic can act on it or anything inside—locator spells, fire spells, obliteration spells..."

Wait. Like Bouchard?

"How does your family know about that spell?" I asked, recalling what Eun-Ji had told us about it. "Barely anyone knows about it, it's super complicated and hard to pull off."

"One of my family members long ago learned of it when they worked in the government," he replied a little too proudly, until I remembered that his country *liked* the humanitarian Nasirs and kept magic legal. "He worked closely to the president, our first one after we abolished the monarchy, so he earned the spell as a means to protect his household as an important member of the government."

Eun-Ji's explanation made it sound like Joseph Bouchard had invented the spell himself—but if that were true, a mage would've felt its existence when they tried to create it. Unless the one here has different rules or conditions.

Regardless, I sank with gratitude that Alejandro and I were

actually safe again.

"I wish I could tell you how you were found," Kamose added, "but I only know all *present* circumstances without an enquirer, and I can only know how someone is trying to find you if they're presently doing it. But asking that question is risky. You would have to pay the nore's price twice if you still want the first answer you came here for. In theory, Annisa could find out what happened with her time traveling ability, but only if she knows the exact date and location to travel to. And there are infinite possibilities for both."

"You can transmogrify present circumstances if they're small enough, right?" I asked, and he verified. "But... changing things and preventing the government from finding us again isn't an option unless you caught them *in* the act."

"Yes. I could destroy the entire security department to prevent it from happening again, but—"

"No." I immediately shook my head. Those consequences were more than implied.

I sighed, crossing my arms. *So we'll be at risk again once we leave.* I'd come here for one answer but now had at least three questions that only Kamose could answer.

"*Amiga*," Alejandro uttered, taking my attention. He leaned forward in Kamose's chair. "I'm sorry that I forget—I *forgot* to ask you, but do you feel well?"

"Yeah, I'm fine now. I think it was the constant shift in time zones and not being used to traveling that way."

"Kamose has an idea," he said a little more slowly, like he was reviewing every word for its correctness. "I told to him that you felt a... same way when we teleported to Mount Steele. When I asked you for your help because you're a mage."

I glimpsed Kamose. "Okay..."

"I think you were subconsciously helping him every time he teleported," Kamose said, "and you never realized it. You did it as if on instinct because you had already done it once, so your magic had an idea of how to do it again. It's almost like, after that one time, facing another mission with high stakes told your magic to help again."

So I had helped him get us to Winnipeg. *And every time before and after that.*

I didn't know why shame pooled in my stomach at those words until I realized that Kamose had it on the nose: because Alejandro had been right, and I hadn't listened to him. His magic *had* been making me sick, and I'd made him make our last jump when I wasn't ready and left him to deal with the consequences of it.

I couldn't even nod my approval. "Well, I'm okay now."

"Good. Then for the other side of that coin,"—Kamose took a spot next to me on the foot of his bed—"are you okay?"

I'd heard that inflection with that question before. I'd spent half of my life hearing that question from my best friends and asking them the same thing when the question mattered most. I'd heard it a hundred times since coming to Bouchard, but not once had I answered it with the full truth. Right now, though, that felt like my only option.

I shook my head.

Kamose wrapped an arm around my shoulders. Alejandro stood and sat on my other side, sliding his arm just under Kamose's and around me.

"Guys—"

"Tell us," Kamose said.

I think up until that point, I'd been waiting to be able to answer that question without completely falling apart. Facing it head-on now, though... I was kind of too worn out to keep waiting for something that wasn't guaranteed.

"It's Mr. Dawson," I muttered, my thumbnails fiddling with each other. "Finding this fifth person without getting caught. Getting back to Bouchard without getting caught or leading anyone there. And then... the memories and I'm still not over how someone was literally—"

—shot and killed in front of me. For me. And now I was living with one of the two survivors of Alexa's family, a constant reminder of what happened that morning, a constant reminder of everything that had happened last year and everything I'd lost because of it.

I couldn't fix anything that was wrong until I had answers that Kamose wasn't allowed to give.

As if reading my mind, he started rubbing my shoulder. "Well," he said gently, "I can tell you that Mr. Dawson is still okay. That's because you're staying behind."

I shook my head, barring my thoughts from escaping. "We're pretty sure he's at the White House because it's under the same protection spell over Bouchard and your house, and we get darkness every time we use a locator spell on him and only that he's in Washington, DC. Does that mean you can't interfere when they do anything to him? Or make a way out for him?"

"I want to," he said, leaning into the words, "I do, but no. For some reason, I can only hear about his status, nothing else.

Not even my magic can cross that border."

"You can't see anything, your magic just gives you status updates?"

"Essentially."

My jaw tightened. I hated how it made sense: Caldwell had made half the country his enemy, and it was the half able to attack long distance. The White House needed that spell to protect it from people like me.

"We will find the fifth person," Alejandro assured me, lightly bumping my shoulder. "They will... help us to continue so that we can help everyone."

"I know it seems cruel," Kamose added, "but it isn't for nothing. None of this is. I promise, I tell you everything that I do for your safety, for your family's."

For the boys' sakes, I nodded. There wasn't anything else I could do when tears were pressing against my eyes and I had to lock my jaw to stop it from shaking.

"Okay," I said, forcing evenness into my voice. I raised my shoulders, telling them both to let go. "Let's find out who this person is."

"I'll try," Kamose said, "but remember, my magic doesn't allow me to know the *identities* of the other wielders who are like us. Such as when I asked you for the next one just like us when we first met."

Right—he'd joked that I was destined to tell him about the next ally because he didn't have access to that information on his own. It was the only piece of external information his magic *didn't* allow him.

"But you knew if he was a friend or an enemy," I argued,

pointing my thumb at Alejandro, "when I asked you on the cruise after I started having visions about him."

"Yes, so..." Kamose began slowly, like he was gathering the words as he went, "I *theorize* that Annisa's vision 'unlocked' access to this person, similar to how your visions did for Alejandro. So I may be able to tell you a fact about them, but not who they are. Otherwise... we'll find our next step."

Alejandro nodded with understanding. "Try it first."

"One of you," Kamose said uneasily, caution glowing in his dark eyes, "needs to pay the nore's price and answer a question I choose."

Alejandro held out an arm in front of me. "I will pay it," he said.

"No," I told him, "you've already done—"

"The Nasir family and my family are safe," he argued in Spanish. "Kamose can ask me a good question. And if I'm ever caught, I can escape with my teleportation before I'm interrogated. You don't have that option."

"What he said," Kamose remarked. "If he was telling you why he should pay the price."

"*Sí*," Alejandro replied, just as quickly shaking his head. "Yes, I mean."

I didn't bother opening my mouth; arguing was pointless.

"You want to know where our fifth ally is?" Kamose asked. With Alejandro's agreement, he closed his eyes and took a deep breath.

A second later, his eyes shot open. He blinked a few times, furrowing his brows.

He's acting like his magic lied to him.

"Okay," he mused. "That's interesting. Somewhere called 'Victoria Land' in Antarctica."

My head shot back. "*Antarctica?*"

His reaction made sense now: what was a powerful wielder doing all the way in a nearly inhospitable continent at the bottom of the world?

Kamose closed his eyes again, waited for a second, and then nodded. "Yes, that's where they are. Alone in a *small* abandoned research facility. You should ask them what they're doing there when you find them."

"Hang on," I said, "do you have an exact location? We can't find *one* wielder in a territory that large, how are we even supposed to know when we've found them?"

"I'll keep an 'eye' on you until you get there," he replied. "When you find them, I'll change something in the room to let you know that you found the right person."

"But what about *locating* them once we get to Victoria Land?" I asked dubiously.

"They're a wielder of powerful magic," he said, shrugging. "Even in a group of other magicians, you can sense the magnitude of their magic and easily find them."

I narrowed my eyes, dumbfounded. "How?"

His brow furrowed, catching on to my confusion. "Aren't you a sorceress?"

"What does that have to do with it? Is there a spell that lets us detect other people's magic?"

"No, no, *amiga*," Alejandro said, turning my attention to him. "I think—he is saying about your... how do you say it—ability as a sorcerer."

My ability as a—?

I looked between the two of them, no less baffled. "What're you guys talking about? Sorcerers are the only class of magic without a distinct ability."

They stared at each other with as much bewilderment as I felt—if not more somehow. What was so confusing to them about common knowledge?

"Emma," Kamose began, "no. The sorcerer's ability—like how druids can have dreams of the possible future, nores can access all present circumstances, mages can create and destroy spells—sorcerers can detect if a person is a mortal or a magician."

C H A P T E R

Twenty-Three

ed-hot fury flashed across my vision. It was the only time in my life I'd ever seen red because of rage, and it was scorching every inch of my skin.

"Her entire identity as a sorceress".

This was it? This whole time, *this* was it? I'd had the ability to detect if my friends were really mortal or not. I'd had the ability to detect who was actually a wielder at Callistro like I was. I'd had the ability to detect if the Delphines were wielders from the start, and I never could because I never knew!

Why would my parents keep something so *essential* from me?

I can just, what, "feel it"? I thought mockingly in my head. *We just feel for if—?*

I froze deeper still in my spot on the end of Kamose's bed.

Kamose. Alejandro.

Omari. Li. Michaela. Anthony.

I'd felt something with all of them—either something that called to me with a connection or something strong enough to physically push against me. Had that been the sorcerer's ability waking up in me? I'd been *detecting their magic?*

I didn't feel anything around Joshua or Dakota because they both stored their magic in Bouchard's vault.

This whole time. Something so simple this whole time. I thought that, with everything else that had been going on, none of us in my family had encountered the topic since we'd argued about it the day we got to Bouchard; we'd accidentally let it go amidst settling in and then planning this trip. But no—now I knew it was because my parents knew I didn't need my ability while at the base, and they didn't want to get into a fight about it with me by telling me the truth.

Because I'd *definitely* needed it over the last two years.

"Emma?" Kamose asked carefully.

I kept my mouth shut to avoid snapping at either boy sitting next to me. No wonder Mr. Dawson had wanted me to know: something so basic, common knowledge, and yet something that could've helped me avoid the *lifetime* of paranoia about every friend and classmate I'd ever had, avoid everything the last year and a half had put me through! And my parents *hid* it from me?

This wasn't life-changing knowledge for sorcerers, but it was life-changing knowledge for *me.*

I sprang up from the bed. "We need to leave."

"What?" Alejandro asked.

"We need to find whoever this fifth person is so we can fix

everything and get back," I stated.

"It's 11," Kamose argued, "it's too late to go out now, and by yourselves."

"Today, we traveled for hours," Alejandro added. His words wobbled as he tried to force his English through quicker. "We're safe in this place. We need to feel better first."

"You don't get it," I snapped. "I spent my whole life thinking sorcerers were the only class of magic who didn't get a distinct ability, we could only cast and nothing else. I found out last year there was something about my identity as a sorceress that my parents always knew about, but they decided to keep it from me because I 'wasn't ready'. You're telling me that's it, that's all it was? My parents stripped me of an entire layer of protection, one I *inherited*? Do you know how much I could've avoided if I'd known that? If I could've used other people's magic against them like how mine's been used against me?"

"Your parents never told you?" Kamose asked, confusion scrunching his features.

"Not once," I spat. "Because they thought—"

I couldn't repeat the words. How could Mom or Dad EVER think that it'd be best to keep this from me?

"I just wanna finish this mission," I said, pacing back and forth. "I'm exhausted, I'm angry, and I can't do *anything* here."

"All reasonable," Kamose said, eyes following me, "and all the reasons you should stay here. You're the only one here who's had Hunter training. Do you really think you're in the right mindset to continue a life-threatening mission right now?"

"You were hurt," Alejandro said awkwardly, "when I teleported to here. You're okay now—you should wait longer."

I didn't want this lecture again, mostly because I didn't *need* this lecture; I already knew everything they were telling me. I just wasn't being fully honest with them: I wanted to finish this mission so we could get back to Bouchard and I could rip my parents' heads off. I was on the other side of the world with no other choice but to live in this rage, unable to unleash it on the people who deserved it, who'd sentenced an innocent man to be punished for their mistakes.

We could've come up with better plans, I kept thinking, regret chained to every thought.

I couldn't do this right now. I couldn't be awake if this was all I had to face.

"I'm going to bed," I said, walking around Kamose's bed and climbing back into it. "I'm not gonna spend the next few hours waiting, wake me up when you're ready to leave."

Before either Alejandro or Kamose could reply, I threw the covers over myself and cast a sleeping spell.

A rectangular man in a beige suit sat across from me at the other end of a steel table. The thickest pastel-yellow file I'd ever seen lay in front of him, two Secret Service men stationed behind him.

"—Target Echo, Target Adeline, and now Target Cipher," the lead agent was telling me. "Are any of those names already familiar to you?"

"I've heard of—"

Flash.

I swallowed, trying to clear some kind of blockage in my

throat. A clear plastic bag with something inside obscured by the overhead light lay in front of me. "She didn't offer her help," I spat. "I know her—"

"Then you should've known that this was a long time coming," the agent shot back, narrowly cut off by another flash.

"—to tell him anything he wants to know about Adara."

Shock had numbed my mind for a reason I didn't know. Instinct spoke for me when I asked, "D—directly?"

Flash.

Secret Service stood along the curve of the bright Oval Office. A tall, gaunt man with sallow yet sharp eyes faced me with two men gripping his deflated arms.

"Emma," he rasped, "don't—"

Flash.

"Long before you knew I knew something," I said with suspicious caution.

"Yes," Caldwell replied, "because Americans trust me to keep them safe from threats like her—"

Flash.

"Shoot him."

I jerked in my agents' grip. "NO, please! I can prove it, just let me—!"

Another white burst swept the room. Cold stone supported my back, my hand pressed to my burning side. Mr. Dawson's voice was fading above me. Stun rang in my ears.

I'm shot.

"Keep talking to me!" Mr. Dawson commanded, pushing away my hand and firmly pressing my side for me. "Don't go to sleep, don't close your eyes—!"

I barely processed the words as another flash blinded me.

Glass shattered somewhere in the distance. Someone's cold hand supported my neck. A sting shot from my side as Jak, above me, apologized over and over again. What had to be an army of Secret Service footsteps pounded against the ground.

"Emma, please," Jak cried, grabbing my left hand. "Look at me, look at me, hold on to me—"

The world submerged me in a disorienting darkness. It boomed with a gunshot and my name, bounding across all directions. I felt my subconscious turn every which way, chasing it to no avail.

The darkness shifted. My brain processed the firm grip on my shoulders.

"Emma, wake up!"

My eyes shot open to a dim, familiar room. A soft blue light illuminated the desk ahead of me, unable to reach the walls on either side. Flatscreen TV in the left corner, a nearly closed door in the right—I knew this room this time. These covers.

I looked to my right. Kamose released my shoulders like I had zapped him.

Why was he staring at me like that?

"Kamose?" I whispered, much raspier than I was expecting.

"Have..." he began quietly, staring at my eyes yet somehow not looking at *me*, "have your eyes always glowed yellow when you wake up?"

I furrowed my brow, ready to ask what he was talking about, until it landed: vision. Hybrid. Druid.

So that one's yellow.

"Um..." I whispered, rubbing the sleep from my eyes, "when

I have a vision—I guess."

He paused with the thought for only a moment. "I heard you crying in your sleep. Is that why? Are you okay?"

That stupid question again. Why was everyone always asking me that? Why was my answer to it still wrong?

And why did Kamose have to ask it at the right time?

The blue night-light across the room probably let him see the glisten forming in my eyes, so I kept my gaze straight and on his chest to avoid eye contact. I tried to focus on anything else but what I wanted to ask him. I couldn't let him see how pathetic I was, only hear it when I whispered, "Can I cry?"

He sat down in the padded chair still next to the bed. His hand came up to rest on my shoulder, rubbing it. "Of course."

It took me a second, but I did. Eventually, I convinced my tears that they were safe to fall. I stopped forcing deep breaths and I let myself hiccup, I let the pressure in my head build up until it was too much to keep myself upright and Kamose had to stand again and lean me against his stomach, rubbing my back. I let my body shake as I grabbed his pajama shirt, I let the salty water stain my cheeks and neck, and I let myself cry.

The frequency of that vision this year was too telling: Dawson was at the White House, and facing Caldwell was becoming a wider path on my journey. No part of me would ever be prepared for that, not even if I spent this entire year planning an ambush on the man and ordered everyone else to leave him to me. But like always, I was powerless against it. Just like I had been with all of those visions about that morning in December.

Kamose didn't say anything. Didn't try to comfort me, didn't lecture me, didn't offer the generic "there, there"—didn't ask that stupid question again. He just let me cry.

"I'm messed up," I whispered, tightening my hold on his shirt. "I've never been this messed up before. It sucks, I hate it so much, I don't know what to do."

He carefully sat beside me on the bed, prompting me to scoot over. He never moved past the edge, keeping one foot on the floor. Instead, he turned and wrapped his arms around me, leaning his cheek on my head. I know it wasn't the right time to notice, but he somehow maintained a trace of his spicy cologne even in the middle of the night. It was kind of comforting right now.

"Nothing feels like the right thing anymore," I said, taking in a sharp breath, "none of my plans, none of the situation, it's all *wrong*. If it's not a nightmare, my visions torture me with the likely future, I can't do *anything* to reunite my family or take down our real enemy without sacrificing the people I love or myself, I feel like I'm slowly losing my rationality to my emotions because I can't help it—I don't even know why I'm crying in front of someone I met a couple of hours ago."

Kamose pulled back enough for his knuckle to wipe away a stray tear. "We're friends all the same, no?"

Friends. Honestly, he felt too good to be true for a friend.

"You barely know me," I murmured. The longer I stared into his black eyes, the more my breaths started to slow—the longer he waited for me. "How are you so good at this?"

A soft smile lifted his full, flat lips. He had to pause before saying, "Because you and Annisa and Alejandro are the same kind of people my family are: humanitarians for humanity, not for one side or the other. Instead, in every sense of the word. Not only does that have my respect,"—he squeezed my shoulder—"but also my full support."

For some reason, that reminded me of Sarah—how she'd reacted to me being Tristan Atera's daughter. How she hadn't blatantly freaked, turned back to the gazebo to tell our friends, or even screamed at me with fury and repulsion. Instead, she'd cried. She'd told me that it all made sense, everything finally made sense. Then she was angry, but only because I'd "harbored it" for so long instead of sharing the burden.

I told her to read my letter with that perspective and know exactly why I'd kept everything from the three of them that I had. I'd begged her to keep the truth from Breanne and Opal for the same reasons. Then she was forced to let me go so my family and I could run. If Caldwell hadn't exposed my identity to the country yet, my secret was safe with her—because she hadn't been angry once she knew. She'd been relieved. She didn't care about what I was; my humanity was first on her mind. Maybe she was a humanitarian, too.

Sometimes I forget why I'm still fighting in this. It turned out, I just needed someone with the same heart to remind me.

I looked back up at Kamose. Last Sarah had told us, she was going to break things off with Adrien. She would definitely think Kamose was cute—and she loved tall guys.

"Do you have a girlfriend?"

Kamose jerked back from me, then quickly blinked away the surprise on his face. "No, but I don't mix business and pleasure."

I rolled my eyes. "Not me—that friend you talked to, to get my phone number."

He thought back on it for a second before his brows shot up. "Oh. Sarah?"

I smirked. "You remember her name."

He gestured to himself with his free hand. "I am in a position where I have no choice but to."

Fair.

"But I'm glad you're feeling well enough to play, how's it called... 'matchmaker'," he deadpanned quietly. "You should do it for Alejandro first, then you can find me."

I tilted my head. "Alejandro?"

Kamose looked down at the sheets, his mouth parting with an answer he, apparently, hadn't intended to give me. "I promised him that I would keep his answer to me a secret—the nore's price he paid for information about our ally. Let's just say that he... was interested in someone, but she's not a possibility. So he might appreciate your *recommendations*."

Alejandro likes someone? And I wasn't allowed to know who or ask him about it?

I felt a faint smile touch the corners of my lips; amidst everything going on, somehow we'd found the time to talk about crushes and romance. Normalcy wasn't completely out of style for us yet, which was a bit of comfort.

"If that's all," Kamose whispered, standing, "I should let you think about how you'll safely make it to Antarctica."

"Just like how we made it over here," I replied. "If we get caught again, we know how to handle it."

"Okay." He meandered down the side of his bed. "Then think about how to activate your sorcerer's ability when you get there so you can find our friend."

I bit the inside of my cheek, remembering why I'd forced myself to sleep in the first place. I hated that that was something I had to try to do rather than simply *do*.

When Kamose reached the bedroom door, my mouth opened without thought. "Kamose?"

He turned with his hand on the knob.

"Thanks for being here for me."

The soft blue night-light illuminated his smile as he nodded, saluting with two fingers. I lay back down on his mattress. There were only two reasons I was able to close my eyes again: visions didn't occur twice in a row, and I wanted to believe that Kamose had left me with enough good thoughts to affect my dreams in the same way.

Twenty-Four

The Nasirs made me and Alejandro stay for a whole day "for our health" before letting us leave bright and early for Antarctica—which was poor planning in my opinion, considering it was 8 at night back at Bouchard and my subconscious was convinced that we needed to be getting ready for bed (on top of being tired from waking up at 6).

Alejandro and I teleported three more times—without me helping this time—down the length of the continent to reach the town of George in South Africa. After we suited back up with our winter gear and grabbed a couple more supplies, next up was the jump to Showa Station in Antarctica and then roughly where Victoria Land should be. On the bright side, I was *pretty* sure we didn't have to worry about the government coming after us while we were there.

I opened my eyes after the second jump in Antarctica. Ice-cold air whipped against my cheeks, already numbing the tip of my nose. A wilderness of white stretched out on all sides with the coast roaring far off in the distance behind us. Since it was late summer in the Southern Hemisphere, Antarctica was a merciful twenty-five degrees Fahrenheit. I was used to that, having grown up in a forest-insulated town where snow fell. Alejandro, who had barely ever experienced the *thirties*, would just have to hold out until we found the research facility.

"Emma?" he called in Spanish, pulling his hood farther over his head. The temperature exposed his every breath out. "It's really cold—I might need to warm up before I can teleport easily again. If we get into trouble before we find this person, things won't end well."

"Hold on tightly to the hand warmers," I said, holding mine in the pocket warmers of my waterproof gloves. The warmth seeped into my fingers, the only thing preserving their dexterity, and my backpack was at least preserving the heat on my back. "Kamose said that this person is in an *abandoned* research facility, so we should be able to safely warm up there with them."

"Do you feel anything?" he asked, taking his first march forward. It was a struggle to hear him both over the wind and through the beanie covering my ears.

"No," I admitted, following him. Ice and snow reached out for miles on all sides. Empty. "I don't even feel your magic right now. Either we're not close enough, or..."

Or I'm still a failure at my own class of magic because my parents never trusted me with the basics of my own identity.

Anger coursed through my blood again. My magic could give me nightmares about Caldwell and Secret Service, about getting shot, but not a single vision about meeting this ally? When they were part of the reason I *was* a hybrid?

Alejandro took a large step over a fresh pile of snow, accidentally kicking some up behind him. "We know that we're in the right area. Let's keep walking until you feel something or we find a building."

"We need direction," I said, matching his steps. "What if we tried... telepathically calling out to them?"

He briefly turned to look at me, taking shorter strides. "Won't it be risky? Aren't there many *American* researchers here?"

"We're not in America," I replied, lunging over another small hill. The grips in my boots were hard at work to keep me steady. "They won't care if we use magic around them. Just use our cover. Worst-case scenario, we erase their memories, knock them out with a sleeping spell, and keep looking."

Maybe my magic already does sense theirs and I just can't feel it, I thought. Well, I wanted to believe that; maybe then my will alone could reach out to this person and my telepathy would automatically connect with them.

Right?

I miss you, Mr. Dawson. The first thing I was doing with him once we got him back was a magic lesson.

Alejandro huffed with a dense cloud swirling in front of his lips. I braced my mind and tried my first call.

—*Hello? Is anyone nearby?*—

Silence whooshed back with the wind, nearly pushing me backwards.

—Showa Station, do you copy? This is Emily Creek from Halley Base. Our vehicle has a busted tire. Does anyone copy?—

"Anything?" I called to Alejandro as we marched with increasingly shorter steps.

"No," he answered, his breaths deepening. "Do you feel anything now?"

I cast my gaze to the crystalline ground, trying to focus my will and sorcerer's magic all in one. Nothing. Absolutely nothing reaching out into the distance, nothing warning me of a great presence nearby.

I looked up, my eyes catching a gray spot in the left corner of my vision this time: a one-story building stood in the left distance—three or four miles out.

"Alejandro!" I tapped his shoulder, bringing his eyes up to me. I took my other hand out of my pocket and pointed. "That could be it! We know someone will be there."

"But are they good or bad?" he asked.

"Keep calling out with telepathy," I said, trying to quicken my sluggish, heavy steps. "We know what to do if they're enemies."

He matched my pace, and I focused my telepathy onto the structure and its surrounding area. *—If anyone can hear me, please, we need a spare tire, or transportation to Showa Station. We're low on supplies and freezing.—*

Nothing. The fog of my and Alejandro's breaths thickened the more we panted.

—Are you able to provide any help?—

"Maybe they're all... away right now," I breathed. "Do you hear anything—?"

With his next step, Alejandro's thickly layered body collapsed into the snow. I barely had time to call his name before I hurtled toward the icy ground and the world swallowed me in darkness.

C H A P T E R

Twenty-Five

Bitter cold stung my cheek as I came to, the smell of rubber so potent that it almost burned my nostrils. My eyes pried themselves open, landing on a dark-gray fabric wall. A couch, I realized when my vision focused.

I noted the black underneath me and pushed myself off the floor. A *floor*. Despite how I'd probably just been kidnapped and thrown into a facility room where nobody could hear me scream, my first thought was *Ew. How many people have walked on this?*

Upon pushing myself to my knees, my coat's hood falling off my head, I found Alejandro beside me and doing the same.

Wait. Where are our things—?

I opened my mouth to alert him before a girl's firm voice commanded, "Don't move. Show me your hands."

My gaze snapped forward. On the other side of the pocket-sized room, a brunette stood against the plywood wall with a pistol aimed at us. The industrial winter coat, gloves, and boots she had on made her no less intimidating: she knew what she was doing out here.

On our knees, Alejandro and I held up our hands in surrender. The girl's square jaw was set tighter than a vault door. Her harsh cobalt-blue eyes, with short and messy bangs falling into them, flashed amber. A truth spell seized my tongue.

"If you try anything, I will either shoot you or throw you out to freeze to death," she stated. "I'm still deciding. Who are you?"

Is that...? The lightest French accent I'd ever heard. Did she used to live with people who had the typical American accent she was trying to impersonate?

Mission first. Let's see: she's a wielder, she seems to be alone here, and Kamose said he'd give us a sign...

Wait. That presence—that same strong aura, connection, something I'd felt before but couldn't describe. Almost enough to physically push me back. But was that because I had Alejandro next to me? Could I finally sense his magic again?

I prayed and hoped against hope that, at any second, Kamose would change something about our circumstances, that he was even "looking" at us right now after Alejandro had texted him saying that we were leaving South Africa. But if he didn't change anything, we had the wrong girl, and we couldn't tell a stranger our mission, wielder or not.

"We're not here to hurt anyone," I began. "We're looking for someone who's supposed to be in this area."

"That doesn't tell me who you are—*are*," she said, forcing a harder American "r" through. Her eyes narrowed at us, her square jaw hardening. "Answer that, and who you are looking for—"

The steel pistol in her hand suddenly melded together, prompting her to yelp and drop it. We all watched as the handle straightened, swallowing the metal in a straight stick: a rod.

Thank you, Kamose!

"Who did that?" the girl exclaimed, holding up her hand next as if it were a weapon.

This was her. This defensive and probably secretly terrified girl was it.

"It wasn't us," I assured her quickly, keeping my hands up. "Please, listen. I'm Emmalynn Atera and this is Alejandro Vidal."

No reaction to either name. That could mean a number of things.

"We don't know why or how, but we and two other friends have powers supposed to be impossible even for magic. We're trying to find someone else who's like us. One of our friends, Annisa, is a druid who had a vision you were in. Alejandro and I went to our other friend, Kamose, who's a nore that can change present circumstances. He told us you lived here, he said he'd change something once we found the right person, and that was it—he changed your gun into that."

The girl's face contorted in skepticism that had a vengeance. "What did you say?" she mumbled. "Impossible magic?"

"Yeah, like what Kamose just did—you know that's impossible otherwise."

"Yes," she hissed, her crisp voice stiffening with more of her accent seeping through. "So I know that was a trick—a *trick*."

She corrects herself on words that sound... "too French". Why does she hate her accent so much?

"We can't lie," Alejandro said in the fastest English I'd ever heard him speak. "Please, I can show to you—"

"Then give me my gun back," she snapped.

"I can't—" he stuttered. "It's—I'm—"

He looked to me for help, and I didn't hesitate. "Our abilities are different for each of us. Only Kamose can change present circumstances. Annisa can time travel, Alejandro can teleport, and I'm a hybrid wielder. I can perform all seven class abilities."

The girl glanced between us. Then, she nodded at Alejandro. "Show me. Teleport to the couch next to her—her."

He shakily exhaled, nodding quickly. An amber swirl of bright waves and shimmers briefly encased him, fading when he disappeared. Just as quickly, a light flashed on my other side: there he sat in the middle of the couch.

The girl stumbled backwards and into the wall. "How—" she stammered, "how did you do that?"

"I can," he said, shrugging timidly like he wasn't allowed to do even that.

"And you," she told me with doubt denting her brow, "you can—you have all the classes of magic?"

"Yeah—"

"You're a mage, a seer, a warlock—all these things?"

"Yes—"

"You can't stay here, I want you out." She grabbed a switchblade from her belt and flicked it open. "Go back home, now."

"No!" I cried, trying to stand. She pointed her blade right at me, and I froze on one knee. "Please, hear us out. I'm begging you, just a couple of minutes. You became my only hope of moving forward when Annisa had a vision with you in it. You have no idea what we've been through to get here, I—I don't even know where to start—"

"Why you came to find me," she stated, keeping the knife firmly pointed in my direction. Her scolding eyes moved to Alejandro. "And trust me, you do not want to try anything by teleporting."

"I understand."

"Do you..." I began, my mind spinning as it tried to find a starting point that she'd accept, "do you know *anything* about what we're talking about? About having an impossible ability, a name only the magic world knows us by—maybe even about being a one hundredth generation of your family?"

I watched a small lump pass in her throat. "I wouldn't know," she muttered.

What? Why not? Was that a no to everything?

"Have you ever heard the legend that a group of magicians is meant to unite the world?" I asked. "So mortals and magicians can finally coexist?"

She snickered. "There's no such thing."

According to magic there is, I wanted to argue, but impatience was the last thing that would help me right now.

"Well, that's what we're meant to do," I told her instead, my legs starting to tingle from staying in my position for too long. It was also way warmer in here than it was outside, and I was itching to unzip my coat amidst the added heat of adrenaline. "Please, we're physically unable to lie right now. We had to travel across the entire width of Canada—"

"Canada?" The girl straightened. "You came from—*from*

there?"

"Yeah, we—"

"Get out," she snapped, jabbing her blade in the direction of the door.

I finally found the courage to stand. "No, wait, you're not listening—"

"I don't need to!" she retorted, stepping forward. "I want nothing to do with that godforsaken country, I am here for a reason!"

She'd *picked* Antarctica, of all places, to live in...? Or had she been forced here?

"We're not *from* there, we're being forced to stay there," I said, bolting my feet to the rubber ground. I could feel sweat start to gather on my torso, desperation flushing through me. "My family and I were chased out of the United States. Alejandro teleported all the way from Spain to stay with us because he's our only way of getting anywhere while we're stuck in a magician refuge for fugitives like us. You want nothing to do with Canada, fine, but we can't leave yet—Alejandro needs time to recover when he teleports long distances."

I definitely wasn't going to admit this to either of them, but I was feeling a bit drained from the journey across the arctic, too.

"I promise," I told the girl, "we aren't dangerous; we don't want to hurt you; and it would take *forever* for someone to follow us all the way out here, even with a locator spell because this place isn't formally established anymore—is it?"

"No," she stated. Right—she would have already taken that precaution to protect herself.

"Victoria Land is a sizable territory," I said, softening my gaze on her. "So—can you spare a few hours here for us to settle and recuperate? After traveling so fast for so long because we weren't safe anywhere else?"

It took a second, but she finally slightly lowered her switchblade. Alejandro and I waited as she glanced between us. I wondered when she was going to swipe her bangs out of her eyes.

"Fine," she spat. "But I have lived here defending myself against animals *and* people for the last three—*three* years. If you try anything—"

"I swear on the truth spell," I said. "You can trust us."

She all but shot daggers at me with her glare. Why wasn't the truth spell enough for her?

What has she been through that landed her right here?

Alejandro carefully stood from the couch. "Can we know your name?"

"No," she said firmly, closing her switchblade and sliding it back into its sheath in her belt. "You can rest here and that is it."

"Do you have our stuff?" I asked carefully.

"You'll get it back when you leave," she stated.

All I could do was hope she hadn't taken anything. We only had essentials like food and extra clothes in those backpacks—and Alejandro's phone—but depending on this girl's living conditions, I didn't know how valuable those things were to her.

"How have you been living here for so long?" I asked. "And... by yourself?"

Her stare lingered on me, like she'd made a mistake somewhere and accidentally given away too much information already. "Magic helps," she said, unzipping her heavy coat. "But I depend on my own hands most of the time. I didn't have to build this place—it was abandoned."

"Why here?" I asked, unzipping my coat slowly to avoid startling her. "Antarctica, of all places? It sounds like you still need to hide from people even though you're someplace so remote."

She slid off her coat, straightening her dry bust-length hair. "It's the only place nobody will find me. Not without impossible magic."

A knowing silence trailed after her words. In my peripheral vision, Alejandro glanced at me, but I didn't return it.

"Sit."

We obeyed, taking adjacent seats on the dark-gray couch.

"You said there were—*were* others," the girl said. "What else do you know about them?"

Alejandro kept his eyes on me, telling me that he was relying on me to tell the whole thing. "Again, we don't know how any of this is possible," I replied, "but there are patterns: we're all a one hundredth generation of our families, we all have a name we're known by in the magic world to protect our real identities, and we're all supposed to be the most powerful magicians of our classes. I'm supposed to be the most powerful sorceress; Alejandro, the mage; Kamose, the nore; and Annisa, the druid. All we know is that you're the next one we're meant to find. Both Annisa's and Kamose's magic told us."

Still standing in front of the plywood wall, refusing to approach us any more, the girl tightly crossed her slim arms. "Then I'm a break in your patterns. I don't know anything about that. We will leave it at that."

An uncomfortable few seconds followed, so overwhelming that Alejandro eventually had to look down at his hands in his lap. When I did the same, I felt the girl burning a hole through my head with her eyes. I'd never encountered such a powerful glare in my life, not even Momma's. Would we ever be able to incorporate this girl into our world?

"Can we..." I forced myself to ask, dragging my eyes up to hers, "help with anything? Since you're letting us stay here?"

"I already did my chores for the day," she said curtly. "Unless you're willing to steal more resources from the closest facility."

Oh, that's one way she survives...

"If you're staying for a few hours, you'll be here for dinner. All I can spare—*spare are* vegetables. No meat. Don't ask."

Geez. Point taken.

Wait a minute. "Do you have a garden?" I asked.

She stiffened. "Why?"

"I'm part warlock," I said. "I can bring plants to harvest and replant them. That way you don't have to worry about running out of anything."

Her jaw remained tight as she stared at me in thought. Then, she loosened. "Fine. I'll show you."

I glimpsed Alejandro next to me. He subtly shrugged like he'd be shot on the spot for moving. We stood and followed the girl across the room and to a doorway on the left. Progress was progress... right?

C H A P T E R

Twenty-Six

The kitchen was barely big enough for the three of us to sit at the small wooden table and leave room for a counter, fridge, stove, and microwave. Kamose hadn't been kidding when he'd said this place was *small*.

In the garden, I'd managed to grow cabbage, carrots, tomatoes, and onions (which definitely wasn't something I thought I'd have to use warlock magic for), giving us vegetable stew for dinner. At least our alleged new ally—who still hadn't given us her name—was willing to share her spices and water, and finally released us from the truth spell after Alejandro showed her how to use cumin, bay leaf, and a dash of chili flakes to liven vegetable broth.

"When do you plan to leave?" she asked between the two of us as we ate, breaking the quiet. This time, though, her voice didn't carry the harsh edge I'd already come to know. Gardening and then cooking together had done some good for the three of us, but she was no less eager to get rid of me and Alejandro.

He met my eyes from across the table, relying on me again to answer.

"Um," I said, "I *did* assume after dinner. But I forgot that it'd be dark everywhere else on our side of the world."

It was almost 8 o'clock at night, but we were still basking in broad daylight thanks to being at the bottom of the globe; that didn't help me remember.

"Why is that a problem?" the girl asked. "You'll teleport to somewhere with light and other—*other* people."

"Yeah, but..." I wasn't sure how to phrase my argument without sounding like I was trying to stay here for longer than we needed to. But if we were going to get her on our team, let alone find out her impossible power, we did need to. "That kind of *is* the problem. The people awake at this hour wherever we go will be strangers and potentially... Well, a lot of *good* people are asleep right now, put it that way."

"We can go to a place with light," Alejandro added slowly, needing to think carefully about his English, "but it can still be a— *dark* place. Do you know?"

On top of all that, the teleportation lag was catching up to me at an alarming rate.

The girl took another bite of her stew. Nothing more, which was a good sign. From what I'd gathered about her so far, her silence meant no resistance or rejection—we were moving slow, but we were getting somewhere.

"What about your families?" she asked after swallowing.

"They know where we are," I replied. "We're okay if you are."

Another bite. Still no rejection.

Then, her brows scrunched together, and she set her spoon against her ceramic bowl. "They think you're here for—*for*—the reason you told me? To find another one of your group of special magicians?"

Well, putting it that way, it almost sounded condescending, like we were forming a magic club that only a select few were allowed to join. If that was how she saw it, no wonder she wanted us gone as soon as possible.

"That's not completely it," I said. "It's to find someone else like us because they have the same destiny we do. Which we all need to be a part of."

"To 'save the world'?" she deadpanned. Her harsh cobalt-blue eyes took turns between me and Alejandro, landing on him. "How did you find this out, that this was a thing?"

"I, um…" He looked across the table at me again like I knew that story, but I was wholly intrigued: I didn't know how any of my allies knew their destinies like I did. "Um… my best friend in Spain is a druid. When we met each other, he had a dream about me. We had—um, I mean—we *were* ten years then. We told to his parents the dream, and they told to us the story about Azariah. They knew about him. They said that he will unite the mortal and magic worlds."

His spoken English was still rough, but I was proud of his progress over the last couple of months.

"How did they know about Azariah?" the girl asked.

"Everyone knows in Spain," he replied. "He's a—*¿cómo se dice?*—story, I don't know the right word. He is a story that… Spain shared during centuries and today.”

“Legend,” I offered.

“Yes, thank you,” he said. “He’s a legend.”

The girl turned to me. “But you have a different version.”

“In a way, I guess. In America, it’s Adara. American magicians have known about her for just as long.”

“How do you know that she’s you?”

I took my spoon, stirring my broth that was separating from the seasoning. “My godfather’s a druid and told me.”

“You aren’t telling me something,” she said, giving me the bravery to match our eyes.

“I don’t want to talk about him.”

“You used present tense, so he isn’t dead?”

I kept my gaze on a floating carrot slice. “The US Government took him into custody.”

“So he’s still alive—”

“I don’t like talking about him,” I stated. “I can’t do anything to save him yet.”

“Then why do you need me—?”

“Because he’s not the mission we need you for.”

I clamped my mouth shut. I’d said those words with more bite than I’d intended, and that was a fast track to sending us five steps back—something we couldn’t afford when we’d only taken two steps forward.

I reset, putting on the professional demeanor I’d used for discussing my grades with my teachers at Callistro. “We need your help for something bigger than... ourselves. This is for other people, it’s for *our* people.”

“Again, to ‘save the world’?” she sneered. “That’s not possible to do—"

"Clearly it is if magic gave us these abilities," I argued. "We're impossible people meant to do an impossible thing."

"Why do you want to?" Her glower instantly put me on edge—like she already felt that she was winning this conversation and didn't need to put effort into it. "Why would you want to join two worlds that want nothing to do with each other? They just want to hurt each other, they want to take advantage of each other. You can't tell me that you've never been hurt by mortals with the pers—*persecution* you face every day. Your own government wants you dead for what you are. And the people they hate have taken advantage of their—*their* abilities and the people who are power—*powerless* against them. I bet you've been hurt by your own people, too. Why work and sacrifice for something that doesn't want it and will kill you for trying?"

I almost didn't have an argument against any of that—until the tears pressing behind my eyes reminded me that that was exactly why I was doing this. "Because I *have* experienced and witnessed firsthand what this world is doing to itself. That's the problem, you're thinking of it as two sides like everyone else does. We're not two sides, we've always been the same species, the same whole, and we're hurting ourselves. Not 'the other side'. Our world may not want it but we need it. An unfulfilled need *will* kill you in the end no matter how long it takes. Whether it's a minute or a few millennia."

She dropped her spoon into her bowl. "I'm not killing myself for people that only want me when I have something for them. Why do they deserve my help?"

Deserve? It wasn't about deserving. Even if it were, nobody "deserved" to die purely for what was in their blood! My family didn't deserve a lifetime of being hunted. Alexa didn't deserve what happened to her when she was seventeen and Anthony's father thought she was a powerless mortal, an easy target. The Delphines were praised until Caldwell found out what they were; they didn't deserve to be killed just because of *that*!

My anger bristled. Alejandro must have seen it, because he stepped in before I could open my mouth: "You were hurt."

The girl's head snapped in his direction, fawn hair flying. Part of me wondered how he didn't split apart then and there under her scowl. "You don't—"

"We are hurt, too," he said, gesturing loosely to me and then himself. "Magic is legal in Spain, but in some cities, no. I live in Valencia—it's legal there. But so much people don't like us. My best friend and his family needed to move when mortals—set fire on his house. We met after that."

I scolded myself for my shock. Wielders had experienced that kind of treatment for centuries; why was I so surprised about it now? Why had those words pelted me?

Because I've only ever heard of *the government doing those things to my people.* When it came to the public, those stories stayed in history textbooks. They never came out of a friend's mouth—someone who was just as real and present as I was, anything but a memento of the past. It was real, it wasn't just history.

Alejandro nodded toward me. "Emma's family needed to leave America, do you remember? She needed to leave her friends, her school, and her godfather. You don't know why. But it was terrible and—only she is allowed to tell to you."

"Stop," the girl hissed. "Neither of you know what I escaped, either. You act like you're helping people who deserve it without realizing that none of them do. Nobody is perfect, *nobody* is completely innocent."

"Neither are we," I argued, "but magic picked us anyway. Like it saw that we would do something with it despite that. Doesn't that make us *more* obligated to help?"

"You're asking the same question and expecting a different response." She turned her attention back to her bowl, scooping up another bite. "You can save the world all you want when you leave, but I won't be the—*there*. Eat."

Alejandro shifted uncomfortably in his chair, leaning forward slightly. "Um... Maybe the base can help you. You should live at a place that's warm and—it can feed you." He gestured vaguely to his face. "I can see no food in your body."

Her eyes darkened, a storm brewing behind them that gripped her words. "It wasn't this continent that starved me."

That was the first crumb of her story that she'd dropped for us. Somehow, with it, she'd made me *want* to shut up.

But we are *gonna need her in the future*, I thought, my hand subconsciously rising to the silver heart around my neck in the silence. *If she's this adamant now, what're we gonna do then?*

"Let me ask you something," she told me. I dropped my locket. "Why do *you* want to 'fulfill your destiny'?"

I furrowed my brow. "Because—I have to. Nobody else can unite these people like we can. We have to."

"No," she stated firmly. "Why do you *want* to do that?"

I blankly stared back at her, unsure if I needed to tell her an answer so obvious... until I realized that I *didn't* have that answer. *So that we can all coexist without wanting to murder each other*—but there would always be people willing to kill for power, and magic was the best source of power. *So that we can clear up the misunderstandings between us*—but our world *wanted* to fabricate misunderstandings, and magic easily made them believable. *So that we won't blindly hate each other anymore*—but that was a condition inherently part of human nature, and magic was just the best excuse for it.

"Adara. Save them."

That. That was why—because Alexa Delphine had been willing to die for this, for Adara *to* save these people. She'd seen people worth saving until her last breath, and that was the only reason she'd given me the torch.

So that I can save my family and friends.

Throwing away my impatience, I took my last bite of stew. "Okay," I began, setting my spoon into my empty bowl and taking a deep breath. "I get why you don't want to come back to a world like ours. Honestly... I don't, either. I wish I didn't have to. It's taken more from me than I can tell you off the top of my head. It's taken things from my friends who were never supposed to be involved, it's ruined my family's lives. But that's the reason I'm coming back: if nobody else, not even for myself, I'm fighting for them, my family. They're not innocent,"—last night at Kamose's flashed in my mind—"ha, they're *definitely* not innocent, I'm actually furious with them right now. But... they do deserve it."

"That's the difference between me and you: I don't have a family to fight for."

"I'm not saying you have to—"

"It's not my job to convince you why I'm not going, it's your job to understand," she snapped. "You're arguing against a story you know nothing about—"

"Because you won't *let* us know anything!" I said, fighting to keep my volume steady. "Look at you, you don't know our stories. You don't know how I was missing a parent until two years ago because he was being hunted, how I've been a prisoner my whole life because nobody can know who I am, how many times I've been lied to and manipulated by the people I care about, how *two* people I love have been physically tortured for me, how I lost the first father I ever had TWICE to the world you hate so much! You pressured me to tell you about my godfather, *that's* why I don't want to talk about him. You don't know about any of that but you refuse to see why we're doing this anyway, we're doing it *despite* it! That's the fight!"

"You suffered because you had a family to love you," she argued. "I didn't, but hatred almost killed me anyway."

"Don't come with us to *help* us," Alejandro said, quickly stepping in. "Come with us to... see our lives, where we live at. See if you like it. See where we come from."

"I'm not leaving," she said.

His lips pressed tightly together, eyes trickling down to his stew. I watched as his features fell with an unfamiliar melancholy. "We didn't want to leave, too."

Strangely enough, when I opened my mouth to reinforce that, my thoughts kept me silent. Not like I was fighting a losing battle, but like... I didn't have an argument anymore.

I glanced around the tiny kitchen, at the life this girl had deliberately chosen for herself because the world had hardened her with her scars. And I found myself... envious. Envious of her solitude, her ignorance, her ability to simply be. The lack of magic's will weighing on her shoulders, a weight Alejandro and I had just placed. We didn't have any of that even at Bouchard.

Why would *we be given these powers, just the five of us? If we're supposed to lead the world into unity, why do we have such a stark advantage over everyone else?* Could magic really fix what it had broken in the first place?

The girl's eyes landed on me again, but I put mine on my bowl. With every second, my mind anticipated her possible answers. Part of me wished that there were at least a clock to tick instead of the quiet that blasted my thoughts into my ears.

Finally, her shoulders rose with a breath. "Okay," she said, gaze still on me. "Warlock. If you win in a duel with me, I'll let you take me to your base for thirty—*thirty* minutes. And I'll give you my coord—*coord*inates so you can find me again if I ever change my mind."

I looked up at her. *So she's a warlock.* Did she know that she'd just given that away? Why would she let me grow the vegetables for the stew when she could have done it herself?

She wanted to guard everything *about her. Maybe we're still making progress if she's exposing her class now.*

It was almost too good to be true, which meant that it was. "Can you promise that under a truth spell?" I asked.

Her exhale and lack of denial gave me her confirmation, and I cast it.

"I will go with you for thirty minutes, that's it," she said, as stiff as a board. "And I'll give you my coordinates. And... I'll tell you my name."

I glimpsed Alejandro as if he could verify that she really was telling the truth.

"You'll do all that if I beat you in a warlock duel?" I asked.

"If you *win*," she said, taking my empty bowl with hers as she stood from the table.

Aren't those the same thing?

Whatever—that was all fine with me. Warlocks are a rare and powerful class of magic, but all this girl had were spells. I had will, and it had never been more determined to move something.

CHAPTER

Twenty-Seven

I tried convincing myself that digesting my food was raising my body temperature as the girl, Alejandro, and I stood in the snowy field outside of the research facility. Evidently the sun was almost *always* out in Antarctica during the (Southern Hemisphere) summer, which was both a blessing and a curse; its rays shone harshly on the crystalline snow, casting a blinding white haze over the field. I already knew what my first move would be: blocking that sun.

"There is one rule," the girl thirty feet away from me announced. Alejandro safely stood at the front door of the facility. "We can't attack each other. We'll go until one of us gives up."

"Got it," I called. "Who goes first?"

"The real warlock," she shot.

In her heavy winter coat, she raised her gloved hand to the sky, waving it in circles. With a flash of amber in her eyes, a gust blew past me, augmenting the Antarctic chill. Our shadows stretched tall on the ground, dimming. I looked up at the sky: light-gray clouds had formed overhead, ready to impede on the sun. It was almost like she'd read my mind.

She dropped her hand, telling me that it was my turn.

Then I'll finish it.

I copied her gesture, raising my own hand. *Tumescere.*

Our shadows disappeared into the graying atmosphere. The clouds billowed in front of the sun, rolling in like a dust storm. More emerged from their sides, crossing the sky and darkening to a stormy gray.

I internally smiled at myself with pride. *My first swelling spell with element manipulation.* Only a warlock's magic allows traditional spells to control nature.

I dared to catch my opponent's eye as she stood stiffly in her heavy clothes. No discernible expression—she wouldn't let me see if she was impressed or worried.

"You can give me a challenge," I shouted.

"That's the point."

She kneeled down, waving her hand over the area in front of her with another flash of amber in her eyes. She stood. From my distance, nothing showed until it started to spread: green spikes poking through the snow around her. Vibrant grass now hid her boots, stretching out in front of her and to the halfway point between us.

Easy.

I kneeled, hovering my hand over the snow. Despite my

gloves, I could feel my magic reach out to it, flow deep below the ice. It latched onto the frozen soil underneath, calling sprouts from the sprigs willing to obey.

Cresce.

With a surge of the warlock's will, the blades strengthened and slithered through the snow. Fresh grass poked through the ground, leaving me with a patch.

"You're too slow," the girl called dully.

Before I could be offended, her palm rose toward the sky and she wiggled her fingers. Another patch of daisies unfurled at her feet, a couple of blue flowers and dandelions blossoming suit.

Without thinking, I reached my hand down, inviting my magic to grab the first seeds it could find. I urged the flowers forward, anticipating the small handful of buds rising from the ground between my grass blades. Their yellow petals unfolded into the daisies the girl had conjured a whole area of.

This isn't gonna work, I told myself. *I summoned whole tree roots onto the highway during a federal pursuit—if I'm supposed to win, I have to restrain myself less.*

I reached my hand down again, determined to match the girl's work—

"No," her firm voice shouted.

I looked up. She raised her hand toward the sky again, this time flicking her wrist with another flash of amber in her irises.

From the clouds above, white specks drifted in slow motion down to the earth. Snow.

"Go ahead," she called, "stop it."

I raised my hand, my magic already detecting the weight of the storm brewing in these clouds. Before I could secure my grip, the girl raised her other hand up. The snowfall doubled, pressing so heavily against my power that my hand faltered.

Come on!

Desine!

Half of the downpour's weight crumbled away, letting my magic tighten its grip.

I can't lose!

I thrust my other hand, shaky to my surprise, up into the sky. The girl flicked her wrist again. Strong winds pushed against my force. Just as I steeled my will for another attempt, the girl threw her hand toward me. With a flash of amber, the ground under me sank. I stumbled, instinctively stepping back. Snow gave way to water with my every step until, with my next one, I slipped and crashed into the pile behind me.

Snowflakes clung to my coat and hair as my opponent raised her hand again. Another frigid wind blew, swirling the snowfall. Sitting up, I lifted my arm against the gusts to calm the storm. The weight seized my strength; she'd increased the downpour again.

Wind howled in my ears, throwing back my hair, but the flurrying snow had stolen my vision. I barely heard Alejandro shout my name from the door of the facility. I was losing.

No, I'm not *losing this!*

I got to my knees, using a strengthening spell to push my arm up. I commanded my will forward as I gazed up at the stormy clouds overhead. "*Desine!*"

My hair dropped to my sides as the wind stopped. The white streams faded from above, their remnants floating down.

"*Tumescere!*" my opponent yelled.

"*Desine!*" I shouted, stopping the next bout before it could begin. I threw out my arm toward the snow beneath the girl. "*Lique!*"

Like a time lapse, the ice melted, dropping her a foot into the ground.

"*Congelo!*" I said just as her wide eyes snapped up to me.

Her grass and flowers frosted over, withering into the ground. The snow blocked my vision of the spell freezing the water around her boots in the ground, but by the way she jerked her body, it had worked.

I cast my eyes up to the dark sky. "*Serena.*"

The clouds whitened at my command, rolling apart from each other and dispersing from the sun. Blinding rays shone through, casting their glare onto the ground again.

I looked back down at my opponent thirty feet away. Her nostrils flared with her breath that clouded in front of her mouth.

"So?" I shouted.

She looked down at her feet. Amber peeked through her bangs and downcast gaze. Water now sloshing under her, she climbed out of the small well she'd made, kicking snow into it as she went.

Alejandro met me at the halfway point. We waited for the girl to finish her march over.

She peered down at us, taking full advantage of the couple of extra inches she had. "You leave *first* thing tomorrow."

"What?" Alejandro and I said, my heart dropping.

"But," I stammered, "you said you'd let us show you the base if I beat you—"

"No," she snapped, eyes hardening with her square jaw. "I said if you won. You didn't win."

"That's the same—!"

My mouth clamped itself shut. In her game, they weren't. She'd made our deal with rules she was never going to tell me.

"That's not fair," I said, "you said there was only one rule—"

"Stop it." Her breath temporarily blocked my view of her. "You lost."

She turned toward the door behind Alejandro, trekking to it. He hopelessly glanced at me like he was silently begging me to try something else.

Desperation clawed up my throat, and I rushed after her as she grabbed the handle. "Please! You don't understand how important this is, everything we had to—"

She faced us again with a tired glower, holding up her gloved hand. "*Listen to me*," she muttered. "We have both been through unimaginable things we aren't ready to share. That is that. You can stay the night, but you leave in the morning."

She opened the door and marched into the facility.

"What do we do?" Alejandro whispered in Spanish.

I shook my head, just now noticing the sweat under my shirt and tempted to take off my coat. "I don't... I don't know. I guess we don't—*have* to do anything anymore."

"What do you mean?"

I turned to him. "She won't come with us whether we need her or not. But it's not like we need her for a mission right *now*, like saving Dawson. We only need her once we're meant to... fulfill our destinies. We came here to recruit her for that because it was the only productive thing we could do."

"You heard what she said. She doesn't *want* to be the person we need her to be. She doesn't want to help. It sounds like it's for reasons only she can overcome, but she can't overcome them if she doesn't want to."

"Remember," I said, honestly reminding myself just as much as I was reminding him, "we tracked her down because it was the only step we could take while we were powerless against everything else, because we knew we were supposed to meet her eventually. We did what we could. Now we're stuck in another stupid waiting game until she's ready to join us."

"What if she never is?"

My chest clenched at the thought—but considering magic clearly had a bigger plan, I had to believe that things wouldn't come to that. If this girl really was supposed to help us, if she'd been given a gift nobody else in the world had, we would *need* her. And if we didn't have her during a global renovation...

I huffed, trudging past Alejandro and to the front door of the facility. "Then we pray we planted the right seeds today and that we planted them in time."

Twenty-Eight

I couldn't remember the last time I'd felt like such a failure; after twelve hours with our "ally", we still didn't even know her first name, let alone her power. And that "duel" had been nothing more than a tactic to make us shut up and follow her demands. Was there such a thing as reasoning with her after that? I couldn't wrap my head around the fact that someone who was just like us, *one* of us, didn't want to help her own people.

With morning, though, I had no choice but to. She wasn't coming back with us because she had been through things I knew nothing about, things she couldn't even bring herself to speak of— she simply wasn't ready. My only choice *was* to understand that; it was the only choice that would take us a step forward, no matter how small it was. Still, it wasn't any easier for me and Alejandro to walk into the entryway of the research facility as we prepared to leave, sliding our backpacks on.

We turned around to face our host. Miraculously, she wasn't scowling at us; she just looked at us like we were research colleagues about to traverse out onto the continent and gather more samples for tests.

"Thank you for letting us stay," Alejandro said in English, giving a respectful nod.

She returned it, eyes lingering on him like they were speaking telepathically. "Before you go..." she began. A flash of amber in her irises followed, pushing the weight of a truth spell onto me. "Swear that you won't tell anyone where I am."

"We won't," I said genuinely.

"I agree," Alejandro added. "We want you to be safe here."

"I have been for three years—*years*."

I looked at Alejandro, at the gentleness and sincerity in his warm-brown eyes that made him mean every word. There was... something new between him and this girl, something I hadn't witnessed the beginning of. Had they talked in private sometime between when we went to bed and now?

She does seem more agreeable toward him. And, well, I couldn't blame her. Remembering last night and her reaction to my magic ending the duel, the Hunter in me didn't have enough pieces to put a story together, but the girl in me reminded me that there was one.

"One more thing," I said.

She stayed quiet, stolid.

"I'm sorry—for when things got heated. I didn't want to *force* you into anything, it's just that... my family is my whole world, so anything that threatens them puts me in fight-or-flight mode. And I tend to fight."

I was pretty sure I was hallucinating it, but her harsh eyes softened on me. She slightly nodded in response. "Me, too. Thank you."

"Are you sure you don't want to see the base?" I asked. "In case you're tired of *having* to fight to survive when there's someplace that you don't?"

"It's safer for me to stay in a place where I do," she replied. "Then I never forget how to."

I wanted to argue and tell her that taking a break didn't automatically mean forgetting, but her mind was in a different place. She felt like she couldn't let go of that fighting instinct, and I understood that firsthand.

"Okay." I reluctantly looked at Alejandro beside me, our next step looming over us. "Then we should..."

He opened his mouth as if he were about to tell me something, but then his gaze landed on the girl in front of us. "You are a strong person," he began. "You let us stay when you didn't believe us. I don't know what happened during your past, but I'm sorry for it. I know that we're working for people who... have your story also, but I think that many of them—they aren't strong like you. I'm glad that we met you because now we can teach them to be like you."

Her brow softened a touch. Before she could give me too much time to read her, she hummed an acknowledgement.

They definitely *talked when I wasn't around. But about what?*

Well, if we weren't leaving on hostile terms because of it, I didn't have a reason to complain.

Alejandro offered me his gloved hand. I took it, meeting my eyes with the girl. "Thanks again," I said.

"'Runelle'."

Our gazes froze on her. She'd even pronounced the name with full French force. I tilted my head, too scared to ask her to repeat—

"'Runelle' is a special name I was given when I was little. I think that's the name you want."

Alejandro smiled in my peripheral vision, and I matched it. We'd built one bridge, after all. It wasn't her real name, but (what I hoped was) her name in the magic world was almost as good.

I didn't completely fail.

"It was nice to meet you, Runelle," I said, excited to try the name like it was a new toy.

With her lips straight, her eyes flashed amber, releasing me from the truth spell. "Keep your word," she said, stepping back.

"We will," Alejandro said, squeezing my hand.

I closed my eyes, orange seeping through my eyelids as the sensation of the ground beneath me blurred.

The time zone shift was the wildest we'd encountered since leaving Bouchard; while it was 8 in the morning when we left Runelle's, it was 11 in the morning the *previous* day in the Yukon. Alejandro needed to start taking bigger breaks as we traveled the length of South America and then from the bottom of Mexico to Cottonwood, Arizona. We could barely tell the difference between night and day at this point, so I only knew that it was 2 in the afternoon from the *panadería*'s clock mounted on the wall behind the pastry display counter.

"*Gracias*," Alejandro told the stout cashier with a bright smile, under the disguise of a burly dark-skinned man. Since Argentina a couple of hours ago, we'd eaten from the food supply we'd packed for the trip, but he'd been eager to go out and grab food the whole time. Now in Arizona, he was probably thrilled to be where so many people spoke his language (despite the dialectal differences). He pocketed the receipt the woman had given him and turned back to me with a nod toward an empty table in the middle of the bakery.

He let me have the chair facing the front windows, as being a hybrid gave me "more tools at my disposal". After sitting and dropping my paper bag of pan dulce onto the table, I let my eyes close and mind stop. I didn't even bother taking off my backpack, sinking into the padded chair and resting my chin on my hand. A woman somewhere beside me talked to someone in a perfect American accent about needing to get an oil change after this.

My eyes opened. American accent.

Cottonwood, Arizona. North America.

I'm back.

I hadn't been in the United States in over two months. I would've freaked out about being back in the country I was federally wanted in if not for the appearance spells we had on. We'd stolen our looks from a father and teenage daughter, both with feathery dark hair and matching brown eyes. It wasn't weird as long as I didn't remember that Alejandro was a year and a half younger than me.

"Is something wrong?" he asked me in Spanish with a foreign

mellow voice, setting his bag down beside him on the floor.

I shook my head, keeping my eyes on the edge of the table. "It's just weird to be back."

"Oh, right..." He leaned back in his chair, meaty fingers opening his paper bag of pastries. "I can't imagine what it must feel like after everything."

"I'm not even in the right state but I feel like I'm home," I said. "I'm three time zones away but I feel close. Probably because I am, I guess, in a way. I can be there almost instantly with you."

He hummed his acknowledgement. Eventually, he nodded to my bag. "Do you like pan dulce?"

"Yeah." My fists clenched on the table, and I swallowed. "I'm waiting for my stomach to settle first."

"You better not be helping me again," he said, tilting his head down at me.

"Well, if I am, you're welcome."

"Don't," he told me gently. "I don't need it, and that's not your job."

"Have you ever wondered if my help is the only reason you haven't passed out?" I asked lightheartedly.

He shrugged with one shoulder, biting into a generous-sized empanada as big as his new palm. —*You can think that. But your stomach needs to relax soon if we're going to teleport faster. If you can eat, please do.*—

I sighed, because he had a point, and I wasn't going to make the same mistake twice. I took out a pink concha shaped like a croissant with pink dough weaved between the brown, and bit off the end. For something called "sweet bread", it was fairly light, and my stomach was thankful.

"They did really well," Alejandro remarked in that mellow, warm voice. "Empanadas used to be my favorite. They're very different depending on where you go to in Spain. It depends on each region's local produce. In Valencia, my grandparents fill theirs with chorizo and corn. They used to have their own bakery, and I would sit in the middle of the store every day with free empanadas and tell everyone that walked by, 'Welcome to my grandparents' bakery! This is my grandparents' bakery!'"

He got a chuckle out of me with that one—and wow, did it lighten a load.

"Your grandparents gave you free empanadas?" I asked.

"No, there was one rule." He held up a finger, licking at the crumbs on the corner of his mouth. "I could only eat the ones I helped them make. That was how they tricked me into working there for free. I didn't realize it until I was eleven."

"That's smart!" I said, grinning. "What's your favorite now?"

"Mmm..." He waited until he swallowed his next bite. "They're called 'magdalenas'."

"'Magdalenas'?" I repeated, testing the word. There was a charm to it.

He nodded. "They have different names in other parts of Europe. It's... ah, I remember, 'madeleines' in France. In Spain, they're in the shape of a muffin, but they taste more... 'rustic'. I don't know how to describe them. My grandmother used olive oil to make them. She said that that made all the difference."

"Huh." *Madeleine*, I thought. "That's a really pretty name for a pastry."

He nodded, taking another bite of his empanada. "The baking history and culture are rich in Spain. It's why my family and I were so disappointed when my grandparents' bakery was condemned because of water damage. It wasn't a safe building anymore, and we couldn't afford to repair it and replace what had been damaged."

I pressed my lips together. "I'm sorry."

He waved it off, swallowing again. "My grandparents, we still bake together all the time. I met most of my friends because of my grandmother's pastries, everybody wanted to try them when I took them to school. Still, coming to places like this is a... how does English call it,"—he switched languages—"a 'treat', yes?"

I caught myself smiling again. This moment almost felt *too* normal, a sharp contrast to what we'd experienced over the last few days. I needed it, though, I needed this, something to remind me that I was alive and human and I had a life beyond my missions. I still had reasons to keep going, things to find beauty in.

Alejandro took the last bite of his empanada. I couldn't help but remember all the times Sarah, Breanne, Opal, and I went to Dom's Bakery or grabbed coffee together, sharing similar moments. How normal those had felt, too. How we'd bonded over the smallest things like who got the slice of cake with the prettiest whipped cream dollop, or dripping water onto our scrunched-up straw wrappers to make a "worm".

We were all in the same country again.

I took another bite of my concha.

"*Amiga*," Alejandro murmured, leaning forward on the small table. Despite his new burly status, his mellow voice had no trouble communicating his gentleness. "What's wrong?"

I shook my head.

"Please tell me."

Clearly I was doing worse than I thought if I couldn't maintain a cover as simple as *that.*

That's not good. I need to fix that.

"It's weird—and hard to be back," I eventually admitted.

He reserved a few seconds to himself. There was another pastry in his bag, but he didn't take it out. A moment passed before he nodded with confirmation at me.

"You miss home?"

I didn't want to verify, to accept it or the fact that he knew me that well.

"What if we visit your friends?"

My head shot back. "What?"

"We'll be disguised," he said, shrugging. "We'll visit them pretending to be your allies or other friends. We can say that we were sent to update them on your situation."

"Alejandro, that's..." I said, half of me earnestly seeking an argument for that—because more than anything, I did want to update the girls, let them know that Momma, Mr. Dawson, and I were still alive. "No, we'd be putting them in danger."

"How?"

I took in a tight breath, fighting to maintain my logic above all else. —*We still don't know how CSIS found us in Watrous, and the fact that it hasn't happened anywhere else terrifies me. Nobody was supposed to know that we were in Canada! Now you want to go back to my hometown, where everything started, where the government is probably waiting for me to go back to?*—

—*We'll be disguised. If anyone finds us, we'll put on the invisibility cloaks and teleport.*—

I opened my mouth before our silence could seem awkward

to anyone, keeping my voice low. "We would still be associating them in all of this—"

"Aren't they already?"

"What?"

—*Last year, when you were a target—weren't all of you targets because you knew something about the Delphines?*—

—*That was just about the Delphines, that wasn't related to being a lead to the Atera descendant.*—

In full honesty, there was only one reason the girls *weren't* in immediate danger already: if not for Jak deleting all of the body cam footage from that morning at the hideout, Caldwell would've no doubt seen Opal and Breanne. We probably would've never been able to teleport out of the country before he announced their capture and demanded us to surrender as a ransom for their lives.

It still worries me that he hasn't done that yet with Dawson, either.

"I have a question," Alejandro said. "If we meet somewhere nobody knows about, who will know we were ever there?"

"The same way they found us in Watrous."

"Then why wasn't that the situation for everywhere else we traveled to?"

"That's what scares me so much!" I hissed. "Why there, why not anywhere else—and if Watrous could happen, why not with my friends?"

"Because you know the places that nobody else knows how to get into."

I paused, giving myself the room to think. Logically speaking, especially if we were disguised and teleported straight into someplace not even the government knew about... would we leave behind a trail at all? Couldn't we cover up our tracks faster in a place

I knew like the back of my hand?

Watrous, a cruel voice taunted in my head. That echoed memory almost sounded familiar.

Unless... what if this place already had high security and would give us time to teleport out before someone breached the front doors?

This is a bad idea. This is an extraordinarily bad idea. Every fiber of my being screamed that—at least, every rational fiber. Because, unfortunately, the fibers that missed my best friends, that missed home, outnumbered my rationality. We'd be fast. We'd be somewhere private and secure. If nobody knew that we were visiting them, no government force could catch us in time.

They're the only sisters I've ever had.

You could put them and the entire school in danger.

Minutes. *That's all I want. They deserve to know we're okay.*

If anyone does find out, we'll "take care of" them. Just like how we did in Watrous.

Nobody's on our tail. I'm taking advantage of that while I can.

"Use the Wi-Fi and open the satellite map on your phone," I told Alejandro. With every second that passed, a plan solidified more and more in my head, and a backup plan formed with it in case all went south. "I know where we can meet."

CHAPTER

Twenty-Nine

Half an hour later, the ground formed again beneath me—this time, with a touch of something plush. I opened my eyes: the familiar dirt, twigs, and pine needles of the Callistro Forest. When I dragged my eyes up, the Callistro Academy manor sat in all its glory a two-minute walk away.

I was home.

Home.

Nashville, Tennessee had had plenty of appearances to choose from for our "undercover agent" disguises. Then came the trip to Capperson, North Carolina—the easiest and shortest jump of the entire journey.

Now I faced the manor of my old school. I'd asked Sarah to cover for me on the off chance that Caldwell wouldn't expose me to the public first, and I was about to find out if that had been for nothing. I'd convinced myself that I'd made my peace with my best friends all knowing. It was easier to believe now that I looked like a middle-aged CEO in slacks, a blouse, and a long black coat; I wouldn't have to face them as myself. Alejandro disguised as a blond man with a beige winter jacket and belted dress pants helped, too. All I had to do was maintain my composure once I saw the girls for the first time in two and a half months.

"Come on," I told Alejandro at the thought, gesturing to the tree stump sitting on our right. "It's down here."

We opened the stump like a compact mirror, exposing the long cobblestone staircase underneath. A cold, damp draft blew up into our faces, and I pulled my long coat tighter around myself. Alejandro let me take the lead, following me in before pulling the entrance shut above us.

I didn't get that many steps down before noticing the dim glow of the lanterns down the tunnel.

The lights are still on. From when Mr. Dawson first turned them on.

I swallowed the emotional breath that tried to escape; I needed every ounce of focus I could grasp.

"Nobody knows about these passageways," I whispered to Alejandro as we descended the stairs, our steps echoing far down the stone corridor and making me wince. "Caralyn Callistro built them for Adara, so now I need to contact Breanne and tell her how to come down with—the girls."

I cursed the way my voice faltered at the end of that statement, the way my body hesitated when we reached the bottom of the staircase.

Alejandro placed his now light-skinned hand on my shoulder, all too knowing of where my head was at. "You deserve this," he assured me again with his new gruff voice. "It will be okay, they won't hate you."

He didn't understand... Federally, magic was legal in Spain; he didn't have best friends who couldn't know who he was, and I wondered if he ever had.

I closed my eyes, trying to brace myself. Even these old, musty passageways felt like home. They were, I told myself. The way the humidity clung to my cheeks, the cold blasting against my face and challenging me to move quickly to get to where I needed to go—everything was heart-throbbingly familiar.

—*Miss Shaw?*—

I almost hoped—actually, I prayed—that she hadn't heard me, that she wasn't even in range. Then a high, clear voice answered, —*Hello...?*—

I bit the inside of my cheek. Sweet little Breanne's voice. It didn't feel real, *her* telepathic voice in my head didn't feel real. How had we ever gotten here?

I spent a moment gathering myself before sending my reply. —*I'm Agent Carmela Jordan, here with my partner, Nathan Garcia. Your friend Emma sent us with an update.*—

Alejandro raised a fawn-brown eyebrow at me with a silent question, making our first right turn with me. I nodded, verifying that I had a connection.

Silence rang on the other end. It grew louder with every step we took down the passageway, on our way to the one that ran behind the Atera family tree in the Hunter's Room. I imagined Breanne running herself in circles trying to explain to Sarah and

Opal what the voice in her head had told her.

I wish I had time to visit Cara and Steven, too. Or even Moren or Ingrid.

Alejandro and I turned down the second and last right turn available. Our target passageway was dead ahead. Halfway down the tunnel, Breanne's voice came back: —*How do I find you, where can we meet, are you in the school?*—

—*Down in the Hunter's Room,*— I began as Alejandro and I reached the archway of our destination, —*there's a secret passageway that runs behind the Atera family tree. Slide the tree to the side, and we'll be under the light at the end of the tunnel.*—

—*We're coming. Give us two minutes.*—

Two minutes. That was all I had.

As we stepped into the passageway running behind my family tree, the light that had once illuminated Caralyn Callistro's framed documents hung at the right end. I didn't dare look to the left, like my mere glance would bring my friends straight through the entrance. It felt like it could.

Alejandro and I walked all the way down, landing just below the light. We took off our backpacks and set them down against the wall. I exhaled, pressing my hand to my racing heart.

"It's okay," Alejandro tried to tell me again—in English this time. His blond hair shone brightly under the light, contrasting his now gravelly voice. "They are your best friends. Be happy."

"What if they all *do* know who I really am now?" I whispered with a quiver I couldn't control. And if I didn't figure out how to control it within the next ninety seconds, our cover story would be blown before we could even step into it. "I'm not Emma right now. They'll have no problem exposing what they really think about me to a stranger."

"Then... you'll know who is really your best friend," he replied slowly, careful with his English. He gave me a subtle smile. "Sarah stayed your friend. She wasn't mad."

"No, but..." I hugged myself tighter, swallowing the words. There's a reason irrational fears are called "irrational": no matter how much logic and reasoning our brains muster up against them, the chemicals inciting them flourish nonetheless. Almost everything is powerless against them, including how much I wanted to be excited to see my best friends again.

"You have been friends for... so long," Alejandro said as I put my hands into my coat pockets. "You don't know when you will see them again. You can't talk to them when you are Emma. Try to enjoy it now."

He had a point: I had to maintain my cover in front of them at *all* costs. I couldn't cry unless I had a cover story for that, too, and I definitely couldn't hug them. That stung. But for our sakes, even for my friends' sakes in a removed way, this had to be the absolute best performance of my life.

I have to. I have to. There's no other choice now—

Grinding echoed from the other side of the passageway. I whirled around. Three girls in crimson Callistro uniforms shuffled inside before sliding the entrance shut behind them.

The smallest of them—with bone-straight blond hair, a soft jaw, and the roundest pair of blue-hazel eyes I'd ever seen—dared a step forward. "Hello?"

C H A P T E R

THIRTY

No matter how tightly I clenched my jaw, it shook. No matter how badly my feet itched to run to my best friends to hug them, they couldn't. No matter how terrible a job I was already doing at maintaining my cover, I had to fight it and do better. For their sakes, for my sake, for Bouchard's sake at this point, because I was still a Hunter even if I was training in a different underground room now.

The cobblestone walls of the passageway seemed to close in on us as the girls trod toward me and Alejandro. Suddenly I had trouble breathing through the thick dampness, trying to solidify myself in Carmela Jordan's shoes. I fought tooth and nail to not grab the locket around my neck, reminding myself that the appearance spell had "removed it".

Stopping a few feet away, Breanne slightly looked up at me with innocent eyes, tacitly asking a hundred questions. Sarah stood three inches taller than her on her left with impeccable bronze skin, heart-shaped jaw firmly set and framed by her thick ebony waves. Her defined pear-green eyes were as unreadable as fine print from a mile away. On Breanne's right, Opal was an even combination of the two, like she wanted to trust someone who'd said her best friend had sent them but her training was wisely telling her otherwise. Those purple eyes on her porcelain face were lifeless in the dim light, almost like they *were* contacts like everyone at the school believed, not the tell that she was supposed to be a high priestess someday.

I miss you, I thought over and over again. *I'm sorry. I'm sorry. I miss us. Please don't hate me. Hug me. Invite me up to the room, to do homework together or get into the teaching schedules again and manipulate test dates—*

I ripped out those thoughts and plugged in Carmela's backstory. Like always, I wasn't Emmalynn Atera to them. I wasn't even Emmalynn Marie; I was spontaneous Agent Jordan.

Breanne opened her thin lips to speak, but Sarah held out her arm in front of her. "Emma sent you?" she asked, just low enough so that the passageway didn't carry her voice with the acoustics. But the even tone and lack of physical tells told me everything I needed to know: Sarah Duncan was practically born for the Hunter career, and she was hunting right now.

"Yes," I answered simply.

"Our Emmalynn Marie sent you two to update us?"

I blinked to suppress my surprise at the use of my old last name. *Either she's protecting me from Agents Jordan and Garcia because she doesn't know that it's okay for them to know... or she's protecting me from Breanne and Opal because they don't know.*

"She and her family are finally in a position to let you know, yes," I replied, testing the waters.

"So she and her mom are safe?" Sarah asked.

Only mentioning Momma when she knows I left with Dad and Becca, too... Which group is she protecting me from?

I did know she was testing me, seeing if I'd reply with the right specifics. A fixed question like that closed off other answers—answers I wasn't supposed to know if I wasn't an ally.

"Both Emma and her mother are safe," I replied with a firm nod. "We can't tell you where for the sake of their safety, but they're protected."

"Interesting." Sarah's tone softened so slightly that I was pretty sure you only could have heard it if you'd remembered to pay attention. "She told us her mom would make the trip back to let us know they'd made it out okay."

I let a subtle smile trace my lips. "Considering Amy Marie's background as a Master Hunter and an instructor here, Miss Duncan, I don't believe she'd be so careless."

Breanne and Opal stiffened. I wanted to believe that they were seeing the signs that they could trust me and "Agent Garcia", but they were following Sarah's lead, and she hadn't been fully convinced yet. Good, because any Hunter with access to Callistro's records could have found that information.

"True," she said. She tilted her head, letting an ebony wave fall over her shoulder. "So they met you two wherever they are now, Agents Nathan..."

"Nathan Garcia," Alejandro said with his new gruff voice.

"And Carmela Jordan," I added.

She raised her chin slightly. "Why? Were you one of the agents on our cruise last semester, so they trusted you?"

The question caught me off guard until the pieces clicked: the cruise and Carmela. The whole reason I'd picked this name for this meeting was that night of the ball on the *Elina*, where my class had been tested on our method acting and had to stick to our roles no matter what. I'd been Carmela Jordan, a spontaneity-loving teaching assistant. I guess Sarah *had* seen my card, or at least caught a glimpse of it.

Had Breanne or Opal?

I squared my eyes solely onto Sarah to send the signal. "I almost wish I was, but I don't like planned trips. They're always more fun when they're spontaneous."

"That makes sense," she said, her eyes starting to soften. "So do we call you 'Agent'? Or..."—her voice slowed just enough for me to catch it—"what do people *usually* call you?"

"We *address* them as 'Agent Jordan' and 'Agent Garcia'," Breanne whispered, like she should've known (and she did). Sarah only shrugged at her before locking her eyes with mine again.

A nickname...? She's looking for what people usually call—?

It dawned on me: Sarah and I had been on the ballroom floor at the same time that night, each with a gentleman who'd asked for a dance. Johan, I remembered. I'd told him my name was "Carmela" but that people called me "Carmie". Sarah must have overheard at some point. She was verifying my identity.

Alejandro glimpsed me with a silent question, sealing the natural confusion everyone else in the passageway had. I played along with Sarah, meeting her gaze. "Well, my friends call me 'Carmie', if that's what you mean," I said, letting my eyes move to the other girls. "But Miss Shaw is right, 'Agent Jordan' is appropriate here."

Sarah's lips subtly curved upward, eyes brightening with recognition. She knew. Now she was my best friend.

I can't believe she remembered that.

"I think we should let them talk." She turned toward Breanne and Opal. "Who else has questions?"

Why isn't Breanne or Opal secretly using a truth spell to verify that we're trustworthy? I mean, I was thankful for it because any one question could back me and Alejandro into confessing who we were, but at this point in our lives, a truth spell was practically the first step in interacting with anyone new.

"I have a question," Breanne said immediately—solidly. That was a bold surprise. "Can we talk to Emma? Or did she send anything with you?"

"It's *extremely* dangerous for you to make contact right now," I told her. "Even this meeting is a risk I didn't want to take, but she insisted."

"So she knew about this passageway?" Opal asked with dark brows knit together.

"She discovered it just before the incident in December," I replied. Blatant lie, but if Breanne and Opal really didn't know about Emmalynn Atera, I wasn't risking anything.

"So you know about that morning, too," Breanne noted. I wasn't used to such a direct tone from her, especially not with a stranger, let alone an agent. "What really happened?"

Her own test. Seriously, how had my smallest best friend grown up so much in the last two and a half months and I hadn't been here to see it?

"Well, it's true," I said a little softer. "Emma and Amy are associated with the Ateras and their daughter, and they are now formally wanted by the US Government for the information they're harboring about them. The Delphines and William Bleu are dead. Thomas Dawson was captured and is now being held captive by the government."

"Can you get him out?" Opal pleaded. "He's my uncle, I can't believe they haven't killed him yet!"

"We're trying, Miss Dubois," I told her with a melancholy I at least didn't have to fake. "Believe me, our operatives have been trying to figure out a plan that'll not only pinpoint his location but also yield a realistic and probable escape. If we don't approach this as perfectly as we can, we risk his life and our agents' lives."

"You have to hurry," she urged, small lips stuck in a frown. "If you wait too long, he *will* die."

"We understand," I said gently. "But Emma wants you to know that she and her mother are okay and found trustworthy allies to help. And she's been anxious to know how things have been doing over here with you all—what happened after the three of them disappeared."

I braced myself for the worst, fully expecting to hear it. As if to confirm that I had every reason to be worried, the girls looked at each other without letting a single word by. The speaker role seemed to pass between them like a grenade until Breanne held Sarah's gaze.

"We know they're clean now," she mumbled.

Sarah crossed her arms, taking a deep breath. "Breanne and Opal got back here safely. I told them about Headmistress Marie's plan with Mr. Dawson. After that, it was a waiting game through break until second semester began."

"An awful waiting game," Opal muttered, lightly shaking her head.

"The school board got a temporary replacement until they found our new headmistress," Sarah said. "Same thing with Mr. Dawson's teaching position."

New headmistress. The words felt like a punch to the gut for some reason.

"But the three of us have gone through the semester kind of just hoping they'd all... show up again. We haven't heard anything until now. Everyone's been asking about what happened to them, but we literally don't know..."

Those words sagged a little, like she was tacitly begging me to break character so I could tell her. Part of me wanted to.

I'm sorry, I almost said.

"Are they coming back soon?" Opal asked.

I looked at Alejandro like he had insight on that, but we were just as clueless as each other.

"It's not safe," he answered. He kept his English simple, sticking to structure that he knew without hesitance was correct. "You need to believe that, please."

"There's a chance Emma won't be able to come back for the rest of the year," I forced myself to say—more so for myself than anyone else, because I needed to keep that in mind.

"She has to," Breanne argued. "She won't be able to graduate next year if she can't catch up on this semester."

It'd been hard enough to stay on top of schoolwork while I *was* going to Callistro. Catching up on an entire semester before June was out of the cards unless I doubled up on my coursework at Bouchard, but I wasn't sure if there was even a point to that. Once the entire country knew my name—and it almost sounded like it still didn't somehow—high school graduation was off the table completely.

"Believe me," I told Breanne, "the situation is way less than ideal for her, too. She wants to come back as soon as possible, but she can't risk involving the three of you in the government's agenda. A Grand Hunter pack was one thing, but this is now a matter of national security. If you get involved because of any one back door, we risk pulling in a lot more innocent people."

"All we've *ever* gotten are secrets," Opal stated. "I get it, I get why, but she doesn't get that we want to fight this *with* her."

Her voice grew until it transferred into a high lilt that I'd only ever heard from her when she was lying. This time, though, I couldn't tell if that was the case or if it was her emotions rising like mine were the longer I stood in front of them, having to lie to their faces like old times.

Sarah's arms loosened around herself as her eyes fell to the concrete ground. She'd used Opal's same argument the night I left. I guess my friends didn't *have* to know the full truth to still want to carry my burdens with me.

"She does understand that," I assured Opal. "But it's not about just you three anymore. The scales are much bigger. So are the stakes."

"So there's a chance we'll never get her back?" she said, crossing her arms.

"It's unlikely. But there's always that chance, yes. I think all of you knew that as soon as you signed up for this career."

Silence settled over the damp passageway like a wet blanket.

And with that, the atmosphere shifted over an edge, like we'd used up all of our words and there was no going back. After all, with so little to say without endangering anyone, we really had no choice but to keep it simple and blunt. Which meant...

No. I need more time with them. I can't go yet.

"You're *sure* she's safe?" Breanne said—loyal to the boldness I wasn't used to from her. "And nobody's tracked her?"

"She traveled an impossible path," Alejandro answered next to me with a faint smirk. I was surprised by his bravery but thankful for it, and for the authority his new voice carried.

"Okay." Breanne's small shoulders sank, and she started picking at the light hairs on her wrists. "Can... can you take a message back for me?"

"Sure," I said.

To my surprise, when she looked down at her picking, she immediately transitioned into rubbing her arm instead. "Please tell her I'm sorry. Make sure she knows how *deeply* sorry I am about that morning. Please. She'll know what it means."

Except I didn't—what did she have to apologize for? I was the one who owed her an apology for that morning, for being stupid enough to leave an enchanted bracelet with Alexa's magic in it on my nightstand for her to ignorantly put on last summer. If not for that, she likely would've never had to deal with that morning with Opal in the first place. Why was she sorry?

"Will do," I assured her anyway.

"Wait," Opal said timidly. She glanced at Sarah and Breanne, both giving her a small nod of encouragement. Opal stepped up and took out a small gray fabric bag from her blazer pocket. "I got her something in case I ever would see her again. *Please* make sure she gets this, it's really important. She can wear it with her locket and have another piece of home."

The plea in her purple eyes twisted my stomach. I wanted to tell her that it was me. I was fine, I already had her gift.

"I'll give it to her the second we get back," I said, taking the bag and offering a smile.

Opal looked back at Breanne, who looked at Sarah. Anticipation stretched among the five of us, as if we all *did* know who was really standing here right now and we didn't want to let go yet. I'd prepared myself to go as long as a year without seeing my best friends, but I wasn't sure that seeing them so much sooner was the blessing I'd thought it would be. Maybe I *would* have to go a year this time.

"Thanks for updating us." Breanne stepped back, prompting Opal to follow. "Please take care of Emma and her mom—and Mr. Dawson as soon as you can."

"We will," I said, because I couldn't bring myself to give any other answer.

My heart clenched, jaw threatening to quiver again, as my friends started to turn around. Right when I stopped myself from reaching out to them, from squeezing in one more word between us, Sarah took a breath in, stopping them.

"I've..." she began, half-turned, "I've been thinking a lot lately about how things used to be. We barely go out anymore now because it's not the same without Em. She left so much... behind." She locked her eyes with mine, intention burning in them. A sad half smile touched her lips as she sniffed, like she was reminiscing. "Like when we'd go to Dom's Bakery. She loved that place. But she had to leave that"—she let her eyes shift sideways, tilting her head—"behind, too. I guess we eventually stopped going there because it was too hard without her."

The Language of Ambiguity, chapter five: turning one word in your sentence into a homonym so you can say one thing around others but your receiver will understand something else. Sarah was speaking in code.

Behind. Dom's Bakery. Going with me.

Got it.

My stare drifted between the three of them to let Sarah know that I'd gotten her code but my words weren't one themselves: "You know what, if we can, we'll stop by and pick something up for her. We'll tell her it's from you guys."

"She'd love that," Opal murmured with a smile. "Thanks. Their cronuts were her favorite."

She remembered.

"Noted," I said. "Thanks for your updates, too. She'll be glad to have them."

I watched the three of them walk down the passageway to the other end before Alejandro and I grabbed our backpacks from the floor. I took him with me to the archway on the left to start heading back.

—So,— he began in Spanish, —*we are going to another bakery?*—

—*It's good timing,*— I replied. —*You can recharge more, and I can see what Sarah has to tell me.*—

C H A P T E R

Thirty-One

I'd missed Dom's cronuts more than I'd realized. They were definitely a nice precursor to the conversation we were about to have with Sarah—whatever she wanted to talk about.

This is the first conversation we're having one on one since I told her the truth, I thought as Alejandro and I left through the back door. The cozy private area back here ran behind the stores in a wide strip of burgundy cement, pairs of benches neatly placed down it with evergreens lining the edge. I found the bench I'd sat on with Jak after I'd gotten back from the cruise, a few yards in front of us. Alejandro and I picked the one across from it so we could see the open road, Main Street, far down at the end of the area. We set our stuff down by our feet, and I exhaled my nerves.

"I have to warn you," Alejandro said with his gruff voice in

Spanish, taking out a cronut from his white paper bag, "I'm ready to cast a sleeping spell and a forgetting spell on her if this doesn't go well."

"I get it," I said, shivering as I leaned against the hard wood of the bench. My heavy coat still existed under the spell, but the thin appearance of the long black one made it harder to believe and feel it. "But I bet you that she just wants to talk before I have to disappear again."

I straightened with remembrance, facing him more. "Don't forget, only use Spanish. Half a dozen people in Capperson speak it, so if anyone walks by, we should be okay."

"Good, I have waited this entire trip to hear you say that," he remarked, chewing. He brushed a few blond strands away from his light face. "I still can't believe that Sarah figured out it was you because of a name... Also, there is *too much* sugar in this."

I chuckled. I actually couldn't help but regret a little that we were still under the appearance spells; I wanted my last conversation with Sarah to be *completely* real, face to face as ourselves. She knew that it was me, but it wasn't the same.

Steps thudded on the burgundy cement, and I looked up. Sarah strolled toward us like a runway model, ebony mermaid waves subtly blowing back under her white wool cap. With a mint-green duffel bag over her shoulder, she kept her hands in the white winter coat she'd gotten in Greece during the cruise, nude-colored wedges carrying her strong steps.

All I could do was stare until she reached the bench across from us. A bittersweet smile pulled apart her mauve lips, pear-green eyes glistening.

"Hi," she whispered.

That was it: the straw that broke the stone dam behind my eyes. My nose stung as my vision blurred, because my best friend was talking to *me*. Not Emmalynn Marie, but Emmalynn Atera, and she still loved me.

"Hi," I whispered back in a voice that I hated wasn't my own.

She stretched out her arms when I stood. I threw myself around her, inhaling the sweet perfume she'd probably refreshed herself with before leaving. Despite her strong grip, her chest expanded with a deep breath that almost pushed me away.

A minute must have passed before we pulled back. With a bronze knuckle, she wiped away a tear that had yet to escape, sniffing with a red nose. I followed suit with my thumb under my eye, inhaling to control myself.

"Is Spanish okay?" I whispered in the language, exhaling shakily. "To be safe?"

"Yes, of course," she replied, briefly glimpsing the boy—or, I guess, man—sitting behind me. "You've been busy."

"You've been loyal," I said, almost like I couldn't believe it. "I don't think I understand—do Breanne and Opal... not know?"

"No. After the news broadcasted what happened at South Mountains State Park, I really thought Caldwell would expose you and your mom, and Dawson—but none of you were mentioned. It was all about the Hunters, the Delphines, and William."

What...? But he knew we'd been there—his Hunters, at the *very* least, knew who'd really been down there that morning. And I highly doubted that they were protecting us because they were secretly allies, too.

"I suppose that's..." I began, trying to find the right word for it, "good."

Way too good to be true—which meant that it was.

"I think so," Sarah said. "But... I'm pretty sure you don't want to relive what happened."

I took in a deep breath, the memories whizzing by in a warning. "No."

"Then let's sit."

"Are you sure you can be here right now without suspicion?" I asked, taking my spot beside Alejandro.

Sarah took the seat across from me, setting her duffel bag down next to her on the bench. "You're actually part of the reason that I can. My parents are picking me up for the weekend, but you coming back as... this and mentioning 'Emma and her mom', I pretended that I needed to process it. So I left early to 'think'."

I gave her a tight smile. The guilt over how I couldn't have this honest conversation with Breanne or Opal yet stung as much as my nose did.

"So you saw my card that night on the cruise?"

"I picked it up after Anthony took you to the deck. It must have fallen out of your dress pocket. Before that, though, I overheard you tell the boy you were dancing with that you went by 'Carmie'." A grateful smile warmed her face. "Thank God. Those two tests were what told me you were *you*. I wouldn't have been able to tell otherwise."

"I think you would have," I said. "You're too perceptive to things like that."

"Except for the biggest plot twist of the century apparently." She scoffed under her breath. "I've looked back so many times since you told me. A lot of things make sense now. But it also still feels impossible."

I nodded, unsure of what to say. I was nowhere near used to talking about Emmalynn Atera with my best friend, in a different language or not.

Sarah nodded at the blond man sitting next to me, arching a brow. "So who's this?"

"He's in disguise, too," I said, eyeing Dom's back door in the distance on my left for anyone who might decide to walk out. I comforted myself with the probability that there was no one in these stores right now who spoke Spanish. "This is Alejandro. Believe it or not, he's a sixteen-year-old boy."

"I turn seventeen next month," Alejandro added gruffly, like it was imperative that Sarah knew that.

"Oh," she said simply, her eyes widening slightly. "Wow. Magic is crazy... Um, Em, where is Jak?"

It was comforting to know that her priorities hadn't changed that much since I'd left.

"He's safe with us, too. I can't tell you where, but he's okay. He's actually been anxious to know about Adrien and Wyatt."

I wondered if it was the right topic to bring up, considering that the last I knew, Sarah was planning on formally breaking up with Adrien, but she didn't seem fazed. Instead, she blinked as if remembering him for the first time in a while. "They're good. About the same. Adrien and I broke up in January but Breanne's still with Wyatt. They were really surprised that Jak's parents were dead, but apparently the shock about Alexa and William hit Redway pretty hard. Nobody knew that they were hunting, let alone that they were Alexa Delphine and William Bleu—you know, since they worked at Redway under aliases. Adrien and Wyatt are just scared for Jak. I think a part of them thinks he's dead."

That made sense. At least Sarah could tell them the good news.

"I wish we could visit them and tell them," I said, glancing at Alejandro. I stuck my hands between my thighs for added warmth. "Is what you said about how Callistro is doing true? And how you guys are doing?"

"Yes. Obviously everyone is making crazy theories, but there's nothing linking you to what happened that morning, so nobody has made the connection. As for Breanne and Opal..."

Uh oh. Why was she slowing down? Why was she hesitating?

"Breanne feels so guilty about that morning," Sarah said dejectedly. "She feels like she could have done more, she could have fought—she could have stopped you and your mom from needing to leave."

"No," I said quickly, "that's not—there was *nothing* she could have done about what happened."

"We told her that," Sarah said, shrugging. "But your letter said that you were friends with"—her voice dropped to a whisper—"*Tristan Atera's descendant* and you knew where she was hiding, and you didn't want to involve us in that. That's what hurt her. She felt like she was never someone you could trust with that information. And, as useless as we were the first week of sophomore year, she felt worse because even if she had known, she would have been too scared to do anything. Just like she was during all of fall semester last year. She feels like all she has *ever* done is be afraid, especially after what happened during freshman year with her ex-boyfriend. She's capable of doing more but her fear holds her back. So she's been spending this semester toughening up."

That was why she'd been bolder toward me and Alejandro

than I'd expected. Breanne Shaw, of all girls. Pride swelled in my chest, drawing a smile on my face.

"Wow," I whispered.

"I know, I'm proud of her, too. Opal's been... stuck since she found out about Dawson. She's definitely not over losing her uncle *and* her best friend on the same day."

"Is she okay?"

"She tries to be." The ground stole her gaze, like she had to recall the details first before she could tell me the story. "Since the Delphines are dead, she isn't scared of anything now except for Dawson's safety. She's found her place as the school gossip girl again, that keeps her busy. But she has a fake smile every day..." She looked up at me, her voice falling a level. "Is what you said true? About trying to save him?"

I sighed, looking at Alejandro for help. He pursed his lips.

"It's really complicated right now," he eventually said. "We can only tell you that magic revealed that he's in custody, probably at the White House. We can't rescue him until we know his exact location and that we can get him *and* escape without being caught. But magic also warned us that saving him right now would lead to his death."

"How?" Sarah asked incredulously, a divot forming between her perfectly shaped brows.

"It causes an order of events that kills him," Alejandro replied. "That's all we know."

"I'm guessing you know everything about the Ateras, too."

"I'm a friend. That's, um... that's all I can say."

"I really hate to say this," I told Sarah, "but there's a *lot* more that I can't tell you because it's twice as dangerous as telling you my real identity. It's not just about me or my family anymore, we're protecting a lot more people now. I think we're even protecting Callistro by keeping things confidential. Can you trust me when I say that?"

She sighed, gripping the edge of the bench. "Yes."

"I'm telling the truth."

She nodded. "I know. That's why I convinced Breanne and Opal not to put you under a truth spell when they thought it was a good idea. As soon as Breanne said 'Carmela Jordan', I suspected something. I'm glad I did—they would have exposed you both in a heartbeat."

This girl was still protecting me even when I wasn't around. I *knew* I'd picked the right friend to confess to.

"Hey, how did you find those underground passageways?" she asked dubiously. "Caralyn Callistro didn't have any riddles about those."

Oh boy. That was a story in itself.

"I don't think I have time to explain," I replied. "Let's just say that Caralyn was an ally of magic."

Sarah paused, a moment going by before she leaned back. "You're kidding me," she deadpanned. "When it started as a *Hunter* school? When everyone there wants to destroy magic?"

"*Now*, yes," I said, right when a couple strolled out of the café next to Dom's. They were heading for Main Street. We were behind them, but I lowered my voice just in case. "But that was never Caralyn's intention."

"Then why—?" Her eyes narrowed in disbelief. "She built an *entire* school for Hunters to hide her secret? That's... extreme."

I tilted my head. "What do you mean?"

"She could have written her secret in a letter or a journal somewhere and had her family keep it safe or something. An entire infrastructure feels like an extra mile, and overcompensation."

I opened my mouth to respond with Caralyn's two documents until I realized that I couldn't—because I actually didn't know the answer to that "why" question. After all, Cara and Steven had found out the truth from a journal that had been passed down Caralyn's line. Caralyn *had* decided to take the discreet route; why go overkill and build a whole school—the *first-ever* school—for Hunters?

I can't believe I've never thought about that before. I wonder if this is—somehow—hidden somewhere in the first copy of her autobiography EunJi gave me.

But I couldn't read through it and see until we got back to Bouchard...

I pressed my lips together, knowing what was next. "Maybe you can figure that out while I'm gone."

Sarah stared at me, realizing that this conversation couldn't last forever. "How much longer will you be gone?"

"I don't know. But believe me—it was my dream to graduate from Callistro with you guys. It still is. I don't want to give it up that easily."

"Good." Then, she looked down at her knees. I was about to tell her not to leave yet, that we probably had a couple of minutes before we had to get back, until her duffel bag sitting next to her stole her attention.

"Um..." she whispered, unzipping it. A white envelope sat on top of a book and a stack of folded clothes. "I have something I wanted to give you in case I saw you again, too. This was supposed to be your Christmas present last year, but I guess it worked out better this way."

She took the envelope and then the book—a yellow book with a blank cover—which she handed to me first. "Because journaling is so important to you. After everything that happened on the cruise, I thought that this would help you sort all that out since your green one is full."

My fingers tightened around the thick journal. My best friend knew me too well.

"Thank you," I told her with a stuck smile, resting her gift in my lap. "Mr. Dawson got me one for Christmas, too, but I already filled it. So it did work out better this way."

Sarah's smile faltered. Then drooped. "That's the, um..." She tentatively extended the envelope to me. "That's... the other thing. I think there's something he wanted you and your mom to know."

I took a second to reach for the envelope, like taking it would make it disintegrate. No, there was no way...

To Amy and Emma

It was impossible to mistake this handwriting. I'd read it every time I needed a pass to go off campus sophomore year. I'd read it in the notes in the margins of my essays and assignments last semester. I'd read it on the gift tag when I unwrapped my journal in December.

"We found it hidden in his dorm," Sarah told me. "When we went back to the school to grab your stuff like you told us to."

My eyes traced every letter in Mr. Dawson's handwriting. How old was this? Why had he never given it to us?

"None of us read it," Sarah quickly assured me. "Whatever's inside belongs to you and your mom. I'm glad you finally have it."

"Yeah," I mouthed, having to clear my throat and force volume into it. "Thanks..."

Alejandro's stare weighed heavily on me in my peripheral vision. When the pressure behind my eyes built, I blinked it away. "Thank you," I told Sarah again, trying to muster a smile until I looked up and caught her teary gaze.

She only had one reason to cry, which meant I now had two.

No. Don't. Please—

She sniffed, pulling back the sleeve of her white coat and checking a golden watch. "Okay," she whispered, wiping a stray tear from her cheek, "I have to go. My parents are picking me up soon and we always meet at the fountain."

No, I thought again. *I can't let go yet. I can't let go again.*

But when Alejandro stood, I did, too.

There was still too much I wanted to say, too much Sarah had to know. She now knew *me*, she needed to know everything I'd ever lied to her about because of magic, didn't she?

She grabbed her duffel bag from the bench and slung it over her shoulder, then held out her arms again. I had to admit to myself that I was stalling. I was about to accept her hug until I saw my hands, how they weren't my own. I couldn't let our goodbye happen like this.

I looked over Sarah's shoulder. There wasn't anyone in the back area. My gaze traveled along the line of stores on my left, searching for security cameras. Five total.

I closed my eyes, picturing each camera in my mind. *Desiste.*

I faced Alejandro to tell him, "Just for a second."

Converte, I said over myself, reversing the appearance spell. My hands faded to a slightly lighter skin tone, their subtle wrinkles melting away. I couldn't imagine what the transformation looked like on my face for Sarah—until I looked up at her relieved stun.

"See?" I whispered in English.

Her lips stretched into a bittersweet smile. "Hi, Emmy."

I wrapped my arms around her, letting the tears grip my body with full force. By the way Sarah shook in my hold, she was doing the same thing. I couldn't smell her perfume anymore because of the sobs congesting me, but her embrace was just as sweet.

"I missed you," I rasped.

"I missed you, too."

All too quickly, she broke away, taking in a sharp breath. "Okay," she breathed, wiping her flushed cheeks dry, "I have to go, you probably do, too. Um..." She moved her duffel bag strap farther up her shoulder, ambling backwards. "I'll... I'll see you later, okay?"

"I promise," I told her, swallowing another bout of tears. "We'll be back soon."

"Please."

Immediately, like she couldn't afford another word, she turned around and hurried down to the street. Instinct snapped awake in me, and I cast her appearance over myself before she could turn left and disappear around the building.

I deeply sighed, replaying the last few moments in my head. At least I got to see my best friend and she got to see me. At least I got to do that with one of them.

"*Amiga?*" a soft yet gravelly voice said beside me.

I looked down at the letter in my hands—my now bronze and

perfectly manicured hands. I'd always wondered what it would be like to look like Sarah Duncan. If only the circumstances weren't what they were.

My eyes traced Mr. Dawson's handwriting again, noting every detail the pen had made. Inky black with a blotch at the end of the "y" in "Amy".

"It was too short," I said, switching back to Spanish. "But I'm glad we were able to talk."

"Are you going to open the letter?" Alejandro asked.

I chewed on the inside of my cheek, facing him. "It's for both me and my mom. But this is now the *very* last thing I have from him, and..."

"You can say it."

I exhaled, deciding. "I can't wait."

These were the last words I had from my godfather, from the man who'd helped raise me. If the letter was to both of us, why couldn't I read it first and then let Mom read it when we got back? The fact that he'd left a *letter* of all things behind screamed something; anything he wanted to tell us, he would've told us in person, over a phone call, or even telepathically. A letter would have been the only option if—

My chest locked. If he'd known that he wouldn't be here to tell us whatever was inside.

He couldn't have... He would've—

I mindlessly sat back down on the bench, my fingers running along the lip of the envelope. Alejandro took his spot again as I pulled out the folded sheet of binder paper.

Full of his handwriting.

Amy and Emma,...

I looked up, taking a deep breath. Alejandro rested a gentle hand on my shoulder, reminding me that he was still here—that we didn't have any time to waste.

The Band-Aid. Rip it off.

I swallowed and put my eyes on the next line.

I'm sorry if you're reading this and I'm still not there to tell you all this in person. But I'm not dead, so chin up.

My breath hiccupped in my throat, teetering on a chuckle that I wasn't sure I was allowed.

I know your first instinct will be to come after me. Don't. I can't emphasize that enough, don't. If you want to save me, you have to let me go. I have a plan, but it'll only work if I have just myself to worry about.

Is that plan why he'll die if we go after him...?

He couldn't have known what would happen that morning. It sounded like he'd known. How?

After Emma told me her vision, I needed insight about it that wouldn't cost you. I had the least to lose out of every-one—so I'm writing this after seeing Ingrid.

No. He'd paid the seer's price for us again? What did he depend on most now that he'd given up until her prophecy passed?

I think I managed to save all of our lives with it, but I won't know until I see you again. I know what I'm signing up for. I know it'll be hell. I'm okay with it. I'm happy to do it. It'll save my family, and if you let me get myself out, it'll be worth it.

I don't know specifically what Caldwell's planning, but I know this is part of it. It depends on luring you all to him. He's going to use me as bait, so no matter what, do not give in. The second you do, everything I've done is for nothing. No matter what happens, no matter how much time has passed, let me save myself. Figure out what Alexa is really doing until then. Figure out what Caldwell's up to while I do the same thing. Do not worry about me.

I'll see you again next year. Trust me. I love you, Emma. I love you, Amy. Please give Tristan and Becca my love, too.

I'll get through this. I promise.
– Thomas D.

A tear fell onto his name, rippling the paper. And then, when I looked at the letter as a whole, splatters of my tears were threatening to eat away at the page.

He'd gone on that mission with us that morning *knowing* how it would end.

I couldn't breathe. I fell into Alejandro beside me, my sobs overcoming my voice. Blinding my vision. Tightening my fingers around my godfather's last words to me, around his plea to leave him suffering.

I barely heard Alejandro murmur, "*Lo siento mucho, amiga. Lo siento.*"

If not for me coming to rescue Dad and Breanne and Opal that morning, if I'd just listened to Mom and stayed at the manor, Mr. Dawson could still be with us. He could've made it back to his family, come with us to Bouchard. The three to have escaped that morning could've been him and my parents, nothing would've changed if I'd stayed behind.

Had he known that me coming would sentence him to capture? Had he just... not cared?

He'd done it anyway. For me.

I have to stay behind this time for him.

That didn't ease the grief any more; it *intensified* it because I had to burn every instinct telling me otherwise. With Alejandro's grip around my shoulders, the hard bench beneath us soon blurred, no longer supporting me. I almost couldn't tell if it was Alejandro teleporting, or our situation that had left me suspended over a bonfire, ready to throw me in next.

Thirty-Two

My mind still felt foggy after we got back to the Yukon that night. While taking the elevator down into the main lobby, I didn't know how I'd greet my parents; they'd lied to me about my ability as a sorceress when it could've altered our entire course with Alexa—but Mom had been right about me staying behind that December morning. Part of me didn't know who was in the right or wrong, but a big-enough part knew what I was angry about.

Alejandro and I were about to sit in two of the armchairs of the empty lobby when three people called our names. When we looked right, my family was coming out of the second residential sector entryway. Eun-Ji must have telepathically alerted Dad and Aunt Becca that we were back after I'd asked her to let us down.

And yet, after everything, the first thing I felt upon seeing them all was relief.

Dad wrapped his firm arms all the way around me and picked me up. I felt Momma beside us, hugging us when he put me down. They squeezed me like they had the morning Dad had come home for the first time, yet my stifled joy was suffocating.

I kept my eyes on the dark-yellow rug when they finally let go. Aunt Becca offered her arms in the corner of my vision, taking my attention. She was the only one I could hug without restriction; like Mr. Dawson, she'd definitely only kept quiet about the sorceress thing because of my parents.

"I was really worried about you, kiddo," she murmured, kissing the side of my temple.

"Me, too," I said as she broke away.

"Thank you, Alejandro," Dad told him in English, exhaling with a hand on his chest like he'd just gotten back from a run. "Whatever you guys did out there, it wasn't possible without you."

A lot more stuff would've been possible if I'd known, I couldn't help but think. Would we even be at Bouchard right now, would we have ever needed to find it, if I'd known sooner?

"Emma is a great leader," Alejandro replied, rubbing his palms on his winter pants. That reminded me to take off my backpack and unzip my coat.

I draped my coat carefully over my arm, mindful of Mr. Dawson's letter in one of the pockets. Then I realized that there were only three people in front of us.

"Where's Jak?" I asked.

"Showering," Auntie said. "He has great timing huh? To be fair, though, none of us thought you'd get back when it's almost time for bed."

Good. Then I can have this conversation with them now.

"I'll go to the kitchen to—recover," Alejandro said in English. "*Buen trabajo, amiga.*"

"You, too," I said.

I watched him walk all the way down the lobby and past the secretary desk until he reached the concourse in the back. Part of me wanted to go with him, too exhausted to have a fight right now; the other part was too exhausted of waiting to *have* that fight.

"So?" Momma asked. She sat in one of the armchairs across from the pair Alejandro and I had picked. Dad took the chair next to it, Aunt Becca balancing on the arm. "Were you able to find the other person like you guys?"

I was still anxious to tell my family about the answers we'd finally gotten, but for all the wrong reasons—and I'd gotten all the wrong answers. It didn't feel right to give them everything they wanted when they never gave me what I was owed.

"We got to Kamose," I said anyway, because I had to. "He told us she was in Antarctica, and we found her. She supposedly didn't know anything about our destinies because she lost her family a long time ago. I don't know if she knows about her impossible ability or not, but she said she'd consider letting us show her Bouchard. That was it."

"You don't sound like yourself," Aunt Becca noted. "Did something happen while you were out there?"

"Except for almost getting caught in Saskatchewan, no."

"What?" my parents said, sitting up.

"Two CSIS agents came in looking for us."

"How?" Dad asked, brows tightly knit together.

"We don't know," I replied flatly, holding on tighter to my coat draped over my arm. I was starting to get cold down here in the humidity. "Kamose can't find out what happened in the past, and it never happened again. So we just don't know."

"How did you escape?" Momma said. Almost like we were back in her classroom my sophomore year and she wanted a full report on how I'd done on the practice hunt that day.

I made myself give her the story, but recapping was the last thing I wanted to do; I just wanted to go to my room, pretend for an hour that my parents didn't exist, and then come back to have the conversation I actually wanted to. Which would also be when I'd give Mom Mr. Dawson's letter, because no way was I ready to fight about *that* right now.

"Without anyone chasing you after that?" Dad asked, a smile playing on his lips. "Wow. I'm... glad you managed to knock those guys out anyway when magic wasn't an option."

The memory flashed in my head for a second before I had to shut it off. I let Dad's praise roll off my back.

"I'm super proud of the way you handled this mission," Momma told me. "You're shaping up to be the Hunter I always saw in you."

I traced my coat with my eyes, not knowing what to say.

In the upper edge of my vision, my parents looked at each other, passing notes with nothing but their eyes. To my surprise, they included Aunt Becca at the end, like they were all speaking a language they'd come up with while I was gone.

"So," Auntie began slowly, "when you saw Kamose, did he happen to mention anything about Thomas?"

"He said he's still not facing death, but he can't do anything to help him or know more about him because of that protection spell over the White House."

Dad huffed, slouching in his chair. Momma rubbed his hand resting on the armrest that Auntie hadn't taken over.

This was flat out the most difficult conversation my family and I had ever had—not topic-wise, but effort-wise. It felt like we had to drag ourselves through the mud just to find our next sentence. Despite what I wanted to bring up, I couldn't find the right sentence to lead with.

Then Momma looked at Dad again, murmuring something under her breath. He nodded. Her gaze squared onto me.

"Em," she started, like she was preparing an inauguration speech, "do you remember when you and I went looking for Jak down in the hideout under Capperson?"

Okay, *that* was the absolute last question I'd expected. "Yeah..."

"You used a lookout spell to make sure nobody else was in the mine, and I asked you if you felt something."

Had I not already known the truth, I would've never connected the pieces: not just feel the presence of anyone the lookout spell revealed, but feel a wielder's magic with the sorcerer's ability.

I fought to keep realization—and renewed fury—off my face. *She refused to tell me even when it came to saving Jak's life, when it mattered.*

I opened my mouth to reply, but my emotions finally demolished the wall in my head and took full control: "You're too late."

Momma paused. "What?"

"My ability as a sorceress? You're too late. I know what it is, and it doesn't matter anymore. You can't change a thing by telling me what I should've known the second I understood what magic was and that I had it."

My parents' faces fell, Aunt Becca stiffening.

"Em, the reason—" Dad began.

"It doesn't *matter*," I snapped. "Dawson's in custody, the Delphines are dead, we're stuck down here, and you missed your chance to help me prevent all of that! Kamose and Alejandro had to tell me what it was so I could find our ally in Antarctica, and they didn't even know that I didn't know something that's *common knowledge*! Why would you hide that from me?"

"We were protecting you," Mom stated in her mom tone that, well, rolled off my back like water. "You've been a show-off since you were little, that's a huge reason I kept you out of public school until your sophomore year. The last thing we needed was you deciding who you could trust based on whether or not they had magic."

"I was a *kid*," I retorted, leaning toward her. "You never even gave me the chance to prove that I could be trusted with it. And who's 'we', because Mr. Dawson thought it was a bad idea from the start, this was *your* decision!"

"It was ours, Emma," Dad said, going rigid against his usual demeanor. "We both decided it."

"You didn't even know I existed until my sixteenth birthday!"

"That day was what told me you weren't ready." His rugged, icy-blue eyes carved into me, trying to strip my anger of its authority. "In the beach house basement, the second you got your magic back, you *instantly* told Alexa you had it by throwing her down the hallway. She wanted to keep us both there after that, when she'd originally thought neither of us had anything to give. Remember?"

My jaw quivered, laced with the infuriating truth that I had no comeback for.

"When I told your mom about it, she told me you didn't know what sorcerers can do. We decided together that we'd tell you when you were ready."

"It's a basic fact of life," I argued, my words flying out of my mouth. "How do you not see how much you took away from me by hiding it, how much of our situation was caused because of that? You stripped an entire layer of protection from me because you wanted to keep a secret!"

"You need to take a good and *long* step back, little one," Mom said, holding up a finger at me. "If the beach house wasn't enough, how about you think back to when you met Cara and Steven, meeting two *strangers* in the middle of the night without backup? Or Annisa, another complete stranger who knew who you were and whom you met up with without telling anyone? Remember how much you wanted to tell Opal the truth until you were forced to realize that you couldn't completely trust her—?"

"Remember how I immediately told you about Breanne getting Alexa's magic because I knew I needed help for a plan? How I didn't automatically trust Kamose and tried to investigate Alejandro when he first showed up in my visions? How I included you and Dawson as much as I could on the cruise because I knew I couldn't handle everything? How I even got to a point last year where I couldn't trust that Jak was Jak without a truth spell?"

"Or how you and Jak met in the first place and you trusted him because of those circumstances?" she shot back.

"He was under a *trust spell*," I spat, my fists clenching under my coat. Rage was ready to boil over, trickling into my words.

"You trusted him, too. *Becca* had to try and get you to think clearly when we first told her about him—"

"Emma," Aunt Becca began, but Mom was first.

"Okay, say you're right." She leaned back in her chair like she'd already won the argument. "I should've told you years ago, now what? What does that fix, how are we supposed to change anything now?"

"That's my point!" I exclaimed. "You only decided to speak up when it was too late to tell me—"

"I'm not a druid or a seer, Emma! It's not like I could've predicted everything going wrong, let alone you knowing being the ultimate remedy for it! This had zero room for risk or error, it was life or death."

"You didn't tell me even after I met Alexa, and the one person who *was* smart enough to know better is the only one in danger." Against my rationality, I tore Mr. Dawson's letter out of my coat pocket. "Dawson knew. He went to Ingrid and found out he'd be taken, but he went on the mission with us anyway to save us because he *loved* us. Now he's paying the price for it when it's not his price to pay!"

I stiffened when my parents and Aunt Becca froze in front of me. "What is that?" Momma muttered, voice low and fierce amber eyes aflame.

My jaw shook with the choice of my next words. The front of the envelope—the side with my name and my mother's name—was facing my family. I think that was why I didn't care how this conversation would end: I knew it'd be ugly no matter what road I picked.

"He explained why he went with us—"

"Where did you get that?" Dad said, every consonant puncturing the air.

Exposed. The word plummeted into my stomach and hardened with regret. My anger had blinded me just enough to drop me into the worst possible pit. Capperson would be a whole other fight. *You just exposed yourself.*

I brought the envelope to my chest. Silence.

"I want to know where you got that," Dad stated, strong features carved by determined anger, "and why it's already been opened."

"This was mine, too," I began, almost creasing the paper with my grip. "I had a right to read it, especially when you hid—"

"No, no, that's not how this works, Emmalynn," Momma hissed, her voice rising as she stood—and shaking with a lack of control I'd never heard from her before. "You don't get to decide who's 'punished' for keeping what, you don't get to harbor something that's from an endangered family member just because you're petty, and you DEFINITELY don't get to use that family member as leverage against me and your father!"

With that, the fire of my anger consumed the reins on my irrationality.

"Here, read it," I spat, throwing my coat to the floor and the letter with it. "Read it and then you'll see why he's been a better parent to me than either of you the last few months."

I strode past them, off the rug, and toward the residential sectors. My parents furiously called after me, full first name and all, but I continued into the entryway and down the hall like I had no parents at all.

Thirty-Three

Despite the exhaustion weighing on my body and the fury blinding my way to my room, my thoughts were thriving. They were flurrying around so fast that I didn't see the boy next door who'd opened his door and stepped out into the hall.

"Emma?"

My hand froze on the doorknob. That voice. I almost wished he *had* been there when I first got back.

I looked up and to my left. Jak was standing in his doorway with damp hair and a navy-blue T-shirt on, water spots speckling his neckline and chest. Kind brown eyes stared back at me like they were hallucinating me, dreaming me up.

I let go of the knob and ran to him, throwing my arms around his neck. He embraced me with equal measure, burying his face into my neck as if to solidify my presence. I was thankful that I'd been able to shower at Runelle's last night, because he deeply inhaled like he needed to know that I was right here, that we were breathing the same air.

"Don't ever do that to me again," he muttered.

"Do what?"

"Leave for something like that for days without any way of telling me you're still okay."

I let my arms rest around him. His hands slid to my waist as he pulled away enough to offer space, but then his hands fell. I almost reached for them, but I wouldn't be able to justify it. And part of me was still too angry.

"Then don't stay behind next time," I said, releasing him.

"What's wrong?" His light-brown finger brushed away a tear I hadn't realized had spilled.

I swallowed the next bout. "I, um... Stupid fight with my parents. They kept my ability as a sorceress from me when it could've helped us avoid... a lot of things since all this started."

"Is Alejandro here? Did everything go okay?"

"Yeah," I said, instinctively twisting my locket. I didn't need to worry him about Watrous. "It's—I'm sorry, I don't know, I'm sorry—"

"Don't apologize." He reached up and wiped away another tear with his thumb. "It's okay. You're here."

I was, but it wasn't the relief I'd thought it would be the last few days. If anything, I'd never felt more like I couldn't breathe this far underground. I was here, but I wanted to be with him.

I sniffed, swallowing the rest of my confessions. "Can we talk about it?"

He stepped backwards and then nodded inside. "Come on."

Probably a little too eagerly, I strode past him and into his room. He left the door open behind him as he followed me and then gestured to his bed for me to take a seat.

"We visited Kamose, the nore I told you about," I began, steadying myself at the foot. Jak took a respectful spot next to me, leaving two feet between us. "He told us where to find our next ally, who ended up not even wanting to ally with us. And on top of that, all Kamose could tell us about Dawson was that he's still alive because we're staying away."

"That's good, isn't it?" Jak asked gently, a whiff of his fresh out-of-the-shower scent wafting into my nose. "Aside from us not being able to save him yet."

I sighed, my thumbnails fiddling with each other. "If you didn't read the letter I did."

"Letter?"

"We stopped in Capperson," I admitted, turning to face him better. "I *had* to see my friends and know what's been happening at the school, so we met up with them under appearance spells and got an update. But Sarah figured out that it was me and left a code for us to secretly meet up, and she gave me this letter Dawson wrote to me and my mom..."

Thinking about those words that I wished I could burn into my memory, I had to set my jaw. I looked ahead at the lamp on the corner of the credenza, focusing on the light as if to will the tears back down into their well.

"He knew he'd be captured, because he talked to a seer," I said. "But he went on the mission anyway because he knew it was the only thing that would save all of us."

"Em…" Jak whispered, sighing. "You don't blame yourself for that, do you?"

"No," I told him, firmly matching our eyes. "I blame my parents—for never telling me that sorcerers can detect if someone's a magician or not. This whole time, my *whole* life, I was supposed to be able to do that, and my parents hid it from me because they thought I 'wasn't ready' for it. I could've figured out the Delphines on *day one*, but they kept that from me. Do you know how much we could've avoided if I'd known?"

Jak pressed his lips together, eyes fixed in front of him. He let out a long breath, almost like he was having to calm *himself* about this. "I don't."

"A ton!" I reminded myself to keep my voice quiet with his door down the hallway open. "The insight I would've had, the choices I could've made, the stress I could've saved myself—"

He rested a gentle hand on my knee, sending a small zap of electricity through me. "Do *you* know?" he asked.

My face scrunched with confusion. "What?"

"Do you know how much you could've avoided if you'd known?"

"Jak—" I began, dumbfounded. I didn't know where to begin with arguing something so obvious. "Yeah. If I'd been able to detect if people had magic, the playing field would've been *drastically* different—"

"Well, yeah, that's a given." He took his hand off my knee, resting it back in his lap. "But do you *know*?"

I wasn't sure if I was understanding him—but if I was, I didn't like what I was hearing, and I needed to make sure that he wasn't actually saying it. "Pretend I'm five."

"You know things would've been different because the circumstances would've been different. But how do you know it would've been a good different? How do you know for sure that things would've turned out better, if not worse somehow?"

He *was* saying what I didn't want to hear. But I didn't know how to tell him to stop.

"The you back then could've made the same mistakes, just with different tools," he added, like I was actually five and he was having to calm me from a meltdown. He lowly raised his hands. "I promise, I'm not trying to discredit how you feel or tell you not to be hurt. But I don't want you to be mad like this if you don't have to be, where it steals your ability to see the good when you need it most."

I scoffed under my breath. "Like what?"

"Like the fact you came back in one perfect piece." The back of his index finger brushed against my cheek. "And you came back to the same number of people you left."

I don't know what it was about that statement that made everything in me pause. I guess I'd assumed throughout the last few days that Alejandro and I were the only ones in immediate danger and temporarily forgotten that Bouchard wasn't immune to the outside world. Honestly, in a way, my family had been at just as much risk as we'd been.

On top of that, Jak had every right to point that out: nobody from his household had come back after leaving for a mission that morning. He hadn't lost family that day, but like he'd told me when he'd shown up at our house, at least he'd had *some* people before then. Even if he hadn't liked them.

I matched our eyes, making the connection: *"Don't ever do that to me again."*

"Yeah." I looked down at my lap.

"Maybe your parents did the wrong thing, but it was for the right reasons," he added. "That was always their only intent, you know that."

I shook my head, trying to get it into the right headspace to resist my pettiness and just accept his words. "Did you read Aristotle or something while I was gone?"

"Not much else to do here," he joked.

For some reason, when I tried to smile, a tight constriction kept my lips locked. Evidently my pettiness wasn't ready to accept the possibility that my anger wasn't completely in the right.

"Are you okay?"

I bit the inside of my cheek. That stupid question again. That one question that, if the right person asked it, could unravel me like a ball of yarn. And Jak was the right person in so many ways.

The back of my hand met my mouth and nose. Despite the tears pooling in my eyes, I swallowed again and tried to push them back. I couldn't break again. I already had in Capperson, I was fine, and it wasn't going to change anything right now.

"Em."

It was easier to push down the tears when I had to look at Jak. Wow, did I miss hearing "Merlin" from him, but I wasn't brave enough or ready to ask him to bring it back.

I nodded to his question, but I couldn't verbally assure him.

His hand went back to my knee. "Talk to me. Please."

I dropped my hand, stopping it just above his. I didn't know if I was allowed to, but then I decided that I didn't care: I rested my hand on top of his, on top of his skin that his shower had left soft and warm. His shampoo wafted into my nose again, enticing me all the more toward a direction I wanted but was afraid of. I wanted to tell him something, almost anything, but I didn't know what I could that was fair and felt safe.

So I closed my eyes. I closed my eyes and honestly hoped that Jak would kiss me. He always knew how to take away my worst thoughts and memories with just his words and lips. Within seconds, he could put me somewhere familiar, somewhere I wanted to be.

Space remained between us, and I opened my eyes, looking up slightly. Jak's eyes stayed on our hands, defined jaw clenched so tightly that I was scared his teeth would shatter.

Does he still feel the same way? Did he give up completely...?

I quietly exhaled my regret. Those thoughts were starting to become too heavy to store. I felt myself lean to the side, my head falling onto Jak's shoulder. His skin was still hot under his shirt, his fresh musk leaving my mind buzzing. He wrapped one arm around my torso, resting his cheek on top of my head. We sighed at the same time, like we both had a world of things we wanted to say to the other.

Please, I couldn't help but think. *Make me forget.*

Almost like he'd heard me, his thumb started rubbing my shoulder. That was all he could tell me, as far as he could go. I wanted to give him more than that, tell him how much I needed him right now.

I needed to feel him, feel how much he cared.

I raised my head, leaving inches between us. "Kiss me."

"Em..." he whispered, casting his eyes down again. His arm

fell from my shoulder. "No, please don't do this."

"Do what?"

"You just got back, you're unwinding from high stress, you still have to settle in." He refused to meet my gaze like it would demolish his resolve the second he did. "I can't take advantage of that, you and I know what you really need right now."

"I don't care," I argued, "that's everything I wanna forget about, I just wanna forget for a sec."

"I told you," he said gently. "Forgetting just puts you in a vicious cycle of coming back to reality harder and faster—"

"Then let me do it this one time. I've spent our whole time here being reminded of why I can't make my family whole again, I can't even help my own people who are suffering right now, that is *all* I can remember and all I'm allowed to think about every day." I took his hand in his lap into both of mine. Finally, his eyes rose to me. "Please."

His lips barely parted with his hollow breath. I held his gaze until it faltered, falling to my lips in a single blink.

"No," he whispered—yet his eyes never came back up to mine. "I can't... I want—"

Neither of us realized that his hand was rising to the side of my face. I leaned forward right as his fingers grazed my skin, and then they cupped my face with full force as his lips took mine.

The second he threw out his rationality, I threw out mine. I didn't think as I shifted in my spot on the bed, taking his face into my hands as he continuously pressed his lips against mine. I pushed against him when he pushed against me, his hands trailing down to my neck and sending a shiver up my spine. His breath deepened, his fingers tightening on my skin. My hands slid down to his warm, damp chest, tempted to pull him closer to me, to never let him go again. I had him and he had me, and this was all we needed, each other's safety in the middle of a dark night.

His teeth grazed my bottom lip. My thoughts cut out. He never let his lips leave mine as his hands fell down my arms and then my waist. His body leaned forward as I gripped his shirt, his hand sliding to the small of my back—

"No," he blurted, breaking away and abruptly standing from the bed. "No, I can't. I can't, Emma, I can't."

"Why not?"

"Because I won't be able to stop if I do."

My chest squeezed. My heart thumped harder and harder with every second of the last few moments—moments that started melding into the memory of our last kiss, at my house.

My teeth clenched with guilt. *I did it again.*

"I'm not—" Jak stammered, briefly turning away from me with his hands on his head, "I'm not gonna do this to you again. Or myself. This isn't what we need right now."

Part of me cursed how rational and levelheaded he was, just like how he'd been the night he'd found out that he was an or-phan—yet after he'd kissed me like that. I cursed how he knew his weaknesses yet still had power over them, cursed how he knew what was best for me and was strong enough to uphold it. Cursed how he was right in a world of wrong but I couldn't make him my world.

I shook my head, lips parting with the start of a hundred words that I didn't have.

"No," Jak said softly, "you don't have to say anything. It's okay."

"It's not okay."

For a moment, he held my gaze like it was the only thing he *could* hold. And then, despite the last minute, he sat back down next to me on the edge of his bed—because Jakson Bleu refused to let me drown if he knew I was in the water. When I couldn't hold myself up, he was always ready to lend his own strength. Even when it meant sacrifice. And I didn't make it any easier on him.

"I don't know, I don't know how to do this," I admitted. "You were right and I made you—"

"Hey, no," he gently assured me, twisting to face me in full. "No, you didn't. That was us, that was both of us, we're both trying to keep our heads on straight right now."

Us. I wish it could be us all the time.

"I'm sorry," I whispered.

He gave me the tightest smile I'd ever seen—like he'd never had to try so hard to find a silver lining in his life. "Me, too," he said softly. "We're... still healing."

"You were right and you tried to warn me, and... you're a lot better at healing than I am." I shakily exhaled, rubbing my face. "It sucks, it really sucks."

"Don't give me that much credit," he said, gaining my full attention again. "I did a lot of it when you couldn't see it, especially the past few days. Clearly I'm not perfect at it, I definitely have... weak spots." For a second, he just looked at me—letting nothing else happen except our eyes holding each other's. "But as long as it's your best, it's enough, Em. As long as you know when you do make mistakes and the people you care about forgive you for them. That's how it works—"

Muffled footsteps pressed down the hall outside Jak's room,

prompting us to scoot away from each other. Soon the door around the corner squeaked before shutting. Of all people, Aunt Becca was the last person I'd expected to walk into the room.

"Hey, so..." she began slowly, my coat draped over her arm, "things are tense. Is it okay if I stay here for the night?"

"Um—sure," Jak said hesitantly. "Why?"

Auntie looked to her right, at the wall his room shared with ours. "I don't think Amy and Tristan are gonna be done before we go to bed."

Thirty-Four

I'd never heard my parents fight until that night. Jak and Alejandro decided to hit the gym despite the late hour because Becca and I weren't ready for sleep.

After they left, I found Opal's present in my coat pocket. The girl had great timing, because I *really* needed to feel like my friends were with me right now—so I opened the gray fabric bag and found a silver necklace with a flame charm at the end, a diamond embedded at the bottom. I guess Dakota had been right about fire suiting me as a symbol.

Having Opal's present somewhat helped. I felt like I was grounded to Jak and Alejandro's room because I was the one who'd *prompted* my parents' fight. It turned out that they disagreed on the extent of my punishment—or even if I should be punished rather than just disciplined—which spiraled into how we were dealing with our overall situation here, which led to a lot of uncovered minor disagreements and conflicts that neither had shared over the last couple of months, and now they were fighting about everything. Their voices were fairly muffled even though we were right next door, so I could only hope that none of our neighbors would be woken up.

I wish I could've handled the conversation better. But I also couldn't ignore how much they'd hurt me.

I think Aunt Becca and I were anticipating that my parents would eventually stop and come in to tell us a plan of some kind. But the door stayed closed, and Aunt Becca stayed lying down on Jak's bed, staring up at the ceiling illuminating us with round yellow lights. I picked at the threading of the reading chair in the corner. My thoughts ran in a loop, trying to find an ending, only to wind up at the beginning of another thought that would ultimately bleed into the next.

"Kamose said Thomas was safe?" Auntie asked, breaking the quiet.

I looked up at her. "Not dead, at least."

"You said that protection spell stops him from physically intervening at all?"

I hated remembering that fact. "Yeah."

She left us in the tense quiet again for a few moments. It almost seemed to blast my parents' stifled voices, so I didn't expect the smile that soon broke out on Auntie's lips. "I miss him."

Even though she couldn't see me, I nodded my agreement.

"I didn't trust him for a *second* when your dad first told me about him, even when he said he was a druid. I interrogated that boy until he turned blue."

I sat up a little in the reading chair, getting a better view of her on the bed. "Really?"

"Oh yeah. And then, by the third time I hung out with him, he was like another little brother to me."

Silence settled over us again—save for Mom and Dad. As much as I wanted to keep drowning them out, I let Aunt Becca lie there and gather her memories, soon reaching for my locket and the flame necklace for comfort.

"He's been nothing but a brother to me since." Her voice softened into something I'd never heard from her before, a mix of melancholy and reminiscence. "He was there for your mom when I couldn't be. Which was often."

"That's not your fault."

"No, but I still wish it wasn't true." She turned her head of mostly blond hair to me. "You know he was the one there the day you were born?"

"Mom told me something like that."

"No, as in"—she sat up, swinging her legs over the edge of the bed—"he was the one who helped her through labor *and* while the midwife delivered you because her husband couldn't be there."

I paused, my brain tripping over the words. Mr. Dawson had been there for Mom like *that?* A substitute for Dad?

An integral part of this family since the beginning.

"So believe me," Auntie said next, "we're *all* suffering from his situation. We all regret it. I bet you that's part of the reason why your parents are so mad right now."

"Why?"

"Because part of them feels the same way you do. Like if

you'd known sooner that we can detect magicians, he might still be with us. But that's what regret does, it stings. They can't do anything about it now, all they can do is move forward and ice it. And everything you said to them—especially after reading Thomas's letter—doesn't make that process easier."

I knew what she was really saying. But the last thing I wanted right now was a lecture when I was hearing my parents fight next door because of me.

"I love you," Aunt Becca told me. "I'm not saying any of this to make you feel bad. Just give you some perspective. We're all trying our best right now, no one more than you."

I looked up at her from my lap. "What?"

"After the mission you just went on because you knew you were the only one who could go, yeah," she replied, like it was obvious. "You have a lot on your shoulders but you're still con-stantly working for other people. We know you're working hard to make things right, you have to fix your own mistakes *and* the rest of the world's. Just remember that we are, too. Just like we have to forgive your mistakes, you have to forgive ours. Okay?"

I bit the inside of my cheek, dropping my necklaces. I could understand those words—I knew those words, and I think that was why I was able to accept them. Thankfully, it was Becca; I was always able to admit when I was wrong if it was just her.

"Okay," I murmured.

Only then did I realize that the room had gone silent. *Silent.* My parents had stopped yelling, so there was a chance that they were in a better mood. How long ago had they stopped?

I should... take advantage, I thought, shifting to stand from the chair. *Apologize.*

"Gonna go say you're sorry?" Auntie asked.

"Yeah—"

The doorknob down the hallway twisted, the door opening with a creak. Hesitant, timid.

I straightened as two pairs of footsteps walked on the tight carpet and toward me and Aunt Becca. Momma and Dad appeared around the corner and into the room.

"Hey," Momma said, tiredness dragging down the word. Her usually sharp, honey-colored eyes were swollen, but the red in them seemed mild. "We're sorry if you heard all that."

I fiddled with my fingernails, unable to look either of my parents in the eye as I told them, "I'm sorry I *said* all that."

It was just as I'd hoped and just as I'd dreaded: they walked over to me and wrapped their arms around me. Hugged me tighter than I felt I deserved, which was nothing at all. They were so quick and easy to love me again just like that, whereas I still had underlying resentment about the whole thing that was merely being trumped by their forgiveness. I didn't know what to do with that resentment, but I knew that I didn't want to let it ruin us.

"We're really bad at telling the truth," I muttered into Dad's chest as Aunt Becca joined the hug on his other side.

"Yeah, well..." Momma whispered, resting her cheek on top of my head. "None of us ever had the best examples. All we're able to do now is our best."

"Therefore...?" Auntie said, her arms barely hanging on to the three of us from Dad's side.

Momma nodded once against my head. "We're sorry for not handling things better about your identity as a sorceress, Em."

"Thanks," I replied, pushing sincerity into my voice.

I was starting to get hot from being smushed between them all. But we stayed in the quiet together, for once nothing willing to interrupt us. It was the four of us for the first time in a long time, and nothing else.

Dad sighed heavily. "That letter hurt," he whispered. "Really hurt. I hate him and love him for knowingly doing what he did."

None of us had anything to respond with. I fully agreed.

"Let's not make anything harder than it has to be," he said with finality. "Things are hard enough."

"Agreed," Momma said, letting go. The rest of us followed suit, and her softening eyes rested on me. "In that spirit, when can we know how you got that letter?"

It wasn't a question, it was a request—one that I was grateful for the timing of so I could say, "After we sleep?"

Thankfully, she merely touched my cheek with the back of her fingers, maintaining her weary smile. "Good. Then we can practice your new superpower."

It took a couple of weeks for the tension to fully dissolve, and part of that was because my parents were *conflicted* on how they felt about me and Alejandro stopping in Capperson; after all, it'd gotten us Dawson's letter and the verification that we hadn't been publicly exposed yet, but they hit every nail on the head that I had while telling Alejandro why we shouldn't go in the first place.

We'd picked the right time for our trip, though; the security ward had detected intense activity within a thirty-mile radius of Bouchard, and the investigation team came back with the report that the Canadian Government was in the mountains. Eun-Ji put everyone on magic arrest after that—especially Alejandro. His teleportation sent out significant waves that Bouchard needed to do without if the government was going to pass us by peacefully.

But in the couple of weeks that followed after that, half of the Hunter ward was sent out undercover to conduct further research regarding both the Canadian and US Governments. April was almost halfway over when my parents, Jak, and I were called into Eun-Ji's office about it.

What surprised me when we walked in was how Anthony was already standing beside Eun-Ji's desk, bent over in deep discussion with her.

Whatever they found can't be good.

Anthony straightened as we entered the gray room, brushing a few strands of spruce-brown hair into place. His solemn forest-green eyes felt heavier than usual as he set his jaw.

"Thank you all for coming," Eun-Ji began in her chair, squaring her shoulders, "let's get started."

She gathered the papers in front of her and held them out, inviting Momma to walk up to the desk to take them. "Our Hunters just got back from their undercover mission in Washington, DC. They were arguably successful and found a few more pieces regarding Caldwell's presumed nationwide purge, which these transcripts our agents recorded will either confirm or disprove. I figured your insight would offer what nobody else's here can."

That's *why Aunt Becca and Alejandro aren't here.* Momma, Dad, Jak, and I had been the last people to talk to the Delphines and come into contact with Caldwell's Hunters in December (even Jak via footage); we had pieces no one else did.

The room fell quiet as Momma scanned the documents in her hands. The circular yellow rug underneath her did hardly any favors to brighten the atmosphere as she started her investigation:

"What is this first one transcribing?"

"A summary report between our Agent Viskov and the White House's director of Secret Service, Ron Carrey," Eun-Ji replied. "Viskov is one of our closest leads to the White House's private affairs. Director Carrey pulled him aside last week to discuss the idea of 'expedited efforts' regarding Caldwell's overarching plan for the country this year."

Momma scrutinized the transcript. "What is Target Echo and why is it highlighted?"

"That's what the US Government has labeled Alejandro for some reason. We need to note that he's now a criminal in the United States despite his citizenship in a protected country due to how he's colluded with and helped American magician fugitives."

"Okay..." Momma mused. "Then 'Target Adeline' must be Emma based on the context here."

Neither made sense to me. What did "Echo" have to do with Alejandro? Why would they pick "Adeline" for me?

"'Expedite efforts'," Momma mused, reading again, "'thorough search and analysis of'—"

Her head snapped up to Eun-Ji and Anthony, and I stiffened. "'Surrounding range of the coordinates'?"

Dad's brow discreetly furrowed in the corner of my vision, Jak glancing down at me on my other side. What coordinates...?

"We were able to connect that to why we've had a sizable amount of activity in our vicinity recently," Eun-Ji answered. Anthony stayed eerily quiet next to her desk like he was waiting his turn to deliver a bad blow. "Hence the extra security measures we've implemented lately."

Momma slowly turned on the rug to face us as she read.

"'Echo might have ties to the prime minister's findings, which we need to verify as soon as possible in case he's the one the prime minister is looking for. If he is, he's a lead to who *we're* looking for, and that means the Ateras are in full collusion with them all. So if Echo is close to Adeline, that means we have a direct link to'"—Momma's voice quieted to a squeak as she locked eyes with me—"'Adara.'"

The blood in my veins ran cold. Adara was a well-known legend among wielders, not mortals—and yet the US Government had her name. They knew who she was, that I was a lead, that Alejandro was a lead. *How?*

"'The president wants all hands on deck to make sure Project Ember pulls through. The entire nation is at stake, and if we don't protect America first, the rest of the world doesn't stand a chance. Echo and Adeline are top priority in the coming months.'"

I didn't know how I was still upright after losing all feeling in my body. It felt like someone had shattered my senses, blocked my brain from sending any signals to the rest of me.

For the country's "protection". We have to die so they'll feel safe?

Dad broke me out of my head when he said, "'Project Ember'—okay, now we have the official name of their plan."

"Look at the page under the transcript," Anthony told Momma. She obeyed as he added, "That's the conversation between me and Alexa before she sent me to Bouchard with Tristan's magic. Carrey didn't tell Viskov what Ember was because it's highly confidential, he and Caldwell are the only ones who know the details. All anyone else is allowed to know is that it's a plan to find Adara and other powerful magicians so they can, allegedly, protect the country."

That sounded in line with Caldwell's fourteen years of genocide—but that wasn't news to even the common American citizen. The government had new and greater efforts planned for this. What made Project Ember different?

"Hang on," Jak said, holding up his hand, "I saw everyone's body cam footage from that morning, including Alexa's, and they were all muted. How did you get this transcript?"

"Alexa did that," Anthony replied. "She bet on you being first to watch it if we didn't come back so you'd know to find the Ateras. She trusted you'd be smart enough to delete it after, but in case Caldwell's Hunters got to it first, she didn't want them hearing anything she or anyone else might've said. So she muted the mics before they left for the mission—everyone's but mine because we'd already agreed who was gonna be the deliverer. Notice how mine was probably the only footage you were missing."

That woman's mission had been to protect us until the very end. *And yet she beat me and Opal nearly to death—and settled on stabbing Steven as a means to incapacitate him.* How could her history with us clash so violently with the hero she'd been at Bouchard?

"Which worked out, because Viskov isn't the last person Ember was mentioned to," Anthony added, nodding to the transcript in Momma's hands.

She read it for a few seconds before looking up at him. "Alexa told you to tell Eun-Ji about Project Ember when you got here. This isn't new to either of you?"

"Anthony came back with the news," Eun-Ji replied. "But we didn't know enough about it to bring it up when we first introduced Caldwell's recent dealings to you. We had to narrow down our options first—now we have a second mention, and from the source directly, which means we have a target and something to look out for."

"Exactly, because Alexa somehow knew about it," Momma said, the furrow between her brow deepening. "Or—she knew that it existed and Adara was involved in it."

"She and her siblings had gathered their own pieces over the last few months at that point," Anthony said. "She told me she'd explain what they understood once we all got to Bouchard."

But they never did.

"So the only other people in America who know what Project Ember is are dead," Dad muttered, remorse tugging at his words, "and that transcript is all we have of it."

"It's all Caldwell."

"Whatever you do, do not let Caldwell catch you."

Alexa told me that just before her final moments. She'd been desperate for me to get to Bouchard so the base could tell me more about what they'd already found—and, I now realized, for us to help them piece it all together. She'd told Anthony that they would all make it to Bouchard, but there was no denying it: while she had been talking to me in that empty concrete room, she'd known she was going to die. Maybe she'd known that her entire family was dead. And me and my family making it would be the only way for Bouchard to piece everything together since the Delphines couldn't deliver their updates themselves.

"There's a decent amount of information here," Momma noted. "It looks like Caldwell's on the hunt for powerful magicians in the hopes of securing the nation. Alexa said, 'With Adara, the country's magicians are destined to fall, and that gives mortals full confidence and control.' She started saying that Caldwell is searching for something before William came in."

Even though he was dead, I couldn't help but curse the man in my head.

"Yeah," Anthony said, "it *sounds* like Caldwell believes Adara's gonna lead a full-on rebellion against mortals. So it still stands to reason that he's going to do a nationwide sweep of magicians so she has none to lead."

"And use her to do it," I breathed in realization, my eyes widening. "With her magic."

"How did you get 'with her magic'?" Jak asked me. "He has to be planning on killing her—"

"No," I said, turning slightly to face him, "Alexa said, '*With* Adara, the country's magicians are destined to fall.' If Caldwell was planning on killing her, that would've been 'without'. He knows she's strong enough to wipe out her own people. She has to be with the destiny she has..."

That's why, I realized—that was why Alexa had been so desperate to find Adara, to take my magic. For most of last year, at least, when I'd tried to throw her off the scent and *turn* her onto Adara instead of me. That was the moment I'd told her that I was a lead to her greatest target. She'd acted power hungry the whole time to figure out how to secure Adara's magic without arousing Caldwell's suspicion and leading him straight to *his* biggest target.

I wished, I wished, I *wished* she could've just told me. I wished that at one point, she could've pulled me aside and let me know that it was all okay, even telepathically warn me. But the Hunter part of me was too great for me to ignore the fact that she'd clung to her cover for the same reason Mr. Dawson hadn't telepathically talked to me during the spring final last year, when I thought he'd betrayed me: Alexa needed real results out of me, real fear, a real fight. Not for my sake, but for hers—the pack had practically been under twenty-four-hour surveillance from William, the agency, *and* Caldwell.

And look at what happened the second Caldwell did find out about the Delphines.

"It's a miracle they're not investigating Callistro from the looks of it," Momma mused, scrutinizing the pages again. "Considering we used it for a cover for a while."

"That's because they don't know about Caralyn Callistro's alliance with magic," Anthony said. "The proof of which Alexa burned."

I straightened. "Caralyn's documents I found in the underground passageways? Alexa *burned* them?"

"Well, yeah," Anthony said, like it was obvious. "That information would've set Callistro on fire. We got what we needed and made sure nobody else could get it ever again."

I guess that's a relief... One less thing to worry about the government getting their hands on. And I technically had a "copy" of Caralyn's documents recorded in my first journal.

"You found them where, Emma?" Eun-Ji asked, arching a thin brow.

"Caralyn built a secret system of passageways under Callistro that was mainly accessed with magic," I replied, recalling the night I'd first found those papers. It felt almost as old as the school was. "There were these two letters exposing her real intention behind founding the school—did... did you already know about them?"

"We updated her as soon as we got them," Anthony told me. So *that* was how Eun-Ji knew about Caralyn's alliance with magic.

And yet, her dark eyes squinted with doubt, almost as if she didn't believe the allegations despite knowing them. "On top of her *Hunter* school, she built underground tunnels only magic could unlock...?"

The room fell to pensive quiet as she looked away and shook her head. I could almost hear the gears turning. Her soft, round features scrunched together in confusion. "There are things I've never been able to make sense of about her, and that's one of them: what could have prompted her to make such a dramatic change from being ready to kill a mage to fighting for his people? And to help the 'Soul of Unity' she believed in by building an entire school?"

Huh. Sarah had said the same thing...

And yet Eun-Ji kept the first-ever copy of Caralyn's autobiography without question until she could give it to me. I guess that had been one of the things she couldn't make sense of, though. In fact, I wouldn't have been surprised if Eun-Ji had more questions about Caralyn Callistro than I did at this point, but I was getting tired of these questions; I didn't have the answers, and I was pretty sure that there was no way for me to get them.

"Hypothetically," Dad began thoughtfully, "if the school goes under investigation, what are the chances they'll find something?"

"'Something' as in condemning plans against the government? None," Anthony said, resting a hand on the edge of Eun-Ji's desk. "Not even my mom ever found Caralyn's second document while she was going to Callistro, just the first one, which still made it sound like Caralyn was against magic. If Caralyn made incriminating secrets that easy to find, even with magic at the school, someone would've found it by now."

That meant I *definitely* wouldn't be getting the answers to my questions any time soon. It was like Caralyn had only given us the punchline and figured trust was good enough for us to laugh at the joke anyway.

"Her documents do confirm something for us," Eun-Ji said. "She blatantly admitted that the Ateras are the 'ultimate connection' to hope for magicians, and proceeds to address the Soul of Unity, Adara, directly like she knew she'd be a Callistro Girl."

"And that Em would be part of it," Dad added, rubbing his stubbled chin. "It doesn't sound like she knew that Emma specifically would be Adara. But now Em's tied to whatever 'findings' in Spain Alejandro's unknowingly involved in."

Eun-Ji briefly bowed her head. "I almost hate that this is all verified," she mumbled. "Our worst theories are plausible. I guess we'll know for sure based on..."

When she looked up at me, the rest of the room followed. I fought against the urge to shrink back as Eun-Ji asked me, "Do you remember *exactly* what Alexa told you before she died? Word for word? Anything about Caldwell?"

I fixed my gaze on the floor and twisted my necklaces together, racking my memory. "She said if I remembered nothing else, remember that 'it's all Caldwell'. 'Do not let Caldwell catch you.' She was always protecting my family's magic, not me, because her plan was to take it and then send it here to..."—my voice slowed with realization—"keep it safe from him."

The weight of everyone's eyes lifted, darting to Eun-Ji. "Caldwell needs strong magic for a nationwide sweep. The Ateras' has the power he wants, and Adara's is potentially the key to pushing past magic's old limitations. And if there are more like her, like

Alejandro, in different countries, they can conduct this purge on a global scale."

The words turned over and over in my stomach. *Impossible abilities.* Combine all of us somehow to achieve the complete annihilation of an entire people, half the global population.

"That's why the government uses magic to *find* magic," Jak realized. "Strength in numbers, so them taking everyone's power creates a stronger army of mortals and nobody left to fight back."

This conversation was pressing me into the ground. What were we doing here? What were we thinking? Us against the US Government planning the genocide of almost two hundred *million* people? When they had the numbers and all we had was... me? Alejandro? Annisa and Kamose? We hadn't even been able to recruit Runelle for this, and she was just one of five! And then how were the five of us supposed to stop something on a global scale, handling *billions* of lives, when so many of our people were powerless or dead?

"Save them."

My swallow burned my throat. *I never fully realized what being Adara meant until now.*

"I want you all to stay here."

I looked up at the authority that had gripped Eun-Ji's voice. What scared me, though, was when nobody argued—when even Anthony simply stopped and listened.

"Until we solidify a plan," she quickly added. "This is now something that concerns anyone you're involved with, which means all of Bouchard. If you're caught now, you won't be the only ones. I more than understand how much you want to save Thomas, but now more than ever, we need to trust that our safety is the best way to serve him. For the time being."

She was dead right. Caldwell was going to keep Mr. Dawson alive until he had us, and Mr. Dawson had written that he needed to get himself out. That was my only hope left, but it *was* hope.

"Until then?" Momma asked. "Are we letting Caldwell continue perfecting this and waiting until it happens?"

"No," Eun-Ji said, laying her small hands flat on her desk's surface. "In fact, I want you and Tristan both promoted to active Hunters so you can provide our team with some valuable insight, and so we can start anticipating. We may know what Caldwell's planning, but that means nothing if we don't know how he's going to do it. Figuring that out is now our biggest priority."

"Done," Dad said, nodding.

"What about me and Emma and Alejandro?" Jak asked, loosely gesturing to himself and then me. "We can't just do nothing, can we?"

"I actually think that's the best thing you *can* do to protect Emma's and Alejandro's magic," Eun-Ji told him, meeting her eyes with mine. "For now, Emma, stay low, okay?"

She was chief of the entire base, so it wasn't like arguing was an option. But I could bypass a few things:

—*Will you keep me updated?*—

—*To a reasonable extent,*— Dad answered. —*But we're keeping you on a need-to-know basis for this. This time, you have to believe that without arguing.*—

As much as I hated to admit it, that was fair. I just hoped that both my parents and I had learned what we should and shouldn't keep from each other.

Thirty-Six

There was only so much Momma and Dad could do as housebound Hunters, and there was only so much evidence the undercover agents could gather in so much time. It was worse for me, Alejandro, and Jak, who had all been assigned to do literally nothing, when all I *wanted* to do was help in the ways that Callistro had taught me. But when May came around, I wasn't allowed to think about Callistro in any capacity—not until I could find out if I was close to making up the credits I needed to be on track to graduate next year. At this rate, though, that window was closing faster and faster.

So of all things, I turned to teaching for a distraction; Li's grandparents had expressed last month that they wanted her to have the "weapon" of a multilingual tongue. Of course, Michaela heard "weapon" and instantly wanted to join us in the library on Saturdays. I soon found, though, that whenever I *really* focused on these girls, I could feel that magic connection with them—what Dad and Becca told me was my improving sorcerer's ability.

"You need '*te*' in front of it, remember?" I whispered to Michaela, pointing at the pronoun before "*gusta*" in her beginner's Spanish textbook. "That pronoun is just as necessary in Spanish as it is in English. Otherwise you're saying, 'Do like cats?'"

"I thought '*te*' meant 'tea'," she whispered back.

"That's '*té*' with an accent. '*Te*' without an accent is the object pronoun for the informal 'you'."

"I thought Spanish was supposed to be easier." She leaned back in her wooden chair and blew her straight blond hair out of her face. "How do you speak it?"

"I had a much better teacher," I admitted quietly. Even though Momma had taught me Spanish, Monsieur Goubeaux's maintenance exercises in class helped me retain it. That bled into the memories of his class—of his "language face-offs" with Sarah, who always spoke in a language he *didn't* know to mess with him.

I mentally shook those images away and leaned forward to get a better look at Li, sitting on Michaela's other side. "How are you doing, Li?"

"*¿Te gustan gatos?*" she whispered slowly with an outright Canadian accent, beaming.

"Good job!" I chirped softly. "You remembered '*-an*', but don't forget the article '*los*': '*¿Te gustan los gatos?*'"

"I wanna do French," Michaela whispered, shutting her textbook. "French is more fun."

I snickered. "It's also twice as hard. Are you sure?"

"When in Canada." She slid out from her chair, taking the Spanish textbook off the table and walking over to the bookcase behind Li.

Alejandro would've been disappointed if he were here instead of visiting his parents; Eun-Ji had been able to allow that this week after government activity finally ceased around the area a little while ago. I wanted to take that as a good sign, but I couldn't stop thinking about what message Kamose could send back with Alejandro. Especially since we'd been cut off for so long.

If anything significant happened, Kamose would've manipulated circumstances somehow to reach us. I repeated that to myself to maintain my sliver of hope.

"Thanks for teaching us again, Emma!" Li whispered, regaining my attention. She leaned forward with her crossed arms tucked under her on the table. "I like your new necklace."

I looked down at my neck, at the flame necklace overlapping my locket. I was surprised she'd only just now noticed it, but the longer I stared at it now, the more the corners of my lips turned upward. I missed my best friends more than anything, but at least I had something from them so it could feel like they were with me in some compacity.

"Thanks," I whispered to Li. "It means a lot to me."

"How many languages did you learn at Callistro?" she asked quietly as Michaela pushed her textbook back onto the shelf. "I wanna learn five like Caralyn did!"

I tilted my head. "How do you know how many languages Caralyn knew?"

"I found it somewhere in her autobiography," she replied, which turned Michaela around before she could grab a beginner's

French textbook. She skipped back over to her seat as Li added, "She learned the most common languages so she could talk to every magician she caught."

"'Wielder'," Michaela whispered, reminding her of the new (and better) name my friends and I had given our people.

"Oh, right, wielder."

"Hang on, I'm confused," I whispered. "How did you get a copy of her autobiography?"

And why would a nine-year-old want to read something so long and from the nineteenth century?

"Come on." Li stood from her chair, prompting me and Michaela to follow.

Was I crazy? Joseph Bouchard keeping the first-ever copy solely for me was wild enough, but the base having its own copy here in the library for the residents to read? Why would a wielder safe haven have the autobiography of the world's first Hunter school founder when nobody knew that she had secretly been an ally of magic? Unless it was to show how the enemy worked and how they thought, like what Momma wanted for me by enrolling me in Callistro in the first place...

On the right side of the large room, Li led us to a bookcase three away from the library entrance. She stood on her tiptoes and pointed at a book two shelves higher than the top of her head. "That one, it's the dark-red one with gold letters."

I was already recognizing and grabbing it before she could finish. The book weighed just as heavily in my hands as it had the very first time I'd held it: in Callistro's library the first week of sophomore year. *White Lies for Sacred Ties.*

"Do you guys know," I whispered, mindlessly flipping to the

chapter listing Caralyn's riddles for the secret passageway entrances, "who approves the books that come into the library?"

"This is the history shelf," Michaela replied, pointing at the slim black label on the edge of the shelf citing her claim. "That means these books are about Bouchard's history, so they're automatically accepted."

I looked up from the book and into her wide brown eyes. "This one shelf is *just* about Bouchard's history?"

"Yeah. If you want other places' history, that's all the other shelves here, they're for 'Social Studies'."

No way.

That's *why Joseph Bouchard kept the first-ever copy for me here? He and Caralyn really were involved with each other somehow?*

I'd never read Caralyn's autobiography from cover to cover before, and every time I'd flipped through Joseph's copy over the last few months to see if there was something different in it, nothing had popped out. But I was starting to think that I couldn't get away with just skimming anymore.

My eyes scanned the shelf of history books in front of me. It'd take way too long to search through all of these books to find even *one* connection between Callistro and Bouchard.

"Does Joseph Bouchard have an autobiography, too?" I whispered to the girls.

Michaela pointed at the beginning of the shelf. "His is the blue one."

Relieved, I slid it out, put it on top of Caralyn's, and flipped to the first page.

May it first be recognized and acknowledged in sound

mind that I, Joseph Maurice Bouchard, was an explorer, a student of nature and Mother Earth, infinitely prior to my days of chiefhood and protection.

Oh no. He was a lot wordier than Caralyn was.

"That's the only ever copy," Li whispered, like it was a huge secret only the three of us could hear. "He wrote it and then it was published just for the base."

Smart. Something only for his people to have.

I closed the book. "Do you guys mind if I cut the lesson short today? I wanna do some research on this."

"It's boring, trust me," Michaela whispered, starting to amble backwards and toward the library entrance. "Research always is."

You'd be surprised, I thought as she spun on her heel and skipped with Li over to the propped-open doors.

I slid into the chair right in front of me at a long table, setting down Caralyn's autobiography next to Joseph Bouchard's. Never in my life had I been tempted to read a full piece of nineteenth-century prose, let alone dissect the sentences to figure out what it was saying, but I had to this time.

I wished I could ask the book my questions directly as I briskly read through the first two pages of Joseph's narrative: all about how he was a traveler and explorer and came to the United States from France when he was a little boy.

But how did the base come about?

I flipped to the table of contents. Early life, education, first apprenticeship (at a printshop to see how he'd like it), achieving his first role in the US Government—I skimmed through the first few pages of each chapter just in case. His family had been mind-numbingly wealthy and frequently made trips back and forth between France and the US, which inspired Joseph's love for travel and the natural world, especially considering his warlock side. His father held a high position in government and eventually persuaded him to take a jab at it to at least help preserve the family's wealth and give him a steady income. That all led to Joseph finding a way to blend his two worlds, magic and government: he became part of a council that Congress had assembled to add an amendment to the Constitution that would permanently legalize magic in America—

Wait, wait, wait, wait, what?

No way.

Acknowledging the horrors transpiring across the Atlantic, even among our own brothers here, despite the example of our neighbors in the north, our council sought a truce between the two hemispheres of humanity, to permanently withhold prejudice between the most basic versions of existence. Ever-increasing injustice in the South incited action no longer solely against those different externally, but those of us in Congress harboring our differences internally.

Before we twenty-one had a name to call ourselves collectively, the devil's hour struck upon us, sentencing all but one to a grave that would bear witness to none but me, its sole survivor. Within an hour, our constitution, vows, records of our existence, our solemn duty to our country and the first step toward revolution, was reduced to ash by the hand of avarice, blighting the future of generations, that they would have no definition of true equality.

The council was slaughtered because someone couldn't stand the idea of magic surviving in this country. And Joseph had been the only one to escape.

And the twenty sentenced to death, their bodies mutilated and strung upon the pole of freedom's flag in Washington, would never be able to incriminate themselves by testimony. Rather, as I watched from the distance, cloaked upon my steed, my brothers' fates blew with the wind and carried me to North Carolina.

I sat up in my chair. Maybe there was something here.

When the first sentence didn't give me a direct answer, I skimmed ahead until my eyes finally snagged on something:

...two figures amidst the grove of trees, conversing in hushed tones. Steel's hooves alerted them, rendering me hostage. That was, until I encountered their kindness, and away they hid me upon my enemies' arrival.

The lady possessed an intellect and wit that spanned wider than the thickest book in my father's library. A cunning dark-skinned gentleman accompanied her, both of which eventually proved their companionship and earned my own. Sympathizing with my story, and foreseeing the direction of the nation, they determined the construction of a sanctuary, the location of which they entrusted my experience with navigation to decide. Many a night passed that I sat by candle light with the world printed on parchment before me, my research determining straight the answer: a grand peak situated in the heart of a jagged mountain range, in the northwest corner of our northern neighbor. None would uncover its inhabitants, oblivious to the conditions only the warlock's magic can provide.

The same magic that makes it possible for us to drive up here from British Columbia at all. I smiled to myself.

The lady, therefore, with her stunning intellect, determined the construction plans with the help of my and her ally's input regarding what is most imperative to a magician's lifestyle.

My eyes glanced over the rest of the chapter: he wouldn't give the woman's name, or the identity of the man who had been with her. It definitely sounded like Caralyn and Samuel, especially if Caralyn *had* somehow been involved with Bouchard's establishment, but I couldn't assume anything yet.

I skimmed through again: Joseph's travels to Canada to survey the area, the insight he gathered along the way from the magicians he stayed with, the struggle to establish an underground base in a mountain...

Here!

I and forty-nine others formally established and inhabited the facility of Bouchard that monumental Wednesday, September 5, 1827....

I froze. What? That... that was the date the Callistro Academy was founded.

I jumped to the next sentence.

We took great refuge in the notion that our efforts were not, nor would they be, in vain. Our faith remains in the right proprietors of the future, arriving in the name of liberty, resolute for justice, for they will guide the hand determined to rescue her nation.

It takes a great will to uncover what hides, even the truth though it flatly resides.

I blinked. Why would he make that sentence rhyme and put it all by itself? It didn't fit his writing style, either.

It almost sounds like...

I looked over at the worn red cover of Caralyn's autobiography. It sounded like *her* writing.

I wanted more than anything to assume that she was the woman Joseph had met in the North Carolinian forests—but if I built my theory on the wrong foundation, I would lose infinitely more once it came tumbling down. There was no room for risk with this.

I reached for Caralyn's book, but my mind swam with the blurring historical prose I'd already analyzed, and I dropped my hand. There were too many coincidences, and if there was anything I knew about Caralyn, it was that she had purposely left behind clues of her past for me to uncover in the future. But for her to have known that I'd end up at Bouchard one day, to leave something here with Joseph...

If she was involved, I'm missing a piece.

I'd figure it out; the beginning of the evidence was staring me right in the face, and there was no doubt now that the first-ever copy in my room had an answer. Right now, though, as I took Caralyn's and Joseph's books and stood from the library table, I needed to make sure that I came at this with fresh eyes and an alert mind.

Maybe it was the anticipation of finding another step forward amidst all the waiting, but part of me was excited to finally check out something from the library.

THIRTY-SEVEN

hen I told Jak the kind of research I wanted to do today, he wanted to tag along... which made me happier and more nervous than I wanted to admit. Our kiss in his room a few weeks ago still lingered in the back of my mind every time I looked at him. I cursed the fact that, with things picking back up ever since then, talking about a potential relationship had gone from the back burner to the fireplace. As always, no matter how closely he stood next to me or how long he smiled at me in the way he did, I had to pretend it was another exchange between "good friends".

As we entered the busy art room together, I clutched Joseph's autobiography with both copies of Caralyn's to my side, noticing Dakota at an easel along the left wall. Joshua stood behind her with his arms around her, one hand guiding hers as they held a paintbrush against the canvas.

"Hey!" I said amidst the subtle conversation floating around.

Dakota's head of fawn-brown hair turned to us, alerting Joshua. Her blue eyes brightened with her grin. "Hi, you guys!" she chirped, setting down the paintbrush and revealing the canvas in full: a campfire in a night-time forest clearing. "What do you think? It's one of the things we wanna experience together if we ever get to see the surface."

"It's beautiful," Jak said, signing the words as he went. "You two look cozy."

"We've been together for a month now," she replied dreamily, turning and tilting her head up for a kiss from Joshua. Her light hand rested on his cheek as he obliged. "Joshua offered watercolor when I failed at digital art. What're you doing today?"

"Some reading," I said, shifting the books from my side and into my hands.

"Oh, yeah, reading together is always a *lot* more fun," she simpered, signing it as she spoke. Joshua pecked her freckled cheek as if in reward. "We'll let you get to that."

"Thanks," Jak replied, maintaining his friendly smile like he hadn't caught the implication. I offered a wave before starting for the beanbag chairs in the back of the room.

Don't read too much into it, I repeated to myself. *They don't know they're taunting you with their couple-y stuff because life refuses to give you a break.*

Jak stayed close to me as we crossed the buzzing room. A cluster of beanbag chairs sat beside the rocking chairs Dakota usually crocheted in with her other friends. For some reason, Jak's eyes felt heavy on me as I plopped down into a purple beanbag. I tried to avoid his stare as I flipped open Joseph's autobiography and to the tenth chapter, where I'd found his random rhyme after Bouchard had been established.

Jak sat in the yellow beanbag next to me before taking both copies of Caralyn's book from the floor of my seat. "Where are we starting?" he asked with the excitement of a schoolboy.

"I really don't know why you wanted to come," I said. "I'm just looking further into these and seeing if I can find an explicit connection."

"Well, because studying *is* always more fun with a partner," he replied. "Wyatt and Breanne told me so."

Wow. Their names felt so... distant. I was surprised that Jak had brought them up to begin with. I guess he was finally at a place where remembering them did more good than harm, which I was thankful for.

"So where did you last leave off?" he asked me.

"Um..." I skimmed through the chapter for "September 5, 1827", then pointed at it and leaned over to show him. "This is the last *interesting* thing that caught my attention. Read the sentence after it."

Jak's eyes slightly jittered across the words before a subtle divot dented his brow. "Maybe he liked poetry."

"Have you ever read Caralyn's autobiography?"

"Well—no."

"Do you remember the riddles she wrote for the secret passageway entrances around Callistro?"

"Yeah."

"Okay. *That's* what this sounds like to me." I read the line again: "'It takes a great will to uncover what hides, even the truth though it flatly resides.' It sounds like Caralyn's writing, like one of her riddles. She's the only one I've ever read who talks like this, and Mrs. Durrett made us read a *lot* of nineteenth-century prose, so I have context for what does and doesn't sound generic for that time period."

Jak flipped through the first-ever copy of Caralyn's autobiography, barely giving himself time to read a word. "So Bouchard and Callistro both have the same founding dates. Did you finish reading that chapter?"

"It was mostly about logistics and how the first week of establishment went."

"What about the next one?"

"I was gonna read it today. You could read from Caralyn's if you wanna help—the chapter where she formally established Callistro. Tell me if any details stick out, and if there's any difference between the two copies."

He flipped to the front of both books. "Gotcha."

I started on the eleventh chapter—or, rather, the twelfth when the eleventh's title was about how Bouchard maintained and gathered their supplies throughout the next year. And then the thirteenth when the twelfth's title warned me that it was just about the establishment of the administration system. It was like that all the way until I found myself at the author's note in the back.

What? Would I actually have to read through this whole thing to find something?

I highly doubted that Joseph would flat out state his secrets in the author's note as a final goodbye, but I probably had a bigger chance with that than reading about the rotating lumber team that was sent out every week to gather fuel and material.

I have yet to determine if my words, being the only testimony of a council that sought to uphold the American Constitution in a light most truthful and unbiased, for liberty and justice for all, will serve the generations to come or condemn them. Without any record but my own account, we should have no reason to believe the council's existence at all, that anyone strived for a future permitting life, liberty, and the pursuit of happiness for all. I write these words, therefore, solely to immortalize their truth, why we pursued all that we did despite the abundance of trial and tribulation: the people of magic must hide, those unable to find courage to match their opponents in physical skill and mental wit, taking refuge in a sanctuary against the direction their world is in chase of.

Okay... So despite the risk he posed in immortalizing his testimony, Joseph published his narrative to reaffirm Bouchard's purpose: safety, a place for powerless wielders to take refuge in. Those "unable to find courage" to... well, it almost sounded like he was referring to wielders willing to fight back against Hunters.

Then Caralyn most likely did help him establish Bouchard—considering the mission she'd given herself with Adara. She had believed in the same thing.

I'm still missing something, though. That final piece confirming that it'd been Caralyn and no other woman. Something was incomplete, like I hadn't found—

"Em?"

I looked up at Jak, my heart skipping a beat. "What?"

"You said any detail that sticks out?"

Using one hand for each copy of Caralyn's book, Jak put his thumb next to a sentence with the unmistakable date of my birthday, leaning toward me. "Like Caralyn writing the exact same rhyme after Callistro's date of establishment?"

Wait—what?

No way. *No way*—there it was. I should've read her autobiography when I'd had the chance at Callistro; I could've saved myself a lot of time here!

"Okay," I said, "what do you know about Joseph Bouchard?"

"He has the same name as the base," Jak answered. "Do you think that's a coincidence?"

"You're turning out to be the worst research partner ever, for one. Two, he was part of a council of Congress meant to draft a constitutional amendment that would permanently legalize magic in America. The entire council was slaughtered and he was the only one who escaped, and then he met this woman in a forest in North Carolina. Now I *know* it was Caralyn, these two were one hundred percent connected. She helped him establish Bouchard."

"Wow, she worked *really* hard to keep her cover to the public," Jak mused, scanning the pages like they would change at any moment. "To go so far as to build a whole school against magic when she was actually on its side."

"It was probably too late to change the purpose of the school to something normal like a house, and so suddenly," I said. "She would've been found out if she'd tried that."

"Maybe... But I feel like their connection goes beyond the idea to found the base. Like, what does this line mean?"

"'It takes a great will to uncover what hides, even the truth though it flatly resides'..."

Caralyn only had a few people she could entrust her darkest secrets to; Joseph, on the other hand, had a story that he hadn't revealed in his autobiography despite knowing that only magicians (and trusted allies of magic) would read it. And they both strongly believed in a system of justice, one that they both had to fight to uphold and would never live to see fulfilled. That definitely took great will, but a will to uncover what hides? The truth though it flatly resides...?

"Why would they both say that?" I whispered, mostly to myself. "In both of their autobiographies, in the same spot..."

"What were you reading just now?" Jak asked, gesturing to the book in my lap. "Why did you skip to the end?"

I flipped through the yellowed pages. "Everything else was all stuff about the base and Joseph's life here, so I figured the author's note might have something. He basically said that he wanted to establish Bouchard so that wielders would have a safe place. Specifically wielders who can't fight the enemy head on."

"Okay." Jak slowly nodded. "Have you ever read Caralyn's author's note?"

"No."

But after I did when we swapped books, it was everything I'd expected from a woman trying to maintain her cover to the public as a renowned Hunter: a message about the dangers of magic and how her testament sought to provide "necessary context for measures seemingly so extreme". Then the last sentence was about how magicians would have nowhere else to hide once Callistro— "perhaps even additional schools"—were established.

It's interesting that she'd almost connect their two last lines in their author's notes—like she was encouraging wielders to hide at Bouchard.

Except she'd given no hint about Bouchard's existence anywhere, not even in the documents she'd hidden in the underground secret passageways.

She was great at acting. Too great.

"I feel like," I began, huffing and leaning into my beanbag, "we're not any closer."

"Why, because we can't figure out one sentence right now?" Jak said patiently. "Now you know these two were involved with each other, no argument. They were working with some kind of common goal with their two establishments, and they left you one line to figure it out with. Because clearly, a Hunter school wasn't the sanctuary Joseph wanted to offer."

"But Caralyn didn't hint anywhere that Bouchard existed," I argued. "I feel like she should've left it in at least one place, or hidden it in a riddle. That was how she hid the underground passageways and nobody found out whose side she was really on."

Jak shrugged. "Probably what that one line is referring to: it takes a strong will to figure out the truth here. But I'll bet you anything that you're the one with that will."

No kidding. My will was practically half of my magic at this point, a superpower on its own. It was even strong enough to cast spells that didn't exist.

I paused but just as quickly had to shake the idea from my head: Caralyn couldn't have meant for me to use my will to find this missing piece. There was absolutely *no* way for her to have known that Adara would be a hybrid who could cast spells that didn't exist.

Honestly, I was starting to think that *she* had been a wielder. As ridiculous as I wanted to count the notion, wasn't *everything* on the table at this point? There were too many possibilities and what-ifs and questions we couldn't solve unless we were to go back in time somehow and ask her ourselves.

I froze. Wait. *Couldn't* we? Me, Alejandro, and Annisa—who was in the same country as us this time. Alejandro and I could pack for another trip and—

"Uh oh."

I lifted my head to Jak again. "What?"

"You have that look."

"What look?"

"The look you get when you have an idea as insane as you taking Alejandro and jumping to the other side of the world for intel."

Okay—knowing the full truth or not, Jak wasn't supposed to know me *that* well.

"You know that's one of the reasons you're such a valuable asset," I said. "You believe in the potential of my craziest ideas *like* jumping to the other side of the world for intel."

"I'm not making any promises," he said, tilting his head down at me. Almost as quickly, though, his eyes softened on me. "Look, whatever you're thinking, don't make any plans yet. You'll figure this out—without potentially killing yourself. The important thing is that Caralyn didn't wanna kill you guys, and hundreds of people, including us, have someplace safe to stay today."

Well, with that, it was set: I was *definitely* jumping to Ontario with Alejandro, because there was no way I was letting Caralyn harbor this many secrets that she'd straight up confessed she had. I'd figured out most of them on my own already; the rest, she could give me herself.

C H A P T E R

Thirty-Eight

"I don't know, *amiga.*" Alejandro took another swig from his water bottle, resting his bare forearms on his knees. His basketball uniform suited him surprisingly nicely, and his verbal English had improved twofold since we'd gotten back from Antarctica. He was speaking it a lot more often with his tutor, his team, and even my family. "Last time, we had success, but they almost caught us, do you remember?"

"That's why this time would be safer," I said, my bottom already sore from the hard wooden bleachers. I'd taken a solid ten minutes to explain everything to him, and I really didn't want to take another ten persuading him. "At least Annisa's in the same country, unlike Kamose. And didn't you say you were getting stronger with your teleportation, traveling all the way to Spain all those weeks to visit your parents?"

"Yes, but..."

When a rebuttal didn't find him in time, he took another drink from his bottle. Water seemed to be what gave him his answer: "Your president will make the governments look for us everywhere. They know that we're in Canada. Well, they know that we went here."

"I'm not saying we leave right this second. But whenever we do, it'll be helpful for both us and Bouchard. Caralyn knew something about Adara, which means she might've known something about the rest of us. Who knows, we might even find a clue about how Caldwell's gonna carry out his plans this year."

"Annisa needs a date to travel to. How will she find the right one?"

I sighed, resting my elbows on my knees and looking out at the basketball players skirting across the brightly lit waxed court. That was a question I'd been contemplating since I first thought of the idea yesterday, and I only had one real solution:

"I have a rough timeframe. The books gave some context clues that we can research and probably find an exact date from."

"If it's wrong, Annisa has to go to—more times. To find the right one. Is it—worthy? To make her do that?"

I didn't want to answer that; I knew how *I* felt, but I couldn't force any of the others to feel the same way.

"It *could* be worth it," I said. "Because if I'm right about this, Caralyn did know that there'd be wielders two hundred years later with, specifically, impossible powers. That involves us. If she, of all people, knew about that, how do we know nobody else ever did or *does*?"

Now Alejandro paused, staring down at the drinking spout on his water bottle. There were too many possibilities now: Caralyn could've seen a seer, she could've *been* a seer, she could've known someone who knew the truth like Jak's mom had—she could've not known the truth at all and hoped for the best! I seriously doubted it, but too many "impossibilities" had popped up since two Augusts ago, and I was ready to consider anything.

"It isn't possible..." Alejandro muttered as if to himself, shaking his head. "A mortal who knows about you, or Joseph Bouchard knows about you..."

"We have to do this before the base goes under magic lockdown again," I told him. I had a nauseating instinct telling me that our freedom wasn't going to last. "This could be our *one* chance to get definitive answers."

Eventually, he turned to face me. "Okay. Find the date first. We will go to Annisa when you know. Then we can go to there and be fast."

I tensed. We couldn't wisely assume how long or short this trip would be. But I *had* to go, for the same reason I once asked Steven to create a mental locator spell so I could track Alexa at any time: to make sure I caught something my allies couldn't. To hear everything for myself so that *I* wouldn't miss anything. If this trip was going to happen, I had to play by Alejandro's terms.

I met the softness in his sharp eyes. "Okay."

"Find me when you know, and then we can tell your family."

That was the plan. There was a lot we needed to figure out, especially if Caralyn had known as much as I was concerned that she had. And if she'd known something we didn't, that something could potentially help us with Caldwell.

"Let's do it," I said as Alejandro climbed down the wooden bleachers.

◊

After a couple of days of studying the autobiographies for solidified context clues, I was anxious to get to Annisa's: both books mentioned something about a specific "encounter" of sorts late at night during a vengeful thunderstorm—"as if the earth herself opposed our alliance, seeking to erase all evidence of magic's refuge," Joseph had written. "Or perhaps she significantly opposed receiving her children prematurely." Prior to meeting with Caralyn that night, he'd witnessed the slaughter of an entire street of wielders—an organized riot that a Master Hunter had led to "inspire" the people. Annisa was sure to be able to research that and pinpoint a date to try... as long as history had deemed that night's slaughter worthy to record.

After the miracle of persuading my parents to let us go, Alejandro and I set off for Ontario with Caralyn's autobiography. This time, we left no room for chance and packed enough snacks so we could teleport to purely remote locations. Alejandro said he could get us to Annisa's in three jumps. And with how much practice he'd had this year, he needed less time between landings to recover. The freedom of the great outdoors with no civilization to threaten our existence this time around probably helped with that, too.

It was in a wild birch forest clearing in Saskatchewan that he told me, "Remember, don't take off your hood until we know there is no one around. We'll be in front of a window when we land, so stay low."

The ground disappeared and then solidified beneath me for the third and last time. Instantly, my feet sank into a dirt patch in front of an exterior gray wall. A large window sat above us.

I'm glad he warned me about that.

I looked out in front of me, over the bushes, at the wide, open street. A row of one-story suburban houses faced us on the other side, quiet. Staying low, I slid off my invisibility cloak's hood and scurried onto the bright-green lawn. When I looked behind me, the window blinds were shut.

Okay, good.

I stood on the grass, prompting Alejandro to do the same as he adjusted his backpack. He ran a tired hand through his spiky hair, sighing with contentment. "The weather is much nicer here," he remarked. "Why did Joseph not build his base somewhere else? Not in the mountains."

I nodded to the dark-wooden door at the end of the white porch railing. "You can find out once we get inside and Annisa takes us to him."

He stepped with me alongside the railing, passing two more windows as we went. The side of what was likely the garage sat ahead, a driveway stretching out from it and into the empty street. Alejandro and I climbed up a few stone steps before approaching the front door, and I rang the doorbell. Only seconds later, the lock clicked.

I'd only met Annisa in person once before, but when she pulled open the door and looked up at me, I'd never seen her pale-brown face and maroon eyes so illuminated (or illuminated at all, for that matter, considering how timid she'd been when we had first met).

"You made it," she chirped with a light Indonesian accent, motioning the two of us inside with a small hand.

I stepped over the threshold, holding out my arms. She embraced me with a tightness I hadn't expected from a girl so small, an inch shorter than Alejandro.

"I can't believe I'm finally seeing you again," I said, squeezing her before letting go, "after all this time. The day we met feels so long ago."

"For me, too." Her eyes fell onto the boy walking in behind me and closing the door. She sheepishly grinned at him, her voice softening more somehow. "Oh, wow—Alejandro?"

"Yes," he said, holding out his hand with a grin similar to the one he'd worn when I'd first met him. "It's nice to meet you."

"Yeah, it's... nice to—meet you in person," she said, shaking his hand. She then placed hers on her heart and pushed a straight lock of her long black hair behind her ear. "Um—welcome, this is my home."

She extended her arm toward the small hallway reaching leftward, leading to one half of the house. Polished wooden floors carried our voices with mild acoustics, the light-gray-painted walls reflecting a soft cold. I could see the start of a living room at the end of the hallway, and the entrance to another hall.

"Where's your family?" I asked, taking a step forward.

Annisa held out her arm, pointing at my shoes. I noticed then her black socks, and the small pile of shoes under a bench sitting against the wall. "Um, you can't... go in unless you take off your shoes."

Alejandro and I obeyed, sliding them under the bench.

"My siblings are at school," Annisa told us, "and, um, my parents are at work. I'm homeschooled because—my magic. My parents... don't want to risk me being caught."

Right: she and her family had chosen to give up their magic back in Indonesia in exchange for their lives, but Annisa had miraculously and somehow gotten it back after they moved to Canada. Now she was the only wielder in her family.

"That makes sense," I said. "And they're okay with us staying here in case we have to? We don't know how long we'll be."

"Oh, completely," she replied, walking ahead of us and toward the living room. "They're—actually really excited that there are others... like me."

"Great," I said, following her down the short leftward hallway with Alejandro behind me. "Then let's get started, we have a pretty good lead for where—or, I guess, when—to go."

The living room paralleled a dining area on our left that we passed as Annisa continued through an archway and into a dim hall. "That's good," she said. "If we can make sure it's the right date, we won't have to spend time experimenting. And—I won't run out of energy."

At the right end of the hall, she led us into a bedroom practically glowing pastel yellow with the sunlight illuminating white wooden furniture and decorations. Despite Annisa's quiet demeanor, her bedroom was a lot cheerier than I would've expected; all her bed in the middle was missing was a smiley face on the comforter. I was almost surprised that her corner desk straight ahead hadn't been painted yellow, too.

An open laptop sat on the surface. *Perfect.*

"Okay," I began, striding over to it with Annisa, "Joseph

wrote about a night that he met up with his 'North Carolinian ally'—Caralyn Callistro—where there was a huge storm, so big that it destroyed a handful of buildings. Right before meeting her, he saw a Master Hunter lead a group of mortals to slaughter the wielders living on Whitman Street. Capperson was just a settlement back then, but I'm really hoping that night was recorded somewhere so it can give us a date."

"Okay, okay," Annisa said eagerly, pulling out her chair from the desk and plopping down. She woke up her laptop and then let her fingers fly over the keyboard, entering her search. "That's... likely. Since it was part of the Hunter movement. And—if the storm was that big."

Alejandro stationed himself at the corner of the bed, dropping his backpack onto it and unzipping it. "*Amiga*, do you need Caralyn's book?"

"Sure, for when we find something."

He slid it out and handed it to me. I took it, setting it down beside Annisa's laptop right when she jumped.

"Right here," she said, pointing at the screen. I leaned down to better see the colonial-themed website that had clearly been coded with HTML. Annisa's pale-brown finger moved along as she read a block of text sitting above a picture of an old newspaper. A church had been photographed on the front page. "May 18, 1819, at 11 P.M., Mark Buckley—the Master Hunter—led a group of people to Whitman Street as a form of protest and empowerment. To prove that mortals could fight against magicians without fear. That night is called the 'Whitman Cleansing'."

The words curdled in my stomach. I hoped my teeth wouldn't break as I clenched them.

"A thunderstorm happened right after," Annisa noted, a concentrative divot forming between her thick brows. "It set half of the street on fire, and an abandoned church on the outskirts of the settlement."

"There," I said, "Joseph Bouchard wrote that they met up in an abandoned church at midnight, it nearly collapsed on them."

"We have the date and the time?" Alejandro asked.

"Yeah, I can—take us there," Annisa replied, swiveling in her chair to face us both. "I can use the photo to go there—to that church during the date and time I want. But it might... feel intense. Also because... I've only taken my brother and sister into the past before."

"Do you use energy while you're there?" Alejandro asked.

"It... it should be fine," Annisa assured him. "We can always take a break and go back—if we need to. But I don't think we have to worry. I've gone—further back before." She peered up at me from her chair. "Are... are you ready?"

I had no idea what we were going to find in 1819 except for concrete answers about who Caralyn Callistro really was, down to her essence and what the Callistro Academy had been to *her*. And that opened a door to a lot more possible answers—why we all had the powers we did, why it was us who had them, how we were supposed to use them. Caralyn and even Joseph were desperate to keep Adara's mission alive for some reason. We needed to know for sure, once and for all.

"Ready," I told Annisa. "You have no idea how long I've been looking for this."

"Okay." She stood, offering me and Alejandro her small hands. "Then let's find it."

We locked hands, and she turned her gaze back to her laptop, to the photo of the church in the newspaper. "Close your eyes," she told us. "The transition will be... weird."

After teleporting with Alejandro so many times, I was tempted to sneak a peek anyway—but time travel was vastly different from teleporting. That was proven the second the world around me suddenly spun together, my insides surging, and I squeezed my eyes shut.

C H A P T E R

Thirty-Nine

A sturdy floor caught me just before I could fall through it. Nausea sloshed in my stomach, untamed by the frigid storm winds raging around me. A rainy torrent blared in my ears, almost drowning out Annisa as she shouted, "It's okay now."

I opened my eyes once the nausea settled. Splintered planks stared back up at me amidst the dark of night. Another sharp gust flew by, blowing a few waterdrops onto my skin. I blinked, glancing up: we were just barely protected by a small overhead creaking above us.

Shivering, I looked down at Annisa next to me, Alejandro on my other side. Double doors stood in front of us. A small field sat behind the church, bleeding into a forest.

"Inside," Annisa called, "so we don't get soaked."

"They won't see us?" Alejandro asked, reaching out to stop her before retracting.

"No, we're... on a different level of reality. In a 'second version'—it coexists with the past, so we can touch anything,"—she grabbed the brass doorknob of one of the doors—"but nobody here will see it, or us—in their reality. Because they're in the one that already happened. Come on."

I was freezing and we *were* getting soaked, so I was grateful when Alejandro didn't argue.

Annisa held open the door, and we dashed inside. A dilapidated, splintered ceiling groaned above us, the muted pounding of rain beating against it. Empty, dusty pews sat left and right, a couple askew and their wood chewed. And as if we'd stepped right into a movie scene, the busted window in the back of the building allowed just enough moonlight in to illuminate the brunet woman standing at the pulpit.

I stopped. *Caralyn Callistro.*

"Emma?" Alejandro asked, pausing with me.

I knew those intense brown eyes, the elegant bun with bangs that framed her triangle face. The regal dark-green dress accompanying her natural air of dignity from the portraits I'd seen all around my school. Now she was standing in front of me, twenty feet away.

She wasn't just part of a story. *She's real.*

The front doors banged open. The three of us spun around, narrowly jumping back and out of Joseph Bouchard's way in time as he barreled down the center of the church. His heavy boots left a trail of muddy footprints, his coat dripping with rainwater.

It's him, I thought, my mouth agape. *We're actually in 1819!*

"Caralyn," Joseph began with a silvery voice I hadn't expected—with a heavy melancholy that I almost had. He stepped onto the platform and up to the pulpit, meeting her there. With a set square jaw and strong nose, he peered down at her with his hat pressed against his chest, leaving inches between them.

She paused, staring at him. "Are you well?"

Annisa, Alejandro, and I carefully approached the front row of the church. I tightened my breath upon the sweet yet smooth voice Caralyn had asked the question with. I hadn't had any expectations for her voice, but I wasn't sure I'd expected that, either.

"Caralyn..." This time Joseph cried her name, water dripping from his blond ends that went down to his neck. He closed his eyes, his head falling forward and onto her shoulder. Without hesitation, she wrapped her thin arms around his shaking form.

Oh... I quickly remembered. *The Whitman Cleansing happened an hour ago.*

"What troubles you?" Caralyn asked, shutting her eyes tightly as if from the pierce of his shallow breathing. "Please."

He straightened, his hand passing over his face. "Whitman Street is now a ghost town—in every sense."

"What do you mean?" she asked, her thin brows pinching with worry.

"Mark Buckley gathered a militia of mortals and led them in a murderous raid. Every one of my people who resided there is dead. Unrecorded and forgotten. Not even their blood stains the road thanks to the storm. None of them are left, none of my people have a place here any longer!"

His voice resounded across the wooden building and up to

the ceiling, a high-up groan giving way with it. Annisa, Alejandro, and I carefully sat down in the frontmost pew. I saw a hard lump pass in Caralyn's throat, one hand coming to rest on the pulpit. Her other bunched the lacy fabric over her chest as her sharp jaw locked. I wondered if, if not for the downpour raging outside, I would've been able to somehow hear her thoughts.

Does she hate what happened as much as he does?

"Samuel has regained his fallen friends tonight," she murmured.

This was *after* Samuel's death? He'd died while the three of them were friends?

"That son of a wench Mark Buckley betrayed *his* friends," Joseph spat. "Yet another Hunter portraying himself as a magician, only, this time, brave enough to murder with his own hands."

I can't believe that back then, mortals pretended to be wielders so they could infiltrate and then kill us. Now it was the opposite, because it was the only way wielders could survive.

"Joseph—"

He threw his arms out. "If not the senseless murder these federal workers conduct on magicians, it's lying as a snake in the grass to pit us against each other! Allow us to doubt our alliances and trust in likeliness alone so that we ultimately kill each other for it!"

"Yes..." she replied. "I've taken notice. The movement against your people has surged with violent urgency as of late."

"Your people*", not "our"*—*Caralyn wasn't a wielder. But how did she find out everything she did and get so involved with them?*

"The enemy's methods are evolving," Joseph said. "They do not depend on brute force alone, they've added manipulation and subterfuge. Our population has never declined so rapidly. They've enlisted us in their war without our knowledge or consent. Our mortality rates have become fatal because of it. We're trembling at the precipice of endangerment and our own hands aid in that, all at the fault of our disagreements. Unless matters change, we won't survive this decade, something *must* be done."

I fidgeted with my locket and the flame necklace for comfort. My body was tense with the itch to hear a long-awaited answer.

"What are you suggesting, Joseph?" Caralyn asked.

"My dear," he said, taking her hands, "I know we stand years prior to when we wanted to begin construction, but you must allow the trip to the northwest mountains before my people's existence is wiped from the face of the earth."

Thunder rumbled lowly in the distance as the divot between her brows deepened. "'Allow'?" she asked. "The facility belongs to you, it's your decision what you ought to do—"

"No," he stated. "Not for this. To successfully establish a haven for the remainder of magicians as soon as possible, I need your help."

Caralyn withdrew her hands. "Joseph."

"Hiding is now our only means to ensure long-term survival. An establishment such as this will cost the same number of years as the school due to the foundation—"

"Exactly why I must stay and build the school," she argued. "Hiding alone won't save you. You'll only delay your extinction."

"You mean to say that producing Hunters by the masses will *alleviate* the matter?"

Exactly! I couldn't help but think. Did Caralyn really believe that keeping her cover until Adara came to pass would outweigh the effects of the Callistro Academy?

"In *this* way, yes." She pressed her hands to her silk sides. "Fortifying a magician's resolve and their confidence—"

"Caralyn." Joseph's voice betrayed its quiver as he grabbed his blond hair. "My love, this may not be the solution we originally thought it to be. This may induce hysteria among us instead!"

Whoa, whoa, whoa, wait a minute—had he just said "my love"? Caralyn, his *love*?

"You let your fear blind you." She lifted her hand to the side of his face. "Remember what you know. Just as it is in the real world, so it will be at the school."

I paused, earning Annisa's glance next to me. What did she mean by that?

"You don't understand," Joseph began, moving her hand away. A heavy wind blew against the church, sending another creak across the building. "For every second we waste without a haven, we sacrifice another innocent soul. I beg you, allow our leave, accompany me to the mountains—"

"The academy is a catalyst, don't pretend that you've forgotten," Caralyn retorted. "You've yet to fully understand—"

"You didn't see what I saw!" he bellowed, slamming his hand against the pulpit. I jumped, and I'm pretty sure Annisa and Alejandro did, too. "Pistols and bayonets slaughtering dozens; backs arched as women and children screamed in terror; the blood of my brothers and sisters washed in the rain, never to record their memory to anyone, rinsing the sins of their *murderers*! Another round of the night I fled from Congress!"

"You needn't speak to me on the tragedy of loss," she stated, her hands balling into fists against her gown. I shivered, holding my necklaces tighter in my hand. "My closest ally and confidant is dead as of last night because of an ignorant spy—one not only working against his own people, but who also believed that the color of Samuel's skin warranted his death all the more. They had him killed because he dared to be human. It is now my responsibility to tell his expecting wife that her husband will never return to her, that her child will never meet their father. And this will be the everyday of this country unless someone dares to change it, and so I have. The school *must* tell the Atera descendant—"

"Think beyond long-term conditions!" Joseph said. In full honesty, I cursed him for not letting Caralyn finish her last sentence. "If our solution doesn't suffice, there will *be* no long term to think for. For all we know, if you and I don't act accordingly now, my own descendant may never live to aid the Ateras' as she is destined!"

My heart skipped a beat as thunder rumbled above, vibrating the floor. *Aid the Ateras' descendant.* Not only did Joseph—which consequently had to mean Caralyn—know that an Atera descendant specifically would be Adara, but a *Bouchard* descendant had the same destiny as her? That meant we had another ally—one that was already at the base and had been the whole time!

I looked over at Alejandro on Annisa's other side, his eyes already trained on me with seemingly the same message. But Annisa sat between us slouched, blinking slowly, a slight furrow pinching her thick brows together.

I leaned toward her ear. "Are you doing okay?"

"Yeah. I can do a—few more minutes."

I looked up at Caralyn and Joseph at the front of the church. This was starting to sound like a full-blown argument; I wasn't sure we *had* a few minutes.

A clap boomed in the distance, startling us all. I reminded myself that Annisa, Alejandro, and I were safe—probably—but Caralyn and Joseph couldn't say the same.

Wait. Are we safe from getting zapped if we could get wet and Annisa could open the door?

I stared after Caralyn and Joseph as they locked eyes with each other, silently begging them to finish up.

"The school plays too vital a role, Joseph," she said, as steady as ever. "But if it worries you to this extent, we'll amend the plan. We'll begin construction now if our enemies won't give us the time we wanted. Bouchard will become the overt sanctuary for your people, but it should also run a confidential training ground to help its residents and the academy in the long term."

What? Did that mean one of Bouchard's missions was to send undercover staffing to Callistro, like how Mrs. Durrett was a magician but also the sophomore-class English teacher?

"Real Hunters will be walking the halls of your school," Joseph argued.

She gently held up her hands. "Only if you deem the capabilities of Bouchard's future residents worthy of the risk. Meanwhile, my school will maintain a cover to the public as one for gifted young ladies learning how to protect themselves in this world. No one but the federal government may be aware that we are the teachers of their Hunters, which inherently assures them, to their knowledge, that matters and the population are under control. That should slow the onslaught and create a partnership with the government so we may receive insight internally. But absolutely no one—no one beyond my ears, yours, and anyone I permit henceforth—is to know the academy's mission."

"Then how should anyone in future generations know what it ever is?"

Caralyn turned to face us. For a split second, I thought she could see us. Then she walked to the edge of the platform, kneeled down, and took the brown leather book lying next to the pulpit.

"Ah," Joseph noted, as if in remembrance. Of what, though? What was that book?

"Everything resides in here," Caralyn began, standing. "I've journaled the truth regarding my alliance with magic and what the academy truly is, and all that I've gathered about Adara. My only struggle now is sealing it from prying eyes and ensuring that hers are the only ones that will read it."

In the corner of my eye, both Annisa and Alejandro whipped their heads over to me, but Caralyn had ensnared my full attention. That journal had every answer about her that I'd ever looked for. How was I supposed to find it? Did it even still exist?

"I have it, it's simple," Joseph said. She released the book into his hands. "An illusion spell will disguise this as whatever you'd like it to appear as, as long as it's similar in nature. A reversal spell can undo it, but nobody will know a spell is over it to begin with."

Caralyn turned back to the pulpit, intense eyes trained on it with concentration. "Another book..." she mused. The church squeaked, her gaze rising to the double doors on the other side of the building. After another moment, she faced Joseph again.

"If we're to disguise this as another book, there must be a discreet way to deliver the message to Adara, even if it's centuries from now."

"What say you?"

"The seer I spoke with regarding her lineage—I'll ask him where she may find this one day. Wherever that is, that's where we will hide it. You and I must lay down the truth in a manner the world won't come to know, but Adara will understand—especially in the case that Runelle won't be there to deliver the message directly and help her."

My jaw fell agape. *Runelle.* The girl we'd met in Antarctica.

That girl is Joseph Bouchard's descendant.

"Emma, did you hear that, too?" Alejandro asked. "Runelle—Joseph's descendant?"

All I could do was nod, too stunned to speak. What had happened to Runelle for her to hate her family so passionately? Did she know who her family really was? Did she know the significance of the name "Joseph Bouchard"?

"A discreet hidden manner such as..." Joseph said, setting Caralyn's journal onto the pulpit, "your own book."

"My account," she answered with revelation. "My narrative regarding the academy's establishment and what I hope for its Hunters—a falsehood to any real Hunter who may read it, but something inside only for Adara's mind to understand. But would that be impetus enough for her to investigate?"

"I'll write my own as well," Joseph quickly said. "For the residents of the facility, should she ever find herself there, or at least a clue for Runelle to provide her."

Caralyn nodded. "If I document my life in printed copies, the illusion spell can hide the journal amidst them, few as they will be. In fact, I should excuse its disguise further: it will be the first printed, a 'test copy' of sorts."

My heart stopped.

Caralyn Callistro's journal. All these months, I'd had *Caralyn Callistro's journal.*

"*Everything resides in here.*" Resides *flat* in a book exposing the truth. As in "the truth though it flatly resides"!

"I'll hide it where the seer instructs me to," she added, "and there will always be someone to protect it there until she arrives. As long as our most trusted allies safeguard this across generations, I have faith this will ultimately land in her hands."

I instinctively looked down at my lap before remembering that I'd left Caralyn's "first-ever printed autobiography" on Annisa's desk. All I had to do was a reversal spell on the book, and it would reveal the truth!

I turned to Annisa with the news practically bursting at the seams—but her small hand now rested on her forehead with her head hanging down.

"Annisa?" I said.

A lump passed in her throat. "I have—" she rasped, barely able to conjure enough volume over the storm outside, "I think I have a minute."

I anxiously looked back up at the front of the church. Lightning flashed through the busted window behind Caralyn and Joseph, scaring us all again. The storm picked up. A large wet spot saturated the wood below the opening. Rain was pouring in sheets outside. A gust of icy wind blasted through the window.

"We should leave," Caralyn called, taking her journal from Joseph. "But I know exactly how to hide my message. Do you remember the riddles I proposed for hiding secret tunnel entrances throughout the manor?"

"I do," he replied, placing his hat back onto his blond head.

"We can hide our clue in a similar manner. I trust in Adara's wit and will to find the pattern. She is a daughter of magic, a soul of unity—I can only pray that these things are in her blood."

Soul of unity. Coming straight from her, the words burned with nostalgia in my chest.

"Then let's begin." Joseph took her hand. "We only have—"

Lightning zapped the grass just beyond the shattered window, inciting Caralyn's scream. Annisa slumped against Alejandro—she was the only one *actually* running out of time.

We've been here for too long.

"Annisa," I shouted, standing and taking her arm while Alejandro did the same. "We have everything, let's go!"

"Are..." she breathed, wobbling as she stood with us, "are you sure—?"

"Yes, let's *go*—!"

Footsteps pounded against the wooden floors. We looked up in time to catch Caralyn and Joseph leaping off the front platform.

He wrapped his arms around her torso as she took his face, both meeting each other's lips. Thunder clapped as if in retaliation, prompting their release.

"Promise me," he said over the downpour, "that we will make the ultimate return to each other."

"With all that I am," she replied.

Lightning struck outside the front doors, sending them flying open. With another zap, the ceiling fractured apart like a crack in the sky. Fire blared above us like the sun, heat combatting the frigid storm and lighting up the night.

The roof was collapsing.

Caralyn and Joseph sprinted past us. Before I could shout

Annisa's name again, Alejandro swooped her up and stumbled down the center aisle. Instinct moved my feet before I could think. My fingers grazed Alejandro's coat just as the world swirled together in a blur.

FORTY

Short-threaded carpet caught my hands when I fell, capturing my breath as I panted. We were back. Barely, but back and safe in Annisa's—

Annisa!

I looked up in time to catch Alejandro getting to his knees beside the bed, shaking. A panting Annisa lay between us on her back, unable to make the attempt to stand.

"Are you okay?" Alejandro asked her, sliding one arm under her back. I noticed his damp hair and realized that mine was no better. Oh well. We'd dry by the time we got back to the base.

"Yeah," she whispered with a single breath. He slid his other arm under her knees. I forced myself to my own, pushing her up into his arms so he could stand with her. I got up and leaned against Annisa's desk, giving Alejandro room to lay her down onto her bed. Evidently, training with Jak at the gym had done him a lot of good.

"Thanks," she breathed, closing her eyes.

"Thank *you*," I said, coming to her side. "Joseph was right, I would've *never* known there was an illusion spell over—"

I glanced behind me at the desk, finding Caralyn's autobiography. No—her journal.

Alejandro grabbed the book and handed it to me. "Try it."

I took it. *Converte.*

A sheer layer of amber magic gleamed over the crimson cover, just brightly enough to block the transition. The texture shifted under my fingers, roughening into chipping, stiff coffee-brown leather. A latch hung loosely in its hook, holding the book closed.

I had it. *I have it!*

"What—does it say?" Annisa panted.

I carefully slid out the leather strap and opened the cover with an ancient creak.

"To you who was always meant to read this." Written in Caralyn Callistro's own handwriting.

I carefully flipped the yellowed page over. The date sat in the top righthand corner: September 4, 1817.

She'd kept her secrets for that *long?*

Catching Annisa's and Alejandro's expectant stares, I didn't waste time: "'Only two months ago, Samuel Baelford begged for his life at the other end of my pointed arrow—what began as a relieving pastime that I weaponized for the hateful, divisive cause of this nation. Through a series of magic and evidence conducted on both myself and his own person, I was obligated to believe

Samuel and his findings on my father, Henry Callistro. The night after our meeting, Samuel approached me with the visions of a druid, upon which he verified with a seer, of an American daughter meant to change her country, even her world, beyond forgetting. That night Samuel disclosed unto me earth-shattering secrets only the dead may be entrusted with, prophecies with the authoritative hand to uproot our strongest trees of ignorance, fear, and pride. It is on these pages, and nowhere else, O Soul of Unity, that I release them all unto you.'"

This was it. I finally had all of Caralyn's secrets right in front of me, the one and only textbook in existence on her. All that was left to do was sit down and read the whole thing cover to cover.

"We got it," I said, my voice shaking with excitement. "*Everything* about her is right here. And we found out another thing about our fifth ally."

"Runelle is Joseph Bouchard's *granddaughter*," Alejandro said with wonder, facing Annisa. "She's the one in Antarctica. We can—how do you say it?—use this for her."

A soft smile touched her lips. "I'm glad we—found so much."

"Thank you," I told her, coming up to her and squeezing her hand. "This was literally impossible without you."

It tempted me to wonder if Caralyn had somehow known that Annisa would time travel back so we could figure all this out, but that was an answer I'd probably find in the journal.

"I'd read it all right now," I said, "but there's some stuff in here I know my family wants to know. And there's probably a lot that they'd know what to do with. I didn't know this would take such a short amount of time, I wish we could've met your family before we left."

Annisa shook her head, her black hair falling over her shoulders. "It's okay. It's... better to overestimate. They'll understand."

I squeezed her hand again, looking up at Alejandro next to me. "Are you ready?"

His eyes drifted to Annisa. He rested a careful hand on her bedspread. "Annisa—your power is incredible. Thank you for helping us. And... I'm glad I'll work with you soon."

She opened her gentle maroon eyes enough to see him. "You—you, too."

He took my hand. Now he was ready.

—*I want to rest longer before we start the trip back,*— he told me in Spanish. —*But let's not bother her. I can take us somewhere else safe.*—

I glimpsed him. —*Are you sure?*—

—*Yes. We'll be fast.*—

That reminded me. "Are you sure you don't need anything before we leave?" I asked Annisa.

"Just a nap." She made a halfhearted shooing motion with her hand. "Go ahead. I'll... see you again. Later."

Leaving her with a smile, I steeled my stomach as soon as glimmering amber waves encased me and Alejandro and the ground beneath us disappeared.

Dinner had just begun when we got back to the base, but my family was thrilled to see us so soon after we'd left. The six of us gathered in the bedroom, my parents taking a comfortable spot on the foot of their bed and Aunt Becca and Jak on the other. Alejandro and I stood in front of the credenza up front and told the story.

Then, I held up what used to be the first-ever copy of Caralyn's autobiography. "Caralyn's journal was hiding under an illusion spell."

"This *whole* time?" Dad asked, squinting his eyes and rubbing his square chin. "It was hidden for two centuries?"

"Yep." I carefully opened the book to the front page. "That's why Joseph entrusted it to each chief to give to me, so I'd ultimately end up with it."

"Okay, wait a minute," Momma said. "So *how* exactly did Caralyn find out about Adara if she wasn't a wielder herself?"

"Her first entry." I read it aloud, ending where I had at Annisa's. "Samuel was her ticket in because he knew a druid and he verified that druid's visions with a seer."

"That tracks, I guess," Aunt Becca remarked, leaning on her palms on the bed. "Druids have been having visions about Adara for forever. That's how we know about her today."

"It's the same for Spain," Alejandro said, keeping his hands in his jean pockets. "About Azariah."

"But it's interesting that a druid had a vision of you right after Samuel met Caralyn," Becca added, her brows furrowing in concentration. "And then told Samuel about it. That tells me Samuel himself was involved somehow in the vision, which would make sense if him meeting Caralyn had... triggered it somehow. That's possible, right, Em?"

"Yeah..." My mind started running. *Because Samuel would help Caralyn help me with Adara's destiny.* Visions are often triggered by specific events or turns *of* events—so if Samuel and Caralyn meeting really had prompted a vision of Adara, that vision had also exposed their involvement with her somehow. Maybe it had shown them making plans in secret, possibly even the night they'd find Joseph Bouchard in the forest.

"That sounds familiar," Jak noted next to Becca, resting his chin in his hand. "Eun-Ji had visions of my mom around the same time some important stuff happened, like after they met and when I was born."

"Well, that takes care of how Caralyn knew about Adara," Momma said, "but she knew an awful lot about you specifically, Em, or it at least seems that way. What else did she write?"

I looked back down, at the start of the next paragraph. "'I admit, however, that my involvement was not the sole prompt'—"

A few lines down, my peripheral vision caught on a name. *"John Atera."*

As in my seventh-great-grandfather-who-founded-the-magician-hideout-under-Capperson John Atera?

"No way," I muttered.

"What?" Momma asked.

I read through the paragraph as fast as I could before looking back up. "John Atera, the one who founded the hideout under Capperson, was friends with Samuel. Samuel met with him and a druid the day Caralyn spared his life, and then that druid had the vision that night. The druid was the one who told Samuel that Adara would be an *Atera* descendant."

"So if Caralyn was on your side and knew you'd be an Atera," Dad began slowly, "she was allies with us from the start."

Wait a second—if all this was true, then...

I shook my head. "It still doesn't make sense to me why she thought mass-producing Hunters at the school was a good idea because it'd 'strengthen magicians' resolve to fight back' and send me a message or something. Like, contributing to that would scare a lot of us, but she was betting on the chance that some would let it motivate them instead. I feel like she was too smart for that, something's not right about it."

Something wasn't right in front of me, either: Momma was pausing. Dad was pausing. Aunt Becca was throwing them both a cautious glance.

"What?" I said, even Alejandro and Jak sharing questioning looks at them.

"Can I see the journal, Em?" Momma asked, reaching for it. I gave it to her.

Her eyes scanned the pages, Dad's scrutinizing them next to her. After a few seconds, Momma flipped the page. To my surprise, when they seemed to reach the end, Dad gave a negligible nod. Mom, on the other hand, exposed nothing.

Not until she looked up at me and said, "Okay... There's some context you need to know before going any further on this."

My shoulders dropped. "Are you kidding me? You've been keeping something else from me this whole time? Something about *Caralyn?*"

"It wasn't just you," Dad assured me with a surprising calmness. The last thing I expected was for him and Mom to look at Jak and add, "It was everyone at the schools."

I'm sorry—*schools?*

Jak stood from the foot of my bed, joining Alejandro's side. If not for the sudden weight of the atmosphere, I would've laughed at how Jak was almost a whole head taller. "What're you talking about?" he asked. "Callistro *and* Redway?"

"Remember when Caralyn said that no one other than those

she trusted would know Callistro's real mission?" Momma asked me. "Those she trusted meant the true allies of magic. Select staff members. At the school today, there are only about a dozen people who know the truth, including me and Thomas—"

"What's the truth?" I said.

She flipped to the previous page of the journal. "'My brother, sister, and I were raised understanding that happiness is a privilege, humanity invaluable, and hypocrisy a tool of the devil.'" She turned the page. "'Upon understanding whose war I stood on the frontlines of, not by choice but by ignorance, all the greater became my determination to build a catalyst. Not all will show a surrendered magician clemency as I managed with Samuel. Most will pull the trigger once his target is on his knees. Your people, Adara, whom it is my humanitarian duty to aid, need not a safe haven to infinitely wait out your predator, but the arsenal to survive amidst them. Hiding only reveals who must be found; hiding in plain sight claims that none are missing at all.

"'I've taken the duty upon myself to provide these four walls in which you will be taught, instructed, and strengthened. I solemnly vow to you on these pages, O Soul of Unity, to establish an academy that will arm its Hunters with the wit of a Callistro, the caution of a Baelford, and the determination of both. Here your people will be safe, disguised as the enemy unto each other, but above all, to the predator. You will know how your enemy works and, therefore, repossess control of your lives. You may survive. You may hunt to protect. You may replenish your army against injustice to uphold all that you stand for as an ambassador of magic.'"

"Hiding alone won't save you. You'll only delay your extinction."

"You mean to say that producing Hunters by the masses will alleviate *the matter?*"

"*In this way, yes. Fortifying a magician's resolve and their confidence—*"

No—how? This whole time, since it was founded...

"The Callistro Academy," I stuttered, "is a Hunter school for magicians?"

FORTY-ONE

"It always has been," Momma began, closing Caralyn's journal with an infuriating calmness. "Somewhere magicians are safe undercover while learning about the enemy in case they ever face worst-case scenario, and how to survive under those circumstances. Caralyn tripled a magician's survival chances with the school, and she inspired a small chain of them to follow."

As if I didn't already have a hundred questions beating against my skull, Momma had added another one: "All the other Hunter schools in America are for wielders?"

"Half of them are," Dad replied. "Which doesn't say a lot, considering there are only, what..."

"Fourteen," Momma finished for him. "The newer schools

don't have the same purpose because they don't know. The wrong people are directing them."

I hated it—absolutely hated it—but things were making sense, stitching together fiber by fiber: Caralyn had never hinted at Bouchard's existence or hidden it anywhere in her autobiography because she hadn't needed to. The Callistro Academy was a sanctuary for wielders in itself; those wielders didn't need to know about Bouchard when they were already at a version of it, one that would teach them how to survive in an open world.

"No, somebody has something wrong," Jak said with a harsh crease in his brow. "Sarah and Breanne? Me? Hello, William?"

No. Don't tell me. First Opal, now Sarah and Breanne? The whole time, don't tell me—

"That's the caveat," Momma said, setting the journal into her lap. "Ten percent of the student population are mortal to make the threat real. Just like in the real world, you would never know if you were speaking to a wielder or a mortal—so you always assumed mortal for the sake of your own safety. Sarah and Breanne were part of the ten percent who were mortals. I'm guessing you and your friends were for Redway, Jak."

"Just as it is in the real world, so it will be at the school." That's *what Caralyn meant.* The truth had stared directly at me in 1819.

"But sorcerers can detect other wielders," I argued. "How has nobody ever exposed this before?"

"Believe me, that was hard," Dad said. I remembered that *he'd* been a sorcerer at a Hunter school, just like me. "But necessary. Any sorcerer with common sense would know to keep everyone's identity a secret. If any part of the truth came out, it'd be a death sentence for all of us. The ones who needed help to process it, like me, went to a teacher who had magic. We were sworn to secrecy for all the obvious reasons. Otherwise we risked expulsion and—further repercussions. That was that."

"Wait." I cursed the shakiness in my voice. "So—Opal? You knew Opal was a druid the whole time?"

"If the head is a trusted ally, they're given a file stating every student's status," Momma replied gently, like she was trying to give me the time I'd never have to understand all this. "So yeah, we knew Opal was a druid. But not that she was Thomas's niece."

"Ava Baleen?" I asked. "Teresa Darci?"

"Both wielders," she said.

"Amelia Baker, Caroline Walker, Elizabeth Moody?"

"Yes, no, and yes."

My head darted to Aunt Becca sitting in front of me. "Why were you always so against me going to Callistro if you knew?"

"I didn't until your mom got tired of me giving her a hard time about it," she remarked. "Which is an *accomplishment* on my end. She let me believe otherwise about the school for so long because as long as my stance was genuine, you'd keep believing it, too. I finally broke her last year after you told us about the whole Alexa-riddle thing on the cruise."

That's *why Becca stopped pushing it.* And unfortunately for me, she was dead right: her resistance to me going to Callistro always made it out to be the ruthless Hunter school it was supposed to be in its world.

And to my anger's dismay, deep down, I knew that my parents were right to keep this from me: for all the same reasons they'd never trusted me with my identity as a sorceress, and this was another reason that they hadn't. I'd always been terrified of exposing myself in front of two hundred Hunters-in-training, but for all I knew, I *would* have back then if I'd known. I'd been too naïve then. I probably would've compromised the greatest cover of all time.

I internally facepalmed over and over again. *I hate it when they're right.*

"I need something better," Jak said with his arms crossed. "Callistro, I can see, but Redway? How was William hired as headmaster if that's the school it actually is?"

"Every board has their process for deciding their head," Momma answered, shrugging. "Redway's might've seen William as an ultimate test of sorts, considering his background. You know he would've exposed everyone in that school if he'd known."

Yeah. Exactly.

Jak shook his head. All of this information about his dad, most of it likely earning William an even lower place in his heart (if he still had one), and—like Jak had told me a few months ago— he couldn't get closure on any of it.

"How're you doing, Em?" Aunt Becca asked me carefully in a manner that reminded me of Momma.

I huffed, letting my arms fall. "I don't—" I began, but I didn't know how to end that sentence. "I wish I could've known about this sooner. But..."

Momma nodded. "You see why we couldn't make you an exception to this."

"I'm just—" I glanced at Alejandro and then at Jak, holding his gaze for no other reason but comfort. He understood me the best out of everyone in the room right now. "What do we do with this? We're on shaky-enough ground hiding ourselves from the

US Government, now we have to hide a whole school from them because we're leads to it?"

"Callistro wouldn't still be standing if it wasn't prepared for federal threats," Dad assured me. "We told Eun-Ji the situation, and she sent a couple of agents to keep an eye on the school just in case with everything going on, another handful back undercover at the White House."

"We can only pray it'll hold out until we deal with Caldwell," Momma added, taking his hand. "Callistro and the others have always known how dangerous the game they're playing is. If worse comes to worst, they have a plan."

I read between those lines fluently: there was no guarantee. Sarah was safe if worse *did* come to worst, but Opal and Breanne would be done for.

"I want to take action," I finally said, my resolve solidifying once and for all. "We know too much now, and everything else is in that journal. The whole reason we went back in time was to find out exactly what Caralyn knew—about me, about Adara, possibly even—"

My eyes widened with remembrance. "Runelle!"

"The girl you met in Antarctica?" Auntie asked, Alejandro perking up with me.

"Yes," I said, my brain spinning faster than the words could leave my mouth. Runelle was still our key to moving forward; if she hadn't been lying about not knowing anything about her destiny, about having no family, there was a chance she didn't know who her real family *was*—not when Joseph had known to pass something down to Adara, who wasn't his own descendant like Runelle was. And if we brought her information about her real family, we could be holding the key to getting her onto our team and solidifying a plan against Caldwell. Which meant Antarctica was our next step—all of us.

"Okay, this is gonna sound crazy," I began, meeting everyone's eyes, "but I think our time at Bouchard is over. We have to get to Antarctica and get Runelle. Caralyn and Joseph *mentioned* her and how she's supposed to help Adara one day with the same destiny. The girl in Antarctica is actually Joseph's—"

A high-pitched alarm blared over the speaker in the corner of the bedroom, making me stumble into the credenza behind me. My mind went numb with the connection: that was the base's code black evacuation alarm.

No. No—

"Move!" Momma exclaimed, leaping off the bed with Dad.

Right as I turned toward the hallway, Alejandro disappeared with an amber flash.

Where is he going?!

"Mom—"

"Go!" she shouted, shoving me toward the hallway with Jak.

He threw open the door and darted into the hall. A handful of people who had chosen to eat dinner in their rooms were already surging toward the lobby, on their way to the eating hall, where the entrance to the panic room was hidden in the back. I'd always wondered how it could possibly fit eight hundred people, and now I was about to find out.

We soon broke into the main lobby from the sector's entryway, any residents not already in the eating hall flooding toward the concourse. The alarm blasted across the lobby, the white fluorescent lights switching to red with each scream. I looked behind me at my parents, but Momma commanded me forward again onto the dark-yellow rug.

A familiar sweet voice rose above the alarm—calling for us.

Eun-Ji.

She rushed toward us past the remaining residents, weaving between the armchairs to meet us at the coffee table in the middle.

"What happened?" Dad shouted.

"We fell into a trap," she said, gesturing toward the concourse in the back. We followed her. "Both the US and Canadian Governments were staying low for the past month, waiting for us to resume normal functioning. Seeing as Emma's back, they must've detected the surge of magic Alejandro released upon teleporting and used it as a final pinpoint to solidify our location."

When we left and *when we got back.* Barely a couple of hours apart.

"Most people are already in the eating hall," Eun-Ji said as the defense team marched in from the security sector entryways. "It has twice the security and can only be found and unlocked with magic, let's go."

I couldn't remember the last time I'd been this conflicted: pull my family with me to the panic room, or stay behind with the emerging defense team to help. We were the reason the governments were here, *we* were their targets, and I couldn't stomach the fact that a handful of people would die—at least a fraction of Bouchard would die—if it meant finding us.

"Eun-Ji—" I began.

She pulled me to the edge of the rug. "Let's go—!"

The alarms switched off, announcing two elevator dings behind us.

Blood congealed in my veins. Mom, or Dad, shoved me forward, Jak stumbling next to me.

"Go!" Momma exclaimed.

"*Nobody move!*"

Forty-Two

I whirled around. Two dozen federal agents stood in front of the elevators, armed and protected from head to toe with visored helmets and winter combat boots. The same amount of Bouchard's defense ward lined the right side of the lobby, pointing their own rifles at them. Magic was only as fast as a bullet; using it as a weapon right now, even as protection, could get us killed faster than we could incapacitate anyone.

One misstep, and we'd all be lying in a bloodbath.

"Tristan, Rebecca, Amy, and Emmalynn Atera and Jakson Bleu, you are officially under federal custody. Step forward, hands on your head, knees on the ground, now!"

"Mom—" I cried.

"Do as he says, Emma," she whispered, slowly locking her

hands behind her head. My family's eyes were trained dead ahead on the agents, warily moving past the armchairs and to the front of the rug. We kneeled. I couldn't bring myself to believe that this was it—that we were surrendering. And yet my only option now was to obey.

"Anyone makes one shot, you're all dead," the frontmost agent in the middle barked. "Lower your weapons."

Alejandro, where are you? I screamed in my head, wishing I could force him to hear it.

"You're dealing with a defense team of strong magicians just as fast with a rifle," Eun-Ji stated from behind me, holding her head high. "Our agents trained alongside yours, and they have another form of long-range attack that you don't. You aren't in a position to make demands if you value your lives."

"And we have half the American and Canadian defense departments above," the frontmost agent shot back. "We have orders to shoot on sight if necessary. *Lower your weapons.*"

Confident, stable Eun-Ji Park hesitated in a way that terrified me. "Lower them," she commanded her team.

On my knees with my hands locked behind my head, I watched the line of Bouchard's defense soldiers obey one by one. I knew there were more waiting to reveal themselves in the halls— but the governments' numbers still dwarfed them. My heart palpitated against my ribs, nausea erupting in my stomach. Anxiety overtook my body, burning my lungs, suppressing my breath.

The left elevator dinged again. A dozen more soldiers marched in. Each one carried an assault rifle trained on us as they joined the lineup.

"Tristan, Rebecca, and Amy Atera," the frontmost man in

the middle began, "under the jurisdiction of Canadian and United States law, as well as the orders of the Unites States president, you are hereby sentenced to immediate death under the charges of sorcery and collusion."

"NO!" I cried, falling forward. "No, please—!"

"Emmalynn!" Momma snapped.

"As you were, Atera," the agent demanded, moving his gun slightly in my direction. With his visored helmet, I couldn't tell if he was looking directly at me, but I knew that gun wasn't lying.

I forced myself into compliance, my shaking body straightening as I put my hands behind my head again.

"Emmalynn Atera and Jakson Bleu," he said next, "by direct command of the President of the United States, you are hereby ordered to come with us back to the White House for immediate transfer into federal captivity. Failure to comply will be treated as an act of defiance against the government, and we will respond with full force."

Wait. What? They wanted me and *Jak?*

"Any use of magic will result in immediate incapacitation. Atera, Bleu, on your feet, now."

Sleeping spell. We have to do a sleeping spell, but I can't do this many people at the same time—

"Now!"

—Sleeping spell!— I told Dad.

—No!— he exclaimed. *—They have almost forty with more coming. Magic is as fast as those bullets. The second we use it, they're opening fire.—*

—We have to try—!—

As if solely to prove me wrong, the two elevators dinged

again. Five more men marched in from both.

We're dead. The words beat across my head, trampling over everything else.

"Please." I forced my right foot forward, getting to one knee. Hot tears streamed down my cheeks. "Take all of us, we'll tell you anything you want to know."

"Direct orders of the president," the leading agent stated. "Emmalynn Atera and Jakson Bleu are our primary sources of relevant intelligence."

"Regarding what?" Jak stated, stopping in his one-knee position with me.

"You have ten seconds to comply and follow us back to Washington," the man retorted. "Ten. Nine."

"Mom," I rasped, looking over. Dread plummeted into my stomach when I saw twice as many tears streaking her cheeks.

"It's okay, Emma," she whispered, her eyes trained ahead of her like she was watching the sunrise. "We'll be okay."

They were going to die. And she knew it.

"Seven. Six."

Mr. Dawson's suffering—him giving himself up for our lives—would be for nothing in the end.

"Four. Three."

No.

It clicked: full realization of why Mr. Dawson had sacrificed himself despite knowing what he'd face—why Jak had stayed silent as two Grand Hunters beat him almost to death for the truth. Family. That bond that made you just as unbreakable, the strength found in sharing each other's suffering.

I knew it the second I looked at the gun that the Bouchard

soldier closest to me held: I would die for my family.

"Two."

Save them.

"If you take one Atera," I called, meeting my gaze with the middle agent's behind his helmet, "you take all of us."

"You don't have that choice," he stated. "One—"

"You won't, either, if I tell my magic to point one of your guns at my head and shoot it."

Like a narrowly diffused bomb, he paused.

I trapped a breath of relief in my lungs as the agents' stances softened—less rigid. Nobody dared to look away from us, but the frontmost man's glare weighed heavier on me. So heavy that it felt like everyone else had dissipated and we were at a standstill.

I pushed myself up to my feet, my hands still locked on the back of my head. "If you try to kill my family, I'm first. You take all of us, or none of us."

In my peripheral vision, my aunt's face had turned to stone. My father had shut his eyes, cheeks wet with tears. And my mother had bowed her head. Her body shook with a subtle tremble that I'd barely ever seen—because her body only shook like that when she needed to sob, something she never let anyone see her do.

I have to, I thought over and over again. *Because I love you.*

Jak rose next to me. "You people took everything from me twice. Emma's the only thing I have left to live for. Wherever she goes, I follow."

I didn't know if the burst in my chest was of happiness that he was willing to end their plans like this with me, or terror that he was just as willing to give up his life. But it didn't matter how dead serious we were—only if the government believed us.

"Lombardi, patch in the Oval Office," the frontmost agent commanded.

A man on the far left held his gun with one hand while pressing a radio on the left side of his chest. The entire room submitted to silence, but he spoke too lowly for me to catch his words.

In full honesty, I was ready. I was ready to aim one of those guns at my head and let my telekinesis pull the trigger. This wasn't Alexa in front of me, a double agent who secretly wanted to help me escape. There wasn't a Hunter looking out for me this time. Now it was just me and how it was out there, life or death—and if I had to, I'd choose death.

"Make your demands," Lombardi called.

I set my jaw to force steadiness into my words. "As long as I'm alive, so is my family. Jak and I will only tell you anything if we know they're alive. And you leave this place alone."

Lombardi exchanged a few more words with the other end of his radio. His response would determine our fates. And that was when I realized in full the chance that I'd be dead within the next sixty seconds.

I'm sorry, Mr. Dawson. I couldn't save you.

Lombardi stiffened, his visored gaze kept somewhere in front of him with his hands on his radio. I swallowed, shooting up a thousand different prayers I couldn't even make sense of.

"Backup's retrieved Target Echo," he announced, "found with a young woman, also a magician, about eighteen."

My heart skipped a beat for so long that it nearly convulsed. Alejandro? Had he seriously come back with Annisa *here* when he knew that the base was under a code-black raid?

"Give me their status," the leading agent said.

"Both have been neutralized," Lombardi replied. "They're on their way down with reinforcements."

They already had fifty; how many more did they need?

The right elevator dinged, its steel doors sliding open with a grinding sound. In handcuffs, Alejandro stepped out with two men gripping his arms. Behind him—

My jaw fell slack when a tall, lean, fawn-haired girl was marched out in the same handcuffs. Runelle.

Regret chained my thoughts. Regret that I *had* ended up dragging her into what she'd spent the last three years protecting herself from.

How, how did Alejandro get to Antarctica and get her here so fast? His limits, his energy—how did he even get her to come?

I was ready to demand the answers from him telepathically until my eyes fell back down to his cuffs. Neutralized magic. He couldn't hear me, and he couldn't respond. All I had was the sharpness of his brown eyes glistening with an apology at me—and Runelle's everlasting cobalt-blue glare, but for once, she had it turned away from me and on the agents around her instead.

Before I knew it, "They live, too" flew out of my mouth.

I felt the frontmost man's eyes harden on me. "Target Echo is as much of a priority as you are," he said. "Since he's brought this young woman with him, we have reason to suspect that she'll be one, too."

I glimpsed Lombardi on the far-left side of the room. His hand was glued to his radio. I wondered if whoever was on the other end could hear us.

"Those are my demands," I said, trying desperately to maintain what little control I had over my voice. "Leave this facility alone, my friends and family live, and I have to have proof that they're alive for me to tell you anything."

Lombardi spoke into his radio. Finally, he nodded. I couldn't tell if it was agreement or a death sentence.

"President Caldwell is willing to comply regarding the Americans," he announced. "But the prime minister orders that any Canadian faces immediate execution."

"No," I stated, "*everyone* lives."

"You've already—"

"Do you need a truth spell to believe me?" I snapped, anger overriding my fear. "You comply within the next ten seconds or I make one of *your* guns shoot me!"

"Emmalynn, stop!" Momma snarled. I knew that anger, and I knew that it wasn't completely for me; the truth simply was, I had to mean these words for us to have a sliver of a chance of making it out of the Bouchard lobby alive.

Lombardi went back to his radio. I planted my feet deep into the dark-yellow rug, stabilizing my body.

"The US and Canada comply."

I kept that breath of relief locked tight in my lungs. My plan had worked—but almost too easily. In fact, I'd made that plan as a final desperate attempt. This was too good to be true, which meant that, especially since we were dealing with the federal governments, it was. There was a caveat they wouldn't tell us; I had to be on guard now more than ever.

Particularly as I figured out where to go from here.

"Nobody move," the leading agent barked again. His line of men marched forward, every step booming across the lobby. "Everyone in this facility is hereby federally detained. The Americans will now be transported to the White House in Washington, DC for immediate debriefing, and are expected to comply fully and without resistance."

The line loomed forward. Every survival instinct I'd ever built over the last seventeen years all but shoved me in the opposite direction, toward the dead-silent concourse in the back. Something deeper, though, bolted my feet to the ground: determination. Now that we'd been caught, it had never burned so furiously to save the people I loved.

Forty-Three

The second we were put into the four-wheel drive cars, we were knocked out. I went from sitting in the unforgiving backseat of the vehicle to waking up in an equally frigid place—in an even harder seat.

My shoulders tingled with a dull ache as I came to, hands cuffed behind me and metal edges digging into my arms through my jacket. I opened my eyes against dim fluorescent lights in the ceiling. A silver table stretched out in front of me. Concrete bricks sandwiched me on either side—and a slight head turn revealed a row of Secret Service agents positioned behind me.

No. Wait. *I've seen this before.*

Only a handful of times, and yet, it didn't faze me. Somehow, the vision I was the least prepared for, I was the most determined to live out.

The silence after I woke up surprised me. Needless to say, this was my first time dealing with the federal government directly and not a branch of Hunters, but I still expected some kind of... movement once their target was conscious again.

With no clock around, I had to count the seconds, and then the minutes. Almost three had passed before the heavy door at the other end of the room squeaked open. A rectangular man in a beige suit strolled in with two officers behind him, a thick pastel-yellow file in his hand—the thickest I'd ever seen in my life. Anxiety burned a hole in my stomach as I caught a flash of the label printed in the center: "EMMALYNN".

"Emmalynn Melicent-Marie Atera," the rectangular man said with a jaw just as square. "Or 'Emmalynn Marie'."

The US Government had finally found me.

"Now that we know those two are the same, we were able to find the right history and intel." He pulled out the metal chair at the end of the table and took a seat. His boxy gray eyes stayed on me as he slid out a black tablet from under the file. He slapped the file down onto the table, a smile presenting itself on his long face. "Welcome to the White House. We're glad to have you."

"Show me my family," I demanded.

"Right, of course, I'm sorry."

He woke up the tablet. After a few taps, he propped it up and turned it to me. A top-corner view of a gray room—cell, more like, with a clear barrier in front—showed Mom, Dad, and Aunt Becca sitting on the bench mounted against the back wall. Today's date and time were printed in the bottom-right corner: 7 A.M. They'd kept us knocked out for the rest of last night.

"And your friends are in their own room talking with my partners. Everyone's safe, okay?"

"Tell my mom to wave at me," I said. Showing an edited video was too easy, especially after I'd been knocked out. For all I knew, it was actually midnight, or two afternoons later.

"Okay," the man told me simply. "No problem, one sec."

You're acting too nicely, I wanted to tell him as he instructed a man behind him. For someone who had an entire file on me, who knew the kind of school I'd gone to for a year and a half and the kind of mother who'd raised me, he was acting like I didn't have any background on interrogation methods. And even if I didn't, building a "bond" with the suspect was too obvious a method to work on anyone above the age of thirteen.

He gestured to the tablet. A black-clad agent had appeared at the clear wall between him and my family, holding a rifle across his chest and motioning with his other hand. My family looked at the camera mounted in the corner of their cell. Momma waved with a sad half smile. Dad and Auntie followed.

I sat back in the chair, the cuffs loosening on my wrists slightly. I'd never felt so empowered and yet helpless in my life.

"See?" the beige-suited man told me, setting the tablet down. "Everyone's safe."

"What about the facility?"

He held up his hands like he was taming a wild horse. "We let them be."

No—something wasn't right about that sentence, or maybe about his delivery. Like he wasn't lying... but it wasn't true.

"We did," he insisted when I didn't respond, his eyes softening on me. He could read me—I reminded myself to keep up my guard, keep up whatever fragments of my cover I had left.

"How do I know you're not lying?"

"You're an expert in that, aren't you?" he asked simply. "You had to be to survive. Just look me square in the eyes." He leaned forward on the table—every muscle in his long face eerily relaxed. A calm that couldn't be faked. "I promise, Emmalynn. We didn't touch them."

That was the problem: I knew he *wasn't* lying. But there was fine print somewhere. There had to be, this field was never that easy—merciful.

I blinked in place of a swallow. *The sooner I finish this, the sooner I find out for myself at Bouchard.* In the meantime, I'd let this man continue to act friendly, because you never let your enemy know what you do. What interrogation techniques was he going to use, and how far would he go with them?

"Look," he began slowly, like he was giving room for me to object. "Not one person has 'federal interrogation' on their bucket list. So let's go with something else—an interview. I'll ask you a few questions, you'll tell me the answer, okay?"

"Interviews don't require Secret Service," I said.

"Just a protective measure," he assured me. "You unleashed a pretty serious threat at the magician facility."

"I'll still honor it."

"Understood. But nobody wants it to come to that. So, since I know who you are, let me introduce myself: Special Agent in Charge Peter Vaughn."

Alias. I knew how security and ranks on the federal level worked.

"Try to relax," Vaughn told me. "It's only a few questions."

One detail he'd purposely left out: the truth spell I felt on my tongue. I didn't know who had cast it, just that I was under it, which made this all the more a fatal game; the government had kept their end of the deal, and that meant that I had to keep mine. For all I knew, if I didn't, they had a gun ready to shoot down my family one member at a time. I had to give my answers away crumb by crumb until I figured out how to escape—to remember the details my visions had already given away.

"I want to start with a few questions about Target Echo, Target Adeline, and now Target Cipher," Vaughn said. "Are any of those names already familiar to you?"

"I've heard of Echo."

"Okay," he said, nodding. "'Echo' refers to your Spanish friend—who can, miraculously, teleport. You've traveled with him a few times with that, haven't you?"

Talking to me like I was a kid definitely wasn't going to get him any answers. Frankly, it was insulting, but my priority right now was letting him figure out on his own that I knew his tricks. That'd buy me the most amount of time to think of something.

"Do echoes have something to do with teleporting?" I asked.

"'Echo' here refers to movement that is... there one moment and gone the next, so to say," Vaughn replied. "How did you find someone like that, someone with an impossible ability?"

Those last two words breathed a chill down my back that I couldn't hide. I prayed that the temperature of the damp room would be enough to excuse it. At the same time, despite their dimness, the lights above seemed to beat down on me.

"What about Adeline or Cipher?" I said, the presence of Secret Service behind me so powerful that it was practically pushing me forward.

"Right." Vaughn relaxed in his chair. "Cipher is the young woman Echo brought in with him. We don't know anything about her, she's a cipher, a code. She's more stubborn than a mule and apparently only speaks French. Our translator is trying to work with her, but she won't budge. Was she that way when you first met?"

Is today his first day as an interrogator or something?

"We have something in common," I told him. "She won't tell me anything, either."

A moment passed where Vaughn's boxy gray eyes analyzed me, temporarily breaking past their false kindness before building it back up. "That's okay," he said, leaning forward and folding his hands on the metal table. "Because I know you can help us with Adeline. She's the only one whose real name we do know, so we disguised it under a new one: 'Adeline' refers to Adara."

Wait—what? "Adeline" didn't refer to *me*?

They think Adara is a different person. They don't know it's an alias in the magic world. I could use that to my advantage.

"*That's* the one I can help you with?" I asked, actually needing clarification.

"Well, yeah," Vaughn replied. "Right?"

I slightly tilted my head. Still asking for an explanation.

Finally, he sighed. "All right," he said, opening the pastel-yellow file. "Let's see if I can clarify. Take a look at this."

He's starting to realize. He's gonna shift into a new technique.

I kept my mind guarded as he grabbed a bar chart and a graph from the pile of documents. He slid them toward me. I don't know why; the table was long, and my hands were stuck behind my back.

"Agent Jang, please," Vaughn said, reading the problem.

The lean man on his left approached the middle of the table and slid the papers in front of me, straightening them horizontally. Five variables along the x-axis of the bar chart: "AA", "A", "B", "C", and then "AAA". AA had a value of zero. Next to it, four different-colored bars stretched up: a short green one for A, a taller yellow one for B, a taller red one for C, and then AAA's purple one nearly capping off the y-axis at one.

I knew this type of chart. We'd studied these in Momma's class second semester of my sophomore year. They were characterized by the AA, whose value was always zero.

Magic density. AA represented mortals, and the other letters represented a tested group of wielders in increasing power.

I've never seen "AAA" on this chart before...

Minding my micro-expressions, I looked over at the graph. Multiple hills ran across it, timestamps dating the x-axis: the electromagnetic waves that magic radiated with a detection gun. A bundle of greens were gathered in the middle. Up top were three different shades of purple, each depicting a sharp parabola.

Three. Me, Alejandro, and Runelle.

"These were your readings upon testing while you were unconscious," Vaughn told me when my analytical gaze still hadn't shifted. "The bar chart reflects the average magic density of a group of mortals, then lower-level magicians, then your average magician, then higher-ups like the Ateras, and then—"

Me.

"—you, Echo, and Cipher."

I finally let my brows straighten. No reaction would just

scream that I was telling myself to hide the truth. My only job right now was to not verify it with my own lips.

"Our readers have never detected something like this before," Vaughn mused. "Echo seems to have an explanation, seeing as he can teleport, but I don't think the same applies to you and Cipher since you both needed him to travel via teleportation. We did test him first, so his results could've jammed the accuracy of our readers when we tested you and Cipher next. Do you have any insight, is there a chance that's true?"

The Reid Technique: using evidence, whether real or fabricated, to lull the suspect into confession. Peter Vaughn knew their gadgets better than I did; he didn't need my opinion.

I exhaled, leaning back and gazing at the data like I had to think about it. And I did—I wasn't sure what answer was a crumb and what was the whole slice.

When Vaughn didn't say a word after that, when he continued to stare at me, I had another piece of his technique: now it was using silence to create uncomfortable voids that would push me into filling it. But the longer he maintained it, the greater my resolve to continue "thinking" was.

I finally made myself shrug, shaking my head. "I don't know if it's possible for it to glitch like that or if the readings are actually true. You know more about this technology than I do."

Which was the truth, and they knew it.

Vaughn cast his soulless eyes down to the sheets of paper in front of me. The atmosphere thickened. I was running out of time; I knew what he was doing, and with every answer I gave, he knew more and more what I was doing. I wouldn't give him anything under niceties, and he was toughening.

"Emmalynn," he said, straightening in his chair. "Your family is depending on your honesty. Remember?"

He's raising the stakes. "Yes."

"Then you know they're depending on whether you uphold your end of the deal."

I tried steadying that Hunter instinct, the one that knew how to stand her ground when she was backed into a corner—how to climb up the wall and flip over the enemy.

Maybe I can connect this to Project Ember somehow. Find out how any of us are involved in it.

"Okay, then what do you want out of me if you already know I'm Tristan Atera's daughter? Just intel about other people?"

"Good," Vaughn replied. "Exactly. Because it's your bloodline that suggests your involvement with people like Targets Echo, Adeline, and Cipher—and your *likeness* to them. And that's a huge lead to President Caldwell's biggest target right now, which is Adeline, Adara. You're familiar with her. Maybe even friends with her like you are with Echo and Cipher—right?"

I couldn't speak without swallowing. So I finally let it go, forcing my voice through for "Yes."

"What do you know about her?"

"She's supposed to be powerful enough to change the world," I said.

"Exactly." He flattened his hands on the table. "Uproot order as we know it and put everyone under her control."

Don't snap. Don't correct them and give them what they want. No matter what this man said or how he said it, the last thing I'd allow was a repeat of the night I confessed to William that I knew where Tristan's daughter was hiding.

"Echo and Cipher are most likely in collusion with her," Vaughn told me. "Not only are we asking as a matter of national security, but if you don't answer, you're subject to charges of sorcery, collusion, obstruction of justice, and even conspiracy—considering our suspicions about Adara. Do you understand what all that means?"

Yeah. You want me to believe that compliance is my best and only option. Unfortunately—because of my family—he was right.

"Save your friends and family," Vaughn said, hardening his voice, "and tell us what you know about these three people. Even yourself, if you've ever come across anything unique about your own magic."

Crumb. Crumb by crumb.

"Magicians have known about Adara for centuries," I began, trying to stick to a textbook tone. "But they don't know exactly *who* she is. She's always just been—someone who was supposed to save them and help them and mortals coexist."

"That was what you were told?"

"Since I was fifteen."

He exhaled. There went that silence again, trying to make me think that I'd left too much room for jumps or irrational conclusions and I needed to justify myself. It almost worked.

"That's all?" he asked.

I cocked my brows like I didn't know what to tell him; obviously I couldn't give him *all* of it.

He tried the silence again. I started counting the seconds, but he didn't let me reach a minute this time.

"Okay, Emmalynn."

He opened the lapel of his suit jacket and pulled out a zipped-up plastic bag. Instinct warned me to brace myself against whatever attempt at the Reid Technique he was going to try next. He tossed the bag onto the table, and Jang slid it over to me.

I leaned forward before realization zapped me like lightning. *The necklace Opal gave me…?*

I looked down at my neck: my "Emma" locket still hung around it. They'd taken one but not the other.

I peered up at Vaughn. "Why did you take that, why's it in an evidence bag?"

"I get it," he said flatly, his hands splayed out in front of him. "You know what I'm doing. I'm not gonna waste my time, so stop playing dumb: you're well aware that this is how we pinpointed your location in the Yukon. Somehow, you found out that the charm has a tracking device, microphone, and camera, the feed of which we kept track of at the Pentagon. The question is, how?"

The world around me shattered into a million shards. No—Sarah and Breanne had nodded at Opal to give me her present; They'd all allowed me to take the necklace. Had… had any of them known?

Why is he pretending that I knew?

"I don't—" I stammered, trying to force my survival instincts past my stun. "I don't understand, what're you talking about? I didn't—I didn't know any of that."

Vaughn's brows shot up. I never thought I'd be so thankful for a truth spell.

"The feed cut out a week after you put it on," he said. "We tracked you jumping to Haines Junction in the Yukon before it completely disappeared—so we know you went with Echo. You have no idea what I'm talking about?"

Alejandro. My body went numb. *Did Alejandro steal this from me at some point? Why would he jump to Haines Junction after taking it? How could he have destroyed the feed in something so small, how could he have even known—?*

I swallowed, keeping my realization far from my face. *Known. Only one person on this planet could've possibly known—but Kamose's magic can't breach the protection spell Bouchard is under. I don't understand, I don't get this...*

It was the only thing I could think of, yet it made the furthest thing from sense.

"No," I told Vaughn. "We never went to Haines Junction."

"Echo clearly did, with or without you. How did he know about the feed?"

I shook my head. "I don't know, I—I never knew... How did Opal get this?"

My body stiffened when the muscles in Vaughn's face relaxed again—like he'd realized something I hadn't yet. Like he now had a weapon I didn't. "We gave Opal Dubois this necklace to give you once she told us about a vision she had received where she'd be getting a 'visitor' soon."

My blood ran cold. *That's a lie. Lie, lie, lie, she wouldn't. That's not her. Sarah and Breanne wouldn't have let me take this if that were true. This is a lie, it's—*

The Reid Technique. Using real or fabricated evidence.

That was it, the necklace was harmless. A flame charm couldn't be hiding a camera, microphone, *and* tracking device in it, it was too thin, the diamond at the bottom was too small.

But then why bring up the Haines Junction story? And the feed cutting out?

"You don't believe a word of this," Vaughn noted, like he was reading my every thought and was determined to prove me wrong. "True or false: you put this on the night she gave it to you."

Don't break. Don't break, don't you dare break!

"Yes—"

"Well, that's when we started collecting our data and realized we had a lot more targets in one place than we thought. Why else do you think we were in alliance with the Canadian Government? We gathered as much as we could before investigating this seemingly random mountain in the Saint Elias range, they located a decent number of fugitives based on our feed, and then we raided the facility with our combined forces."

Why does it make sense? Why would Sarah and Breanne let Opal give me this? Why would Sarah let her give me this?

No, he's manipulating you, this is his job! None of my friends would ever do this unless...

"What did you threaten them with?" I demanded. "Their lives in exchange for help in finding us?"

To my surprise, Vaughn blinked, tilting his head. "'Them'?"

"My other roommates," I said, because there was no way they knew about Opal and not Sarah and Breanne.

"They weren't involved," he replied simply. "Miss Dubois was the only one who approached us and who knew the truth about this necklace. This was all her proposal: her help in exchange for letting your other friends go."

Sarah and Breanne really thought this was just a gift.

Denial refused to release my mind. "She didn't offer her help," I spat. "I know her—"

"Then you should've known this was a long time coming,"

Vaughn shot back. "Your best friend whose memories you suppressed to keep your own secrets, and whose uncle sacrificed his freedom for you?"

She remembered.

Opal remembered everything from the night Alexa attacked us in the forest—including me being Tristan's daughter. Nobody had been there to keep her memories suppressed.

No, this isn't right. Turning us in is a death sentence and she knows it. She wouldn't do all this to us just because we wiped her memories! She's my best friend, someone is lying—

My spiraling thoughts paused, giving way to the last and only time a family member had ever betrayed me like this: her uncle. Mr. Dawson had disguised himself as the Hunter assigned to me for our spring final and made me believe that he only wanted me for my power, that he'd never really been on my side. And it had all been just a test. I'd been furious that he and Momma had approved something like that until they told me...

"We wanted to know if you'd be able to make one of the hardest decisions on the battlefield and fight someone you thought you could trust.... You didn't let past experience or relationship cloud your judgment."

The girl who had access to my things while I was gone. Who had magic so she could use a locator spell on those things. Who was in direct contact with the government.

Watrous, Saskatchewan. The gas station in Brookmere.

My visions warned me about all this.

It was Opal. Opal Dubois had turned us in.

"Seems like we're getting somewhere," Vaughn said, subtle satisfaction lacing his words. "So let's skip the back-and-forth and get to how you're involved with Adara, because there's clearly a connection there. You wrote in a letter to your friends before leaving for Canada saying you were friends with Tristan Atera's daughter and knew where she was hiding—but we know that's you. That leads me to believe you know where *a* certain daughter is hiding."

That was a stretch, but it didn't matter: they were right on top of everything, and Vaughn had stunned me with the truth to a condemning extent. And my body language had already given that away.

"Look, Emmalynn, you're out of hiding places," his clipped voice stated as he stood. I locked my jaw against the tears pressing behind my eyes, against the harsh heat in my cheeks. "We need an answer within the next ten seconds or the world *actually* says goodbye to Tristan Atera."

"No," I said, my gaze snapping up to him. "Fine, okay, yes, I know about Adara, just—leave them alone. I told you, I'm not telling you anything unless they're safe."

"Sounds like you're just stalling to keep them alive for as long as possible without answering our questions." Vaughn leaned on his hands against the table. "Ten seconds—"

"You're asking me to condemn my friends!" I exclaimed, jerking against my restraints. "I don't know how to betray them when all they've done is help me and my family survive!"

"Nine. Eight."

"Stop!" I cried. "Wait, I don't—I can't—"

He awoke the tablet again, standing it up for me to see my family in their cell. "Five. Four."

I shook against the cuffs like I could break them off me. "Please, I just need time—!"

"Two." Vaughn raised his hand toward the agent on his right side. "*One—*"

He paused.

My body locked. The order never came. Secret Service behind him didn't move.

I jumped when he half turned. "Mr. President—"

Caldwell can hear us? I thought, keeping my breath tight. *What is he saying?*

"Yes—"

Every time Vaughn left another stretch of silence, I built my resolve a little bit more—hopefully enough to hold my ground when his conversation ended.

"Yes, Mr. President," he stated. Then, he turned to me.

"The president just saved your father's life," he said, squaring his shoulders. "He's willing to keep your family and friends alive if you agree to tell him everything he wants to know about Adara."

I didn't let my jaw hang open for long. "D—directly?"

"Face to face, everything about her: who she is, what she can do, exactly how powerful she is, her involvement with everyone else—especially you."

"Why?"

"Because I think he knows that he's the only one you *will* crack for." His voice lowered with a threat. "Allow me to give you a piece of advice. The president just saved a twenty-three-year-long fugitive's life in exchange for your intelligence regarding national security after you refused to uphold your end of the deal *you* proposed. You will not get a second chance in the Oval Office, and I know you understand that. Either the first sentence you speak gives the president what he wants, or each of the Ateras gets a bullet in the head. What do you say?"

I didn't know. I really didn't know. It felt like the world around me was moving with a delay and my thoughts still hadn't caught up.

A tear finally won out and spilled over, leaving an icy trail down my cheek. I only had one response to pick: "Yes."

Vaughn's glare stayed on me as he spoke his verification to Caldwell. Then, he glanced at the agents behind me and instructed them to escort me.

"Play your cards right, Emmalynn," he said as Secret Service jerked me out of the chair. "You might just get one more hour."

Forty-Four

Secret Service only took off my blindfold once we were outside and at the start of a shaded stone pathway. It led to a glass-paned door with a white wooden frame. Under the gray sky of early morning, my three escorts walked me down, trees standing on either side of us. Past their slim trunks, the White House loomed tall on the right. I remembered Breanne's exciting stories about the DC field trip she and Sarah had taken in eighth grade. Those stories felt so distant, like fiction.

I couldn't think beyond that point. I couldn't think of anything else but right now, every step I took. I couldn't think of anyone else besides me and Caldwell—but I wanted to think that was because I wouldn't be able to go through with this if I thought of anyone else.

When we walked under the shade of the colonnade, some-thing billowed in my chest—a kind of instinct warning me about the presence inside the Oval Office. I was in Washington, DC, back in my own country yet the furthest from home I'd ever been. And the closer that glass door got, the more that instinct roared in my chest, overcoming the rest of my body. Not fear, not anxiety, not even nausea. It was...

Hatred. A loathing so intense that it was stifling. I didn't know I could hate a man I'd never met before to this extent.

An officer stationed beside the door placed a white-gloved hand on the golden handle and pushed down. With an easy pull, the door opened. My escorts marched me inside.

The first thing I noticed: the row of Secret Service lining the curvature of the room on the opposite side, as if I really were a national threat, capable of ending the president's life where I stood. Which, I realized, I was—or I would've been if not for the neutralizing cuffs around my wrists. On my left sat the oak Reso-lute Desk, one man behind it like he had the whole world at his fingertips. Long nose, downturned brown eyes, horribly buzzed black hair, a long face. At the very sight of him, my knees nearly buckled, that instinctual hatred consuming my body. No, this wasn't just hatred; this was an abhorrence, something actively working against him and everything he was. My people's blood stained his hands and he was proud of it. He believed it was for the greater *good*.

"There she is," President Caldwell announced, grinning at me with pearly whites I wanted to knock out of his mouth. He stood from his desk and straightened his navy-blue suit, exposing his six-foot-tall stature. "Emmalynn Marie, long-lost descendant of

Tristan Atera, it's wonderful to finally meet you. I understand you had trouble communicating with our agents. Special Agent in Charge Vaughn actually started getting frustrated."

"That's because he sucks at his job," I spat. "He had a file on my whole life and he never once remembered that I have formal Hunter training."

"You got away every time Agent Delphine pulled you in for a debriefing, too," Caldwell replied. "But I'm pretty sure I know the reason why for that—finding out what we did about them."

I bit the inside of my cheek. Alexa had told me that morning in the hideout that she and her family were working against this man. Bouchard had discovered something about him that they couldn't figure out. Nobody had pieced it together, and he was taking his time right now, too.

Something's not right. Why isn't he getting straight to the point and demanding for my answers about Adara when he's the one who called me in here?

"I'm not gonna insult your intelligence," he said, strolling around his desk and to the front of it. "You're not gonna give anything up unless you have to. I get that."

It almost sounded like compassion—until he wiggled his fingers at the men holding me and then nodded at those behind me. The two men beside me pulled me to the right side of the Office and between two couches, facing me head-on with the Resolute Desk. Another agent at the glass-paned door muttered into his radio, "Bring him in."

Caldwell kept his eyes trained on the door. We didn't wait for even half a minute before it creaked open. Two officers dragged in a tall and gaunt prisoner.

Gray streaked his ear-length hickory-brown hair, a matching beard lightly carpeting his triangular jaw as sharp as his sallow eyes. A worn T-shirt hung loosely from his torso, black pants matching his slip-ons.

I almost didn't recognize him until something in me snapped when I did—from both my visions and here and now. I jolted forward in my agents' grip, something deep reaching for the man in front of me. Bond, family. Protection.

He's here, it's really him, let me get to him!

"No," Mr. Dawson rasped, "Emma, don't—"

I was jerked to face Caldwell again before he could finish. "Nobody wants to waste any more time, the schedule's packed for today," he said. "Thomas is gonna help you tell us the truth, Emmalynn. I'll ask you a question, and for every answer you don't give,"—he gestured to the agent beside Mr. Dawson—"a bullet will keep track."

The agent unholstered the gun from his belt. With a stomach-twisting click, he cocked it and aimed it straight at Mr. Dawson's chest.

"No," I snapped, "I told you, I'd only tell you if my family stays safe!"

"He is," Caldwell said, an edge impeding on his voice. "So is your family, none of them have been harmed. You're the only one who hasn't fulfilled their end of the deal."

"Don't," Mr. Dawson told me, taking a strained breath in. "Emma, don't give him anything!"

"If she doesn't, her father's next," Caldwell said, turning his brown eyes onto me. "Tell me what you know about Adara's power, Emmalynn."

"Emma—"

"Stop," I told Mr. Dawson, forcing myself to look into his sallow, now dull-blue eyes. I couldn't believe the gray growing into his hair. "You did your part. You're done." I looked down at the royal-blue rug under us, the Great Seal of the United States threaded in the middle. I couldn't let Mr. Dawson look me in the eye when I told him, "This part's mine."

I dragged my eyes up to Caldwell again. "Adara is destined to be powerful enough to ultimately unite the mortal and magic worlds. Magicians consider her a savior."

He hummed, leaning on the front of his desk. "Does she possess impossible magic like Target Echo and probably Cipher?"

My chest clenched with the men's grasp on my arms as we neared the edge of the cliff. I was going to have to jump off soon, and my only option was to prepare for it. "Yes."

"I want her ability and then yours."

I swallowed. Took a deep breath. *Okay.*

"Emma, stop—!"

"I'm a hybrid wielder," I said above Mr. Dawson. "I am all seven classes of magic."

"Interesting. But I asked for Adara's."

All I needed was a glimpse at Mr. Dawson in the left corner of my eye to remember why I was confessing.

"That's it. 'Adara' is just an alias in the magic world." I dropped my resistance against the men who held me, letting my hands unclench and hang. I knew what my future looked like. "I'm Tristan Atera's daughter, Adara."

I wanted to believe that the words only existed in my head. In another vision. I wanted to believe that my mind was projecting

all this in a what-if scenario, that reality was still my dorm at Callistro with my best friends.

"*You're* Adara."

Sarcasm dripped from Caldwell's lips—like he didn't believe
me.

"You? I've allocated millions over the years toward finding
this all-powerful sorceress to protect the country, spent the last
fourteen years in office sending out our best Hunters to find her,
and you're telling me she's right here in front of me? A seventeen-
year-old girl?"

"I can't lie," I shot back, "I'm still under the truth spell they
put on me. I feel like you'd use my last name as enough justifica-
tion after spending your whole presidency—"

I froze, my own words echoing back at me like an alarm in a
canyon. Something wasn't adding up about that. No, there were
a few things not adding up.

"You've been in office for fourteen years," I said, the presence
of every rifle in the room so heavy that I could already feel them
pressing against me. "Long before you knew I knew something."

"Yes, because Americans trust me to keep them safe from
threats like her," he replied, crossing his arms over his suit.

My memory ignited. No matter what version of this vision I'd
had, my magic had always shown Caldwell saying that very line.

The details. Remember the details.

"*Threats like her*". He'd spent millions trying to protect the
country from—

My mind snagged on the words. From an "all-powerful sorceress".

I met his downturned eyes. "I never said she was a sorceress."

"It's a generalization," he deadpanned. "A *magician*."

No. Every sorcerer was a magician, but not every magician was a sorcerer.

"You didn't ask me how I knew so much about her, either," I argued. "She's famous among *magicians*. I didn't know about her until two years ago when I *am* her, but you came into office with the mission to hunt her down, like you'd already been told about her. You're willing to kill my family, so they don't matter to you anymore—you only wanted me and my friends alive, the two with the same amount of power as me and the one who was your last living lead to what Alexa Delphine knew about me—"

"Accusing the president of a felony that grim earns you quite the spot on Death Row," Caldwell said, squaring his shoulders. He wiggled his fingers at the agent with a gun pointed at Mr. Dawson, reminding him to stay in position. The man solidified his stance. "It sounds like you know exactly what's going on with you, Echo, and Cipher, after all. Let's hear it: a hybrid magician, a teleporter, what else?"

When I let my brain start slipping down the slope, the pieces started falling into place: allocating funds for "security" by grandly investing in Hunter technologies to find Adara. Lowering the federal standards to promote Hunters and mass-produce Grand Hunter packs. Keeping select wielders alive upon capturing them, like me, Alejandro, and Runelle. Utilizing Alexa, whose secret mission was to protect my *magic*.

"Emma, if you remember nothing else, just remember that it's Caldwell, it's all Caldwell."

"Whatever you do, do not let Caldwell catch you."

"She's famous among magicians.*"*

What I'd felt upon approaching the Oval Office, it was familiar. Despite the neutralizing cuffs, it was ever so dimly familiar, I knew that feeling, *this* feeling.

"Wait," I urged, turning my head to the men on either side of me, "sorcerers can detect if someone's a magician, if you take the cuffs off me—"

"Answer me or the last thing Thomas sees is a bullet. What is Cipher's ability and who else do you know is like this?"

"You didn't just have the Delphines killed because they were magicians," I said, writhing in the loosening grip on my arms, "they knew what you were really doing with magic, didn't they? That's why they were trying to protect their innocent targets' magic, and you didn't want me or my friends killed because we had power you couldn't let die with us!"

Caldwell's glare squared on the armed agent beside Mr. Dawson. "Shoot him."

I jerked in his direction. "No, please! I can prove it, just let me—!"

A release clicked behind me. The cuffs around my wrists clattered to the rug.

My head snapped up to the man on my right: he'd unlocked me, but now he had his gun aimed at me.

"What're you doing?" Caldwell barked, marching forward, but the man held out his hand.

"As you said, Mr. President, this is a matter of national security," he replied sternly. "As *she* said, she's still under the truth spell from the interrogation. Our first priority is to neutralize any threats, potential or otherwise, terrorist or traitor."

In the corner of my vision, Mr. Dawson's eyes darted to me.

—*They finally told you? You unlocked your ability as a sorceress?*—

"Well?" the man on my right growled, nodding toward Caldwell with his gun still aimed.

The second my gaze met the president's dark eyes, that abhorrence swallowed my being alive. That instinct hadn't been born of hatred, it'd caused it. Somehow, despite the cuffs neutralizing my magic, the sorcerer's ability had awoken in me upon confronting one of the strongest wielders... *ever.* So powerful that even the root of my magic, subdued *and* suppressed for my whole life, could still detect it.

Their blood stains his hands while their magic flows in his veins.

"You're a magician," I stated. "You've been hunting down Adara so you can absorb her magic—!"

"I said SHOOT HIM!"

Caldwell charged forward. The middle glass window shattered with a boom behind him as the agent on my left grabbed his arm. Shouts of an urgent code resounded across the room. A bullet zipped through the broken window.

President Caldwell froze in front of me, jaw stuck open and eyes wide with stun. Two crimson gouges stained the left side of his blazer. Another shot whizzed by, striking the shoulder of the man on my right.

I dropped to the floor just as a fourth bullet ripped through the air right above my head.

Forty-Five

My palms slammed against the blue carpet before cuffed hands grabbed my wrist and yanked me off the floor. Those firm fingers almost felt familiar, but they were too weak. Relief flooded into my stomach when I looked up at Mr. Dawson pulling me. My magic obliterated his cuffs, and we bolted to the glass-paned door.

A bullet struck the floor by my feet. I screamed.

Just as Secret Service all turned toward me, their bodies fell by the triplet. It took me half a second to realize that Mr. Dawson was putting them to sleep. I jumped in to help before he dragged me to the exit.

We slammed the door shut. I froze the lock as gunshots fired from the Office—but not at us. Before the other awake agents had a chance to shatter the door's tempered glass, Mr. Dawson put them to sleep.

Another bullet flew by behind me, striking the concrete of the colonnade. I spun around as Mr. Dawson grabbed my wrist again.

They got Caldwell, why are they still shooting?

The narrow stone pathway stretched out in front of us, curving rightward into the oval road of the White House campus. I searched for a target through the trees alongside us.

The shots are from the right. Someone's shooting from—

My gaze landed on the Eisenhower Executive Office across the street, the landscape concealing the bottom of it. Gunshots continued banging from the Oval Office. Not at us, but at the other side of the street, like Secret Service saw a sniper I couldn't.

Infrared cameras. The sniper's invisible but Secret Service has—

The campus echoed with another shot. A searing pang burst in my left side, knocking me to the ground halfway down the path.

Mr. Dawson's voice was muffled in my ears. I think he called my name—but the shock was ringing in my head, stifling my senses.

I'm shot.

I'm shot. It's me. I'm their target.

My hand warmed at my side with something slick. A gouge's edge burned my skin and what I prayed wasn't my large intestine. Against my will, against my instincts, panic overtook my breaths in shallow pants. Mr. Dawson kept a firm grip around my waist as he lay me down, his other hand supporting my head. I couldn't make out his urgent words. My left side pulsed, stun depriving my every sensation except the two-inch-long bullet that had wedged itself into me. Mr. Dawson moved away my hand, pressing firmly against the wound. I unleashed a strangled cry.

"I know, honey, I know," I think he said, "I have to, just hold on!"

A final reverberating shot boomed from the Office. All was left silent across the White House campus.

Glass shattered somewhere in the distance. Footsteps pounded, shouting ensued, Mr. Dawson's voice intensified in my ears before fully clearing up.

"Keep talking to me!" he commanded, turning his head to look behind him and then back at me. "Don't go to sleep, don't close your eyes, look at me!"

It hurts. It hurts.

They were shooting at me.

They wanted me dead.

From somewhere in the field, my name curdled the air. Jak. Jak and another pair of footsteps sprinting across the grass. A cold hand slid under my neck, another under my back to prop me up slightly. A sting zapped my side, and I cried out. The hands froze on my body, Jak muttering apology after apology. In my bottom peripheral vision, a warm-brown hand reached out while Dawson looked behind him again. I heard bodies collapse with sleep.

Alejandro...?

"Don't close your eyes," Mr. Dawson commanded again, his hands still pressing against my side. "Hang on!"

I'd been shot with a sniper rifle. Even with his pressure, I was bleeding. Too much. My blood was pouring out onto the stone. Every second was getting harder to live through, to endure.

Black encroached on the edges of my vision. I rested my

bloodied hand above my wound. A drop streamed down the side and to my arm, leaving a warm-cold trail in its wake.

"Emma, please," Jak cried above me, one hand holding my head and the other interlocking with my left. "Look at me, look at me, hold on to me."

My eyes pulled themselves to his. Jak. My Jak. I never got to tell him. I was fading into unconsciousness, and I didn't know if I'd wake up again. I wanted to wake up again so I could tell him. So he would at least know. How I felt about him, how much he meant to me, everything I loved about him, how much I loved... him.

Why his torture had affected me the way it had, why I was willing to sacrifice for him as much as I was for my family, why his pain felt like my own—why I'd lose part of myself if I ever lost him. I loved him.

With another pulse of black in my vision, I didn't have time to be afraid anymore. I didn't have time for doubt or questions—only what I knew.

"Jak," I rasped, inhaling sharply.

"Don't talk," he said, his fingers tightening around mine. "Don't waste—"

"Yes," I whispered. And even just testing that word felt less like I was sinking in the deep end and more like I was diving into free waters. "I'll be—your girlfriend."

His grip on the back of my head faltered. "What?"

"I want—to be yours," I managed, my blood sticking my shirt to my skin now. "Because—I love you, too."

"No. No, no, no, stop." He took his hand out of mine to hold the side of my face. He was blurring. "You're gonna be fine, stop, don't close your eyes—"

His voice narrowed into a tunnel, clouding with a haze that swarmed my vision. Three familiar voices melded together in an indiscernible echo as my head fell limp in Jak's hand and my world blacked out.

C H A P T E R

Forty-Six

old wind rushed over my body as I stirred. A hard surface dully pressed against my back. I exhaled with a groan, my left side stiff with taut skin that stretched with every small movement.

I was *alive?* And my wound—it was sore, but it didn't hurt.

My eyes snapped open. Two hopeful faces stared back at me, faces I thankfully recognized: Momma and Runelle.

Where were we? Why had I woken up to just them?

"Em?" Momma whispered on my left. She took my hand and helped me sit up. Her cheeks and nose were teeming with red, honey-colored eyes swollen like golf balls. I could barely recognize the remnants of her voice, ravaged by sobs I clearly hadn't been awake to hear. "How do you feel?"

My senses started waking up, processing a sleeping bag under me on what felt like concrete. The whole room was made of concrete, echoing a cold air onto us.

Were we still in the White House?

I grunted, moving my hand to my side. Under the dried bloodstain on my shirt, my wound was closed. It was... healed.

"Easy, honey," Momma said with a crackly voice. "You lost a lot of blood that your body needs to finish replenishing. It's okay. You're okay."

I glanced down. Other than the ripped hole in my shirt, a nickel-sized scar was all that remained. How long had I been out for?

I looked back up, catching the hallway stretching down in front of me. My memory flared. I'd walked down that hallway before—I'd been in this *room* before.

The Atera family beach house basement...?

Almost two years ago, on my sixteenth birthday, Alexa had taken me down here. I carefully looked behind me: the heavy door that had been hiding Dad in a small, empty room sat closed. A small part of me wondered if anything was inside now.

"What happened?" I asked, my voice hoarser than I remembered. "Where's everyone, how long was I out?"

Momma rubbed my shoulder, her fingers shaky. Her narrow face sagged with melancholy, flyaways sticking out all over her chestnut hair. "You were out for a couple hours. Everyone's in the room behind us. Alejandro's grabbing our things from the base."

I turned my head to Runelle on my other side.

"Hello, Emma."

Her light French accent was undetectable then. Her harsh

eyes on her square face lacked their signature glare and instead stared at me like she—somehow—owed me. A frown pulled down her small lips as she moved her bangs out of her eyes.

Joseph Bouchard's descendant. As much as I wanted the story, to know if she even knew, her family lineage felt irrelevant as I made myself ask, "You're still here?"

"Yeah. You were right about me—about having an impossible ability with my 'special' name. My magic can heal."

A healer. She'd taken care of my bullet wound.

She *healed Alejandro's exhaustion yesterday when he went to get her. That's how he got back to Bouchard so fast.*

"Thank you," I said, my words hollow with disbelief and, well, gratitude. "You literally saved my life."

"I was... obligated to help."

The faintest smile pushed up one corner of her lips. Reassurance, like my words the night we met had actually stuck with her.

"You changed your mind?" I asked.

It took her a second to softly nod. "And I guess we're partners—*partners* now. So..."—she pressed her hand to her chest—"my real name is 'Mila'."

She trusts us enough with it now. It was pretty.

"Why did you choose to stay?" I asked. "When we dragged you back into everything you ran from? Why did you go with Alejandro in the first place?"

"I was furious," she began, still making sure that every "r" sounded like the American one, "when Alejandro and I were caught. But I stayed because..." She looked down at her lap like she was ashamed of her answer. "I stayed for the same rea—*reason* Alejandro convinced me to come: I had to."

I didn't know what that meant, but I refused to question it when she was finally on our team. Alejandro had managed to get through to her, and that was all that mattered.

"I was scared when we met," Mila admitted. "People took advantage of my magic while I was growing up. I thought you and Alejandro came to do the same thing, I was terrified that someone had found me after—*after* everything I went through to hide. But he talked to me that night we dueled. While you were asleep. By the end of it, I... understood him. So I told him what my magic can do. That's why he came to me yesterday, he assumed people would need my help and... I couldn't reject that after our talk. He was going to ask you if it was safe to come down when we got to the base, but those men caught us."

"I'm so sorry..." I told her. I didn't know what she had gone through that had forced her to run all the way to Antarctica to survive on her own, but I knew that getting caught by *two* federal governments was a great reminder of why she had.

"We got out," she said, like everything was okay just because of that.

"Anthony broke Alejandro out this morning," Momma told me. "They got us out while you were with Caldwell. Alejandro's teleportation and Mila's healing are the only reasons we escaped."

"*How* did Anthony break out Alejandro?" I asked. "Where did he even come from?"

"He pretended to turn himself in as a Delphine so he could come after us—when Alejandro left to get Mila, he messaged Kamose about the raid. Kamose must've seen his text when we were on our way to the White House—which was a blessing in disguise since his magic couldn't act on it with the protection spell. I guess he knew that releasing us before we got there would end up in another capture. So he saw Anthony riding in a separate car and knocked out the agents escorting him."

Wow. How different Anthony was from the young man who'd threatened me in the Callistro Forest and enabled my hospitalization last year.

"Kamose broke off the neutralizing cuffs on Anthony so he had his magic. Alejandro said he woke up one of the guards in the car, got the location of the camera room in the facility, and then knocked out the guard again and took his uniform."

Which have their IDs, and face masks for anonymity.

"So Anthony was able to shut down all the cameras so nobody would see him getting Alejandro out," I said with realization.

"Yep. From there it was moving fast enough so Secret Service wouldn't catch us again."

Secret Service.

"Caldwell..." I said, the name ragged in my throat.

"He's dead," Momma told me, verifying my unspoken thoughts. "He was assassinated—"

"They weren't trying to kill him," I said, my body involuntarily starting to shake with the memory. My vision blurred, my heart pulsing in my ears. "They wanted me dead, I was their target—"

"It's okay," Momma crooned, even Mila reaching out to help stabilize me. "No, honey, you were just caught in the crossfire—"

"No, Caldwell moved in front of me and they killed him and then kept shooting," I cried. "They kept shooting at me when we got outside, it only stopped when Secret Service killed them. Those bullets *always* landed near me!"

Momma's eyes trickled down to my wound. A heavy silence,

one that I cursed with my whole being, crashed over the room like a tidal wave. I could understand not having anywhere near the proper reaction for that—but what scared me was how Momma didn't have anything to argue with.

"Who?" Mila asked. "It would have to be someone who got there in time and knew who you were. Who could that be?"

"It doesn't matter," Mom said with more bite than I'd anticipated. "The government did us a favor for once and took care of them. What matters is that we have a plan for where to go next."

The government taking care of our enemy. Ha... My foggy brain could barely put the pieces together. They'd taken care of the sniper because the sniper had shot the president, but they'd been aiming for me. Someone had it out for me, had betrayed *me*. Who would... who could—?

Opal betrayed me, too.

My stomach twisted. With my head free from the pressuring atmosphere of the interrogation, I still didn't want to believe that she had *chosen* to turn us in to the government. She remembered everything I'd done to her, but how did that warrant sending me and my family to the White House?

"This was all her proposal: her help in exchange for letting your other friends go." I bit the inside of my cheek, the evidence resurfacing in my head: her having my things for a locator spell, the timing of everything, the necklace...

Alejandro, I remembered. He'd somehow known about the necklace and taken it to Haines Junction to destroy the feed. He knew something about the situation that I didn't. The second he came back, I needed to ask him, and I refused to let my mind entertain any possibility until then. Most of our enemies were dead, and from the sounds of it, my family already knew what our next step was. That was what mattered.

I looked up at Momma again. "I want to see Dawson. I wanna know what Ingrid told him."

She pushed my hair behind my ear. "She told him what would happen at the hideout. Because of that, he knew that whatever Caldwell was planning would depend on trapping us since his Hunters failed. But we needed to get to Steele, collect what intel we could, and let him find a way out."

"But he didn't," I snapped, recalling his gaunt stature and sunken facial features. "He let them torture him for *months*. We were stuck at Bouchard waiting to hear he was dead!"

Mila straightened as Momma's voice tightened. "Emma, Bouchard had information we *needed*. A lot more than we needed him."

"How did *he* know that?"

She sighed, her thumb rubbing my shoulder. "Alexa found him that morning and told him everything."

My heart clenched for him. *He probably knows she's dead.*

"She told him about Caldwell really being after his targets' magic, how the Delphines didn't know exactly what he was planning—but they were pretty sure it was a collaboration between him and a few other leaders."

I paused. "Do we have what he was planning? Other people are involved in Project Ember?"

"That was their theory," she answered tentatively. "And the other reason we couldn't save Thomas when we wanted to. Ingrid and Alexa both gave him clues for what to listen for, and he ultimately ended up finding out where Caldwell was keeping his main agenda—partially thanks to Bouchard's double agents that were sent out this month. He went back in with Alejandro after they saved you to grab it since Secret Service was distracted with the assassination."

Bouchard's double agents—I wonder if they're part of the reason we made it out alive.

"Then... what was Caldwell planning?"

When Momma swallowed, it felt like a blow to the stomach. Instinct again. Instinct knew what I didn't, something I didn't want to hear.

"Should..." Mila began, "should I leave, Mrs. Atera?"

"Yes," she replied, her eyes falling to my lap. "Alejandro will be back soon, anyway."

Something wasn't right: she wouldn't look at me no matter how long I stared at her, even as Mila stood up and walked to the room behind us. Even as she entered the code on the keypad beside the door and joined my family and Jak inside.

"A few things," Momma began in a whisper, like she couldn't force volume into her voice no matter how hard she tried. "Understand that, for now, we're safe here because the only people who knew about this place are dead—save for Nolan's father, but you and I both know he's too scared to come after us again."

"A locator spell—"

"Alejandro is getting Bouchard's protection spell from them with our things so we can cast it here."

"Okay, but—"

"There's a small grocery store half an hour away that we can get supplies from to prepare for where we're going next. We need to leave as soon as we're in a stable headspace."

"Mom," I said, "what was Caldwell really doing—?"

An orange light flashed in the hall in front of us. Alejandro, dressed in his signature leather jacket and black jeans, had a bulging duffel bag hanging over his shoulder. He walked into the room like he was making a casual delivery.

"I'm so glad you're okay," he told me in English, dropping the bag at my feet and kneeling. "I got your things from the base."

"Wait," I said, carefully shifting to my knees, my wound tugging with every flex of my muscles. "The necklace, the necklace Opal gave me—did you take it at some point?"

There it was: his pause, the deer-caught-in-the-headlights eyes. "*Amiga*," he murmured, "I'm—please don't be mad—"

"Why? How did you know it was recording us?"

His head caught back, and he blinked. "Kamose. He texted me about it—he watched us during the trip to Bouchard from Antarctica, so he saw you get it. He thought it was—weird. He watched Opal and saw that the necklace recorded everything. I saw his text when I visited my parents next time. He told me to take the necklace out of Bouchard so he could—make it normal."

My heart fell into the pit of my stomach. Momma's hand dropped from my shoulder like she'd made the connection with me. Alejandro had taken the necklace to Haines Junction—someplace where he could get Wi-Fi for his phone—and let Kamose know to change it to a normal necklace, cutting out the feed.

I can't believe Kamose kept a protective eye over us even after we left Antarctica.

"We wanted to let you keep it," Alejandro added somberly. "Because you thought it was a present from your friend. It made you happy. If you knew the truth, it..." He thought about the words before huffing and then switching to Spanish. "It would have broken your heart, *amiga*, it would have given you *another* problem you had no control over. We did this for you."

My nose stung, a barrage of tears threatening to snap my last string of control—until I looked at Momma. At the hardness in her strong eyes, the brewing anger at the realization of who our "friend" really was. And I vowed to never waste a single tear on Opal Dubois again.

"She hates me that much?" I whispered to Alejandro.

His gaze softened on me. "She is not your friend, *amiga*."

I locked my jaw, tightened my throat, against the heartstring that had snapped. I knew he was saying that because he knew. I knew it was true.

She conspired with the US Government against me like she wanted me dead.

I didn't know if I could connect the sniper to her or not; sending me to the White House was a guaranteed death sentence on its own. Why hire a hit man? How would *she* have ever hired a hit man?

"We..." Momma began softly, pulling my eyes back to her, "we have to ease Thomas into this."

He's gonna be devastated.

I swallowed, because Alejandro was right about another thing: there was nothing I could do about this right now, not until we got out of here. Until then, though, there was so much more I needed to know.

"Is Bouchard okay?" I asked. "Did the government actually leave them alone?"

His throat bobbed. He switched back to English. "I don't... I saw—a lot of... bad things."

"What does that mean?" Momma asked before I could.

"They followed their plan for a—how do you say it?—a... when the government comes. The government said that Bouchard needed to come for... custody. But Bouchard didn't believe them— they thought that they will die, so they attacked. There were a lot of agents, but the base had many more people. They made all the agents sleep and... and then they—killed them. All of them."

Everyone in this facility is hereby federally detained. "Detained". Technically, the Canadian Government had tried to uphold their end of the deal—but nobody had given Bouchard the message.

I bit the inside of my cheek. I hated how *conflicted* I felt about those words. What other choice had Bouchard had? Erasing the agents' memories was a temporary solution; they'd all remember eventually, one way or another...

So why was the smallest part of me so disturbed?

"Is the base okay?" I asked again slowly.

"They..." Alejandro said timidly, almost like he was scared to say these words in English. "They lost a lot. Many people."

No... No. My heartbeat faltered. *No. I was supposed to protect them.*

"Eun-Ji?" I whispered with a tremble.

Alejandro shook his head. "Defense and Security protected her. They didn't let her fight. But now the base is—exposed. Eun-Ji says that they have a place to go to. But... I don't know."

I swallowed a bout of tears. *I couldn't save them.*

Ignorance really is bliss; I wanted to believe that as long as the base had Eun-Ji, if she said they had somewhere to go, then they did. I had no idea if it was true—Eun-Ji had never mentioned anything about Bouchard having escape routes or backup locations. Right now, though, too big a part of me didn't want to know anything for sure.

"Here." Alejandro unzipped the duffel bag, pulling apart the opening. "I took the most important things."

The first and smallest item on top grabbed my attention. I carefully reached for the yellow-and-orange crocheted flame as if it'd unravel in my hold. "Emmalynn" was spelled out around it in dark-blue yarn. Dakota. She'd survived. Right?

Omari, Joshua. Michaela. Li...

I looked up at Alejandro to ask if he knew until my gaze snagged on a familiar book. Remembrance ignited in my mind.

Setting the flame down beside me, I took the yellow journal Sarah had given me almost three months ago. I flipped through the empty pages, relieved; now felt like no better time to start filling them.

I reached into the bag again, expecting to see the others—the red one Momma had given me for my sixteenth birthday, the purple one Jak had given me second semester before Redway left Callistro, the green one Cara had given me in the hospital, and the blue one Mr. Dawson had given me last Christmas. My fingers froze amidst the fabric of clothes.

I looked up at Alejandro. "Where are my journals?"

His throat bobbed again. No. He shouldn't have had to think about how to reply if he had a normal answer.

"They weren't..." he began, too quietly for my anxiety's sake. "I looked for them, I couldn't... They weren't there."

They took them.

The words slammed against me like a battering ram. The US

Government had every word of my confession in custody—about *everything.*

"Caralyn's...?" I whispered.

"No," he quickly said, reaching deep down into the duffel bag. He pulled out a crimson book from the bottom. "I think that they didn't take it because it looks like this."

I took it from him. *White Lies for Sacred Ties.*

Converte, I said.

A bright amber sheen glimmered over the book, the material roughening under my fingers until the cover faded into chipping coffee-brown leather.

"How?" I breathed, looking up at Momma.

"Your dad," she said. "He recast the illusion spell when he heard the alarm in case"—she nodded at the book in my hands—"this happened."

I huffed. I didn't know whether to cry from relief or despair; my journals were a testament of Caralyn's alliance with magic themselves, and if the government had them, I'd just set Callistro on fire. The school wasn't surviving with my evidence, my confession, of who the founder really was, of how I'd met wielders at a school meant for Hunters—

Sarah and Breanne. Someone had to warn them about who was coming. The SWAT team, FBI, federal agents were bound to swarm the premises at any—

"There was another thing," Alejandro muttered before my mind could spiral further, "um..."

He unzipped a side pocket of the duffel bag and drew out a simple gold-chained bracelet. A small heart dangled from it. "Rebecca's boyfriend wants to give this to you all."

My brows pinched together. "Um—okay. Go ahead, she's in the room behind us."

Unmoving, he kept the bracelet extended toward me. I stared back at him. He'd paused like I'd said something wrong, like I was acting too normal.

I looked at Momma.

"Emma," she murmured, taking my hands into hers, "just listen to me, okay?"

"No," I told myself—against the wicked thoughts that had to be lying to me right now.

Alejandro wordlessly stood and trudged into the room behind us, joining my family as Momma said, "Anthony was able to grab a few weapons and get Alejandro to our cell, but the entire containment ward was proofed against magic—"

"No, Mom," I said at her wavering voice, daring her to tell me my worst fear *was* lying.

"Alejandro couldn't teleport us while we were in the containment ward, but the security door was closing—"

"No, Mom, stop," I said as my body jerked.

"We shot most of them, but—the door was closing, Becca saw we weren't all gonna make it—"

"Mom, *stop!*" I cried, thrashing in her grasp.

"She shoved us ahead before the door closed. The agent we didn't get shot—she already had a couple of bullet wounds, she was..."

My lips opened with the words but never moved to form them. My voice had caught in my throat, stuck there like the rest of me in my mother's hold.

"I'm so, so sorry, honey," she rasped, moving her hands to

cup my hot face. Her tears spilled over and down her red cheeks, her fingers quivering against my skin. "Becca's dead."

Blurred. Black. Nonexistent. The world in front of me somehow became all three. I lost all feeling in my body, any awareness of my senses. I should've felt my hot breath blowing up in my face as I sobbed against my mother, but I didn't. I should've felt the pressure building to a fatal extent in my head, but I didn't. I should've felt the pang as I fell out of my mother's arms and crumpled to the concrete floor, but I didn't. I didn't feel anything except the pulsating thought, the throbbing reality, hammering into my head that my aunt was dead.

I couldn't feel the icy ground under my palms. My chest constricting as I struggled to breathe past my choking sobs. The numb sting of my fist as I slammed it against the ground, trying to break the world in front of me. It wasn't right. This wasn't right. We'd escaped, we'd taken down our enemy, and yet we were worse off. We'd traded our fight and chains for a world more broken than the last. We'd made it out of the den and into the fire, and I was burning alive.

Forty-Seven

I wasn't okay. But I pretended I was stable. That was the only way to get my parents to leave with Alejandro the next day to grab what we needed from the grocery store half an hour away. We were safe under the protection spell he'd learned from Bouchard, so that offered a bit more solace.

While they were gone, Jak stayed down in the basement while Mr. Dawson had gone up to the surface. It wasn't long before I went up the steep stairs to the ashy remains of the Atera family beach house to join him.

Cold, salty wind blew my hair out of my face as I surfaced. With his back to me and his hands in his pockets, Mr. Dawson stood in front of the charred brick fireplace, standing amidst the fallen burnt walls and ceiling planks that used to make up the living area. Dad had given him a shirt and jacket to borrow so he could finally get out of the clothes from the White House facility. If not for the flowing length and the gray streaking his hickory-brown hair, I would've mistaken him for Dad.

I stepped over a fractured board, causing it to shift as my heel scraped against it. Mr. Dawson turned, exposing his light beard that I hadn't gotten used to yet. The original bright blue of his deep-set eyes amidst the cloudy morning had dulled to a light gray.

"Hi," I said.

His nostrils flared as he huffed, turned to face me, and took a step forward. I didn't let him take another, lunging over the debris and around the tarped sofa to throw my arms around him.

"I missed you," he whispered into my ear.

"I missed you, too," I murmured, squeezing him. "I hate you for doing that."

"No." He pulled away just enough to dry my eye with his rough thumb, saving a tear before it fell. "You hate what I did. But it saved you."

Not all of us. We'd finally rescued him, and one of us had paid the price for it.

No. I swallowed hard, shutting off my mind to those thoughts. *Not now.*

"What did you give up?" I said. "Until Ingrid's prophecy happened."

He tilted his head away, his throat bobbing. I knew to brace myself when he let go of me and stepped back, scratching the beard on his sharp jaw. "It's the main reason I was able to suffer through this year. When you told me as a nore that Alexa's mission was to protect your family, and then when Ingrid prophesied what would happen... I realized that I was willing to go through it to keep you guys safe—because I was *dependent*, more than anything else in this world, on whatever would keep my family safe. Including William's ignorance."

I was about to ask for more until it hit me: what Alexa told William after shooting him before setting me free—when she and I were running through the halls and she explained everything.

"It is solely my mercy stopping me from shooting you dead right now for what you did!"

"William ruined everything."

"When you got here, he called in backup." He'd called for Caldwell's best Hunters specifically, like he'd known the real reason the Delphines were hunting the Ateras. Even Alexa had been caught off guard by his betrayal. He wasn't supposed to have figured it out that soon, and then he waited for the right moment to betray them.

Mr. Dawson asking Ingrid about the future gave William access to that information and neutralized Alexa's protection over us. So when Dawson killed William and was caught, he fulfilled the prophecy of his capture... Giving him "back" William's ignorance because William was dead.

My chest locked. I didn't know what to do with those words, where to put them. Where to direct my emotions about them, whatever they were.

"And that information killed Alexa," Mr. Dawson said next, rubbing his mouth. Refusing to look at me. "So I guess I gave up two things."

I didn't have the right words. Not when Thomas Dawson, whom I'd only ever seen crack once, was letting a couple of tears fall freely down his face. Not when Mr. Dawson was letting them steal his authoritative voice. Not when my godfather was breaking in front of me.

At the sight of his tears, the thought burst through the front doors of my mind: *Three things. He lost even more yesterday.*

I tried stabling my trembling jaw to no avail. It'd been a full day since we'd escaped. A full day away yet not one step forward. I wanted, I *wanted* to honor my aunt, but I couldn't without remembering her. I couldn't, I couldn't, I couldn't.

I can't. I can't—

"Honey..." Mr. Dawson whispered, reaching for my cheek.

I shook my head, stepping back. I couldn't say a single thing about her without inciting my own collapse, whether or not her name left my lips. All I had now were my emotions and they wouldn't leave.

"It wasn't—supposed to happen like this," I stated, trying to stick to the facts.

He nodded. His throat bobbed again. "I know."

"No," I said, my volume rising out of my control, "you don't know, it wasn't supposed to happen like *this*. You have no idea what I've done this year to reunite my family, and that'll NEVER be possible now!"

"Emma—"

"She didn't deserve that!" I exclaimed, throwing my arm out toward the sea as if I could conjure my aunt with a flick of my hand. But she didn't appear, and I was remembering her. "Of all people, she deserved a life away from the worst our family had to offer, she waited the longest out of all of us for it and she died for it! She didn't deserve that!"

"She *wanted* it, Emma."

I froze. Seething rage helplessly curled my fingers. "No," I muttered, gritting my teeth. "She didn't."

"She did." His eyes steeled themselves, challenging my anger further. "She shoved her family to safety because she knew someone had to make the sacrifice—and hers would not only save them, but give her a way out."

A way out. A way out?!

"You don't know—!"

"*You* don't know, Emma," he told me, pointing a firm, low finger at me. "Becca was severely depressed."

That accusation set my blood aflame—but Mr. Dawson had spoken the words with a greater weight than I'd expected. It wasn't anger.

It was regret.

Those words had a conviction in them that dared me to think he was lying. I wanted so badly to believe he was lying. I knew my aunt, I *knew* her and she understood me. She couldn't have nor wouldn't have hidden something like that from me and let me lose her to—

"She locked herself up her entire life out of fear until she had no choice but to, her younger brother had seen more of the world than she had by the time he came home, and everyone else in her family was able to live outside of their four walls while she never could." With every sentence, Mr. Dawson's eyes teemed more and more with red. The glisten intensified, and his voice progressively rose over the coastal wind. "She was going so crazy that she took the risk and started taking midnight walks with an invisibility cloak on the nights she couldn't sleep, just to escape it all. She had no life until she got to Bouchard, and then she was ripped from it after less than *half a year*. She had *no hope* left. She saw that door in the facility closing and knew what was on the other side, a life identical to the one she'd finally escaped from! She pushed her family because she knew *they* had a life worth living—"

"So did she!"

"She didn't believe it!" he retorted, making me flinch. "Yes, she did! But *she* didn't believe it." His voice cracked open. Much like his heart that I could hear in his now tear-soaked words. "She saw an opportunity. Not a death sentence. And she knew she was the only one who saw it that way. Her mind was made, nobody—"

His brow pinched with the force of his oncoming sobs. He turned from me and rubbed his mouth again.

The end of his sentence beat in my head like the steadiest heart in the world: *Nobody could have changed her mind.* Nobody could have saved her because she didn't want to be saved.

No. No... My mind felt like it was fracturing. I didn't know how much longer I could keep it in one piece. *Not her. Not her. She wouldn't do that. She'd never,* never *do something like that, she wouldn't do something like that.*

I was in denial because the truth made sense. A lot of things about her made more sense now.

"If I'm not running, I'm fine, Em."

I didn't know if I hated her for it, or hated myself for never picking up the signs two years earlier.

"How do you know?" I forced myself to ask.

Mr. Dawson looked down at the ashy floor. "Your dad."

Dad knew. He'd been there when his older sister had made her sacrifice, he'd seen the look in her eyes in those moments.

Dad knew.

Why?

Through my teary vision, I looked all around me at the burnt remains of what was once the Atera family beach house. We were all here except one.

She was so close. She wouldn't have done that.

That was easier to believe—that her sacrifice had been nothing more than a final act of selfless love, a desire for the rest of us to live. My aunt had done the unthinkable, and I didn't know where to direct this helplessness, this searing hatred for the situation and whoever was to blame for it, because I knew there was *someone* to blame. I couldn't hate her for it. I couldn't even hate myself for not being able to prevent it while I faced off against the most wicked man in the world. No, I hated the world that had locked Rebecca Atera in the house to begin with, and I wanted to set it on fire.

As if hearing my thoughts, Mr. Dawson faced me again. His red eyes and nose were as foreign to me as his hair and beard were. "I'm sorry," he whispered.

For some reason, that apology made him come alive to me in that moment. What he was apologizing for, I couldn't pin down—but he was apologizing to me here and now because *he* was in front of me here and now. He'd made it out. He was alive.

I took a step toward him just as he opened his arms to me, and I fell into them. He embraced me like he was transferring all the warmth he had to offer amidst the cold morning, and I squeezed him back to bury the sobs racking my body. The harder I cried, the more I told myself that Mr. Dawson was here in front of me, and I had that much.

"I love you, Emma," he rasped. "I love you so much."

I held him tighter. "Don't ever—*ever*—leave us again."

"I won't." He pressed his hand to the back of my head. "I promise."

I silently vowed to hold him to that. He hadn't broken a promise to me yet, and if he started with this one, I'd crack open. I couldn't afford to lose any more pieces now. It wasn't right, none of this was right.

"It wasn't supposed to be like this," I whispered.

He pulled away enough to match our eyes, cupping the side of my face and then my chin. "But you came through," he said. "Nothing I did was in vain."

That was true. And Becca's death wouldn't be, either. She'd left a fire in my veins that I'd let burn until I could unleash it and avenge her.

C H A P T E R

Forty-Eight

The small incline of the sandhill offered a bit of support as I sat facing the horizon on the sea. I dug my toes deeper into the sand, one arm clutching my knees to my chest and my other hand mindlessly twisting the locket around my neck. I almost thought about the necklace Opal had given me but immediately forced it out of my head; I refused to subject myself to my anger until I could do something about it, especially because her betrayal had caused my aunt's death—

No. Don't. I closed my eyes, breathing it all out. I couldn't hold on to it. I couldn't fall apart with the rest of the world. I could only put it together if I was in one piece, too. After all, the US Government was no doubt still on the hunt for us, even if I'd been the one to expose Caldwell. If anything, the whole event had probably reinforced their mission. No wonder they believed Adara was trying to take over the world.

Unless Adara is somehow miraculous enough to change their minds from "dictator sorceress" to wanting to establish resolution. Honestly, I was starting to lose hope for that. Did our government *want* resolution? Or just two different populations to control?

"Hey."

My breath caught at the warm voice that had once jumpstarted my heart with a beat of butterflies. Now it left me facing the shards of reality we had to scrape together somehow.

I didn't say anything as Jak took a close spot next to me on the sand.

"Did Alejandro tell you?" he asked after a few moments. "About Julia?"

I looked up at him. There were a hundred possible answers to that, and I couldn't handle ninety-nine of them. "No."

"It was a boy."

A tinge of relief eased my chest. "He found her after the raid?"

"Yeah." He looked down at his lap, like he was trying hard to convince himself that we were having a normal conversation. "He was born early the same morning. All three of them are okay."

At least the Delphines aren't completely extinct. Now there was a new son—

Wait.

"What about," I said, swallowing the blockage in my throat, "Anthony?"

Jak turned toward me like he was about to look me in the eyes, but then stopped short. He shook his head.

"When?" I whispered, my lips barely able to form the word.

"The same time as... her," he murmured. Becca. "Alejandro said the two of them saved him and your parents. Apparently Anthony is the reason you still have your mom."

He took her bullets.

I didn't dare open my mouth again. Neither did Jak. What were we supposed to say right now, all things considered? Since yesterday, nobody had had anything to say beyond survival and planning. My family wanted to give me more time before sharing Caldwell's plans with me, and for once, I agreed with that. Those plans were *about* me—and I needed a bit more time before seeing just how big the target on my back really was.

A salty breeze blew back my hair, ruffling the curled-up tips of Jak's. I remembered all those times I'd thought about how much I liked that about him, a hairstyle I'd never seen on any other guy. And that uniqueness dove so much deeper—I'd never encountered a guy with more patience, more understanding, enough love to sacrifice his wants just for the sake of... well, me.

I looked into his russet eyes and remembered the last thing I'd said to him. At least half of me had been convinced that I wouldn't wake up to the repercussions of it. If anything, though, I knew all the more where I stood when I'd woken up with relief that I'd said it—not regret.

I loved him. I really did.

"I meant it," I said. When he cast his eyes down to his lap, I knew he didn't need me to clarify the topic.

"Em," he began, "you thought you were dying. You *were* dying—"

"I didn't tell you because I thought I was dying." I waited for him to look back up at me. "I told you because if I *had* died, you would've never known."

A small lump passed in his throat, almost like he couldn't let himself believe me. And I couldn't blame him. With that, our kiss in his room a couple of months ago was now the only thing giving me the courage I needed:

"We found out how we felt about each other at the same time," I said. "What happened in November made things painfully clear for me, too. I've wanted to tell you for so long but was always too paranoid that we'd end up in the same situation. But when I was shot, my biggest regret was that I never told you how much I care about you, how you…" I turned to face him, fully settling into my words. "You're a whole part of me, Jak," I whispered. "And I knew what it was when I realized that I might not ever wake up to you again when—when I *need* to. I love you—"

He pressed his lips to mine right as I leaned in, desperate and pleading and fulfilled all at once. His hands took the sides of my face, lips kissing me as if with every second, another fragment of him glued itself into place. I melted into him, let myself start to piece myself back together with him holding me in place. His lips took mine with every ounce of affection they'd had before and, this time, a promise to never leave. Never leave me wondering how long it would be until they'd find me again.

He broke away, exhaling. "I've hoped," he murmured, "for so long to hear you say that."

"You don't ever have to wait for it again."

"No, not wait. That was why it was so hard. I couldn't wait for it because that would mean I expected it, but you're not obligated to me. You never were, that was why…"—he brushed my hair behind my ear—"that was why I could only ever hope. I love you, too, Emma. So much."

A week ago, I would've grabbed his face and kissed him for that. I would've thrown myself into him and relaxed in his hold and let him kiss me back—but now, for some reason, there was more comfort in leaning into him, pressing my forehead to his chest. Wrapping my arms around his torso as he held me, encompassed me like a shield, let me simply be with him.

The breeze blew harder against us, and Jak tightened his arms around me. I absorbed his warmth against the coastal cold, sinking into him in a way that we'd finally unlocked with this conversation. And with no feelings left hidden between us, I couldn't move forward without him.

"I don't wanna do this separate from you anymore," I said.

"Emma." He broke away, taking my face into his hands again. "I was yours the moment you put your head on my shoulder on the Ferris wheel."

"I mean it. I need you."

With a soft smile that restored part of my hope, he pressed a lingering kiss to my lips. "I need you, too, Merlin."

I don't know what it was about that nickname—how it shattered the dam I'd built so strongly behind my eyes, revived a part of my heart amidst the death of another.

But I broke.

I fell into him again, choking on my first sob. I squeezed my chest to try to suppress it, to minimize sound and extent—and yet, with the deep breath that ravaged my lungs, Jak held me firmer. He never let me hit the sand, just kept me against him, strong, secure, safe in a way I hadn't been since the morning Dad first came home and he and Momma held me in their arms on our living room floor.

"No more doing this alone," Jak whispered. "It's you and me. Me and you from here on out."

I raised my head, ready to press a kiss to my boyfriend's lips, and then his eyes caught mine. Eyes so rich against light-brown skin that had finally healed from last November, soft yet firm features that knew how to melt and command, dark-oak hair that suited him so well. I could find remnants of his father in him, but now more than ever, despite never seeing her before, I knew that Jak had more of his mother in him.

Aastha. The truth pulled on my memory again.

I managed a sad half smile at Jak. Amidst everything that had happened yesterday, losing my own family member to a bullet during a hunt... I wanted to tell him the truth about his mother's death. There was a part of me that needed to know who'd fired the gun on my aunt, stolen her from me, and I probably never would—but I had that information for Jak. And if he wanted to, he deserved to know even if he couldn't do anything about it, for that peace of mind if nothing else. I'd spent the last few months protecting him from it, but like Eun-Ji told me the day she gave me Caralyn's journal, only he could decide if he was ready to hear about his mother.

If you ever need to know... I'll tell you. But for now, I wanted this moment, our first one allowed in I didn't remember how long. For now, my promise was enough.

His stare fell to somewhere behind me, and I looked over my shoulder. Momma was trudging up the small sandhill. Most of the red had faded from her cheeks and eyes after a day. I immediately dried my own, steadying my breath as she approached.

"Em." She stopped a few feet away, standing tall above me and Jak. The heaviness from yesterday was still stuck in her voice as she told me, "We really need to talk."

C H A P T E R

Forty-Nine

Salty sea air clung to my hair. Oscillating waves teased at my toes as Momma walked beside me on the damp sand of the coast. "Before I tell you this," she said over the wind, "I need to know you're okay. Or that you know you will be."

For the sake of never having to hear something like those words again, my heart clenched in my chest, deflecting them. I still had most of my family, and I'd unlocked what was important with Jak; those were the only things that emotionally mattered. I was back in the real world and needed to defend myself as such.

"Yeah," I told her. "I know."

She wrapped her arm around my waist. Her voice was unusually gentle. "We just need to hold on until we leave."

Again.

We'd left behind our whole lives in my hometown, and now we'd left behind the lives we'd built at an underground base in Canada. We'd had friends there, close friends, bonds that we hadn't had in a while. Everything ripped away. Again.

Momma took my hand. I moved my gaze to the horizon as she brought my knuckles to her lips, kissed my fingers, and then held my hand under her chin.

"I'm glad you know you'll be okay. Because you need to know the other reason we're hurrying."

The edge of a wave came up and skimmed my toes as she let go of my hand and then slid something out of her back pocket: a small stack of folded-up papers. She unfolded them, their rustle lost to the crashing waves. Then, she handed them to me.

Caldwell's plans. I'm out of time.

I ripped off the Band-Aid and took them, eyes jumping to the first word on the front page.

Federal Intelligence Assessment: Atera Family – Lineage, Activity, and Implications. Anomalous Research Division, US Department of Defense (DoD). Date of first entry: July 27, 1947.

What...? How did this report span so long ago? That was the year the Department of Defense was *established*; my family had been one of their first subjects to research?

Wait. This didn't just document our family's history starting from the first entry. This recorded an entire half century *prior* of our movements—past residencies, occupations, hiding spots when magic was illegal, movement patterns, *most significant demonstrations of magic?*

The information ran scarce as decades passed until my parents' names appeared—which led to mine. And there was a lot more intel recorded under us than I was comfortable with, including Mom being hired at Callistro and Dad's residency at our house and then his apartment.

They must've found all that out this year. There was no way that Caldwell would've had this information and then let it sit for even one week.

I slid the first page to the back and read the top of the next one:

US Department of Defense (DoD), National Threat Assessment Center (NTAC), Office of Intelligence & Analysis (I&A) Report: Anomalous Individuals Across the Nations.

My chest locked, trapping my breath inside my lungs.

Analysis indicates inexplicably high energy readings over the past twenty (20) years, potentially correlating with significant magician lineages across the countries of Argentina, Australia, Canada, Egypt, Indonesia, Spain, and the United States of America. Subjects' existences, of which none have been formally identified, pose an existential threat to geopolitical and international stability. Experimental containment facilities currently underway.

Neutralization Initiative: Preemptive strikes.

Global Collaboration: Leverage intelligence-sharing agreements with allied nations to develop detection and suppression techniques.

UPON SUBJECT CONTAINMENT: Project Ember to be formally initiated.

This wasn't right. All of this was familiar, hauntingly familiar. Like the federal governments across the world already knew about me and my friends, even though none of our names were printed here.

"This is what Dawson found?" I asked Momma.

She nodded.

I flipped to the next report.

M-477A-01: Global Alignment

Dread plummeted into my stomach. Instinct blared an alarm in my head. This had been updated at the beginning of May, this month.

The global initiative designed to protect long-term geopolitical security through engineered conflict and structured post-event consolidation, with the collective goal to eliminate emergent threats after transferring their power, unify authority, and restructure order to ensure absolute stability under our leadership.

Wait a minute. This sounded like…

"Ensure compatibility", I realized. *Project Ember, "transferring their power". Caldwell was looking for Adara so he could transfer her magic to himself—for this plan.*

PHASE ONE: Coordinated National Destabilization

CURRENT STATUS: Yielding results in Argentina, Indonesia, and the United States. Projected escalation within three months.

PHASE TWO: Selective Targeting

CURRENT STATUS: In active pursuit of United States anomaly. Those of Argentina and Indonesia yet to be located.

Familiar. *Familiar.* This was what we were living right now.

PHASE THREE: Catalyst

PHASE FOUR: Consolidation

A plan was printed under every heading, all of which I was too afraid to read and understand. At the end of the second page lay President Nicholas Caldwell's signature with six others: names I didn't recognize but were betrayed by their titles as national leaders. They'd all signed off on a plan to locate and eliminate these powerful individuals whose magic they planned on "transferring" so they could seize control of the world.

"Adara. Save them."

I looked up at my mother, hoping and praying and wishing that I *didn't* understand.

"Caldwell was in collusion with six other national leaders to find you guys," she said. "The US, Canada, Indonesia, Egypt, Spain, Argentina, and Australia."

A girl from the United States, a girl from Indonesia, a boy from Egypt, a boy from Spain, and a girl from Canada who'd fled to Antarctica. Our governments all knew about our existences and were working together to locate us.

"The US Government already identified you," Momma said, "and they know Alejandro and Mila are impossibly powerful like you, so it doesn't matter that Caldwell's dead. This is already in motion, and these other countries will not stop once they find out they have three major leads to the rest of their targets."

I forced my breath out, trying to regain feeling in my body. "They're gonna destroy the world."

"And then use your magic to fix it and become the heroes," Momma said. "You guys are the key to starting the next World War."

ACKNOWLEDGEMENTS

mc pending, I'm embarrassed that you alpha read the draft that you did, but without you, I would've NEVER figured out those chapters that were falling flat on their faces into an ashy firepit—so thanks for being my number one book wifey and caring enough to rip my babies apart.

To my beta readers—McKenna, Amelia, Sabrey, Bryce, Grace, and Bella—thank you for all the feels in your reaction comments, and thank you so much more for the vast number of missed/wrong details and plot errors you caught. If not for you, I would've missed all the plot errors *I* caught in the next three drafts. Thanks for dealing with this book when it was at its Judges 4 so I could get it to its Proverbs 31. (I've been reading and fixing this book for twenty days straight, sorry.)

And thank you to all of my friends who were forgiving and patient with me throughout the last three weeks as I boarded myself up in my house to meet a deadline that, yet again, sneaked up on me. (Looking at you, Orion—you're a real one.) Anyone want boba or Wendy's, hit me up!

Finally, to my readers on social media: you are the sole reason I put so much work and love into this book. Thank you for giving this series life online, for giving me constant encouragement, and for having my stories on your shelves—what a sincere privilege. You are appreciated more than you know.

As we come to the final two books in the *Emmalynn Atera Series* (I'm sorry—WHAT?), I want to take the time to execute them properly. I can't put a release year on either yet, but they're currently in the works—alongside other novels I'm just as excited for. Thank you so much for being here in the meantime, dear reader, and stay tuned!

ABOUT THE AUTHOR

Ariana Tosado is a 23-year-old author, book editor, and content creator for teen and young-adult audiences. She started pursuing her passion of writing novels in middle school. Today, she's homed her focus on the *Emmalynn Atera* Series, marketing *Thy Kingdom Come*, and producing music. She aims to create relatable and encouraging content through her platforms, all with her cat, Sophie, in one hand and an iced vanilla latte in the other.

You can find out more about what she's up to on her website (www.arianatosado.com) or on Instagram (@thearianatosado).

Seven kingdoms are trapped in a death race to unlock a lost kingdom and break a global curse. When a fiery princess, a troubled prince, and their teams collide, can they work together to survive until the end of the race?

www.ingramcontent.com/pod-product-compliance
Lightning Source LLC
Chambersburg PA
CBHW031235310726
48971CB00004B/1030